Pretty Please ME

JERÉ ANTHONY

Copyright © 2023 by Jeré Anthony

All rights reserved.

No part of this book may be reproduced in any form or by any electronic or mechanical means, including information storage and retrieval systems, without written permission from the author, except for the use of brief quotations in a book review.

Edited by Olivia Kalb

Cover Design by Bailey McGinn

ISBN 978-1-7368195-5-5

ISBN 978-1-7368195-4-8 (ebook)

This one's for all the woman out there who ever thought they were broken.

It was never you...

ONE

Maggie

"Are you sure you came? I don't think you made a single peep the entire time."

I pull the navy-blue comforter up to cover my chest with one hand as I prop my head on my other hand and angle my body toward Kyle, my most recent sexual conquest. We've only been out three times, and as the rules of dating go, tonight was the night to put out if I wanted to continue seeing him. It's a simple modern dating formula; I don't make the rules, but I've learned to abide by them.

"Oh, yeah, I came really hard. Twice, I think." I nod in assurance, then rub my hand along his bare shoulder. "You're really good at sex."

Lying isn't normally my M.O. However, when it comes to hurting someone's feelings, it's the lesser of two evils. Besides, Kyle is a perfectly acceptable suitor, and it's not his fault I can't have an orgasm.

I don't exactly know that it's *impossible* for me to have

one, but I'm twenty-eight years old, and I've never experienced the toe-curling pleasure that my best friends love to brag about every chance they get. In fact, with each additional conquest, I think more and more it's some extravagant prank to convince me I'm missing out on something–or make me think I'm crazy. It's either that or... I, Magnolia Anderson, am not genetically equipped with the ability to orgasm. I've grown to accept it over time, but I understand that sex is important for men, hence my fulfillment of the three-date rule tonight.

Kyle slides up, so he's leaning against the headboard, allowing me to admire his masculine form. He's got a decent body covered sparsely with long strands of hair.

I narrow my eyes as I focus on one particularly long nipple hair that hangs down at least three inches. Why is only one extra-long? How could he not notice it among the others?

I'm torn from my observation by the sound of a crackling water bottle, and I look up to see Kyle chugging it as he squeezes it to push even more water into his mouth like a water hose. I guess he worked up quite a thirst.

He offers me the remaining drops from the crushed water bottle. "Thirsty?"

I shake my head. "No, but thank you for offering."

Before I can even finish my sentence, he yanks the condom off and throws it across the room, where it makes a sharp thwack as it slaps the wall, leaving a disgusting snail trail behind as it skids down in slow motion before finally falling into the metal trashcan below.

My lip curls in disgust for only a moment before I catch myself and quickly replace it with what I hope is a smile—though it probably looks like something closer to horror.

I want to look away, but the jizz has left a stain on the wall, and it's only then that I notice all the dried stains surrounding it.

How many used condoms met the same fate? When was the last time he changed the trash can?

I make a mental note to scrub the wall in my apartment as soon as I get home. I could have been surrounded by walls coated in bodily fluids for the last three years and only just realized it.

"Listen, Maggie, I know this is awkward, but–"

I tear my gaze away from the wall to see Kyle staring down at his hands and fisting the comforter as my heart sinks into the pit of my stomach. I know exactly what he's about to say, but that doesn't make it sting any less.

"I just didn't feel a connection with you, ya know? Sex is really important to me, and if it's not good, then I don't see the point of us seeing each other," he finishes.

I try my best not to look hurt as I move my leg underneath the comforter, searching for my discarded panties. The sooner I can get out of here, the sooner this nightmare can end.

"I mean, you just laid there like a plank of wood. No expression, no noise, you didn't even breathe heavily. It felt like I was fucking an inanimate object. I don't mean to hurt your feelings, but truly, I think that was the worst sex I've ever had. It was like making myself a giant bowl of my favorite cereal and then taking a huge bite only to discover the milk was spoiled–"

My toe finally connects with the scrap of lacy fabric I tortured my butt cheeks with tonight just for this disgustingly humiliating occasion. I pull them on, doing my best to keep myself covered beneath the sheets. "Well, Kyle, since we're both being honest, I lied about orgasming, and you're actually terrible at sex... Also, you've had a booger in your nose all night, and I didn't say anything because I didn't want to hurt your feelings." I slide off the edge of the bed like a slug as I search for my clothes on the floor.

I jump as I pull on my skinny jeans, then shove my bare

feet into my boots. My socks are a lost cause among the piles of dirty laundry on the floor. "You should really clean your apartment before bringing women home. It smells like armpits and dirty hair in here. And now that I know what's on your wall... I don't even want to think about when you last washed your sheets!"

"And what does it say about you that you still had sex with me anyway?" Kyle shouts just as I slam the door, the truth of his words clinging to me like static.

I stomp down the fire escape, not wanting to tempt my fate with the sketchy elevator, and open my Uber app. I just need to get home and wash this whole experience off me.

One hour later, I'm freshly showered and sitting cross-legged on my sofa with a pint of Ben & Jerry's Phish Food in one hand and a glass of shiraz in the other. This is not at all how I intended to spend my Friday night, but it's where I am nonetheless.

I lick the spoon clean before diving in for another heaping scoop as a sob escapes me. My face feels tight from dried tears, and I know one glance in the mirror would be just another blow to my ego, so I opt not to move. I wash down the creamy goodness with a gulp of wine and wince. It's not the best choice for drinking the sorrow away, but it's the only thing I had on hand.

I wish I could say this was a new experience for me, but the truth is that I've been here before... more times than I'd like to admit. At some point, you'd think I'd realize my mistake, or hell, maybe even give up entirely, but somehow, my need for companionship always outweighs my embarrassment.

I wasn't always so desperate, but having my two best friends, the two most important people in my life, get married within the last year has been hard. Seeing them so happy feels like someone's shining a spotlight on my loneliness.

I'm used to being needed, and now that Elliot and Gwen don't need me, I don't know where I fit into their lives anymore. It's not their fault, and I'm happy they're both happy, but sometimes I wish we could go back to how things used to be when I took care of everyone and felt needed. I don't know how to feel satisfied if I'm not playing caretaker.

That's why I need to meet someone, learn how to sexually please him, and fall madly in love, so I have a companion to come home to. So I never have to feel this alone and useless ever again.

It shouldn't be so difficult, but I suppose it's my fault for not *practicing* sooner. Sure, I slept with men in college, but after a couple of embarrassing encounters—not so different from tonight—I quickly gave up. I didn't see the point, and because of my limited distractions, I could focus on my goals. I got my five-hundred-hour yoga certification and worked my butt off until I saved enough money to buy this apartment connected to my yoga studio downstairs.

I've done everything right, yet I still can't get a man to sleep with me twice.

I'm pathetic.

You just laid there like a plank of wood. I wince as Kyle's words echo through my mind.

It's not like I haven't heard the same variation of rejection before. I shouldn't be surprised that once I get as far as sex, guys lose all interest in me. I'm like the opposite of Viagra, and I don't know how or what to do to fix it.

I mean, he compared me to spoiled milk! How am I ever supposed to recover from that? It's not like I can talk to my friends about it. All they do is brag about their amazing sex lives with their husbands. I've tried to mention it in the past, but the only advice I got was "*Clear your mind and focus on the sensations*" and "*Try drinking a glass of wine first.*" Believe me, I've tried all that stuff, and it's never helped. So then I decided I just needed to be a little more convincing to the men that I was enjoying myself.

I started watching porn, and there were so many responses to choose from, so I went down the list. I moaned loudly, but that only seemed to scare my partner. Maybe my tone was too deep? Then I added some twitching and eye-rolling, but the guy I was with thought I was having a seizure when I accidentally kicked him in the face. Needless to say, he didn't ask me out again.

So, this time, I tried staying silent, and I guess *that* was creepy.

Maybe if sex actually felt good, I wouldn't struggle so much acting like it does.

With a sigh, I pull my fuzzy blanket off the back of the sofa, wrap it around myself, and turn on the TV, happy for the distraction.

I can tell the wine is finally starting to kick in when the warm buzz calms my nerves. Maybe tonight wasn't so bad... I suppose everything's funny eventually? No matter how disgusting or embarrassing.

Maybe this is just a little speed bump I can learn from? Like what *not* to do during sex. Eventually, I'll get it right. At some point, it's just a numbers game, isn't it?

I take another long sip of wine as I scroll through my social media feed during the commercial break when a familiar image catches my eye.

I sit up a little straighter as I take in the image of Trent Cane. My childhood crush. The captain of the football team and the student council president.

He's tagged in one of our mutual friend's pictures with the caption, *"Ready to mingle."*

I'm only one glass of wine in, but this kind of recall definitely calls for a second. Reaching behind me, I grab the bottle and pour myself another before clicking on his name.

Of course, we're not social media friends–not that I have many of those anyway–so I can only see a limited amount of public information.

Trent was wildly popular in high school but in a humble kind of way. I still remember his piercing blue eyes and how his long tousled hair flipped to the side in the front. He was dreamy and perfect, and he didn't even know I existed.

How could he really? I was the shy, skinny, fair-skinned redhead who sat in the back of every classroom with my nose in a book. I didn't even get boobs until my junior year, all gangly legs and freckles.

I look down at my perky B cups and shrug. They may not be huge, but Gwen's told me many times that I've got a perfect rack for my frame. And Gwen's not one to lie about boobs.

As I study his picture, I bite my lip. Maybe it's the liquid courage, or maybe it's those familiar blue eyes that feel like home staring back at me, but a strange sense of curiosity urges me on.

He looks just as I remember, though he's traded his long tousled locks for a nice crew cut. There are slight creases around the corners of his eyes, and his muscular frame is a bit softer but still lean. He's just as handsome, and seeing him as a man has all my senses on edge.

I dive into his profile, devouring every piece of him that's available for public viewing. I'm taking another sip of wine as I scroll down to three months ago when his relationship status changed from married to single, and my finger accidentally presses the like button.

I choke on my wine as I frantically hit the button again and again, trying to undo the reaction. Liking it and unliking it with rapid-fire speed when a friend request pops up on my screen.

If it were possible to die of embarrassment, this would be my moment to ceremoniously be sucked up into the heavens, where I'd be crowned the Patron Saint of Humiliation. Seriously. I'm two for two tonight.

"Shit. Shit. Shit." I look around the room as if the answer is somehow written on the wall, but it's no use.

I grit my teeth as I click accept. I've already liked a three-month-old post from his divorce. Things can't really get much worse, can they?

TWO

Sam

I sigh as I drag my carry-on bag behind me, exhausted from back-to-back work trips spanning all over the globe, fueled solely by airport coffee and adrenaline from my last meeting. Good things are happening in my career, but fuck, I don't know how much longer I can keep this on-the-go lifestyle up.

The line inches forward little by little as I impatiently wait my turn to board. When I finally make it to the front, I'm forced to surrender my carryon as there's no more room in the overhead compartments due to the packed flight. That's just great. As if I needed another hoop to jump through today.

I follow the string of passengers to the back of the plane, where I find my seat right next to an exhausted-looking mother and two small children. I try to maneuver over them to get to the window seat when the woman taps me on the back.

"Excuse me, sir. Would you mind swapping places with my little boy? It's his birthday, and we're flying to see his father. This is his first flight, and I know he'd love the window seat."

"Sure, uh, I'll take the aisle." I back out awkwardly, waiting for her to slide over, but she just sits there, holding the baby to her chest.

"I'd actually prefer to sit on the aisle if that's okay. Sometimes baby Julian gets motion sickness, and I need to be able to get to the bathroom quickly." She gestures to the bathroom just behind us, and I gather that her seating choice was chosen on purpose.

"Oh, well, then, I guess I'll take the middle."

So much for the power nap I'd planned on sneaking in. There's nothing more uncomfortable than wedging my six-three frame in the already narrow middle seat.

I suppose that's what happens when you have a last-minute emergency in-person meeting added to your calendar. I can't complain too much. This deal will make me at least ten million when it's all said and done. Not to mention the perpetuities.

I step over her and collapse into my seat with a sigh.

"Mama, do you see that?" the little boy shouts over me, pointing at the plane's wing.

"Yes, I do." She nods.

"Mama. Mama. Mama. Watch this!" The kid says as he smashes his face against the small window. He blows hard, making a fart sound against the glass.

"Mmhmm." She picks up her book, balancing it carefully on the baby's head. It's only been five minutes, and she's already tuned him out. I check my watch again, willing the four-hour flight to go faster.

"Hey, Mama, what's that? Mama, are we there yet? Hey, Mama, can I have a snack?" The boy rattles off request after request, and I seem to be the only soul on this aircraft who hears him.

For a moment, I'm concerned his poor mother's hearing is impaired, but when I peek in her direction, I notice the dark circles and bags under her eyes. Her hair is a tangled mess, and it looks like she's wearing last night's makeup. She seems to be even more exhausted than I am.

I'm not really a kid person, but I can't help but feel sorry for her. Perhaps it's a lapse in judgment, or the exhaustion has finally done me in, but I surprise myself. "I don't mind entertaining him for a while if you need a break–"

"Really?" Her eyes go wild as she looks me up and down, no doubt assessing whether or not I'm sane for the offering. Really, who offers to entertain a random hyperactive child who's not theirs... on an airplane? *Maybe I have lost my mind.*

Before I can backpedal, she shoves the baby in my direction and pulls a neck pillow from her extra-large purse, complete with a drawstring hoodie to block out the light. And five minutes later, she's snoring.

Damn, I guess mama really did need a break.

I'm partly annoyed but mostly jealous. Snoring is like bragging about sleeping to people who can't sleep. Good for her... *I guess.*

"Hey, mister, I can count to one hundred. Want to hear me?" the small boy says, and I look around for any help, trying my best to make eye contact with the mother across the aisle. As if they know I've just shot myself in the foot, no one dares to look in my direction. My momentary lapse of judgment has thrown me to the wolves, and now there's nothing I can do but pray for this flight to defy the space-time continuum. So far, luck hasn't been on my side.

"Sure." I agree, "Let's hear it."

Three hours later, the little boy–whose name is Cody, I've finally gathered—has long moved passed counting to one hundred. We've gone through the ABCs, he's informed me more than I ever cared to know about Pokémon, and now, he's educating me on his favorite dinosaurs in order of their existence.

Really, does this kid shotgun the Discovery Channel? Is his dad some kind of paleontologist or some shit? How can someone so young—he's four, we've already been over his birthday party —know all this random information?

Baby Julian jumps in my lap as I do my best to steady his wobbly baby legs. Three hours is a long time for little kids, and by the time we make it to the Cretaceous period, the once giggly baby is quickly becoming tired of me.

I not too subtly nudge the snoring mother's arm, knocking it clear off the armrest, but she only turns on her side facing the aisle and curls into a deeper and apparently more comfortable position.

I'm considering pinching little Julian's leg to force a cry out of him when the flight attendant comes around with the snack tray. "Cookies, nuts, or pretzels?" she asks as little Julian squirms in my lap, trying to make a breakaway.

"Oh, no, you don't." I clench him tighter to my chest and nudge Cody. "Hey, kid, what's your pick?"

"Umm." He places a small finger on his lip, considering his options. "I want–" He sneaks his head around, checking to see if his mother is still asleep before deciding. "A coke and cookies, pwease."

I shrug, "I suppose I'll have the same." The flight attendant serves us our snacks, and I help Cody with his tray, opening his bag of cookies while carefully feeding Julian one at a time. I don't really know if babies should eat cookies, but the package says nut-free, so I figure if he had a major allergy or something, his mom wouldn't have handed him over so easily—to a complete stranger, nonetheless.

"Mmm. Soda!" Cody balances the can of soda in his small chubby hands, slurping it with a phsst-ahh with every sip.

I watch him go in, again and again, taking less and less time between each sip. After a few minutes, he's nothing short of chugging the can like he's at a frat party.

"Hey, buddy. Maybe you should slow down a little on that soda–" I reach to take the can, his eyes growing wider with every gulp.

He slaps my hand away. "Mine!" he hisses, and I recoil like I've just touched a hot stove.

I don't know if you've ever seen a small child turn feral right before your eyes, but it's nothing short of what nightmares are made of. I clench baby Julian to my chest as I watch Cody shotgun the rest of the soda.

"More!" he screams, beating his chest with his fist. His words come out as a growl, and I look around for any help I can find, willing someone to take mercy on me and tell me what to do.

When he strips his shirt off and begins slapping himself in the face, I whip my head around the cabin in search of anyone vaguely resembling a priest. I don't know shit about little kids, but demon possession seems like the only logical explanation for this sudden change in behavior.

I connect gazes with an elderly woman two aisles behind me and mouth the words *"Help me,"* but she snaps her eyes back down to her knitting as if she didn't see me at all.

Baby Julian seems to have picked up on whatever crazed possession his brother is experiencing now, too. He's got my tie clenched in a tiny white knuckle grip coated in slick cookie-crumble drool.

I cough as the fabric tightens around my windpipe and try my best to balance the little guy as he jumps up and down while using my balls as his own personal trampoline. "Helll-p" I gasp, trying to get their mother's attention as baby Julian tightens his grip. My vision begins to blur from the lack of oxygen, and I feel that this right here may just be the end for me.

Death by strangulation from a tiny human. It's certainly not something I can say I saw coming...

"More soda!" Cody screams as he crushes the soda can against his skull like a deranged frat bro.

Somehow *this* is what stirs his mother, and she opens her eyes with a gasp, snatching Julian out of my arms. Precious oxygen flows back into my lungs.

I suck in a deep breath, cherishing the feeling of my lungs expanding, when I feel a sharp, stinging slap across my face. Heat rushes to the surface as a high-pitched ringing shrills inside my eardrum.

"How dare you! Sugar is the leading cause of inflammation, which is the root of all diseases! What were you thinking, giving them cookies without asking!?"

I blink several times, rubbing the welt on my face as the stinging sensation fades, and I try to collect my thoughts. Then, just as the fasten seatbelt lights come on, baby Julian empties the contents of his stomach all over my new suit.

The taste of warm, regurgitated cookies and spoiled milk seep into my mouth, and I sink into my seat. So much for being a good person.

I sniff the cabernet before tasting it, and my nose scrunches up in repulsion. No matter how many times I wash my face, I still can't get the smell of spoiled milk out of my nose.

"Is the wine not to your liking? I'd be happy to get you something else—"

I hold up my hand to stop her. "No, this is perfect. Thank you, Bethany. I'll call you over if I need anything else."

Bethany nods before stepping out in silence.

I'm sitting in the private room of my favorite high-end restaurant in the city, waiting not so patiently on my date which should've been here ten minutes ago. She knows how exhausted I am from traveling all week, and it's not like her to be late without notice. I force my mind to stop the spiral of worry as I check the time once more.

The soft sweet melody of a piano sends a wave of calm over my agitated nerves, and my clenched jaw softens. I rub my aching temples and close my eyes. I'm so exhausted. I can't wait to get home and go to bed.

In the last seven days, I've traveled everywhere from India to France, making a quick stop in Germany and then Puerto Rico to meet with clients. Then I had to rush back home a day early to handle someone else's emergency, and I've been in meetings all day ever since. I was lucky I even had time to shower before this dinner that Natalie sprung on me at the last minute.

Normally, we go out on Saturday night, but something major must've come up for her. It's not like her to stray from out outlined agreement. It's part of the reason I'm being so understanding with her tardiness—that and I haven't had a real meal in nearly forty-eight hours...

"Sam, I'm so sorry I'm late. Traffic was nuts, and I got tied up at the drycleaners—" Natalie drops her large purse in the seat beside her and collapses into her seat.

"It's fine. I was starting to worry, though. It's good to see you, Nat." I stand to greet her, going in for a kiss on the mouth, but she turns her face landing my kiss on her cheek.

Her eyes widen, and she lifts her menu to cover her face.

"Let's see, what do I want to eat? Have they added anything good to the menu?"

I pour her a glass of wine as I study her. She's acting odd. As if nervous about something.

She takes a long sip, downing half the glass in one gulp. "Oh, you know what, I haven't had lobster in a while. That would be good. Don't you think?"

I place my napkin in my lap and quirk a brow. "Is everything okay? You're acting strange this evening."

"Oh, yes, everything is just fine. I'm just hungry, that's all." She offers me an exaggerated smile that rivals a creepy porcelain doll.

I stare at her for a beat before Bethany returns to take our order. When she finally walks away, I narrow my eyes on Natalie. "Spill it. What's really going on? Why'd you insist on having dinner tonight?"

She fidgets with her napkin and grimaces. "I met someone," she blurts. "I didn't mean for it to happen, but we were at this work party together, and we just hit it off."

"I see—"

"I'm crazy about him, Sam. Like, I think he actually may be the one... or at least the one for now. He makes me feel alive, ya know? Like I can be anyone I want when I'm with him." She takes another sip of wine and swallows with a gulp. "We want the same things, too," she says in almost a whisper.

I refill our glasses as the silence builds between us before I finally speak. "I'm happy for you, Nat." I hold my glass up in a toast, and she sighs in relief. "To new beginnings."

We clink our glasses, and I place my hand on top of hers on the table. "You know, all I want is what's best for you. I don't know why you were so nervous to tell me."

She smiles, and this time, it's a real smile because her eyes squint in the corners. "Why are you so amazing? I show up late and tell you I've met someone, and you just pour me another glass of your crazy expensive wine?"

I shrug and clasp my hands loosely over the stem of my glass. "I happen to think this news should be celebrated. It's not every day you fall in love."

She twirls her glass as she leans back in her seat, much more relaxed than five minutes ago. "And what about you, Sam? Do you think you'll fall in love someday? If you met the right person?"

I stare down at the white tablecloth with a slight shake of my head. "No, Natalie, love is not something that interests me. I think I'll stick to my arrangements, but I'm happy for you and–?"

"Conner," she answers.

"Conner." I nod. "I don't have to know him to know he's a lucky guy. I hope he treats you how you deserve to be treated?" I lift an eyebrow in question.

"He does. Don't worry about that." She assures me with a blushing smile.

"Good. Then why don't you tell me how you two met."

THREE

Maggie

Ten the next morning comes a lot earlier when you're nursing a hangover crafted by copious amounts of shiraz, sugar, and humiliation. Nevertheless, there aren't many things that could keep me from meeting my girls for brunch.

I spot Gwen's bright blonde hair when I round the corner to our favorite outdoor brunch place and let myself in through the gate to join them.

Gwen sits in a reclined position with her hands resting on her large baby bump and her feet propped up in the seat beside her. "Hey, Mags, you skinny bitch," she mutters in greeting, and I look at Elliot in confusion.

"She's upset because she split her pants at the farmer's market this morning," Elliot explains as she pulls me into a hug. "It's so good to see you, Mags!" She pulls away to take a better look at me and narrows her eyes. "You seem off... Are you feeling okay?"

I brush her off and take a seat across from a grumpy Gwen.

"Just tired. I've been so busy at the studio lately. We've expanded our schedule, and I just hired two new instructors to teach weekend classes. It's been a lot." I give her a reassuring smile as I pretend to examine the menu... as if I'd actually change my usual order.

My phone buzzes in my pocket. "So, tell me what you've been up to lately?" I ask as a message pops up on my screen. My eyes widen as a wave of panic forms a knot in my stomach. Elliot goes into a full retelling of one of her latest embarrassing foot-in-mouth work stories, but she might as well be a grown-up in a Charlie Brown movie because I can't hear a word she's saying.

I re-read the message again and again, trying my best not to look distracted.

TRENT CANE

Hey, Maggie! I'm glad you reached out. I was dreading having to contact all of our senior classmates individually (you have no idea how long it takes to find these people with all the marriages and name changes). Anyway, our ten-year high school reunion is just on the horizon. It's October 3rd, to be exact.

Here's a link to the invite.

Sorry it's late notice! But that's what happens when a man's in charge! (I was waaaay too ambitious back then, totally should've let Samantha Simmons take the W on Student Council President.)

Anyway, it's good hearing from you.

Talk soon.

P.S. You look great, Maggie. I really hope you can make it.

"–And then I had to send him a formal apology email

explaining I didn't mean it how it sounded." She laughs, and I force out a chuckle to match, so it's not obvious I wasn't listening.

When the server appears with our appetizer, Gwen's entire demeanor shifts as she dives into the plate of cheese fries. She moans as she licks ranch off her fingers, reminding me of some of the women in the porno films I used to watch.

I look to Elliot, who seems equally uncomfortable and feel a little better as I watch her *thoroughly* enjoy her food.

"What?" Gwen licks her fingers and smiles. "Can a pregnant woman not have a foodgasm? If it weren't for the amazing pregnancy sex and food tasting better than it ever has, I don't know if this whole pregnancy thing would be worth it."

I furrow my brow in confusion and take a sip of my iced tea.

"So, pregnant sex really is better? I've heard that, but I didn't know it was true–"

"Oh my God, everything is so sensitive. It's incredible. Last night, Jack was railing me from behind–"

I hold up my hands to stop her. "Whoa. We really don't need details this early in the morning. I haven't had enough caffeine yet."

Gwen goes silent, and she and Elliot turn to stare at me, wearing similar looks of concern.

"Are you sure everything's okay, Mags?" Elliot asks again.

I roll my eyes and shove a cheese fry in my mouth, covering my mouth as I chew. "Yes, as I said, I'm just tired."

I wish I could talk to them about my problems. I really do, but I feel like there's too big of a gap for them to actually offer me any helpful advice. The message from Trent burns in the back of my mind, making me antsier by the minute.

Elliot daps her face with her napkin. "Well, on a safer conversational note." She offers me a nervous smile. "You know how Benjamin signed me up for tennis lessons? Well, I just finished my first month, and I've already improved so much that I can safely play with strangers! I mean, originally, I just wanted to play so I had an excuse to wear my tennis skirt more often—Benjamin goes crazy for me in a tennis skirt."

I perk up a little as an idea starts to form in my mind.

"I mean, when I started my lessons, I couldn't even hit the ball. I was so terrible that Benjamin had to duck because I'd fling the tennis racket with my swing half the time." She laughs as she describes a particular incident when the racket hit Benjamin between the eyes, but my mind takes me in a completely different direction.

Elliot was terrible at tennis. So terrible that Benjamin signed her up for lessons for his own safety... And now she's better. After only a month, she's improved so much that she can play with strangers... safely.

I slap my hands on the table. "That's it!"

Elliot and Gwen go silent as they stare at me. "What's it?" Gwen asks, but I wave her off just as our food arrives.

"Oh, your story just helped me solve a problem at the studio." I lie as I dig into my food, thankful for the distraction.

All I need to do is find a nice, willing gentleman to agree to give me sex lessons with no strings attached. Then I'll feel confident to go out with Trent without scaring him off.

That shouldn't be too difficult, right?

FOUR

Maggie

I tighten my grip on my heavy purse, pulling it close to my body as I maneuver between the swarm of people. Underground Bar is a speakeasy that Gwen used to talk about. It's an exclusive secret watering hole where all the hot singles gather to mingle and find someone to bring home for the night.

My eyes drink in the dark, crowed space faintly lit with only red lights and candles. Groups of scantily clad women and well-dressed men usher around me, bumping against me despite my best efforts to move out of the way. The bar seems extra-crowded tonight, not that I have anything to compare it to other than my tried-and-true haven, Terry's. This place is nothing like Terry's. Rather than cozy and familiar, it feels edgy and dangerous.

Insecurity burns in my chest like acid reflux, but I ignore it. Just because I'm not dressed provocatively, or my hair isn't teased to look like I've just crawled out of bed with a man, doesn't mean I don't belong here. I undo the top button of my cardigan and feel a little better. See, I'm not so uptight. I can let loose a little. I mean, I'm here, after all. That's got to count for something.

I suck in a breath and straighten my shoulders as I set my sight on the bar and force myself to move.

Tonight, my mission is simple: Find a nice man who isn't too creepy—or married—share a couple of drinks, so he's loosened up, then ask him to be my personal sex tutor in exchange for three thousand dollars.

I have no idea what the going rate for sex lessons is. My only knowledge of prostitution comes from *Pretty Woman,* so three thousand feels like a good starting point. I like to think of myself as a quick learner, so I'm hopeful it won't take more than a week. Of course, I'm open to negotiation.

I pull my purse against my chest protectively as I maneuver myself up to the bar and order a drink, sliding a twenty to the bartender. "Keep the change."

The bartender gives me a surprised smile and mouths a *"Thank you."*

I've always been a good tipper, but tonight, I need a little help from the universe and all the karma I can get.

My eyes narrow in on a line of people heading toward the back of the room. There must be some kind of event... Maybe that's why it's so busy tonight? I stand on my tiptoes to get a better look when I spot a familiar face and instantly feel excited. Damian Johnson is offering psychic readings for charity at a booth in the back.

Damian is a fashion icon and an extremely gifted psychic. He was Elliot's first paying client and single-handedly put her company, Clutch Media, on the map. Last summer, he helped us track down Gwen and Jack after they went missing on a work trip. If it weren't for Damian telling us we were looking in the wrong direction, we never would've found them, and I can't even begin to think about that. The man has proven his abilities in spades, and I can't believe how lucky I am that he's here tonight.

With a bit of renewed excitement, I make my way into the crowd and join the line. Not only would it be great to see him, but maybe he can offer me a little clarity on what... or who... to look for tonight. At this point, I'm so desperate I'd do just about anything.

I sip the melted ice from my drink, waiting thirty minutes until I'm finally at the front of the line. Damian smiles wide when he sees me and stands up to greet me.

He kisses me on each cheek, then looks me up and down. "Magnolia Anderson, I've been looking for you all night."

I narrow my eyes. "How did you? Oh... You're good."

He shrugs. "That's what they tell me."

"What is all this?" I motion to the three booths set up with different tarot readers.

"Oh, we're partnering with the bar to raise money for a homeless shelter. They're donating twenty percent of the proceeds tonight, so drink up. It's a good cause."

I smile warmly at the sentiment. There are good people in the world, but ironically, they're usually not the ones hanging out in the most obvious of spaces. They don't need accolades, the spotlight, or the promise of a reward; they're just good because they *actually* love everyone.

"Hey, Bobbi, I'm going to take a break. Cover my table, would you?" Damian calls to the woman set up beside him, and she gives him a thumbs up.

"Come on." He leads me to an empty booth with a VIP rope around it, and we both climb over, settling into the plush velvet seats.

It's quieter here. Despite the fact that we're still in the middle of the bar, it feels a little cozier and safe. A server appears with a tray of drinks, and I snatch a fruity-looking one, needing something to calm my nerves.

"Now, tell me, what exactly do you want guidance for?" Damian pulls out a deck of tarot cards and shuffles them masterfully, staring at me as if he can see right through me.

I squirm in my seat and twirl a fallen strand of hair that's usually tucked behind my ear. "I'm in the market for some *lessons*, and I was hoping you could tell me whether that's a good idea... or give me any advice?"

He quirks a brow. "Go on..."

I swallow a lump in my throat. "There's this guy back home, and I've had a huge crush on him, and he asked me out... Well, there's a reunion, and he said he couldn't wait to spend some time with me... alone... and I don't want to scare him away, so I–"

He perks up in his seat as if he hears something and tilts his head to the side. "Okay, something is coming through. Keep talking..."

"I... uh... I've just felt really lost lately watching everyone move forward with their lives. I don't have anyone to take care of, and I'm not really sure what the point of anything is anymore," I confess. "I mean, I own my own business, and things there have been good. I guess I just thought I'd be happy by now, but I just feel so... lonely." I look up with blurry eyes. I'm not sure when I started crying, but there's something so calming about Damian's presence. I don't feel embarrassed spilling my soul to him like this... even if we're in the middle of the bar.

"Oh, sweet, sweet, Magnolia," he coos. "I think you were meant to come here tonight. In fact, hold on one moment. I'm getting a download." He grabs my partially damp bar napkin and pulls a pen from his jacket pocket.

I watch him scribble rapidly in shocked observation.

Minutes pass by, and he doesn't look up. He just keeps scribbling. I try to make sense of the few words I can actually read: trust, play, release, true love, and I almost fall out of my seat when I make out the word orgasm. He's written it in all caps and underlined it three times in the center of the napkin.

I glance around us as if I'm guilty of something. I feel as if Damian somehow managed to project the word like a bubble over my head, like a scarlet letter signaling my abhorrent embarrassment to the entire bar.

"Well, well, well." Damian pushes himself back from the table, wearing a mischievous smile. "The universe has quite the message for you, sweet Magnolia."

My eyes widen, and I lean forward and whisper-yell, "What does it mean!?"

He shuffles his cards and smirks. "Let's see, shall we?" He spreads the cards out in front of me, and I close my eyes as I use my intuition to select the perfect card, the answer to all my problems.

"Mags? I didn't think I'd see you out at a place like this." The familiar deep voice sends a shiver down my spine. I sneak one eye open and immediately want to crawl under the table when I see my friend, Sam, staring down at me.

Sam is best friends with Benjamin and Jack, making us the respective fifth wheels in our friend circles. I don't know how I would've handled the whole Gwen and Jack fiasco last summer without his help. He's a private person, but just like me, he'll do just about anything for his friends. He had a private helicopter search running constantly and dove at any chance to help me. I like to think Sam and I are similar in our friendships. We're the responsible ones who take care of everyone else, and even more than me, Sam has his shit together. To say he intimidates me is the understatement of the century.

I dive on top of the napkin, using my body as a shield, but judging by his laughter, I'm pretty sure it's too late.

"Now, this looks like an interesting conversation. You two are having a much better night than I am." He slides into the booth, and I shuffle over, making room for him.

Damian props his face on his hand and smiles."Good to see you again, Samuel."

"Hey, man, I've been meaning to reach out and thank you for everything you did this summer." He pats his chest, pulls his phone from his jacket, and types something. "I just sent my donation. I'd love to chat more with you about what you're doing with the shelter. This is a great idea."

"Thank you. That means a lot coming from you."

"So, what's all this?" Sam gestures at the cards.

"I was just giving Magnolia a tarot reading. How about I do a double reading for you both?"

Sam looks to me for permission, and I let out a sigh. "Fine. You can stay, but you have to promise to keep things confidential." I hold out my pinky.

He stares at my extended finger for a moment before laughing and linking his to mine. "I pinky promise to keep all your secrets."

"Good." I huff, then spin back to find Damian studying us with a curious gaze. His lips pull into a smirk. "Oh, this is going to be fun. Ladies first."

I close my eyes and wave my left hand over the line of cards before finally choosing one. I flip it over and look at Damian, but I can't read his expression.

He taps his finger to his lip. "The Six of Wands shows you're embarking on a journey of sorts." Damian's eyes twinkle with excitement. "Notice the man steering the boat. He represents the masculine. This could be taking action..." He bats his eyes. "Or it could represent a man steering you along your journey. Seated in the boat are a woman and a small child. She represents the feminine. This could be intuition or *receiving* something."

My stomach is in knots, and I wish he'd just come out with it already. Why are these messages so vague? Why can't the universe just tell me what I need to know? I sigh in frustration, propping my face on my hand.

"There's a child here. This could represent an inner child being ushered along the journey as well." He smiles widely, "This is a very good card for you, Magnolia." He slides the damp napkin toward me, and all I see is the word orgasm written in all caps in the center.

"Wow, that escalated quickly." Sam laughs.

"Now that we've done your tarot reading, I'm starting to make a little more sense of this." Damian taps his knuckle on the napkin. "Spirit showed me a little girl eating cotton candy at an amusement park. The ocean... or waves crashing along the sand. Bubbles." He turns the napkin to read the smaller words, "Oh, this one was strange, a blindfold or something to do with vision or eyes... and finally orgasms." He blushes and clears his throat. "Lots and lots of orgasms."

Sam chokes on his beer next to me, and I snatch the napkin off the table, shoving it in my bag. "Well, I'm sure there's some cryptic meaning behind that message, too. We can't take everything at face value."

"No, that one was pretty damn clear." Damian laughs.

"So, what am I supposed to do with this?" I hover my hands in a circular motion over the table. "Go on some kind of healing quest to find myself using the power of the female orgasm?"

This time, Sam actually spits out his beer in shock, and Damian throws his head back in laughter.

I wait while the two of them can compose themselves.

Damian finally says, "You know what, Magnolia? Although it's a bit literal, I don't think that's a bad idea at all."

This is just great. Not only is my life's journey the butt of the joke, but Sam got to witness the train wreck firsthand. There's no way I'll be able to keep this insanity from Elliot and Gwen. What kind of person must he think I am after hearing hints of my deepest darkest secrets with the goal of orgasming my way to fixing all my problems?

Damian wipes the tears from his eyes. "I knew I liked you, Magnolia. I think there's so much more to you than meets the eye." He holds his deck out to Sam. "Ok, handsome, it's your turn. What would you like guidance with?"

For a moment, my embarrassment subsides as I wait for Sam to ask his question. What could he possibly need help with? The guy's got it all. The job. The friends. I pause for a moment as I try to remember if he's ever mentioned a girlfriend, but I can't recall hearing about one.

Sam twists his lips in contemplation and finally says, "You know... why don't you just use your psychic woo-woo powers and pick some advice for me?"

Damian's brow rises in surprise as if there's an unspoken conversation between them, "Sure. If that's what you want." He cuts the deck and reveals Sam's card. "The Hermit in Reverse." He snaps his lips closed and tilts his head to the side as he studies the card.

Several moments pass, and I'm almost too uncomfortable. I contemplate climbing underneath the table and leaving, suddenly feeling as if I'm about to hear something I shouldn't.

"The Hermit in Reverse is an interesting card for you, Samuel. In its upright position, it means a search for inner truth or guidance ... but in its reversed position, it indicates loneliness and isolation as if you've lost your way." Damian's eyes soften, and he looks at Sam like he feels sorry for him. "My interpretation of this card for you is to change your ways. The path that you've been on is only leading you toward self-destruction."

"Well, then..." Sam's eyes widen, and he rubs his hand over his jaw.

Damian gathers the cards, placing them back in his pocket. "I should get back. Let me know if you need anything, okay?"

Sam lets me out of the booth, and I hug Damian goodbye. "Thank you so much for everything."

His eyes sparkle with mischief. "Of course, Magnolia. Any time." He places the damp bar napkin in my hand. "Don't forget your road map."

I grip the napkin and laugh before shoving it into my pocket. I fully intend on burning the thing when I get home. "Right. Thanks."

"You know where to find me, and please let me know all the details after you complete your *quest*."

I shrug. "I think you'll be disappointed."

"You'd be surprised," he says with a wink.

When I turn back, I find Sam studying me with a look of confusion.

"What's wrong?" I pat myself and spin around. "Do I have toilet paper stuck in my pants?"

"No, Mags." He laughs and nods his head toward the door. "What do you say we get out of here and catch up... somewhere a little less crowded?"

"Terry's?"

"Sounds perfect. Just let me close out my tab."

FIVE

Sam

Terry's bar may not look like much on the surface, but that's the best part about it. It's cozy and comfortable, like an old leather glove that fits your hand just right. The only patrons are the ones who know about it, so the whole vibe stays pretty mellow. It's the place you go when you want to catch up with good friends or have meaningful conversations with someone you're getting to know better.

It's not, however, the kind of place one would look to find a new submissive. That would be like shitting where you sleep, just a bad idea altogether. I knew my search would be on hold the minute I ducked into Maggie's booth tonight, and that was before Damian's freaky prophecy, or whatever the hell that was.

I order our drinks, then make my way to the back booth, where Maggie sits ramrod straight, wearing a fully buttoned cardigan with her giant purse tucked in her lap. The woman is puzzling, to say the least. I've always found her intriguing, but after hearing her psychic reading, I'm itching to know the rest of the story because I'd put money on the fact that there's a story there.

"Here you are." I sit both beers down on the gloss table in front of her. "This one's a double IPA, and this one's a hazy IPA, I think."

She quirks her lips to the side as she considers her choices, then looks up at me with the cutest fucking doe eyes. "Do you mind if I taste them both before I pick?"

I let out a laugh as I slide across from her. "Not at all."

I watch her carefully sip each one, then go in for another just to be sure. "This one." She slides the hazy closer to her and takes another sip like it's the best thing she's had all day. "God, that's good," she moans, wiping a little foam from her lip.

My dick swells at the sight of it, taking me off guard. It's just another reminder that I need to replace Natalie ASAP.

"So..." I tap my fingers on the table. "Care to elaborate on the whole 'seek orgasms' thing back there, or should I just make up my own interpretation?"

Maggie's eyes fall to her beer as she twirls it around and fires back, "If we're telling secrets, then I'm sure you'll be willing to share who you were hiding from in the bar back there?"

My face breaks into a grin, and I rub my jaw as I consider how much I want to share. I'm a private person, but I can't expect her to share if I'm holding back myself, and my curiosity is growing larger by the second. "I saw this woman I dated on a trial basis. It didn't end up working out, and she didn't take the breakup well. I didn't feel like lying to her or upsetting her again, so I ducked into the nearest VIP section thinking it was still empty." I squint my eyes as I watch for her reaction.

Her eyebrows lift in surprise. "Oh, well then, I'm glad you could make it out unseen." She makes a show of looking behind us. "Are there any other admirers on our tail, or do you think we're safe?"

"I think we're safe for now, but the night is still young." I tap my beer to hers. "Your turn, now spill."

She clears her throat and tightens her grip on her purse strap. "Well, let's see, where do I begin?" Her eyes dart around the bar like she's searching for something... or someone. "I... well... I'm looking for someone to help me out with a problem I have. Someone who's kind and gentle... and patient." She pauses, pulling her sleeves to cover her hands.

"What, like a mechanic or something?"

"More like a tutor..." Her voice trails off, and she seems to be looking everywhere but at me.

I tilt my head. "You're looking for a tutor? In a bar? Don't you think–"

"It's for sex!" She blurts.

My eyebrows jump up, and I jerk back in my seat, but she keeps going before I can get a word in.

"There's this guy back home. I've always been in love with him. We have a history, but the timing was never right." She spins her empty glass nervously as she talks. "He messaged me out of the blue and invited me to our high school reunion. He wants to go with me and hang out after..." She bites her lip and looks up at me.

I cross my arms over my chest. "I... uh... I guess I don't understand where the tutor comes in?"

Maggie rolls her eyes and huffs. "You're really going to make me say it?"

I nod, encouraging her to keep going.

"Fine. I need someone to help me get better at sex." She grabs my beer and takes a gulp, then wipes her mouth with the back of her hand. "I've been told by several people that I'm not very good at it, and I don't want to screw this up."

I blink several times as I try to process this information. I don't know what I thought she was going to tell me, but needed sex lessons weren't anywhere on my bingo card. I'm going to need another drink for this.

I motion for our server to bring another round, then lace my fingers together as I study her. She's so buttoned up and wound tight; I suppose I can see she may not be able to let herself loose in the bedroom, but I can't be sure that's the issue.

"What do you mean you've been told you're not very good? Guys have actually said that to you?"

She tilts her head from side to side. "Not verbatim, but yeah." She lets out a huff and looks off. "Last night, the guy compared me to accidentally eating spoiled milk in his favorite cereal..."

My fists clench as white-hot rage boils underneath my skin. How could any dumb fuck have the audacity to tell her something like that? I may not know firsthand, but I can take one look at her and tell you that *she* isn't the problem. Any man would be lucky to even look at her, much less *touch* her.

I want to find that little dipshit and knock his teeth in for hurting her so badly that she felt like she needed to find someone to give her lessons when he's the one who didn't know what he was doing.

My nostrils flare as a wave of heat rises up my neck, and I force myself to ask the question brewing in my mind all night. "Do you enjoy having sex, Maggie?"

She stills in her seat and gives me a puzzled look. "Yeah, I mean. I guess. It's fine."

"Fine?"

"What's wrong with fine?" She frustratedly pulls at her neatly pinned-back hair, and small tendrils fall around her face.

I bite my tongue, holding back all the things I want to say about how sex should be exhilarating, passionate, hot, greedy, erotic... anything but fine. Which can only mean one thing...

"Do you come every time you have sex?" The question leaves my lips before I can hold back.

Her face drops, and she begins twirling the small piece of hair that's fallen. "Yeah, I mean, not every *single* time, but mostly." She darts her gaze away, looking uncomfortable.

It's blatantly obvious she's lying… and therein lies the problem.

My lips quirk to the side, and I narrow my eyes. "You're full of shit, Mags. It's clear as day." I lean forward and place each of my hands on the table. "Tell me this, have you ever had an orgasm with anyone you've been with? Because my guess would be that you haven't, and you never tell them because you're too nice to hurt anyone's feelings…"

She sucks in a breath, goes completely still, then shakes her head ever so slightly.

I lean slowly back in my seat, "That's what I thought."

Suddenly, my collar feels restrictive as a curious arousal makes my every nerve stand on end. It's a cruel form of torture knowing this about her when all I want to do is show her exactly what she's missing. She doesn't even realize she's just served up my biggest kink on a silver platter, and I can't fucking touch it. My mouth salivates at the thought of it. Like a shark with blood in the water.

I shake the thoughts from my head. I can't let myself even entertain them. I've got to get this conversation back on track.

"So, that's what you were out doing tonight? Looking for some random guy to give you sex lessons?" I keep my voice level and calm, despite the rush of testosterone oozing through my veins.

"Yeah, is that weird?" She sets her purse on the table and pulls out a wad of cash. "I was going to pay him. I don't expect anyone to do it for free."

I rush to cover her hands with mine, fear replacing my

arousal. "Mags, put that away before someone sees! Please tell me you haven't been walking around by yourself all night with all this cash on you–"

"Well, yeah, you can only withdraw one thousand from an ATM, and I wasn't going to tell him my real name." She says it like I'm the idiot. "It's not like I was going to approach anyone creepy, and I was only showing *you*," she scoffs. "Honestly, I was halfway hoping Damian would point me in the right direction."

"Christ, woman, how much were you willing to pay?" I hiss.

She tucks the money back into her bag and shrugs. "Three thousand, I just took a guess. Why? Do you not think that's fair?"

A stinging ache forms behind my temples, and I massage them. "Let me be clear. You don't need to pay any man to sleep with you. We are more than happy to do that for free. Do you understand?"

"You say that, but–"

"Magnolia Anderson, as your friend, I am telling you that is the stupidest way of getting chlamydia that I can think of, and I can't allow it. Just find a nice, decent guy like a normal person. Okay?"

"Fine, since you're here, you can help me pick someone who looks *normal*," she mocks, then gestures to the mass of people moving around the bar.

I tighten my grip around my glass and lean back with a sigh. "Sure. Yeah. Let's find you a fairy-god-fucker..."

One hour later, we're both feeling tipsy and are no closer to finding a suitable prospect than when we arrived.

Maggie's cheeks are tinted a rosy pink, and she's pushed the sleeves up on her cardigan. Her long hair hangs down her back in loose waves, and every time she laughs, I catch myself staring at her in awe. Maggie has this full-body laugh that pulls you in. It's bubbly and contagious and feels like a crackling fire warming your chilled bones.

How could anyone think she was bad at sex? The thought is burned in my mind, and I can't get rid of it.

Maggie slaps the table to get my attention, and I glance to see what she's looking at.

"How about that guy?" She closes one eye and points. "The one in the plaid standing by the guy in overalls."

I shoot her a questioning look before trading out her beer for a bottle of water. "Seriously? That guy? He looks like he doesn't wash his hands after he pees."

She slaps me on the shoulder. "Sam! Now, you're just being mean."

"What? I thought you wanted my male opinion?" I shrug. "But, hey, if you want Ecoli and pinkeye, that's your prerogative."

We watch as the guy grabs a handful of nuts from the community bowl and licks the salt from each finger before diving in for another handful. I send Maggie an *I told you so look.*

She throws up her hands and rolls her eyes. "Fine. You're probably right. What about the guy sitting down in the corner by the do–"

"Married," I answer before she can finish her sentence. "You can tell because he's alone. He keeps rubbing his left finger and playing with something in his pocket. Mostly likely a newlywed, and it's their first big fight." Her head tilts curiously, and I continue. "My guess is that he'll realize he's about to fuck everything up and go home soon."

"And how could you possibly know all of that?"

I shrug and take a sip of my water. "I've spent enough time watching, I guess. When you travel like I do, you realize there are only a few different archetypes of people. It's easy to tell them apart after a while."

"Yeah?" She narrows her eyes and studies me. "What's mine, then?" She absentmindedly braids a strand of her hair. I can't help but notice how much more relaxed she seems. Like she's finally let down her guard and is enjoying herself. It feels good that she's comfortable enough to do that with me.

"Well, I know you, so it's not exactly fair, but you're a good person who puts everyone's needs before your own. You're sweet and thoughtful, and people tend to take advantage of you without you even realizing it."

Her mouth drops open. "I don't know if that's an insult or a compliment. You make me sound like I'm naïve..."

"It doesn't have to be either." I shrug. "There's nothing wrong with being a good girl. It's all about how you feel about yourself in the end."

She sucks in a breath, and her cheeks burn bright pink, sending a jolt of electricity to my cock. I couldn't help but throw it out there to see if she'd react, and fuck me, my suspicions were right. This is a dangerous game I'm playing, but I know I won't let myself do anything stupid. She means too much to me for that.

"And what about you?" she whispers.

I blow out a sigh, thankful to be brought back down to earth. "I'm basically the exact opposite, but like you, I'm loyal to the people I love. I think that's my one saving grace."

"If you're trying to tell me you're a bad person, then I don't believe it." She yawns as she stretches her hands over her head. "You're like the sweetest guy I've ever met, Sam. I don't think anyone could consider you a bad guy."

I think you may be surprised.

"It's getting late. Why don't you let me walk you home?" I slide out of the booth and offer her my hand.

Disappointment flashes across her face for just a moment, and then she smiles. "Yeah, I've got an early class tomorrow, and I'll hate myself for staying out this late. I had so much fun tonight. I think I needed this."

I loop my arm through hers and place a gentle kiss on top of her head. "Me, too, Mags. Me, too."

SIX

Maggie

My apartment is a short walk from Terry's, but Sam and I take our time as if we're both not quite ready for the night to be over. It feels so good to connect with someone like this—and just another painful reminder of how lonely I've been. I wonder if he feels the same?

I guess that's what happens when you focus so hard on your career. You make those dreams come true, but if that's all you have, it doesn't feel quite as rewarding as you thought it would. What's the point of any of it without someone to share it with?

"Thanks for walking me home." I nudge him with my elbow. "Even though you didn't have to. I've literally walked home from Terry's alone more times than I can count."

He shoves his hands in his pockets. "Well, that's because I wasn't around. No decent man lets a woman walk home alone at night. I don't care how many times you've done it."

I glance down at my feet, unsure how to respond, and notice a trickle of water dripping from the bottom of the door, draining in a thin stream to the street. "Oh, no." I twist my key in the lock and slam my hip into the frosted glass door as I push it open. A cold sheet of water pours over our feet, and my heart sinks to my stomach. I don't have to turn on the lights to know this is bad, very, very bad.

"Oh, shit. Looks like you've got a gnarly leak somewhere." Sam steps in front of me and turns on his phone's flashlight, and I follow him, the water covering the top of my shoes.

"Dammit." I shake my hands and flip the light switch, but nothing happens, so I try another. "The lights aren't working," I call to Sam, who's somewhere in the hallway. "I can't see anything. Do you see where it's coming from?"

I turn on my phone flashlight to illuminate the lobby, and it's so much worse than I thought. At least three inches of water covers the floor as water streams down the walls, soaking all my new artwork and furniture.

My brand new mustard modular sofa is absolutely drenched. The rugs, cabinets, merchandise, and the brand-new iMac computer are all ruined.

"No, no, no." I rush to the crystal display to see my collection of selenite bowls and all the other crystal bins filled to the brim with water.

I run into the yoga room, cold water splashing up my legs and soaking me, and crash into Sam's hard chest.

"Whoa, just breathe. We'll figure it out. It's going to be alright." He grips me by the elbows to steady me, but it's too much. My brand new infrared heaters—ruined. The cork flooring I just installed last summer—ruined. Props, speakers, mood lights—all ruined. Everything that I've worked so hard for is completely destroyed.

My legs crumble beneath me as devastation rips the breath from my lungs, and Sam catches me before I hit the ground.

"You're alright, Maggie. It's going to be alright. I'm here. I'm going to help you figure this out." He tightens his grip around me, pressing me flush against his strong chest as hot tears flow down my face.

"Y-You don't understand. This is everything I've worked for. There's so much water. Everything's ruined. Everything." I cry into his chest as his large hand rubs my back.

"I have an eight o'clock class in the morning. What am I supposed to do?"

"We'll figure that out, but right now, we need to find the source of the leak and turn it off." He lifts my chin to meet my eyes. "It's just a building. We'll figure it out. You're going to be okay." He speaks so confidently that I almost believe him.

I wipe my teary, swollen face with my sleeve and nod as Sam slowly releases me.

"I think it's coming from the hallway."

I shine my light, following closely behind him, and bump into Sam's back when he suddenly stops at the foot of the stairs. Gusts of water trickle over the steps, and the *current* seems to get stronger the closer we get to my door.

"Shit. Do those stairs lead to your apartment?"

"Yeah." It's all I can muster because I'm in such disbelief.

Sam takes my keys, and I follow him up the stairs on shaky legs to what feels like my impending doom.

When he unlocks the door and pushes it open, my eyes widen in horror.

Oh, shit. I stand there in shocked silence as water pours from the ceiling in every direction. How long was I gone?

Sam wades inside through the ankle-deep water shining his light on the ceiling. "Do you have a landlord we can call?"

I walk inside on numb legs as water sprays me, soaking me from head to toe. It's so much worse than I could've imagined. Everything I own is ruined.

"No... I... uh... I own this building. I have a tenant who lives above me, though."

"Fuck, that's not good," Sam says as he stares up at a spot on the ceiling. He pulls out his phone and dials a number.

"Hey, Jeff. Yeah, I know it's late, but I've got an emergency. I need you to send a crew over ASAP. We've got a busted pipe on a three-story building. I haven't been up to check, but I'm worried about structural damage."

I follow his gaze to the sagging ceiling tiles and swallow a lump in my throat. I acquired my tenant, Ms. Beasly, a seventy-year-old widow, when I bought the building two years ago. She's never given me any problems and always paid her rent on time. I hate this is happening to her. Where is she supposed to go?

"I don't care if I have to pay holiday pay *and* time and a half. Just send someone over. Preferably more than one, got it?" Sam ends the call, and I look at him through my tears.

"I... I... can't afford to pay for this," I say in a panicked whimper. "There's so much damage. It's everywhere. I don't even know where to begin. I've got to cancel my class tomorrow, and we need to wake up Ms. Beasly upstairs–"

"I'll handle that. Do you have an emergency contact for her or something?" He takes the phone from my shaking hands and pulls me into the kitchen, so we're not standing underneath the dripping water.

"Yeah, she has a daughter. There's a file in my notes with her contact information." I push my sopping-wet hair back and cross my arms over my chest. I stand there helplessly as Sam dials the number and tells her what's going on. How did this amazing night turn into this... nightmare?

He hands me back the phone. "She's on her way to get her now. We'll find somewhere more permanent for her to stay in the morning. My contractor's sending over his plumber now. He should be here any minute."

"Thank you. I don't ... I don't know what I would've done if you weren't here."

His deep brown eyes soften as he rubs his thumb along my cheek. "You would've figured it out, but I'm happy I was here to help you." He pats me on the shoulder. "Come on, let's wake Ms. Beasly and help her pack a bag. Her daughter should be here soon."

Luckily, Ms. Beasly was still awake when we broke the news—though she was far more interested in the handsome gentlemen by my side than the flooding. Sam assured her that his assistant would be in touch in the morning, and we helped her pack a bag. By the time her daughter arrived, she'd loaded us up with a variety of baked goods from her pantry that "would've gone to waste."

I clench the loaf of still-warm, freshly baked sourdough bread to my chest as I watch her daughter's tail lights drive away.

"What am I supposed to do now?" I don't know if the question is for Sam or myself, but he answers anyway.

"You'll stay with me until we figure this out." He takes the bread out of my arms and piles it on top of his armful of baked goods.

I spin to face him. "No, Sam, you've already done enough. I'll just see if I can stay with Gwen or Elliot, or I'll get a hotel room."

"Gwen's going to have a baby any day now, and Elliot and Benjamin are hosting their in-laws while they remodel their house." He looks down at me with soft eyes. "I know you haven't met Benjamin's family, but they're a lot. You wouldn't have a moment to yourself."

I shake my head. "I don't want to impose–"

"Magnolia, I won't take no for an answer. I wouldn't have offered if it was an inconvenience."

Something about how he says my full name commands my attention. It sends shivers down my spine, and my body goes warm all over.

"Okay," I nod. "I'll stay with you."

"Good. Now, let's get you out of here. Your teeth are chattering so hard I'm afraid you'll chip a tooth."

He calls for a ride, and we stand in silence, soaked to the bone and loaded with loaves of bread.

"I hope you like french toast because I don't know how we're going to eat all this bread," he teases.

Sam's apartment is a penthouse suite in the middle of the business district. "I didn't even know you could live in a building like this," I say as he ushers me into the elevator.

"It's not a forever thing, but right now, it serves its purpose of keeping me within walking distance of everywhere I need to go. I hate traffic, so if there's a way I can ride my bike or go on foot, I don't mind exerting a little energy to do so."

It's nearly one in the morning, and I'm so exhausted my eyes feel like sandpaper. On the Uber ride here, I canceled my classes for the rest of the week and sent each client an apologetic text. The last thing I want is for someone to show up only to realize the entire studio is closed until further notice.

"Here we are," Sam says as he ushers me to his door and opens it to welcome me inside. I don't know what I was expecting, but I can safely say this was not it. Sam's apartment looks like something out of a men's lifestyle magazine. We walk into a foyer with a large chandelier hanging overhead that leads into an open floor-plan space. His kitchen is a combination of wood and marble countertops with a giant island. There's an industrial stainless steel gas stove and an assortment of knives magnetically secured on the wall.

"Wow, this is incredible." I'm in awe as I take in the most beautifully designed and decorated space I've ever seen in real life. "Did you hire a decorator or something?"

He laughs and drops his keys in a bowl on the counter before sliding off his wet shoes. I'm wearing sandals, so my feet are mostly dry by now. I didn't even consider that he's been walking around with soaked feet. "I actually did most of it myself. That and my stepmother helped. I completely gutted this place when I bought it three years ago. It's been a fun side project, and I've enjoyed putting all the pieces I've collected over the years to good use."

"You're extremely talented. I mean, I knew you were successful..." I open my arms wide. "But this is on another level. No wonder your investment properties are doing so well."

"Well, coming from you, that means a lot." He opens the fridge, pulls out two water bottles, and hands me one. "Come on. I'll show you to your room. I know you must be exhausted."

We pass through the living room that's somehow equally modern and cozy. There's a leather sofa with a huge ottoman that doubles as a coffee table facing a flatscreen TV that looks like framed art.

I can't help but notice the small personal touches sprinkled around. There are photos of Sam rock climbing on an actual mountain, group photos with Benjamin and Jack, and what must be his entire family all laughing hysterically, wearing swimsuits and beach coverups in front of the ocean.

"Just down the hall on the left here." He opens the door to what will be my bedroom. "Here you are. There are extra blankets in the closet, and the bathroom is just across the hall. My room's right over there." He scratches the back of his head.

"Unfortunately, my bathroom is under construction at the moment, so we'll be sharing yours. I hope that's not too much of an inconvenience–"

"Oh my gosh, Sam, don't even worry about it," I assure him. "This bedroom alone is bigger than my entire studio apartment. I think I'll be okay sharing a bathroom."

His shoulders soften, and a small smile pulls at his lips. "You know, I haven't had a roommate since college. I think this will be fun." He opens the bathroom door, revealing the most beautiful spa-like bathroom with a deep tub in the center and a large glass shower off to the side.

There's no hiding in here. I'll have to make sure to keep the door locked because I don't know if I've ever seen glass so clean. An accidental walk-in would leave us both scarred for life.

"Towels are in here, and there are extra razors and toothbrushes in the bottom drawer." He grins and pushes a piece of hair behind my ear. I must look like a drowned rat by now. "Why don't you go first? I'll see if I can find something clean for you to sleep in."

"Thanks. This is all so nice," I sigh. "I don't know what I would've done tonight without you."

He walks backward, shoving his hands in his pockets. "That's what friends are for, right?"

"Right." I agree. After the door clicks closed, I make sure to secure the lock, locking it and unlocking it a few times just to be safe.

I nearly jump when I see my reflection in the mirror. I look more like a drowned Master Splinter than a rat. My wavy hair is halfway dried and frizzy while my mascara's rubbed off my eyelashes, making me look like a raccoon.

I should be mortified Sam had to see me like this, but I'm too exhausted.

I turn on the shower and step inside, letting the warm water rinse away the remnants of the day. My tense muscles start to relax as steamy plumes in the air around me.

For the first time in my life, my five-year plan is irrelevant, and there's nothing I can do about it.

SEVEN

Sam

"Dude, what's with you today? I don't think I've ever seen you miss so many free throws," Benjamin says as he jumps up for the rebound.

I catch the ball he throws my way and take another shot. It hits the rim straight on and flies across the gym, and Benjamin arches his brow in question.

"I don't know, man. I guess I'm just tired." I rub the back of my neck and walk over to retrieve the ball, then pass it to Jack.

When Benjamin texted asking if I was available to play this morning, I couldn't say yes fast enough, despite being exhausted. I just needed to get some air and clear my head. Last night after I was sure Maggie was situated and in bed, I spent hours calling in favors to find a contractor who could take on her renovations immediately. After going through most of my contact list, I finally found someone who agreed to stop by today to do an assessment.

Maggie was still asleep when I left this morning for the gym, so I left her a note telling her I'd be back this afternoon and that I would have groceries delivered. I just want her to feel as comfortable as possible. I know staying in someone else's home can be awkward, even if it's a good friend.

Our pickup game ended, so it's just the three of us shooting. I don't get to see the guys much these days, so it's nice to bullshit around.

"What do you have to be tired about?" Benjamin teases as he throws me the ball. "Long night having kinky sex with Natalie?"

I bite my cheek as I dribble. "No, actually. She, uh, she ended things." I shoot the ball, which hits the rim straight on and bounces across the court, and they both turn to stare at me.

I shrug. "It's not a big deal. She met someone. I'm happy for her."

Benjamin retrieves the ball and dribbles through his legs. "Are you really happy for her, or are you just telling yourself that because you don't want to break one of your stupid rules?"

I roll my eyes and cross my arms. "I'm genuinely happy for her. Natalie is a great woman. She deserves to be happy. And there's nothing wrong with having rules. Rules keep things clean and simple. You have rules in your business agreements, so why should your sex life be any different?"

"I don't know, maybe because humans are messy and have emotions that can't always be controlled. That's what life's all about, isn't it?" Jack says with a shrug. "Just this morning, Gwen went from screaming at me for finishing the last of the Lucky Charms to crying because she remembered she no longer likes the taste of marshmallows—which is why I ate all the Lucky Charms... Range is what keeps love interesting, Samuel."

Benjamin's eyes widen as he fights a smirk. We both know not to point out just how much *range* Gwen has now that she's pregnant, especially since Jack seems to love every second of it.

I hold up my hands. "Who said anything about love? Look, I'm happy for you both, but I'm not looking for a life of domestication. I've figured out what works for me, and I'm happy with my system."

"I don't understand why you're such a serial monogamist, Samuel. Why don't you download an app and meet up with a nice woman? You can both take care of your needs and part your separate ways. You know, like a normal, single thirty-four-year-old dude," Jack says as he runs to retrieve the ball.

I drag my hand down my face and sigh. "You both know that's not how I work–"

"Yeah, we know." Benjamin and Jack share a look as if they're having a silent conversation. "So, what happens next? Do you have a waiting list or some shit?" Benjamin teases, but he eyes me curiously as she throws me the ball.

"No, I don't have a waiting list." I catch it and shoot. This time, it bounces against the backboard and goes in. "But I was out last night looking to meet someone new. Actually, I ran into Maggie..."

"Maggie Anderson, Maggie?" Jack interrupts. "Where?"

"I was out scouting this new bar downtown and was hiding from one of the women I cut things off early with before Natalie. Anyway, I ducked into a VIP booth, thinking it was empty, and there she was, sitting with Damian Johnson. He was giving her a tarot reading."

Jack stops dribbling the ball and props his hands on his hips. "You're just going to speed past that like everything you just said was completely normal?"

I shake my head. "Anyway, he gave us each a reading, and then we went to Terry's and hung out–"

"What did he say?" Benjamin narrows his eyes.

"Nothing, really," I lie. "Just some generic bullshit about my future."

Jack shoves me and jumps up and down like a little kid awaiting his surprise. "Stop holding back on us, dude! You wouldn't have mentioned that part if it wasn't important!"

I shove him back and rub the back of my neck as I think back to Damian's cryptic message scribbled on that napkin.

"Uh oh! You're lying. Your nostrils just flared!" Jack shakes his head and points at me.

Fuck. I forget these guys know my tells.

"Look, it was nothing, really. The message may have leaned on the sexual side of things, but it's not my place to share Maggie's secrets. So, don't ask." I meet both of their eyes, and they nod.

I let out a sigh and walk over to the bleachers to take off my shoes. "Anyway, after that, she seemed kind of frazzled, so I suggested we grab a drink at Terry's. Then I walked her home, and we found her whole building flooded. A pipe burst on the third floor. Everything was flooded, so I offered her my spare room until she could get a crew to repair everything. I was on the phone half the night trying to find someone. She was so upset. I can't imagine how worried she must be."

"Damn, dude." Benjamin sits beside me and places a hand on my shoulder. "Why didn't you just say that? You know if it's too much trouble for you, Elliot and I are happy to put her up."

I scoff. "It's Maggie we're talking about. She's the furthest thing from trouble. I'm just worried about her. I know she's hard on herself, and I just want to do what I can to help."

It's mostly the truth. I am worried about her, but I know everything with her business will be okay. I've got the best crew in the city working on it, and they'll have her back up and running in no time.

No, I'm more worried about the desperation I saw on her face last night. No woman—especially someone as devastatingly gorgeous as Maggie—should feel like they need to pay someone to sleep with them because they're not *good enough* at it.

Maybe I'm just broken.

Her words echo in my head as arousal and rage ignite within me. I strain my hand reflexively at the thought of just how much fun I could have with her. What I could do for her, how I could wake her up to something she's never experienced. Oh, how easily it would be for me to show her just how wrong she is.

I close my eyes and blow out a slow breath to calm myself.

I can't let my mind go there. I've got to shove this urge down deep, along with all the pieces I buried a long time ago.

I'll need to keep myself thoroughly distracted if this shared living arrangement will ever work. I can't risk our friendship because I'm making decisions with the wrong head. I need to replace Natalie ASAP.

Jack stands to leave and swings his duffle bag over his shoulder. "Good luck with your new roomie, Samuel. I've got to get going. Gwen wants me to pick her up a tub of movie theater popcorn on the way home."

"Why don't you just take her to the movies?" Benjamin asks.

Jack shakes his head and sighs. "She says it tastes better when she eats it on the couch at home because she doesn't have to wear pants."

I laugh because that's the most ridiculous thing I've ever heard, yet Jack doesn't seem to mind one bit. He's wrapped so tightly around her finger that he'd probably buy her the whole movie theater if that's what it took to curb her popcorn craving. "Well, you have fun with that."

"I've got to go, too. Elliot wants to pick out coordinating armchairs for the sitting room. She doesn't want them to match but wants them to look like they belong together... which means I'll be chair shopping all day long."

We say our goodbyes, and I promise to keep them in the loop with the renovations. Once the heavy metal door slams shut, I'm left with the strangest feeling of loneliness. It's something I haven't felt in quite a long time.

EIGHT

Maggie

After everything that happened last night, I was spent. I slept so hard that I think I may have aged backward. I woke up to find a note on my side table informing me that Sam had some errands to run and would be back later in the afternoon. Naturally, my first reaction was to panic that he had witnessed me sleeping so deeply, and I bolted to the bathroom to check for any signs of dried drool. And just as my luck would have it, not only did I discover the traitorous stain, but my hair stood in all directions like a cockatoo. That's what happens when your head is covered in cowlicks, and you go to bed with wet hair. So, here I am, forced to take another luxurious shower.

When I say luxurious, I'm not just talking about the ambiance and water pressure. I feel like I'm in a spa, stocked to the brim with all the best hair products. From shampoo and conditioner to exfoliating body wash and moisturizing body butters, Sam's bathroom is something out of every woman's fantasy.

When I step out of the steamy shower, I wrap myself in a plush white robe. A girl could get used to this.

Bending down, I open the cabinet under the sink and find an acrylic organization system filled with razors, hair ties, extra toothbrushes, toothpaste, and an assortment of pads and tampons. Wow, it's like he thought of everything.

I shake my head when I find the Dyson hair dryer and Airwrap. How many women does he bring home to warrant all this?

I brush out my long strands and flip my head over as I dry my hair and think back to our conversation last night, trying to remember if he mentioned having a girlfriend, but I'm drawing a blank. Come to think of it, I've never even heard him mention seeing anyone. He's certainly seeing someone, though. That's shockingly apparent.

When I'm finished rough drying—in record time, I might add—I play around with the Airwrap. The time seems to fly as I sing along to my favorite playlist and play around with all the fancy products. I'm having so much fun, like how I imagine it feels to be a little girl playing in her mother's makeup.

When I'm finished, I take in my appearance and feel so beautiful. I look like I've just come back from the spa. My hair is freshly blown out, and my skin is scrubbed and moisturized to perfection.

But when I open the cabinet to put everything back, I knock over another container, and its contents spill out with a clink. A silky red piece of fabric catches my eye—does he keep her panties under here, too? I look over my shoulder as if to make sure he can't see me, even though he said he wouldn't be back for a while.

Curiosity gets the best of me, and I reach inside and pull out a long piece of fabric. I hold it out in front of me and assess it like a venomous snake.

It's a bright red piece of silk about two feet long and three inches wide. I spin it around, searching for any details, but it's just a boring piece of silk. Maybe it's her robe tie? I quirk my lips and go back to retrieve the container.

As I pick up the fallen belongings, I pull out a long chain with three clamps on each end and some kind of black leather bracelet-looking things that connect in the center. What is this stuff?

I slide my hand through the center of one as the realization hits me. My eyes widen in horror as I realize what it is, and I panic. I try to yank to cuff off my wrist, but it's tighter than I realized, so I stand up and use my foot to hold the other side down as I yank with all my force.

Then, suddenly, the cuff snaps open. The force sends me flying backward as the cuffs shoot out across the bathroom, hitting the kinky box and sending its hidden surprises flying in every direction.

I cover my head just in time for the toys to shower me, crashing down in clinks and soft thuds like a naughty thunderstorm of sin.

Once the room goes silent, I lay on the cool tile floor in stunned silence. I don't know what I was expecting, but finding my friend's secret kinky sex paraphernalia stash was not it. How am I ever going to be able to act like I didn't find all this stuff? I couldn't lie if my life depended on it. I don't know how to keep a secret, and now I have to look Sam in the face and pretend I wasn't going through his stuff? What if he gets mad and asks me to leave? That's what I get for being nosey.

I sigh as I slowly push myself up and retrieve the strange contraptions, trying not to think about the who's and what orifices they've been inside. When I'm finished, I place the red sash on top and shove it back in the cabinet in the same spot I found it.

Finally, I close the cabinet doors and release a sigh of relief. That was way too close for comfort. I'm going to keep my nose out of Sam's business from now on.

Walking out of the bathroom, I'm surprised to find my clothes freshly washed and pressed, folded neatly in a pile on the dresser with the embarrassing napkin on top.

Oh, great, this just keeps getting better and better. I swipe the napkin up and shake it at the sky. "Haven't I been humiliated enough?"

I plop down on the bed with a bounce and shove my face into a pillow as I let out a feral scream of frustration. Why can't things just be easy for once?

I roll onto my back and stare up at the intricate crown molding as the napkin message plays on repeat in my mind. It's not just some random psychic hoopla. It's Damian. He's literally proved himself time and time again. It may seem insane, but I actually believe him, which is why everything is so confusing. Why did all of this have to happen right now?

As if on cue, my phone buzzes against my leg, and I sit up with an exasperated sigh. Ok, universe, I'm listening.

I swipe open the lock screen and find a message notification from Trent.

My heart hammers in my chest, and I hug the phone to my chest, looking around suspiciously as a million thoughts begin racing through my mind.

When I've finally gathered myself, I take a breath and open the app.

TRENT

Hey Maggie!

I just wanted to check in. I noticed you haven't RSVP'd for the reunion yet.

The green dot next to his name indicates he's currently online, not that I didn't grasp that from the message notification, but then I realize I also have a green dot next to my name.

Shit, I can't just leave him on read when he can clearly see that I read his message. I wipe my sweaty palms on the duvet before typing out a response.

Hey!

It's so good to hear from you. Sorry, I haven't had a chance to RSVP to the reunion. I was originally planning on trying to go, but I've just had a major hiccup with my yoga studio. I feel like I'll be tied up with repairs for the foreseeable future.

Good luck with everything, and it was great hearing from you!

I breathe out a long sigh. There, that wasn't so bad. I hate disappointing people, especially someone like Trent. My younger self would've peed her pants if I even thought he knew I existed, much less cared if I came to the reunion.

I stare at his small circular photo. He's aged a bit, his hairline's receding slightly, but he still looks incredible with his dimples and bright blue eyes. It's too bad I can't make it. It really would've been something to see him again in the flesh.

Another notification breaks me from my trance.

TRENT

Well, I have to say I'm incredibly disappointed to hear that you can't make it. I have to admit I was looking forward to reconnecting with you...

I bite my lip as I let his words sink in. Trent was the first person ever to notice me. Growing up in foster care, I had to move around a lot, which made it hard for me to make connections with anyone, especially friends.

We were partnered up in science class our freshman year and slowly became friends over the semester. He was skinny and a little shy, like me, even though he was on the football team.

He was my only friend back then, and I had the biggest crush on him. I don't know if he was just being nice or if he shared the same sentiment, but he asked me to the spring formal that year.

I was so excited to go but ended up getting moved to a new foster home when my foster family got selected for a new baby. Then overnight, I was rehomed to a new family a few hours outside of Madison. It was a week before the dance, and it happened so fast I didn't have time to tell him.

I lived with that family for another two years until the same thing happened again, and I got moved back to Bramville to a group home my senior year.

By the time I saw him again, I almost didn't recognize him. He'd climbed the ranks to be captain of the football team, his skinny frame now bulky with muscles, and he was dating the head cheerleader. He was Mr. Bramville High, and I couldn't blame him for moving on. I didn't fit into his friend group or his life anymore. He was still kind, but he never really went out of his way to speak to me.

Really? I didn't even think you noticed me after I moved away...

I type the message out and hit send before my brain can register my candor. Immediately I see the three little dots indicating he's typing a response.

TRENT

Yeah, well, high school boys can be pretty dumb. I'm ashamed to admit I was blinded by popularity back then. Of course, I remembered you. How could I not? I was so bummed after I asked you to the dance, and you just disappeared. I thought you were avoiding me until word got around that you had to move. That was my first broken heart. I think I cried myself to sleep for a month.

My mouth goes dry as I reread his message at least five times before letting myself blink and swallowing the hard lump that's formed in my throat. I can't believe this. He actually *cried* over me? Little does he know I felt the same way, on top of all the emotional trauma of uprooting your life at a moment's notice.

I can't help myself. I click on the event page, respond *Yes* to the RSVP, then type out my response.

Wow, I had no idea. It killed me to leave without telling you... Listen, I'm going to see what I can do to make the reunion. I'd really like to reconnect with you too.

TRENT

Seriously!? Wow, you just made my day. Listen, I've got to run. Here's my cell number 555-981-0982. Call or text me anytime, okay?

Will do. Bye, Trent!

Dropping my phone, I let out an excited squeal, my face hurting from smiling so big. Maybe this is where my journey will lead me! With everything going on with the studio, it feels crazy even to be entertaining the idea of taking a trip to rekindle whatever this is with Trent, but isn't that the whole point?

Maybe the universe really does have my back, and I just need to start trusting that everything is working out like it's supposed to.

I grab the fragile bar napkin and place it in the empty drawer of my side table. One day all of this will make sense, and I'll have the memento as a physical reminder.

Three hours later, I've just finished loading the dishwasher when I hear Sam come through the door.

"Hey, Mags, sorry I'm late, but I stopped by that new sushi place you mentioned you wanted to try." He comes around the corner with an armful of to-go containers stacked up to his chin. "I didn't know what you liked, so I got a little of everything."

I rush to help him, but he waves me away. "Sam, you didn't have to do that! It's more than enough that you're letting me stay here. I don't expect you to feed me and wash my clothes, too."

He places the containers on the counter and smirks. "You could just say *thank you*. Maybe I like having you here as a guest. Did you ever consider that?"

I pause in the middle of my search for plates. What an odd thing to say.

"Just over there, in the corner," he directs.

"Oh, got it." I grab two plates and set them next to the spread of sushi. "Will it just be the two of us tonight, or should I grab another plate?" The question falls out of my mouth before I can stop it, and I snap my lips shut nervously.

"It's just us." Sam turns to face me and stills, narrowing his eyes. "Why are your cheeks so flushed? Are you hot?"

"Oh, yeah, I was doing jumping jacks right before you came home. You've got to get that cardio in every day, ya know?" I snatch a napkin off the counter to fan my face, but it's too limp to do much, so I have to wave it faster than what seems natural.

Sam just stares at me with a look of confusion, and I finally abandon the fan idea and start loading my plate with sushi.

Why can't I just act naturally? He doesn't need to know that I know about his dirty bathroom secrets. We're both adults. Maybe I just need to pretend to have found his board game stash. That's it; I'll just pretend it's something else. No big deal.

"Your hair looks nice," he says as he lines sushi on his plate.

My hand freezes, hovering over the spicy tuna roll. "Uh, thank you. I... um... I used your Dyson Airwrap in the bathroom. I hope that was ok?"

"Of course, it's okay. I told you to make yourself at home, and I meant it." He grabs fancy chopsticks for each of us from a drawer, which he closes it with his hip. "If there's anything you need that isn't already stocked, just let me know."

I force a smile. "Great." I don't trust myself to say anything else because *I went through your bathroom and found your secret stash of kinky sex toys* is just on the tip of my tongue.

Sam takes my plate from me and carries it to the living room, placing it on the coffee table. I awkwardly follow and take a seat.

"I thought we could eat in here tonight and talk about the construction plans." He goes back into the kitchen and opens the fridge. "Kombucha?" He holds up a couple of bottles.

"Yes, please." After shoving some kind of fried roll in my mouth, my eyes roll back in my head, and I moan.

"Looks like the sushi's a hit." He laughs as he sets our drinks down on the coasters.

I cover my mouth as I chew. "Oh my God, it's incredible." I shove another piece in my mouth and glance over to see Sam staring at me with a grin.

"I'm glad you like it." He picks up his chopsticks and dives in. "Wow, you were right. This is the best sushi I've had in

Chicago." As he wipes his mouth and sips his drink, I watch his Adam's Apple bob.

A strange electric sensation jolts down my spine, and I stiffen.

"So, I wanted you to know that I found a contractor for the studio. He owes me a favor, so don't even worry about it. He went by today after the plumbers left and assessed the damage. He thinks he can have it finished in four weeks if he can get enough guys."

"Wow, Sam, that's... that's incredible! You didn't have to do that–"

"I wanted to help, and I know every contractor in this city. Really, Maggie, it was nothing."

A warm, fluttering sensation jolts through me from the relief. "I... Sam... I don't know what I would do without you. Thank you for taking care of this... of me."

"That's what friends are for." He pops another piece of sushi in his mouth like what he just said was the easiest thing in the world, no big deal at all.

"Speaking of friends..." A sudden wave of courage comes over me. "I couldn't help but notice all the feminine products in the bathroom. I know we're sharing, and I just don't want to be in the way if you have someone over. I don't want to put you out, and I want you to know that I can make myself as scarce as you need me to be when you have a guest. Just send me a text, and I'll disappear into my room–"

"I don't plan on having any women over while you're staying with me, but I appreciate the thought," he says in a clipped tone before going back to eating his sushi.

"Really, though, I don't want to be a distraction for you. I don't mind–"

"Mags, I'm not seeing anyone right now. Relax. You're not an inconvenience in the slightest."

"Oh, okay," I say in almost a whisper. "Is that because you just broke up with someone, or you're just taking a break–"

He turns to face me. "No, I'm not seeing anyone right now. Is there anything else you'd like to ask me?" He lifts a brow and studies me. I wonder if he knows what I found.

I swallow a gulp and wet my lips. "No. I... I was just thinking that I don't really know that much about your dating life... and we didn't really get to talk about who you were hiding from last night..."

His eyes narrow. "I'm not sure you can handle that information, Mags." His words hang in the space between us.

"Who? Me? I can handle it." My voice comes out a few octaves higher than normal.

I shimmy a little closer and catch a whiff of his cologne. He smells like worn leather and amber. It's seductive and masculine and has my mind going in a million different directions as I sit on the edge of my seat, waiting for him to reveal whatever it is he thinks I can't handle.

He looks down at the glass in his hand. "Not many people know this about me—other than Benjamin and Jack—but I'm not really much of a *traditional* dater."

"So, what, you like to hook up with a lot of women?"

"Not exactly." He takes a sip of his drink, sucking a small piece of ice in his mouth, and I watch as his muscular jaw moves around it until he finally bites it and swallows. My neck warms at the strangely erotic feeling of it.

"You see, I don't like to get attached... or bored." He pauses as if considering how much more he wants to reveal.

A million questions burn through my mind, but I don't dare interrupt him. I'm afraid with one wrong word, he'll back peddle, and I don't know if I've ever wanted to hear a secret so badly in my life.

"I don't like to sleep with several different women. I enjoy learning exactly how to pleasure a woman and delivering on that over and over again. I also really like to be in control."

I suck in the tiniest gasp, drawing his eyes to my heaving chest. His eyes scan my body before landing on my lips and then back to my eyes.

Over and over again. I swallow a gulp, and Sam blows out an amused breath as he takes another sexually charged sip of his drink.

"I'm what's called a dominant, and I had an arrangement with my submissive for nearly a year. She met someone recently, and I was looking for her replacement. The woman I was hiding from was a past arrangement that didn't work out. She didn't like my one-year rule and got a little too clingy."

"You were in a relationship for almost a year, and you never told me?" I blurt out, causing Sam to laugh.

He scratches the back of his head and smiles. "There's nothing to tell. It's not a relationship, just consensual sex with some basic rules for each party to follow."

I lean closer and prop my chin on my hands. "What kind of rules?"

Sam laughs as he leans back on the sofa arm, propping a pillow behind him to get more comfortable. "Just your standard expectations between both parties."

"No, you don't." I jump on my knees and grab his hand. "You can't just skim past the rule part. This is the most exciting thing I've ever heard, and you owe me after I shared my humiliation with you last night!"

He chuckles and shakes his head. "Fine, I'll tell you, but you have to promise not to think differently of me."

I hold out my pinky and grin. "I pinky promise I won't."

Sam rolls his eyes, then loops his pinky around mine. We pull away and kiss our hands to seal the deal.

"The first thing you need to know about the BDSM community is that there are a lot of different ways to be a dominant and a submissive. Personally, I'm what's called a pleasure dom, and I get off by bringing pleasure to my subs..."

NINE

Sam

"Let me get this straight... you get off on bringing pleasure to your partners? Not like hurting them or whatever?" Maggie stares at me with big doe eyes as she hangs on to my every word.

I scratch the scruff on my chin. This is going much deeper than I intended, but she's soaking everything up like a sponge. I can practically see the wheels spinning in her mind, and fuck, if it doesn't have me thinking about things I have no business thinking. "As I said, there are many different ways to practice kink, and everyone has their preferences of what turns them on. Personally, I'm not big into impact play, but I'd be happy to comply if that was something my partner wanted."

Maggie lays back on the opposite end of the sofa to get more comfortable, and I pull her feet into my lap as I mindlessly begin massaging them. Empty to-go containers are strewn across the coffee table, and the TVs timed out and gone to the main menu screen. It's nice having a low-key night in with good conversation and even better company. It's the makings of a perfect night.

"So, what are some of your other rules?" She twirls a stay piece of hair, looking so comfortable and relaxed.

"Well, it depends on what my submissive needs from me." I clear my throat and take a sip of water. "Everyone is different, and my goal is to help my sub grow as much as possible during our time together. For some, that means helping them to prioritize boundaries in their work life, and for others, it could be something as little as pushing them to stand up for themselves." I shrug. "It all depends."

"Do the women tell you what they need help with?"

"No, I like to get to know them first, and then, if I identify something I can help them with and they're a good personality fit, I'll agree to a one-month trial run. If everything goes smoothly, then we'll both sign a one-year contract with the agreed-upon terms."

"So, that's what happened with the woman you were hiding from?"

I nod as I swap her feet and pull the other into my lap. "Yes. She was a little too needy for my taste, and I couldn't give her the attention she needed. It's a rare occurrence, and I probably didn't handle it as well as I should have. It wasn't one of my proudest moments."

"Why the one-year contract? What if you met someone, and you both hit it off? Would you be open to extending it? Maybe getting married someday?"

I shake my head. "No. That's a firm rule that I have no intention of changing. I have my reasons..." My voice trails off.

Maggie pulls her feet away and bolts upright, pushing her hair away from her face in a panic. "Oh my God, Sam, I'm sorry. I didn't mean to pry."

I place my hand on her arm to calm her. "It's fine, Maggie.

It's natural to be curious about these things. You haven't done anything wrong," I assure her.

She blows out an exasperated sigh and falls back on the couch, covering her eyes. "You probably think I'm so lame after everything I told you last night. God, I'm so embarrassed. I never would've told you if I knew you were so..." She gestures to all of me.

"So... what?" I quirk a brow.

"So... I don't know... Experienced? Professional? Basically the complete opposite of me."

I pull her foot back into my lap and continue my massage, and she seems to relax a little. "You should never be embarrassed about something like that. It doesn't take much to know that you've been sleeping with the wrong men if you can even entertain the idea that you're not good at sex." I scoff at the absurdity. "Sometimes women just need to be able to completely trust their partners to feel pleasure. The right man would create an experience that allowed you to have a safe space, to feel protected and supported, so that you could let yourself go and be in your body rather than your head."

I look up to see her mouth hanging open ever so slightly, forming an O. The shocked expression is mixed with intrigue and something that looks a lot like arousal. *Don't look at me like that right now, you beautiful goddess of a woman. I don't think my will can stand it.*

I bite my cheek and let out a long, controlled breath.

She shivers, then shakes her head. "Wow, well, I guess I just need to find someone so perfect and willing to take me on as a fixer-upper project. That shouldn't be hard to do at all," she mocks.

Despite the warning sirens blaring in my head, begging me to leave it alone, I can't help myself. I move my hand from her foot to her calf as I massage the tight muscles, my body growing hungrier as she quietly whimpers from my touch. Fuck, that little noise is more erotic than anything I've ever heard.

I clear my throat. "Why are you so determined to find someone to help you? If you're so crazy about this guy, why don't you practice with him?" The words taste like vinegar in my mouth, but I can't help but wonder.

"I told you, I don't want to scare him off." She sighs. "He's recently divorced, and his ex-wife is gorgeous. He's probably mastered everything there is to know in the bedroom. Meanwhile, I'm still over here using all my lives on level one." She props herself on her elbows, her eyes drifting down in defeat. "I've never had a repeat sexual partner—and that's pretty bad since I've only had sex five times. I feel like every single time, I'm left with a new insecurity. It's hard putting yourself out there, and I don't know how much more of it I can take."

My heart aches for her, and I want to pull her in my lap and wrap her up and tell her how perfect she actually is ... but that's not my place. I grit my teeth to keep from saying something I shouldn't because none of that is actually helpful right now. I could tell her I think all those guys are crazy and that she's perfect, but she has scars that say otherwise. Words are cheap; actions are how you really show someone how you feel about them.

I let out a sigh. "Maybe you could find a way to relax into your body during sex? Focus on the sensations without worrying about all the other stuff—"

"I don't know what the point is. I told you I'm broken, Sam. I wouldn't know what an orgasm felt like if it hit me between the eyes," she interrupts.

My hands come to a stop, and I blink several times as I try to process what she just said. "What do you mean, Maggie? Are you saying you've never had an orgasm at all? Not even by yourself?" A knot forms in my stomach, and I hold my breath while waiting for her reply.

She doesn't look at me, focusing her eyes down as she scratches something off the sofa and fidgets nervously.

"Magnolia–"

"No, Sam, I've never had an orgasm." She collapses back again and covers her face with her arms. "I can't imagine what you must be thinking of me right now. God, I'm so embarrassed." She shakes her head as she covers her face, and I sit there, mouth agape, shocked to my fucking core.

How? How is this possible? How could someone so beautiful and accomplished, so seemingly sure of herself, have never experienced the euphoric pleasure of an orgasm? I have so many questions, but seeing her reaction gives me pause. I don't want to be insensitive or pour salt on a wound, but I feel outraged on her behalf while simultaneously aroused in a way I've never experienced. Blood rushes to my cock, and I shift her foot to the side, so she doesn't notice it as my mind does its best to flash images of what she might look like coming undone at my hands.

I close my eyes and suck in a breath as I try to bring myself down from the fantasy, but when she sits up and looks at me, her long tousled red hair falling over one shoulder, her freckled cheeks burning bright pink, it's like all the air's been knocked from my lungs.

I cough several times and sit up as I drain the rest of my water.

"I'm sorry, Sam. I overshared. Please don't feel sorry for me or look at me differently now. I promise I won't mention it again–"

I hold up my hand. "Maggie, please stop apologizing. You haven't done anything wrong." I stare down at my feet with my elbows propped on my knees and shake my head. "If you were mine, I'd punish you every time you apologized for something so menial..." I mutter under my breath.

"You'd what?" she asks in a breathy whisper.

"Nothing." I grab the remote and click on the TV to reign my thoughts back to a normal frequency.

How is she supposed to know that I'm the Big Bad Wolf, and she just waved the juiciest piece of meat right underneath my nose... and I've never been quite so famished.

Fuck me. This was a bad idea.

We spend the rest of the evening rewatching "Parks and Rec" as I try to distract myself from the wild thoughts threatening to play over in my mind. I don't know how in one conversation, you can go from completely platonic feelings toward someone to wanting to rip their clothes off and see them sitting on their knees, but that's exactly what happened tonight.

It's not that I wasn't attracted to Maggie before; she's fucking gorgeous in a natural, understated way, and she has no idea. Her long red hair's like the equivalent of a human rose, and her vibrant hazel eyes are mesmerizing. You never know if they'll be more green or blue, it depends on what she's wearing, but sometimes, I think they change with her mood, too. Either way, I find myself getting lost in them as I try to memorize the color before they change again.

And that tight shapely body of hers that you can never quite get a good look at underneath her modest clothing has my mind doing cartwheels trying to imagine how she'd look wearing a naughty set of lingerie. The contrast of her sweet personality dressed like a vixen for my eyes only, how I'd show her just how capable she is of feeling pleasure, and I'd revel in the feeling of accomplishment. I'd be doing the world a favor by showing her what that would do for her confidence alone.

I pull my shirt over my head, swap my jeans for gray sweats, then climb into bed, propping my arms behind my head and staring at the ceiling. I watch the fan spin around and around as I scold myself for getting so worked up over someone I care so deeply about.

Maggie is my friend, and I don't fantasize about my friends... and I certainly don't fuck them. I just need to up my search and find someone, so I'm not so tempted around her. Maybe I can make time to go out tomorrow evening, take someone home for the night at least and get some of this out of my system. Then I'll be able to think more clearly.

A soft knock on the door startles me, and I sit up on my elbows. "Come in."

Maggie stands in the doorway wearing the only the t-shirt I gave her. It falls to her mid-thigh, exposing plenty of leg for my imagination to run wild with.

Fucking great.

I make a mental note to get her more clothes first thing tomorrow, some pajamas—preferably the kinds with pants.

She twists her hands and leans against the doorframe. "I... uh... do you mind if I come in?" She looks behind her nervously as if she's afraid of being caught, even though we're the only two people here. It makes it feel even naughtier somehow, which doesn't do my eager cock any favors in calming the fuck down.

I clear my throat. "Uh, yes. Come in."

She slowly tip-toes over the cool hardwood floors and comes to sit on the corner of my bed. I can see the faintest outline of her hardened nipples underneath the white concert t-shirt, and I inwardly groan, breathing a heavy sigh out of my nose.

"Is there something you need, or–"

"I didn't know you had so many tattoos." Her eyes widen as

she takes in my exposed torso.

"I like to keep them hidden so that they can't be seen in a suit," My answer comes out clipped. "Is everything alright?"

"Oh, no, everything's fine." She waves a hand, then twists the hem of the t-shirt; it inches higher and higher by the second.

Having a nervous, fidgeting, half-dressed Maggie sitting on my bed is in no way helping me fight the carnal desires currently plaguing me, a torment so cruel yet so deliciously exciting nonetheless. My breath hitches, and my heart races in my chest, and my fingers itch to reach out and touch her soft, satin skin.

"So, I was just laying in bed, and I couldn't stop my mind from racing, playing back everything we talked about tonight..."

"Yes, and?" I press.

She looks down at her hands. "I... um... well, then I had this idea. It just popped into my head, and I couldn't stop thinking about it..."

I take a deep breath as I wait in silence for her to continue, not wanting to put any more pressure on her considering how nervous she seems.

She pushes the heels of her hands against her eyes and rubs them before folding her hands back in her lap. "I was thinking that maybe we could help each other out. You know, with our problems?" Her voice trails up in question, and I tighten my grip on the sheets.

"With what problems?"

"God, this is so embarrassing." She shakes her head, keeping her eyes trained on the comforter. "I was thinking that I could be your new submissive... *temporarily*. You know, just until the reunion, and you could maybe teach me how to have an orgasm?"

"Maggie, I–"

"I promise I won't be clingy or weird," she assures me. "You won't have to impress me or anything, and I don't even have to take my shirt off if you don't want me to." She shakes her head. "I won't make a peep. I'll follow your rules and do whatever you tell me to do. I won't give you any trouble, and I don't have any expectations of you." She shrugs. "And if I can't orgasm with you, then at least I'll know I'm the problem. Then you can just teach me how to act like I've had one."

"Maggie–"

"I trust you, Sam. You're the only one I trust to do this for me, and after hearing what you said in there about how you treat your submissives, well, that just confirmed it."

I shake my head. "Maggie, I don't think I can–"

"Wait." She holds up her hands, her eyes pleading as she bites her lip. "Just don't... don't say *no* tonight. Sleep on it, and if you still feel the same way in the morning, I promise I'll never bring it up again. We can forget all of this happened. Deal?"

It feels like she stares right into my soul, melting my icy heart from the inside out.

"Fine. I'll sleep on it... but I'm not making any promises." I lay back down with a sigh.

"Thank you, Sam." She jumps on top of me and plants a kiss on my cheek. "Sleep tight. No pressure, okay?"

I force myself not to watch her ass sway as she leaves and clicks off my lamp with a disgruntled sigh. What the fuck is happening right now, and in what universe is *this* my life?

I try to like hell to push the conversation to the back of my mind as I toss and turn, making an absolute mess of my sheets, but I can't get the stupid, idiotic, dangerous idea out of my head.

By the time the clock strikes five the next morning, I sit up, yank open my side table, pull out my contract, and read over it.

I can't believe I'm even considering this... I get up and grab my laptop, bringing it back to bed as I type away, amending it just for Maggie.

TEN

Maggie

I pace back and forth, biting my fingernails as I stare down at the gorgeous designer dress left on my side table this morning.

I haven't even been able to bring myself to look at the dress; it's still folded neatly inside the box because the sealed envelope with my name on it has my brain short-circuiting.

I don't know what it is, but after my conversation with Sam last night, I think I know what it's about...

So, he's either giving me a formal rejection letter and this fancy dress as a sympathy gift... or there's something in that envelope that's going to scare the absolute shit out of me, and this dress has something to do with it.

I throw my head back and let out a frustrated grunt to no one as I plop down on the floor and hold the envelope in my lap. What was I thinking last night being so forward with him? I can't even blame it on alcohol because we didn't even drink! No, last night I was drunk with desperation... and maybe a little desire.

There was something about how Sam described his lifestyle. It was like something deep inside me woke up, and my entire body felt on edge as curiosity danced in my mind. I've never felt so... *aroused*.

After we went to bed, I lay there and tried to turn my brain off, but the idea just wouldn't leave me alone. I realized that if I wanted to get better at sex, I would need to do something more drastic than simply dating guys I meet on dating apps. Maybe it was time to step away from the amateurs and enlist some professional help. After hearing about Sam's lifestyle and all the rules he set in place to keep things simple, I realized that that was exactly what I needed.

I knew I'd regret it if I didn't at least put it out there for him to consider, so even though it was completely out of my comfort zone, I forced myself to march in there and lay my cards out on the table. I knew he'd be shocked, but I wasn't expecting the pained look on his face. Mortified, I went back to bed, internally scolding myself, and tossed and turned most of the night as my embarrassment ate away at me slowly and painfully until I finally passed out.

I rub my thumb across my name as my heart races in my chest. Whatever is inside could change everything in my life, my friendship with Sam, or who knows what else.

I suck in a breath as I slide my finger underneath the seal and pull out a packet of papers neatly stapled together at the corner with a letter attached to the front.

Magnolia,

After much consideration, I've decided to agree to your proposal, provided you're in agreement with the attached contract and conditions.

It's important you understand this is merely an

agreement between two friends and nothing more than that. My biggest wish is for you to be happy, and if I can help you with that, then I'm pleased to do so.

Please review the aforementioned contract and make any notes or modifications you deem necessary. I'll send a car to pick you up for dinner at six p.m. sharp, where we will discuss the contract in its entirety.

I've provided you with a dress to wear this evening, as well as undergarments and shoes. I also had my assistant stock an assortment of new makeup and beauty products in the bathroom since all of yours were ruined due to the flooding. I've also included a lipstick that I believe would look fantastic with your complexion. Please wear your hair down this evening.

Read over the contract thoroughly, and come with any questions or amendments you have.

Please know that if this seems like it's too much, I will not be offended in the slightest. I look forward to seeing you tonight.

–Sam

I hold my hand over my gaping mouth as I reread the letter three more times as reality finally sets in. I pull the dress out of the box to reveal a royal blue long-sleeve beaded fabric with a high neck. A pair of nude strappy stilettos with a delicate bra and panty set is tucked underneath. My cheeks flush with embarrassment as I hold up the lacey bra and panties my exact size. He must've checked my dirty clothes before sending them off to be cleaned. I force myself to stop overthinking it. This is the kind of stuff I have to get past, especially since having sex with him will be far more vulnerable than knowing he looked at my underwear.

I place the clothes back into the box and grab the contract. Flipping to the first page, I begin to scan.

Section One: Code of Conduct

- The Submissive will submit to the Dominant in every way
- The Submissive will address the Dominant as Sir unless there is not enough privacy or given explicit permission by the Dominant
- The Submissive will dress in a wardrobe provided by the Dominant
- The Submissive will let the Dominant care for her and provide whatever he deems fit
- The Submissive will follow the Dominant's sexual commands unless the Submissive is uncomfortable and utilizes the safe words (Green, Yellow, or Red). In which case, the Dominant will immediately stop the scene, and both parties will have a discussion and renegotiate limits
- The Submissive will use her manners at all times
- The Submissive will not speak about herself in a self-deprecating way and will behave with confidence at all times
- The Submissive will not put herself in harm's way or behave negligently

The nature of the relationship between the Dominant and the Submissive is strictly contractual. There will be zero tolerance for the expression of deeper feelings during the time the contract is in place. Failure to uphold this expectation will result in immediate termination of the agreement.

Punishment for the breaking of any of the rules will be determined/administered by the Dominant at the first available opportunity.

I swallow a gulp as I stare down at the list, gripping the thick stack of papers with my clammy hands. It's all so formal and stated so explicitly, as if we're negotiating a business deal rather than a sexual agreement.

The Submissive will Submit to the Dominant in every way...

I sit the papers on the bed and flap my hands as I try to calm myself by pacing back and forth across the bedroom. I know Sam—or I thought I did anyway—and this... this seems so intense...

A cool shiver works its way up my spine, and the hairs on my arms stand on end as a wave of excitement jolts through me. I'm terrified yet exhilarated, and the intensity is making me feel like I may explode.

Am I really up for this?

I walk over to the giant window that stretches from the floor to the ceiling to take in the magnificent city beneath. The breathtaking view is a constant reminder of how big the world is and, inversely, how limited my experiences have been.

Maybe this is what I need to push myself, to really start living life to the fullest and experiencing the full spectrum of human emotion. Maybe this will show me exactly what I've been missing. Maybe this is the journey Damian was talking about.

It's scary, that's for sure, but I trust Sam, and I know he wouldn't do something to hurt me. I pace back to the bed and pick up the contract, its heft a physical representation of the weight of my decision.

I dive back in with a more open mind and continue reading.

Section Two: Safe Words

The use of safe words will be expected during the entire duration of the contract in public and private settings.

- Red will indicate an immediate stop to all activities
- Yellow will indicate an approach to the limits and will be used as a warning to slow down/check-in
- Green will be used to indicate pleasure/encouragement

Okay, well, that seems smart and not too intimidating. Knowing I always have an out relieves some of my nervousness, though, for the life of me, I can't imagine what I'd need to use them for. It's not like I have a long list of sexual experiences to compare to, but they've mostly been uneventful and over within a couple of minutes.

I flip the page over, and my eyes nearly bug out of my head when I see the long list of sexual limits, which includes some things I've never even heard of.

But why are they all marked out?

When I get to the second to last page, I find a note written at the bottom.

The Dominant is willing to participate in the following sexual activities with the Submissive for the duration of the contract.

- Kissing
- Touching of breasts, nipples, and genitals
- Oral sex where the Submissive is the recipient
- Light anal play
- Vaginal intercourse

I bite my lip as I read through the tiny list, and I don't know whether to be embarrassed or relieved that he doesn't think I can handle any more than the basics. I make a note to ask him about it tonight. A thin sheen of sweat breaks out on my upper lip as I work my way down the list and sign my initials by each act, pausing for only a moment when I get to light anal play. It's not something I've ever considered, nor can I understand why it's on the list, but I trust that Sam knows what he's doing and probably knows more about these things than I do. I sign my initials without giving it any more thought and move on to the next section.

Section Three: Limits

Please indicate any and all limits from the list of sexual activities. If the limit is not already listed, please provide it will as much detail as possible.

I read through the list, and since I only have five choices of what Sam's willing to do with me, I don't see any reason to list any other limits, not that I'd even know what they'd be anyway. I knew I was inexperienced, but after reading this contract, I'm wondering if I'm even living in the same world as everyone else. I feel like an alien who thought she was human all her life and is just now realizing she's different.

Oh, well, I may be a little behind, but you know what they say, *the best time to plant a tree is twenty years ago... and the second best time is today.*

I flip back through as I read over my answers when the sexual health agreement catches my eye.

Both the Submissive and the Dominant agree to undergo sexual health screening prior to any shared sexual activity.

I jot down an amendment in the margins, surprised he overlooked something so basic, but it must've been an oversight. I set the papers down, ready to sign when we meet later today. I have no idea what happens next, and for the first time in my life, I'm actually okay with that.

When Sam said a car would come for me, I expected something more along the lines of an Uber, not a top-of-the-line black Range Rover with blacked-out windows that probably cost more than my entire commercial property. During the short drive to the restaurant, I read through the contract three more times as I try to calm my anxious nerves.

It's not that I don't trust Sam; it's more that I'm afraid to disappoint him. Up until now, I've never had to see the guys I slept with again, but I'll still see Sam all the time, no matter how this shakes out. *What if I'm so terrible he can't stand to be around me anymore, and he distances himself from our friend group?*

I shake my head as I tighten my grip on the folded contract. Sam wouldn't do that. He's taken so much time and care to prevent that from happening. Besides, this is literally what he does in his normal life. He's a professional. A sexpert, if you will.

As the driver pulls up to a quaint Italian restaurant, he says, "Here we are, Miss. Anderson."

He jumps out to open my door, and I take his offered hand as I step into the cool night air. A refreshing gust of wind whips at my long pin-curled hair, and I push it back over my shoulders as I step into the lobby to find the hostess waiting for me.

"Miss Anderson, Mr. Jordan is already seated at his table in the back. If you'll follow me, it's right this way."

His table. How much does someone have to spend in a place like this to have their own table?

I follow the hostess through the elegant restaurant to the back, where she opens the double doors leading to a private room dimly lit by candlelight. The deep burgundy walls are adorned with oil paintings of the Italian countryside that look like they belong in an art gallery... and probably do.

Looking like a movie star in his tailored black suit and tie, Sam is sitting at a round table set for two, fully immersed in whatever he's reading on his phone. He looks so effortlessly polished yet casual, and I don't know how I've never noticed how strikingly handsome he is.

"Your server will be by to check on you shortly," the hostess says before stepping out and closing the doors behind her.

He stands to pull out my chair, giving my a full scan, and my heart kicks up a beat. "Wow, Magnolia, that dress looks stunning on you."

I think back to the contract. *The Submissive will dress in a wardrobe provided by the Dominant.* "Thank you. It's beautiful. I hope you didn't spend too much on it."

Sam's smile falls, and he places his napkin in his lap. "You don't need to worry about things like that. I'm an adult, and I'll spend my money on whatever I want." He pours us each a glass of wine. "Now, tell me, did you read the contract? Do you have any questions for me?"

I open my mouth to speak, then close it, unsure where to begin. "What made you change your mind?" It's not exactly the question I planned on asking, but I'm curious. Last night, he seemed so against the idea; I really wasn't expecting to wake up to a contract on my side table.

"I care about you, Maggie, and the thought of you going out and finding another incompetent tool who may hurt you wasn't something I needed on my conscience. If I can help you gain more confidence and love yourself a little more, then that's the least I can do for one of my best friends." He takes a sip of wine and smiles warmly, melting my nervous jitters away.

I let out a sigh of relief as I sip my wine, suddenly feeling a little more normal. This is my friend, Sam, and even though this little arrangement is out of my comfort zone, I know he won't hurt me.

"I see you've brought the contract with you. Why don't we take a look." Sam pulls out his own copy and passes me a pen as he walks me through the expectations, reiterating everything thing I agreed to in writing.

"Some of the rules are a little odd and seem like common sense, don't you think?"

"Could you give me an example?"

I use my finger as a guide as I read, "*The Submissive will eat two healthy meals a day*." I look up. "Is this a blanket rule or something?"

Sam crosses his leg in a figure four position and leans back in his chair, looking sexy as sin as his eyes scan me. "No, that's a rule I specifically added for your benefit. I want to make sure you're taking care of yourself, and from what I've observed during my time around you, you don't always prioritize meals.

Do you not think that's fair?" He quirks a brow, and I wave him off.

"No, it's not that. That seems fair."

"Then what's the hesitancy I'm sensing? Let me be clear; I'm by no means asking you to restrict, only to add nutritious foods to two meals."

I wipe my sweaty palms on the seat cushion. "Yeah, I get that. I guess it just feels a little strange knowing you noticed something like that. I don't think anyone's ever paid so much attention to me. I don't know how I feel about it."

Sam's eyes seem to drink me in as if in challenge, and a smug smile pulls at the corner of his lips. "Maybe you just haven't realized it, but you're incredibly noticeable, Maggie. Some may even consider you bewitching." He eyes me over the rim of his glass as he takes another long, slow sip of his wine.

"Great." I take a long gulp of my own wine. "Thank you for clearing that up for me."

Sam leans forward, focusing once again on the contract. "Anything else you'd like to discuss? Do you have a clear understanding of the safe words? In my experience, the use of the color system is the easiest thing to remember."

"Is it common for safe words to be used? I mean, does that usually happen?"

Sam sets down his pen. "It's not common, but it's something that happens from time to time. With the sexual activities we'll be performing, I don't expect you'll need to use them, but since I'm not a mind reader, I think it's important to have communication in place, so we're both comfortable." He purses his lips and places his hand on my arm. "I know this seems like a lot, but I want you to know we can go as slow as you like. Ultimately, the submissive is the one who's truly in control."

I nod and flip to the next page. "I do have one amendment to add under the sexual health section."

Sam flips his page and clicks his pen, ready to edit the text.

"You say we both need sexual health screenings." I look up to meet his eyes. "Which I appreciate. But there's no mention of birth control requirements." I tilt my head to the side. "I'm not on birth control, nor do I plan to start taking it. I don't like the way it makes me feel, and frankly, I don't have enough sex normally to warrant all the side effects. Is that going to be an issue for you? Are you willing to wear a condom every single time—for the entire time?" I add the last bit because they always say the same thing, *just let me start without one, and I promise I'll put it on before we're finished.*

I won't risk it. It's a firm boundary he'll have to accept, or the whole deal is off the table.

A small smirk pulls at the corner of Sam's mouth. "I'm pleased to see you taking your health and well-being so seriously. I'm proud of you for communicating that boundary, but birth control isn't something you need to worry about with me..."

My eyebrows knit together in confusion.

"I had a vasectomy when I was twenty-one."

It takes a moment for his words to sink in. "Why? What made you do something so extreme when you were that young?"

He spins the wine glass by the stem without taking his eyes off me. "Lots of reasons, actually. I didn't want children and knew that if I changed my mind, I could either have it reversed or I could adopt. I also wanted to take responsibility for my sex life and not put the burden on every woman I slept with. It was a no-brainer for me since I decided around that time that I wasn't ever interested in having a real relationship. It allowed me to have better sex, and I never had to worry about altering a woman's life by making her choose whether she wanted a child." He shrugs like it's nothing and takes a sip of his wine.

"Wow, Sam, that's incredibly mature of you. Really, I don't

think I've ever met a man who's so responsible? Considerate?" I scratch through the note in the margin. "Well, I guess that's settled, then."

"And you're positive you still want to do this?" He quirks a brow.

"I've never been more sure of anything." I grab the contract and sign my name at the very bottom and pass it to him. He scribbles his own signature and sits back in his chair with a smug grin.

"So, what happens now?" I ask as the server walks in with our food and places our plates on the table before us.

"First things first, we're going to enjoy this nice meal together, and then, tomorrow morning, I'm taking you shopping." He cuts a bite of his salmon and pops it into his mouth.

"Shopping for what?" I ask nervously.

"Everything. Now, eat your dinner before it gets cold."

I pick up my fork as my cheeks heat. "Yes, sir."

Sam lets out a surprised laugh. "I have a feeling you're going to be my star pupil, Magnolia."

ELEVEN

Maggie

When Sam said he was taking me shopping, I didn't expect the full Julia Roberts in *Pretty Woman* experience, but that is exactly what this feels like, only I'm the one who asked him for help.

We've already covered the basics, meaning he's bought me a new wardrobe of jeans, tops, sneakers, and jackets. I try to argue that I don't have anywhere to wear all these clothes, but he insists.

"Come on. This is fun. You have to admit this is fun." He nudges me with his elbow playfully as he pays for my giant pretzel and hands it over to me.

I snatch it out of his hands and pinch off a piece of the warm, salty bread before dunking it in the nacho cheese sauce.

"Mmm," I moan as my eyes practically roll back in my head. "It's getting a little more fun now."

Sam laughs as he leads us to a nearby bench. "Now that I've

seen how much you enjoy pretzels, I may just need to keep the apartment stocked with them." He smiles. "You've just got a little..." He wipes cheese from the corner of my lip with his thumb, then sucks it clean.

"Uh... Thanks." I take another bite, trying to ignore the butterflies taking up residence in the pit of my belly. Ever since our conversation last night, it's like something's shifted between us. I mean, I guess technically, things have shifted, considering we signed a contract. I don't know, though. I guess I thought things would change immediately, and aside from Sam bringing me breakfast in bed this morning and the shopping, things seem kind of normal, except for the cheese licking, of course.

I'm not sure when my lessons start, but I feel like I'm on the edge of my seat waiting for him to command me to do something sexual at any moment, but I have to remind myself that Sam isn't like that, and this arrangement isn't like that either.

I can't help but wonder if he's doing this because he feels sorry for me, but I can't make myself ask, and maybe I don't want to know the answer anyway.

"So, tell me, what's your favorite part of your body?" Sam asks as he pinches off a piece of my pretzel and pops it into his mouth.

I shrug. "Like in a functional way? I guess my heart because it pumps my blood, keeping me alive, and it's my favorite chakra to work on–"

"For the purposes of this conversation, I'm just asking about the body parts that can be seen. What's a part of your body that makes you feel sexy when you look at it?" He wraps an arm around the back of the bench behind me and leans in a little closer.

"Oh, well..." I tap my lip as I consider the question. "I guess my collarbone and my shoulders?"

"Are you asking me or telling me?" He challenges as he leans in and, this time, takes a small bite directly from my pretzel. Holy hell, I can still feel the heat from his mouth on my hand, and a blush burns hot on my cheeks.

"You're so fucking cute when you blush." He smiles as he traces his thumb over my jaw before trailing down my neck until he reaches my collarbone.

I suck in a breath as his velvet touch creates a current of electricity, and my whole body wakes up as if I'm being touched for the very first time.

"You have a beautiful neck, and your collarbone is nearly erotic." His fingers spread over the base of my throat, and I swallow a gulp, afraid to make any sudden movements that'll cause him to stop. It hardly feels legal to be so aroused by such a seemingly innocent touch in public. I guess that just goes to show how much of an amateur I really am. At this rate, I may just have my first orgasm from a nice, firm handshake. Maybe there's hope for me yet...

"So, if we can both agree that you have a great chest... why do you always cover it up with high-neck clothing? I don't think I've ever seen you wear anything lower than a crew neckline."

I bite my lip, feeling awkward under his intense stare. "I guess I've never really thought about it before..." My gaze drifts down, and Sam nudges my chin up, encouraging me to look him in the eyes.

"That's not true. Tell me, Maggie."

"I guess... In the back of my mind, I'm still following the rules I had growing up. Even though I don't agree with them consciously, maybe they've become ingrained in who I am?" I say with a shrug.

Sam nods, his hands drifting to the back of my neck as he gently rubs his fingers through my hair.

I melt into his touch and relax a little more. "The foster mother from my group home loved to remind me of why I'd been abandoned as a baby. She'd say that if my birth mother weren't so promiscuous, she wouldn't have gotten pregnant so young and out of wedlock, and that she was basically asking for it..."

"Are you saying your birth mother was...?"

I nod ever so slightly as I stare down at my hands, the familiar ping of shame and embarrassment burning a hole in my chest. I know it's not something I should be ashamed of. I had nothing to do with it, but knowing something like that, knowing you weren't just unwanted, you were actually someone's nightmare made flesh, doesn't exactly give the warm fuzzy feelings of self-love.

"That's the most ridiculous thing I've ever heard," Sam snaps as he rubs his hand down my back to comfort me. "I'm sorry someone weaponized that to control you. It's disgusting, and it says far more about her than it ever will about you." He links his fingers with mine and plants a gentle kiss on the back of my hand. "Come on. I've got an idea."

Ten minutes later, I'm staring at myself in a gorgeous, floor-length emerald green gown. It has a sweetheart neckline that dips low on my chest, making me feel sexy and confident, and drapey sleeves that give it a soft, ethereal essence. The deep color makes my red hair pop and brings out the green in my hazel eyes.

I smooth my hands down the silky fabric and spin, loving how breezy and light it is, just as Sam knocks on the door. "Are you going to let me see it or what?"

I swing the door open as I walk to the mirrors, and Sam lets out a loud whistle as he follows behind me. "Holy shit, Mags, you look so fucking hot." He moves behind me and places his hands on my hips as he meets my eyes in the mirror. "How do you feel wearing this?" he whispers, his warm breath tickling my neck and sending a wave of goosebumps over my skin.

"I... I actually feel kind of pretty," I admit, feeling a little more confident.

"I can work with that." He tightens his grip around my waist and moves a little closer. "This dress compliments your body so well. If you look this incredible with it on, I can't imagine what you'll look like when I take it off you."

I suck in a tiny gasp as his touch deepens, and my body gets all floaty, his hold around my waist the only thing keeping my feet planted on the ground.

"There's just one problem." His finger loops at the elastic of my panties through the dress, and he pops them against my hip, making me jump in surprise. "Why don't you go and change while I checkout? We've got one last stop to make."

Without a word, I take off to the dressing room and quickly change into my regular clothes. This time, I don't look at myself in the mirror because I already know what I'll find, and I'd like to pretend that I'm confident enough to handle this.

When I return, I find Sam waiting by the door, twirling the bag in his hand and his eyes sparkling with mischief. "Ready?"

I force a nervous smile. "You bet."

My eyes go wide as I take in the microscopic garment made up of no more than ten pieces of ribbon strung together. I squint to read the tag. *Meredith.*

What's a Meredith? Is that a name for the type of lingerie, or is that *her* name?

Everything in here is so tiny. I feel like I need reading glasses to even see the outfits.

Do people really wear stuff like this in their everyday life?

I think about my collection of plain white cotton panties, with the exception of the five pairs of black I wear during my period. They're comfortable, practical, and machine washable... What more does a woman need?

Maybe that's why I've never gotten a second date?

"Maggie, what do you think of this?" Sam calls from the other side of the rack.

"Be right there," I call as I hang Meredith back on the rack with her sisters? Friends? Whatever you call a group of Merediths.

"What's—" I stop in my tracks when I see the black lacey nightie he's holding. "Wh—what are you doing with that?" I awkwardly point, then cross my arms over my chest.

"I want you to try this on. I've already had them start you a dressing room, so just go on back, and I'll be right there." He nudges his head toward the dressing rooms.

"Are you sure, Sam? I don't need all this. I'm not too good for Target." I almost choke when I turn over the price tag for a little nighty that'd be barely long enough to cover my butt.

"Magnolia," he warns in an almost growl. "Do you really think I'd spend all the money I have today on clothes and let you wear polyester undergarments?"

I clear my throat. "They're cotton, actually."

"They're perfectly acceptable to wear when you're menstruating." He shoots me a glare. "Otherwise, you'll wear something nicer. Understand?" His tone is clipped and final.

"Yes, sir?" I quirk a brow in question, sensing that the tone of our shopping trip is quickly trending from the *friend* to *dom* territory.

He stops in his tracks and tilts his head, wearing a surprised look of approval. "Very good."

Sam leads me to the dressing room, where the saleswoman

carefully spreads our selection on the rack. My eyes threaten to bug out of my head as I take in the array of sex clothes... because there's no way any of it is regular underwear. No, this is designed with the sole intent of being taken off to have sex, which makes me wonder how something with such a short wear time can cost so much.

Strappy one-piece body suits with holes cut out in strategic areas, tiny silk dresses that surely won't cover the bits that need covering, thongs, belts, and lacey, see-through bras with extra straps around the midsection...

I slide the curtain closed and hesitantly begin removing my clothes. Undressed, I choose the black silk nighty, the least confusing of all the *outfits*. I've just pulled on the matching lacey thongs when I hear Sam say, "Come out here and let me see when you're ready."

I whip the curtain open just enough to shove my head out. "What!?" I hiss. "I'm not coming out there in this!"

"Magnolia." He growls just low enough for me to hear. "This is a private dressing area. There's no one out here but me..."

"Fine." I sigh, blowing my hair out of my eyes, then slide the curtain open and step in front of the large mirror in the center of the small room.

Sam comes to stand behind me, just like he did before, only this time, his hungry eyes lap me up, carefully settling on every inch of my body in the mirror's reflection. His eyes finally meet mine, and he looks like he's in pain.

It's too much to take. He probably realizes he wants out of our deal. Seeing how ridiculous I look in next to nothing, realizing I don't belong here.

A crimson blush creeps over my chest and cheeks, and I squeeze my eyes shut, unable to take his disappointment any longer.

I don't know if I want to shrivel up in a little ball or run. Sam's grip on my waist tightens, anchoring me in place.

"Open your eyes, Magnolia," he whispers in my ear, his warm breath brushing my neck, sending a shiver down my spine. "Open your eyes and admire yourself." He releases my hip and nudges my chin up, so I'm standing up straight as I hesitantly obey and let my eyes flutter open.

"Good girl." He smirks, then runs his finger over my lips. "Now, look at yourself. Look at how breathtaking you are." He runs his fingers down the back of my arm, barely grazing my skin yet shooting bolts of electricity in his wake.

My breath hitches as his hand caresses my hip, playing with the hem of the ultra-tiny nighty that doesn't even cover my ass. "You look good enough to eat, do you know that?" He tightens his grip on my waist with his other hand as he lets his free hand roam toward the top of my thigh, teasing the hem of my panties.

Arousal floods my system as my eyes adjust to the dimly lit room. My nipples harden under the thin silk as every hair on my body stands on end. He brushes my long hair over one shoulder and peppers kisses on the other. I can't help but arch my head to give him full access to the side of my neck.

"You're so responsive," he whispers as he leans into my neck, sprinkling kisses over every inch.

I suck in a heavy breath as my eyes find his in the mirror's reflection. He smirks when he sees me, then slides his hand over my neck and gently tightens his grip. I can feel his erection against my back, he's hard as granite, and my eyes flutter closed as I take in all the sensations. When he releases my neck, my thighs reflexively clench at my aching center as I try to stand on wobbly legs.

"God, I'm going to have fun with you." He slides his fingers from my hip up my stomach and grazes over the side of my breast before returning to my throat, where he lifts my chin, forcing me to meet his eyes. "You'll wear this tonight." Then he pulls my hair back to center and steps back, clasping his hands behind his back.

"Try on the rest of the garments to make sure they fit. I'm just going to step outside and give you some privacy. I'll meet you at the counter when you're finished."

I nod as I stare back at him and bite my lip before adding, "Yes, sir."

This earns me an approving smile before he turns on his heel, leaving me alone in my soaking-wet lingerie.

I slap my forehead to bring myself back to reality. Holy shit, this man is going to eat me alive... and I can't say I'm mad about it, either. I hurry back to my dressing room and almost have a heart attack when I see he added a Meredith to the pile when I wasn't looking.

It takes some finagling, and I have to refer to the instructions on the tag several times, but I finally manage to get her on with all the straps in place. After looking in the mirror, I take a step back in shock. I spin and take in the view from every angle, pushing my old mindset down to the very back of my brain.

It's bold and confident and completely unexpected... I look sexy as hell in this collection of strings. I try to imagine what Trent's face would be like if he took off my clothes to find me wearing this underneath. Now that's something I bet he'd remember.

After gushing over myself enough, I carefully strip out of Meredith and move her to the keep pile, then carry the winners out to the register where Sam's waiting.

"I'm craving something sweet." He waggles his brows.

My heart skips a beat, unsure of what he means. "You are?"

He tucks a loose strand of hair behind my ear, then touches the tip of my nose. "I am. How about we stop for ice cream on the way home?"

"Oh," I let out an anxious breath. "Yeah, that would be great."

He takes the bag and then throws his free hand over my shoulder, pulling me into his side playfully. "So, what'll it be, chocolate or vanilla?"

TWELVE

Sam

Of two things I'm completely certain. Maggie really loves ice cream, *and* she has no clue how irresistible she is.

I had to grip the steering wheel so tightly nearly lost sensation in my hands at one point on the way home.

This whole day has been a whirlwind of mixed emotions, with some confusing boners tossed in.

I can't decide if I need a good fuck or to take out my anger on a punching bag... or maybe both?

The thought of Maggie being taught something so disgusting by the adults who were supposed to love her—or at least help prepare her for the rest of her life—makes me want to go completely feral. No wonder she isn't confident in her body. She's literally been programmed to think of herself as a walking *nightmare*.

I grip the bathroom counter and stare at my reflection as I take a long deep breath to calm myself. Underneath my eyes, the skin is shaded a blueish hue from exhaustion. I haven't had a full night's sleep since the night Maggie came home with me. It's not her fault my fucked-up brain enjoys torturing me, reminding me that she's just in the other room and just how long it's been since I've had sex.

Thirty-three days... but who's counting.

Natalie really picked a shitty time to end things, waiting until the day I returned from my month-long international trip. I could've at least cleared the pipes with a couple of randoms if I'd known I was coming back to be alone.

I didn't even have time to recalibrate before jumping into whatever this fucked up friendly arrangement is with Maggie, and now, I can't get the image of her in that fucking lingerie out of my mind. I think it's burned into my brain permanently.

We're supposed to start our lessons tonight, but I don't know how I can manage with this raging boner that pops up every time I think of her... which is a fucking lot.

I walk to the shower and turn it to the hottest setting before stepping inside to the billowing steam. The scalding water burns and soothes my aching muscles, and I start to relax. I plant one hand on the cool tile wall and grip my rock-hard cock with the other as I work myself, creating delicious friction. A fresh image of Maggie flashes in my mind, and I grit my teeth as I try to shake her away and replace her with Natalie or anyone from my past, but she keeps coming back, haunting me with big doe eyes and fuck-me lips.

Fuck it. I don't have the strength to fight it anymore.

I deepen my strokes and close my eyes as I let myself succumb to the fantasy.

Maggie's wearing black lingerie sitting on her knees in the living room, waiting for me when I come home from a long day of traveling. She looks sexy as sin with her wild, tousled red hair hanging down her back, waiting patiently like such a fucking good girl for me.

I move a little closer, and she sucks in a breath, her gorgeous tits barely covered by the thin silk ribbon holding them. The hem of the nightie rides up, allowing her supple ass cheeks to peek through on each side. She's wearing a red silk blindfold, and her hands sit in her lap, clasped in leather cuffs. She's ready to be tied up, just as I like it.

"I see you missed me. I missed you as well." I loosen my tie and stride toward her. Once I reach her, I pull her up to her knees by her cuffs. "I see you wore my favorite lipstick."

"Yes, sir," she pants as she wets her lips.

I let out a growl as I unbutton my shirt and throw it to the side before lifting her chin so I can admire her gorgeous face—what's not covered by her blindfold anyway.

I swipe my finger along her plump bottom lip, and she surprises me by taking a small nibble, then sucks my thumb into her hot, wet mouth. "Sorry, sir. I just wanted to taste you." She licks her lips, and her red lipstick smears when I wipe at them again.

Fuck, I love smearing her lipstick.

"Please, sir. Let me taste you," she pants, and my head falls back as arousal courses through me. I quickly unbutton my belt but don't remove it, so I can hear the buckle clinking while she works me in her mouth.

"You're a dirty little slut, Magnolia." I free my aching cock from my pants and place my head in front of her lips, so she can kiss me the way she loves before taking all of me in her soft mouth.

I grip my cock tighter, my strokes pumping faster as the fantasy of Maggie sucking me off plays out in my mind. My stomach tightens, and I'm on the cusp of release when a loud crash rips the fantasy away.

My eyes shoot open, pulling me out of my sex-hazed stupor as I see Maggie slam into the tall, opened cabinet door right before her feet fly out from underneath her. She lands on the tile floor with a loud thud.

"Mags, shit, are you ok?" I hustle out of the shower, snatch the towel hanging from a hook next to it, and wrap myself up with a swift motion before pulling her into my lap.

She winces as she pulls her headphones off. The song "WAP" blares in the small space.

"I'm so sorry, Sam! I was getting ready, and I saw your bedroom door shut, so I thought you were in there working or something, and the bathroom door wasn't locked–"

"Fuck, you're bleeding." A small trickle of blood seeps between her eyebrows and trickles down her cheek. I pull her up, so she's curled into my lap, not caring that we're both practically soaked. I nudge her chin to look at her nose and then let my gaze drift over her to check for any other signs of injury.

It's only then I realize she's wearing the lingerie from my fantasy, the very thing I instructed her to wear tonight.

It takes everything in me not to let my eyes burn holes in the fabric as the faintest glimpse of her little peach nipples pebble into little points behind the sheer black lace. She must realize it at the same time because she tries to jerk away, but I pull her back down. "Not so fast."

I run my hand to the back of her head, pleased not to find any cuts. Though, there is a pretty large knot forming. "Do you feel nauseous at all? Are you dizzy?"

"No, I'm fine. It's nothing..." She tries to sit up, but I pull her back and lodge her tight against my chest.

"It's not nothing. You're hurt. Stop being so stubborn, and let me look at it." My words come out a little harsher than intended, but at least she doesn't fight me. I grab an extra white towel hanging on the towel rack behind me and apply pressure to the wound.

When I pull the towel away, I can see it more clearly and let out a sigh of relief. "Good, it's not that bad. I don't think you need proper stitches. I can fix you up with a little super glue. It's actually the best treatment for a facial wound. It won't leave as big of a scar–"

"It's fine, Sam. Really." She grips my wrist, then reaches up to pat me on the cheek.

My arousal transforms into annoyance that she can be so blasé about hurting herself. What if I wasn't here? Would she have just put on a Tinkerbell bandaid and called it good? Would she have taken the proper care to even disinfect it first?

I grit my teeth and swallow my irritation as I pull her up to stand, holding her close. Suddenly, I'm keenly aware of the little-to-no fabric separating our naked bodies, and my annoyance doubles back to my cock, where it feels the most comfortable.

I decide the bathroom's as good a place as any to clean this up and lift her onto the counter without warning. She lets out a little whimper in surprise as I move closer, pressing myself between her thighs.

My pulse pounds in my ears as my heart races, no doubt confused about just where to send all the rushing blood. I chance a look down and see my cock is still hard, my head peeking over the top of the towel tied around my waist, and Maggie's eyes follow, growing big when she sees me.

I'm tempted to cover myself, but I don't. Instead, I let her look, her eyes fixated on my cock, and I study her, watching the look on her face go from worried to... *curious*?

I can't help my smirk. I'm going to have so much fun teaching her everything she wants to know.

Suddenly, her eyes widen in shock, and her body goes stiff... ok not exactly the response I was hoping for...

I look behind me and follow her gaze as something black

and oblong rolls across the floor and stops just before it hits my foot.

It's a butt plug.

Maggie's cheeks burn bright red, and she covers her face with her hands.

Guilty.

I clear my throat. "I see you've been exploring in here. Care to share what you've been up to, or would you rather me guess?"

"It's not like that!" She parts her fingers just enough to peek at me, and I actually chuckle watching her squirm. "I wasn't using it or anything! I don't even know what it's for!"

"Uh huh, that still doesn't explain how it escaped from its box in the cabinet..." I pull her hands away from her face and nudge her chin, so she's looking at me.

"I was looking for the hair dryer the other day, and I found your *stuff* tucked under the sink. I pulled it out, not knowing what it was. I was mortified when I realized what was in the box, and I may have accidentally thrown it into the air... I guess I must've missed that particular item when I was cleaning up the mess, and then when I came in here, I slipped on it." She crosses her arms over her chest and blows her hair out of her face. "There, are you happy?"

The blood's dripping faster now, soaking through the white hand towel, pulling me back to the moment.

I shake my head. "As much as I'd like to hear the rest of this story, we'll have to save it for another time. We need to stop this bleeding." I grab her hands and position them on the towel pressed firmly to her nose. "Here, hold the towel just like this. I'm going to grab my first aid kit. I'll be right back."

I squeeze her free hand, then turn on my heel and race to my bedroom, where I grab the first aid kit from my closet. Before returning, I throw on some gray sweatpants, so I don't scare her off completely.

I smile as I make my way back to the bathroom to apply the liquid stitches.

Though it's not how I intended our night to unfold, I'm not exactly mad about the progress we've made today, and I can't help but wonder if Maggie's got any more surprises up her sleeve...

Maggie sits on the sofa with her feet curled to the side while I prepare our dinner. After I cleaned up her head, I offered her a fluffy oversized robe to wear over her lingerie. I keep the apartment pretty chilly, and I don't think I can stand watching her shiver all night, no matter how much it'd thrill me to get a better look at those perfect nipples. Truly, I haven't even seen her tits completely, and my mouth is already watering with anticipation. I don't think I've had blue balls this bad since I was fourteen—and maybe still not even then.

I'm still wearing my sweatpants, though I did grab a t-shirt to cover my bare chest. When I told Maggie she'd wear the lingerie tonight, I originally meant after I'd taken her to dinner, but considering the unexpected excitement of the evening, I figured we'd do better with another night in.

"Are you sure you're feeling okay?" I ask for the tenth time, glancing through the doorway. "Do you need Tylenol or Advil? I think I've got Ibuprofen in the bathroom... "

"I'm fine, Sam." She lets out a nervous laugh, and I can't help but find it endearing.

"Kombucha?" I call as I place our food onto two plates. After I got the murder scene cleaned up in the bathroom—I ordered Maggie to rest against her rigorous protests—I ordered takeout from the bar and grill downstairs.

"Kombucha would be wonderful," she replies, then bites her

lip, probably stopping herself from reminding me for the millionth time that she's capable of making her own plate.

I glower at her, an unspoken reminder that I'm in charge, as I bring her a wine glass of kombucha, a bottle of water, and her plate. She accepts my offering, forcing a smile through clenched teeth.

"Good girl," I whisper, kissing her forehead. Then I turn back to grab my drink and plate from the kitchen.

The worn leather sofa sinks comfortably underneath me as I sit across from her, careful not to mess up the throw blanket spread over her legs. We eat in silence for a moment until Maggie finally blurts. "So, are we just going to pretend like I didn't bust in on you... *pleasuring yourself* earlier?"

I pound my fist on my chest as my laugh causes me to choke on my chicken. "Well, that's one way of opening the door to conversation." Tears prickle behind my eyes from the straining, and I continue laughing as I wipe them away with the back of my forearm.

"That's not an answer!" She pounds her small fist on the couch, which only causes me to laugh harder. "What's so funny!?"

"You are utterly adorable; you know that?"

"Adorable?" Her voice shrieks a few octaves higher than normal as she unties the robe belt, giving me a brief glimpse underneath. "Why would you make me wear this ridiculous outfit if you think it's adorable, huh, Sam?" She cinches the tie back and falls back on the couch, covering her face with her arm.

"I'm so embarrassed and confused... and I saw your penis, and it's really freaking me out to think about something that *substantial* coming anywhere near me... and I don't want you to hate me for making you do something you don't want to do." She sits up in a panic and pulls at the roots of her hair. "Sam, do you feel like I'm trying to take advantage of you?" She lets out a little gasp. "Because if you don't feel safe with me here–"

"Magnolia—" I place my hand firmly on her arm, commanding her to look at me. "Trust me when I say there's nothing about you that makes me uncomfortable." I continue to stare into her eyes. She blinks at me several times, and I can't read what she's thinking, so I continue, "I'm quite enjoying the idea of these lessons, I assure you." I hold up my kombucha in a toast, and she quickly grabs her glass to mirror my motion. "So, why don't we eat our dinner, and we'll worry about what happens after that later, okay?"

She nods, then chugs the remainder of the kombucha, wincing as she finishes the tart liquid.

After eating, I clean up our plates and turn down the lights to set the ambiance. Then I turn up the heat, so she isn't uncomfortable without her robe, and make my way back to the couch.

I sit closer to her this time and turn her to face me. Taking her chin in my hand, I study her gorgeous features for a moment before finally speaking. "I was thinking tonight we could practice making out. Are you comfortable with that?"

I see confusion wash over her face as her eyebrows pull together. "I... uh... Sam... I know I asked you for lessons, but maybe I should be clearer." She clears her throat. "I was hoping you'd show me how to be good at *sex*." She opens the robe and gestures to her lingerie, "I thought that's what all this was for..."

She tries to close the robe, but I grab the front of it and pull it off her before she can, tossing it on the floor behind the couch.

"Oh... I..."

Slowly, I slide my hand around the nape of her neck and pull her into me, so she's practically sitting in my lap. I whisper, "You'll not question me again, or there'll be a punishment to pay. Understand?"

She gasps her acquiescence just as I slide my hands under her ass and settle her just above my cock. I wrap her legs around my back, circling myself into a perfect cocoon. My hands trail up her thigh, pausing to squeeze the delicious exposed flesh of her ass, where I fully intend to pay tribute later.

She lets out the slightest whimper, and I can't help but repeat the motion. "So responsive, aren't you? I bet you've never had anyone worship your body, have you?"

I don't wait for an answer. Instead, I continue perusing her gorgeous body, letting my wandering hands land on her rib cage. My cock throbs as I wet my lips and lean in, my mouth finding hers so hot and swollen, needy for my kiss.

She sucks in a breath when I swipe my tongue over her bottom lip, and she offers her pretty mouth to me. Maggie tastes like peaches and sunshine. Like pure joy bottled up at the source. She's freckles and rainbows and soft summer days, all the good things in life wrapped up in the prettiest fucking package that I have no business opening.

I scoop her up in my arms and lay her on the sofa, covering her body with mine. Our kisses grow heavy, and I can't get enough of her. I want to taste her and suck her and never stop feeling this electrical charge that's consumed me from the tip of my toes to my lips touching hers.

I bite her bottom lip, evoking an exhilarating cry from her. Her fists grip my t-shirt before sliding underneath, where she lets her hands explore my hot skin.

My cock's so hard it's making another appearance, poking out of my sweatpants, but I don't mind. In fact, I welcome the sensation.

Moments pass, or maybe hour—I'm really not sure—as I lose myself in her kiss. I've had sex with plenty of women, have kissed easily five times as many, and never, not once, have I ever felt a fraction of the all-consuming desire I feel now.

Without thinking, my hand finds her throat as I rub my thumb back and forth over her sensitive flesh. Losing control isn't an option, so I will myself to take a deep breath and calm my raging desire. I pull my hand away, find her waist, and squeeze, pulling her body closer to mine so that my dick lines up with her perfect, wet pussy.

Every sense is heightened as our kisses grow needy, and I can feel the heat of her pussy on my thigh.

I suck in one final breath as I muster the unspeakable strength to pull away and catch my breath.

"Wow," Maggie says as she pulls her hand up to cover her swollen lips.

I swallow a gulp and let my head fall on the couch cushion beside me. "Wow is right."

I think it's safe to say Magnolia's kissing is not the problem... and now, I'm wondering just what I've gotten myself into. I've experienced more pleasure from a kiss with Maggie than I ever have in sex.

Maybe she's not the one I should be worried about... I don't know how I'm ever supposed to go back to just being her friend now that I've had a taste...

THIRTEEN

Maggie

"Did you carry me to bed last night?" I rub my sleepy eyes as I walk into the kitchen, lured awake by the smell of bacon and freshly brewed coffee.

"Good morning, Sleeping Beauty. I hope I wasn't being too loud in here." Sam hands me a cup of coffee and pulls out a stool for me by the large island.

I take a seat and use the hot mug as a hand warmer, taking tiny, cautious sips of the delicious, perfectly sweetened latté. I never told Sam how I like my coffee, but it's not surprising to know he's paid attention.

"You didn't answer my question."

Sam pours himself a coffee, then spins around to face me. He's dressed in a casual navy tailored suit with a white button-down underneath and no tie. He looks powerful and confident and charming. After our kissing lessons last night and how he moved on top of me, commanding my mouth with his own, I realize that characteristic is enmeshed into his entire being.

"You passed out halfway through the first episode. But don't worry. I don't mind watching it with you again tonight." He winks before turning back to tend to the bacon cooking on the stove.

Last night after our lessons, I figured we'd go our separate ways, but Sam insisted on us watching *Ted Lasso* and cuddling on the couch. It was nice to have that time to come down after the rush of making out. It felt easy and natural. I'm learning that everything feels easy when it comes to Sam. I suppose that's a testament to our friendship.

He grabs two plates from the cabinet and begins piling food on them. "Your cut looks good today. I don't think it'll leave much of a scar. How's the bump on the back of your head?"

"It's fine. Doesn't hurt a bit."

He slides my plate in front of me with a glass of water. "Good. I've got a busy day today, so I'll be home around seven. What are you going to get into today?"

I pile a mound of eggs on top of my toast and fold it like a taco. "I don't know. It's pretty out. Maybe I'll go for a walk in the park or something or find a bookstore." I shrug as I take a giant bite.

"Well, I've already scheduled for your lunch to be delivered from the sandwich shop down the street, but if you're not home, I'll tell the housekeeper to just put it in the fridge for you." He picks up my phone from where I left it on the counter last night and hands it to me. "Keep this on you, so I know you're safe, especially if you go for a walk, and if you don't mind, could you set it in focus mode if you plan on being away from it?"

I look up from my breakfast in confusion, and Sam holds up his hands.

"I'm not going to stalk you; I just like knowing you're safe, okay? It makes me feel better knowing you're out there alone in this big city. Anything could happen. In fact, scary shit happens to women all the time. I'm just being cautious."

"Fine," I say, rolling my eyes.

Sam sets down his fork and braces his hands on the counter, his expression morphing from playful to serious.

I slowly look up.

"I will not apologize for being protective about your safety, Magnolia, and I don't appreciate your careless attitude about it."

"Yes, sir," I whisper.

"That's much better." He puts his plate in the sink, then walks behind me and gently kisses my cheek, the smell of cedar and citrus lingering in his lips' wake. Without thinking, I rub the spot his lips touched. He shaved this morning, and his smooth face feels completely different from last night's scruff.

"Have fun today. I'll see you tonight." He turns on his heel, and then he's gone, leaving me with a flood of memories in his wake.

After finishing my breakfast, I load our breakfast dishes in the dishwasher—I don't care that a housekeeper is coming; it's the least I can do to make their job easier—then grab my phone and head to my room to get dressed.

My phone buzzes with a new message.

SAM

I just wanted to let you know I haven't been able to stop thinking about our kiss last night. I don't know what kind of guys you've been with before, but they're all insane... Have a good day, sweetheart.

I smile, letting the compliment sink in. A girl could get used to this. I bite my lip as I consider my response.

Are you sure I just didn't have a great teacher?

SAM

I may be a great teacher, but I can't take credit for that. I can't wait to find out what other hidden talents you've got hidden up your sleeves... You're just full of surprises.

What are you talking about???

SAM

Your secret smoking hot body and your kissing were both huge surprises... not to mention your curiosity with ass play with the butt plug...

I told you it wasn't like that!!

SAM

I guess only time will tell...

I can't believe you. Do you get off on embarrassing me or something!?

SAM

Or something... As long as you're mine you should get used to it.

Have a good day, sweetheart.

I read the message over ten times, my belly twisting and turning flips at his words. *It's all part of the agreement. You're not really his, so calm down.*

I'm pulled back down to earth when another message lights up my phone screen.

TRENT

Hey Maggie. How's it going? I haven't heard from you, and I was just wondering if you're still planning on coming to the reunion?

Hey Trent! It's so good to hear from you! Sorry I haven't texted. I kind of had a lot going on. Yes, I'm still planning to attend.

TRENT

Great! I'm happy to hear it. Listen, I was wondering if you'd like to go with me? Like as my date? I know these things can be daunting if you're alone, and I want to hang out with you while I've got the chance...

Of course, I'll be your date. It would be nice to catch up with you

TRENT

It's settled, then. I can't wait to see you. I'm actually counting down the days...

I'm excited, too. If you need any help with anything, I'm happy to pitch in however I can.

TRENT

Seriously? That would be incredible

You have no idea how much I needed help! I'll send you a list of caterers and the budget. Seriously, just pick what you think is best. I'm up to my eyeballs in decisions, and I trust your judgment.

P.S. You're the best!

With a bubbling sense of excitement, I lace up my sneakers and pull my hair into a ponytail. It's a beautiful day, and I want to spend it outside

---

Time seems to disappear as I take in the beautiful park surrounding me. There's a slight chill in the air, enough to warrant pants and a long sleeve workout shirt, and the bright afternoon sun warms my skin. I love the changing of seasons. It's like mother nature doesn't know which way to lean, and you get a perfect mix, the best of each.

A light sheen of sweat coats the back of my neck as I do my final lap around the park. It's busier than usual today. A group of bikers passes me on my left, and I laugh as I watch a man chasing a rogue dog who must've gotten off his leash. The frustrated man's wearing a nice suit and shoes that can't be comfortable to run in as he faces the dog in a standoff, both lunging to the opposite sides before the dog takes off again.

I shouldn't be laughing, but the park is set far enough from the roads, and I'm sure the dog will eventually tire of the game. He looks like he's having the time of his life and probably thinks his owner is playing along. It's funny how moments can be frustrating or fun; the only difference is our perspective. The dog is clearly having a great time, while the man is annoyed for an endless list of human reasons the dog will never understand.

The thought surprises me, and I pull out my phone to write it down in my notes. Once I'm back in the studio and teaching, that could be a fun story to tell in class. I type out the thought and give a little backstory, so I don't forget, then slide my phone back into my pocket.

I can't wait for life to return to normal, to have my studio back in working order—and my apartment—but I must admit staying with Sam hasn't been the worst. Other than my short time in college, I've never had a roommate, and I like not being alone in the evenings. Having someone to share a meal with and talk about our days is nice and just another reminder that I'm doing the right thing pursuing Trent.

He actually seems to like me, which is crazy.

Things with Sam may be unconventional, but I can already see my confidence starting to grow, and all we've done is kiss. The compliments help, too, of course, but I really think this will work out.

I make my way over to a large oak tree set off from the walking trail and curl up against the thick trunk. I pull my phone out of my pocket and set it beside me and grab my new book out of my bag.

After leaving Sam's apartment, I walked around the city, did a little window shopping, and then stumbled across the cutest little bookstore. I had every intention of stopping by the studio today and probing the crew on their timeline but opted to take a day to relax instead. I feel like it's what Sam would want me to do, and a part of me really wants to please him. I want to show him that I'm listening, so I think I'll save the worrying for tomorrow and enjoy my little slice of peace today.

I open my book and let all my thoughts melt away as I disappear into the story...

"Hey, lady! Are you okay!?" A bright light shines brightly on my face, and I blink several times, shielding my eyes with my hands.

It's pitch-black outside except for the blinding light that is currently burning a hole in my retinas.

I sit up slowly, my aching back sore from the knobby tree roots, as I try to see who's talking to me.

"Yeah, I'm fine. I guess I just fell asleep." I pat around the grass in search of my phone, but all I find is my book.

"Oh, good. Sawyer thought you were dead, and Devon thought you passed out because you were drunk... I thought maybe you were homeless. Are you homeless?" the kid asks, and I hold up my hand to block the light.

"No, I'm not homeless. Do you think you could stop shining your flashlight in my face?"

"Oh, sorry." The kid moves the beam to the ground, and my eyes nearly cry in relief.

"Do you see my phone?" I pat around the grass and then stand up to look around the trunk.

"No. I didn't take it... I swear... I just came over here to check on you." The kid holds up his hands and shakes his head.

"I can't find my purse either... it was just here." My heart starts to race as panic rises in my chest.

"Sorry, lady, all I saw was the book in your hand, but maybe it'll turn up?" He shrugs and then points behind him. "I've got to go. My mom doesn't like me talking to strangers." He takes off on his bike toward two other boys.

"Wait! Do you know what time it is?" I call after him.

"Eight-thirty!" he yells back as he speeds off with his friends.

I press my fingers on the bridge of my nose. Shit. Did I really just get mugged while sleeping? In public?

I sweep the area one more time before finally giving up and making my walk of shame back to Sam's.

I've barely made it outside the park when a black car shrieks to a stop, and a very angry Sam jumps out.

"What the fuck, Maggie!" He pulls me into him and wraps me in a hug, his body and face communicating completely opposite emotions.

"Where have you been? I've been driving around for two hours looking for you! You didn't answer your phone, and you weren't anywhere you said you'd be today!" There's a slight tremble in his hands as he pulls back, gripping me firmly by the arms.

"I'm so sorry, Sam. I was in the park." I gesture behind me and hold up my book. "I fell asleep reading."

He crushes me to his chest again and squeezes, and I can feel his heart beating violently as he smoothes my hair with a gentle brush of his fingers. "You didn't answer your phone. I called you about a hundred times. Everyone's out looking for you." He pulls out his phone and dials a number. "Hey, yeah, I found her. Can you tell everyone for me? Yeah, she's safe, said she fell asleep reading in the park. I know. Thanks, man."

He ends the call, then grabs my hand and leads me to the back of the car.

"Sam, I'm so sorry. I feel terrible. I–"

"Where's your purse?" He glances behind me, and I let out a sigh.

"I think I got robbed while I was sleeping..." I suck in a wince and scrunch my nose as I wait for it to register.

Sam's jaw flexes, and his nostrils flare. "You what?" he growls.

"I'm sorry. I–"

"*The Submissive will not put herself in harm's way or behave negligently...*" he recites through gritted teeth. "I don't think I have to tell you what could've happened today."

"I know, and I feel so stupid. I promise it was an accident. I'll be more careful from now on. Please don't be angry. I feel horrible that everyone was looking for me..." My voice shakes as I try to fight back the tears.

Sam's warm hand covers my cheek, and he brushes a stray tear away with his thumb. "I'm sorry. The important thing is that you're safe. Are you hungry?"

"Not really, I–"

"Let me rephrase that. What would you like to eat?" He squeezes my shoulder, then threads his fingers through mine, holding my hand like he's afraid I'll float away.

"I could go for a gyro and some hummus?"

He kisses my hand. "Anything you want." He pulls out his phone and places an online order.

"So, are we good?"

"We're good." He ruffles my hair playfully, and I lay my head on his shoulder, relieved that he's not mad at me.

"But there's one more thing we need to deal with." His deep voice cuts through the easy silence.

"Oh? What's that?"

"Your punishment..."

FOURTEEN

Maggie

I stand frozen in place, gripping my robe like a life preserver as Sam sits on the edge of his freestanding tub and draws me a bubble bath. Of all the possible punishments my mind could conjure in the twenty-minute drive to get here, this is quite possibly the last thing I could've imagined.

My palms are sweaty, and I feel as if I could vomit or pass out, or maybe a combination of both.

I look up at the bright overhead lights that will surely expose every imperfection I have and probably create a whole slew of new insecurities. I feel like I'm standing at the opening of an aircraft, about to be thrown out without a parachute.

"I'll step out and give you some privacy. Can I get you anything to–"

"Wine, please... No, actually, do you have any vodka?"I'm going to need some liquid courage if I'm expected to go through with this.

Sam laughs as he opens the door. "I'll see what I can conjure up." He winks, and then he's gone, leaving me alone with my *punishment*.

I wait a moment to make sure he's gone before stripping off the robe and practically cannonballing into the tub, shielding myself underneath the clustered layer of bubbles while splashing an obscene amount of water out in the process. The water's slightly warmer than is comfortable, but my aching muscles cry out in relief. It feels wonderful, so good I almost forget Sam's about to return.

I try to arrange the bubble clumps over my important bits to create a barrier, but the more I move them around, the thinner they seem to become. I'm just about to squirt in another heap of bubble bath and swish the water aggressively with my open hand when Sam's tall frame appears over me.

I drop the bottle, and it clashes over the side of the tub, landing on the floor. I sink low, so even my mouth is covered in the water. "Is there something wrong with your bath?" he teases and quirks his brow. In his hand is a crystal glass, holding what I hope is straight alcohol.

Hesitantly, I take the glass, reaching my arm out as far as possible without moving my bubble-shielded body from its position. I realize that sooner or later, Sam will probably see me naked. I just thought I'd have more time to warm up to it, and I didn't think it would be so one-sided.

I bring the ice-cold liquid to my lips and take a heavy swallow of what tastes like vodka and cranberry. He's added some cinnamon and something else that give it a nice festive flavor. I nod in silent approval and set the glass on the side of the tub as I sink back down like a swamp monster. My eyes trained on Sam as something like pure terror mixed with curiosity prickles in my chest.

He begins rolling up the sleeves of his button-up shirt, showcasing the most defined forearms I've ever seen covered in colorful tattoos. It's only now I realize I've never seen Sam in anything other than a long-sleeved dress shirt. In all the years I've known him, I guess I never considered it strange.

I suppose I never considered him at all.

I don't know how that's possible now. Maybe it's because the water feels so amazing on my skin, or the fact that I'm completely naked with only a few bubble mounds separating me from his view, or the fact that I feel like he's the first person I've ever known whom I can completely trust... but as I study how precise his movements are, I can't help but wonder if maybe all of this time I just didn't have the right partner.

He lifts the loofa and applies a generous amount of shower gel, and I suck in a breath when he reaches under the water and grabs my foot.

"Relax, Magnolia. I'm not going to hurt you," he says gruffly, and I let out a whimper as he massages my sore foot, lathering it with the warm soap.

I take another swig of my liquid courage, then hurry to shield myself underneath my bubble blanket as Sam watches and laughs.

"I knew you'd be nervous, but this is almost too perfect of a punishment." He laughs again, then drops my foot and trades it for the other. A moment passes, and there's only the sound of our breaths before he breaks the silence. "Do you understand why I was upset with you today?"

I nod, keeping my eyes trained on his talented hands. Sam's touch is excruciatingly delightful. It's doing things to my body that I've never felt with anyone, and he's only touching my feet. I can't imagine what it would be like to have him really touch me, and I'd be lying if I said I wasn't thinking about it right now.

"Use your words, please. It's hard to have a one-sided conversation, and I'd like to talk about this," he scolds.

"Oh... um... you were mad because I didn't answer my phone as you'd asked me to," I offer nervously.

"And?" he pries, pressing firmly into my heel.

"And you were worried because you couldn't find me, and no one had heard from me."

"Close." He slides his hand up my calf, alternating between scrubbing it with the loofa and massaging it. He's scooted closer to me now, and the cold air nips at my exposed skin. "I was fucking terrified today. You scared the shit out of me, Magnolia. I don't know what I would've done if something had happened to you. Anything could've happened while you were asleep."

"I know. I'm really sorry."

"I know it was an accident, but when you agreed to be my submissive, you agreed to all the rules." He breathes deep, his nostrils flaring as he slides his hand a little higher, fingertips brushing just past my knee.

I close my eyes, enjoying the sensation as my body wakes up with arousal. I squeeze my thighs together to try to get some relief from the building tension. Sam surprises me when he switches my legs again. I suck in a sharp breath almost forget to keep myself covered underneath the bubbles.

"When I said we needed to discuss your punishment, you looked afraid."

I open my eyes, surprised by the change in direction.

"You looked like you were afraid of *me*," he emphasizes. "Can you tell me why, Magnolia? Because I want you to feel completely safe with me, and I need to know what was going on in that pretty little head of yours."

I bite my lip. "I thought you meant something more like a physical punishment, and I got scared." I shrug. "It's just a reflex, I guess."

Sam holds my gaze, and I don't dare look away. His eyes are soft with something that looks a lot like concern as he studies me, then moves again so that he's beside me. When he reaches into the water to grab my arm, my whole body tenses.

"Tell me about that," he demands, and I don't know if it's his touch that excites me or that I actually feel safe, but I answer honestly.

"I don't really talk about it a lot, but during my time in different foster homes, the adults always seemed to expect more from me because I was the oldest."

His fingers pause for a moment then he gently continues his perusal with the loofa, sliding his hands up my forearms and slightly past my elbow. I take his silence as an invitation to continue.

"It seemed like I was always in trouble for something, always being punished one way or another..."

Sam sucks in a long breath and pulls his hands away, balling them into fists in his lap. I sit up a little, careful not to expose myself, and place my wet hand on his thigh. "Don't worry. It's nothing like that." I shake my head. "I wasn't physically abused or anything. They weren't allowed to hit us, so they had to be creative. I've been grounded from electricity, grounded from eating carbs, dessert, and one time, even cheese. The thing that hit me the hardest, though, was when I was twelve, my foster mom at the time cut all my hair off."

"Fuck, Maggie, that's terrible. Abuse isn't just physical. I'm so sorry you were treated like that."

Wanting to reassure him, I grab his hand, locking my fingers around his. "I guess I'm just hypersensitive because I always got in trouble for all the younger kids in the home. It didn't matter what I did. If one of the younger ones did something wrong, it was always my fault."

I shrug and release his hand as I sink into the warm water.

"That doesn't seem fair," he finally says, and I laugh.

"Nothing about my life has been fair, Sam. I learned to

accept that a long time ago."

I offer him my other arm, holding it out over my chest, and he offers me a soft smile as he continues to bathe me.

"So, that's why you're always trying to take care of everyone," he whispers.

"Yeah, I guess so. I always think there's someone else who needs protecting more than I do. I learned really early on that though my circumstances weren't ideal, they could've been so much worse."

"But that doesn't mean you owe anyone because they had it harder than you," he retorts, and I almost flinch before I realize he's being protective of me, of the little girl I was all those years ago.

He drops my arm, and I hug it over me, murmuring, "Yeah. I guess you're right."

Sliding the loofa along my neck, he scrubs the small area of exposed flesh, and I suck in a breath. "Lean forward so I can wash your back."

I squeeze my eyes shut, bringing my arms over my breast as I sit up and lean forward. The cold air elicits chill bumps over my exposed skin.

"You're so lovely," Sam whispers. "Just when I think you can't get any more perfect, I learn something new about you or see you in a way that no one else has." He lets out a long muffled sigh, and then suddenly, instead of the loofa, I feel his firm hands sliding down my back, massaging and kneading my neck.

This is the strangest punishment I could've imagined, and I'd be lying if I said I wasn't enjoying it. Being the center of attention has never been something I liked, but listening to Sam's sighs and groans of frustration as his eyes stay glued to my naked body is a pleasure I've never felt.

"I can't imagine someone doing anything less than worshiping your body. It's taking everything in me not to climb in that bathtub with you right now." His fingers trail down my ribcage, skating dangerously close to my breasts.

I close my eyes as I urge him to touch me, internally screaming for him to do something to relieve me from this growing tension building between my legs, but he pulls away, the cold air replacing his warm touch like a slap in the face.

Something comes over me, call it courage, lust, desperation, but I don't even recognize the sound of my voice when I say, "Touch me, Sam." It comes out more like a plea than a statement, but I don't care. "Please touch me, sir," I add for good measure. Hey, if I'm going to be forward, I guess I should go all in, right?

"Fuck." Sam mumbles under his breath, then he appears in front of me, eyes dark with hunger. He props his foot on the tub, bracing his back flat against the wall as he balances on his stool. "Magnolia, I would love nothing more than to touch you right now." He bites his knuckle and sighs. "But this is a punishment, remember? I can't reward you for your behavior today and give you something so... easy."

He scratches his scruff and covers his mouth with his hand as he eyes me for a moment, then his brows lift in delight. A devilish grin spreads across his face as he grabs the shower head and turns the warm water back on. He holds his hand in front of it, carefully adjusting the temperature and pressure until he finally gets it just how he wants.

"Touch yourself." He hands me the shower head, and I look at him in confusion.

"You want me to wash myself off?" I guess, and he actually laughs.

"Oh, sweet Magnolia, not quite," he snickers, then takes the shower head, plunging it underneath the water pointed toward my most sensitive spot.

I startle at the sensation, and my breasts bob above the water line as I look at him in complete and utter shock. My bubble blanket is long gone as I sit before him, hot, sweaty, and fully aroused in the bathtub, the shower head pulsing to reveal an entirely new sensation in my body.

Warmth pools in my belly as tingles shoot up and down my legs. I feel as if my every cell has awakened and is wholly exposed to the most exquisite pleasure I've ever known. My clit throbs, begging for relief as the steady pressure threatens to take my breath away.

"Oh my God," I whimper as my breath hitches, not knowing whether to speed up or slow down. I throw my head back against the tub, back arching as the steady pressure slowly unravels me bit by bit. "What's happening?" I moan, but I have a strong feeling I know just what's about to happen, though I can hardly believe it.

"Fuck, Magnolia, you look so hot pleasuring yourself," Sam growls. I let my body move through the waves of pleasure, not caring how I must look as I completely lose control in front of Sam. At this moment, only one thing is on my mind, and I'm so close.

I bite my lip to keep from crying out as pleasure rips through me, my sex pulsing and hungry to be filled. When I open my eyes, I see Sam wearing a pained expression as his hardened cock strains beneath his pants.

I bite my lip, letting my eyes trail down his body and then back up, an unspoken challenge.

With a tortured sigh, he slowly unbuckles his belt, never taking his eyes off me.

I wiggle and writhe as pleasure coats every inch of my skin like warm candle wax.

He unzips his pants and grips his bare cock letting out a sexy groan as his eyes fill with lust.

I watch him begin to pump his cock. His movements slow at

first, then steadily increasing as he works himself harder and faster.

"Oh God," the sight is almost too much, and I want to surrender to my impending orgasm, but I also don't want it to end. I've never seen a man masturbate, nor did I expect I'd enjoy it, but knowing that I'm the reason he's losing control only adds to my arousal.

I maneuver the shower head in small circles to deliver an entirely new sensation and spread my legs wider, so hungry for relief that I cry out a moan, unable to control my body's responses.

"Pinch your nipple with your free hand and play with your breast," Sam commands, and I don't hesitate to follow his orders.

After bringing the sensation to my nipples, I almost lose it but manage to hold on a little longer. I'm so needy for something —I just don't know what it is—that I want to do is explode. All I can hear are our panting breaths as we bring ourselves closer to the edge.

"Christ, your tits are perfect. I can't wait to sink my cock into you and show you how a real man fucks. You could have my hands on you right now, but this is your punishment. I want you to bring yourself to orgasm right now in front of me. I want to watch you fall apart and see the moment you realize what your body is capable of feeling. How you deserve to feel when you're alone or with a man."

The sensation builds, and my whole body tenses, ready to fall over the edge as Sam's sexy voice guides me. "Oh, God, Sam. It's so... so–"

"Come for me. Make yourself come while I watch you fall apart, your perfect tits wet and bouncing as you scream. Next time, you'll have my tongue, or my hands, or my cock to fill you up. That's what's missing, isn't it? You wish you had my cock to stretch you out, don't you?"

"Yes. Yes. Yes," I cry out as every muscle in my body tightens, and a jolt of pleasure rips through me. I feel as if I'm being swallowed up whole, tossed to and fro in the ocean, unable to control my body as pleasure shoots through me in every direction. A bright white light flashes before my eyes, and I can't say what is up from down. Then the tension releases, every muscle goes limp, and suddenly, I'm floating.

I take a few moments to steady my breathing as I return to my body, every sensation feeling slightly different than it did a few moments ago. My eyelids flutter open, and Sam sits in front of me, disheveled and sated, as he buckles his pants. His pristinely combed hair sticks up a little on top, and his cheeks are flushed, lips parted and swollen. His dress shirt is wrinkled and unbuttoned at the top. And among everything, I notice a pain in his eyes that wasn't there before.

I knit my brows in confusion. "You okay? Are you... mad at me?" I manage to ask, feeling extremely exposed. I wrap my arms around myself, and Sam shakes his head as he stands.

"Nothing about what just happened could ever make me feel anything but adoration for you." He holds out a towel for me to step into, and I reluctantly oblige.

After wrapping me in the warm, soft towel, he pulls me into a tight hug. I tuck myself into him as he props his chin on top of my head, then lifts it to kiss me there. "I think it's safe to say you just gave yourself your very first orgasm." His voice comes out deep and calm like he's proud of me.

I tuck myself into him a little tighter, and he squeezes me just as the first of my tears starts to fall. I don't try to hide it as I let my sobs bubble out of me, messy, fitful, and effervescent. Just like that, I've unlocked years of pent-up emotions with my release.

"Shh, I've got you, love. You're safe with me," Sam whispers into my ear as he rubs his hand up and down my back. "It's normal to feel emotional your first time. I can't imagine what you must be feeling right now."

After a minute or two... or maybe even an hour... I finally settle. My breathing deepens, and I wipe the tears and snot from my face with the back of my arm. Surprisingly, I feel safe and not embarrassed at all. I can't imagine being so vulnerable with anyone.

"Come on. You're going to sleep with me tonight." Sam pulls me with him, keeping me tucked tightly underneath his arm as he leads me down the hall to his bedroom.

I stand awkwardly in the doorway, still wrapped in my oversized fluffy towel, as I watch him change his clothes, underwear and all, right before my eyes. Then he pulls a t-shirt from his dresser and motions for me to step closer.

"Come here, you. I want you to wear this tonight." He pulls the towel away, and I stand bare before him for only a moment before he pulls the gray t-shirt over my head, encompassing me in the soft cotton that smells like his cologne. Then he hands me a pair of his boxer briefs, and I slide them up my legs, feeling cozy and warm.

He walks to his bed and pulls back the comforter. I momentarily hesitate, then climb underneath the plush cotton sheets as Sam walks around and climbs into bed on the other side.

He pulls me into him so that my head rests on his chest, and it feels oddly comfortable even though we masturbated together just moments before.

I don't know where the boundaries are any more, and right now, I can't seem to make myself care. All I know are the rules of our agreement and that I trust Sam with every inch of me. We're long past the normal rules of friendship, and now, we're paving our own path to something completely new, something just for us.

FIFTEEN

Sam

I refresh my browser as I stare at my calendar, wishing to slow down time. It's already two o'clock, and I haven't gotten any real work done other than making some phone calls and attending three pointless meetings that could've been emails.

I didn't wake her up with breakfast in bed this morning. Instead, I snuck out before my alarm and left a note that I needed to go into the office for an early meeting. It wasn't a complete lie, I did have a meeting with my accountant, but it was just a touch-base that could've easily been rescheduled. I had breakfast delivered, though, and had the delivery guy confirm when she accepted it.

I feel like a coward, but when I woke up with her wrapped in my arms, I knew I'd do something I would regret if I didn't get out of there soon. I needed the space to clear my head and calculate my next move, our next lesson, before I got caught up in my own carnal needs.

I hang my head and close my eyes as glimmers of last night

flash through my mind. I feel like a teenager with how my dick responds. But how can I not think about it? Last night was one of the hottest nights of my life, and I didn't even touch her. Fuck, I wanted to, though.

A headache starts to form, and I rub my temples in frustration. Not touching Maggie last night was quite possibly the greatest restraint I've ever shown, and clearly, it's still affecting me. But she wasn't ready, and this isn't about me.

Loosening my tie, I sit back in my desk chair, letting my head fall against the seat. I feel like I'm running out of time with her. Her high school reunion is only two weeks away, and she's still so green. I don't think I realized how much stuff we'd have to cover when I agreed to help. It's not that she actually needs help learning how to be good at sex. There's so much more to it than that. I just want her to feel confident before I set her free to date—and fuck—whoever she pleases.

My skin heats up at the thought of her with someone else, and I clench my jaw, not wanting to let myself go there. Of course, this is all for a bigger purpose, and of course, I'm the last fucking man to deserve her, but that doesn't mean I don't feel protective. I am her dom, after all. It's kind of my whole thing.

The truth is I wish I could keep her all to myself. She'd be my most prized possession, a hidden treasure I'd happily keep secret for as long as I live, worshipping and dominating her every free chance I got. But after learning about her background, everything clicked into place. It's the reason she's so generous and is literally the nicest human I've ever known. It's why she puts everyone else's needs before her own and why she's never going to see her worth on her own.

The woman is too goddamn perfect, and now that I know what a treasure she is, I've got to be careful about how I approach this. I want her to see herself the way I see her, the way everyone else sees her. I can practically hear the clock ticking in my ear, taunting me with each passing second.

The office phone rings, and I'm thankful for the distraction.

"Jordan Properties, this is Sam speaking."

"Sam! I'm so glad you picked up!" my dad yells into the receiver. Obviously, he's chosen not to wear his hearing aids today... Lucky me. "Listen, I've got some good news. Do you have a minute to chat?"

I click open my email to reveal a full inbox that I've clearly abandoned for the day and decide to welcome the distraction. "Looks like I do. What's going on?"

"Oh, good. I hoped that's what you'd say. Now, listen, I know this may come as a bit of a surprise, but I've finally decided to retire. As of October second, your old man will be spending his days fly fishing and golfing." His words come out fast, and I can hear the excitement in his voice.

I blink several times as I let it sink in. My father started his construction company from the ground up just before I was born. He's worked his ass off building it into what it is today. It's nothing for him to work twelve-hour days even until now as he approaches seventy.

"Wow, Dad, that's... that's great!" I hesitate for a moment before I press, "So, is everything okay, or are you–"

"Oh, Sam, don't worry. I'm completely healthy. It's nothing like that. I just thought I'd spend the last quarter of my life with Charlotte, is all. Maybe take another honeymoon, travel around in an RV. You know, live a little before it's too late."

My throat tightens as I think about how happy I am for him. If anyone deserves to retire, it's my saint of a father. He's been through so much. When my mother died when I was twelve, my dad had to take care of all four of us boys by himself, all while running a business. He didn't meet my stepmother, Charlotte, until I left for college, but they came into each other's lives at just the right moment.

"I'm happy for you, Dad. I really am."

"So, listen, the reason I'm calling is Charlotte's throwing me a big retirement party. Of course, we want you to be there. I've already talked to your brothers, and Charlotte's hosting it on our property. She's working so hard to make this special, son, and I know you're a busy man... but please, could you try to make it?"

I nod even though he can't see me as an idea starts to form in my mind, "Yeah, Dad, I'll be there."

"Wonderful! Charlotte's going to be tickled pink to have all you boys back home under one roof." I roll my eyes, wanting to argue, but there's no use in fighting it. There's no way in hell my family will let me get away with anything other than staying in my childhood home.

I open Google Maps on my browser and type in his city and Maggie's hometown's location, pleased that my assumption was right, before asking, "Hey, Dad, you think it'd be okay if I brought home a date?"

Silence falls on the other end as I wait. Finally, I hear him suck in a breath, and I can hear the smile in his voice, "Son, we would be delighted for you to bring someone home to meet us–"

"Great, Dad, I think she'd enjoy the beach. Listen, we're just friends, okay? I don't want you and Charlotte to get your hopes up..." I trail off, letting my words sink in. "I... uh... I still haven't changed my mind about all that stuff. I just don't want you to get too excited."

My dad sighs, and I can feel his disappointment from a thousand miles away. "You know, Sam, just because you decided something over a decade ago doesn't mean you have to stick to it. People grow, you're allowed to change your mind–"

"I know, Dad, but not on this." I cut him off. It's always the same conversation with him, and I get it. He wants me to be happy. He wants me to settle down and finally let go of some of the shame, but I can't do that. I don't expect him to understand, or anyone to understand, for that matter. I'm the one who has to live with my decisions, and this is the best way.

"Well, okay, then. I guess I'll see you in two weeks?"

"Sounds good." I confirm and then add, "Oh, and could you tell everyone not to bring up any of that stuff around Maggie? I don't exactly feel like explaining the mistakes I made when I was eighteen to every person I meet, you know?"

Dad sighs again, sounding disappointed. "Yeah, I'll make sure to tell them." He pauses for a moment as if considering what to say next. "You know, son, I think you're being too hard on yourself about all this, but just know that we're your family, and we love you no matter what. I love you, and I can't wait to see you."

"Thanks. I love you, too, Dad. See you in two weeks." I hang up, then send a message to my assistant to mark my calendars for two weeks off. I figure I won't be in much of a working mood after my family visit and then sending Maggie off to meet up with her new beau.

Despite my dad's disappointment, I feel a little lighter having something to look forward to at the end of this. I know it'll be hard seeing Maggie with all my family, but it'll be the closest thing I ever get to settling down, and as the old proverb goes, *It's better to have loved and lost than to have never loved at all.* Maybe this is my penance.

I shut down my computer, deciding to cut the day short. I've got an idea for tonight's lessons, and I'm itching to get started.

I type in the key code and listen for the beep as I let myself into my apartment. I texted Maggie to be dressed and ready by the time I got here, and as I walk in, I'm happy to find her fully clothed in athletic wear, wiping the kitchen counters.

"I hope this is okay." She pulls at her cropped t-shirt. "I don't know if you did it on purpose, but I couldn't find a single workout top from our shopping trip. I guess the only tops that made it to the register were crop tops and workout bras..."

She pins me with a stare, and I laugh, holding up my hands. "Hey, I'm a man who knows what I like, and after seeing you in a crop top at that mall, I couldn't help myself." I walk toward her and pull her into me, catching her off guard. I don't care about toeing the line anymore now that the reality of this has sunken in and I've received a fresh reminder of the end date. I just want to enjoy what we've got while I can. And I don't care if it's reckless. I can lick my wounds and savor my memories for years to come.

I bury my face in her neck, sucking in her clean scent as I run my hand up her back, finally landing on the nape of her neck. "I missed you today. I couldn't stop thinking about our night, I couldn't focus on anything else, so I figured I'd cut the day short, and we could do something physical to get my mind out of the gutter." I give her neck a tiny nibble, then seal it with a kiss.

When I pull away, Maggie's eyes are as wide as saucers. I guess I did come in a little hot and heavy, but she didn't see her get herself off in the bathtub last night. I'm convinced I'm the luckiest man in the world for having the privilege of witnessing it firsthand.

I kiss her on the forehead. "I'm going to change, and then we can go."

She relaxes a little, and I release her, not missing her flushed cheeks or how her eyes scan me up and down when she doesn't think I'm looking. Maggie may not be confident in her sexuality just yet, but I can read her like a book, and she's enjoying her role in our little dynamic.

After I change, we head out to where our next lesson will take place. Maggie's already asked me once where we're going, but I told her it was a surprise. Though I could tell she wanted to argue with me, it seems she's remembered the rules. I suppose I have last night's punishment to thank for that.

As we pull up to my rock-climbing gym, she shakes her head. "I should've known."

"What do you mean?" I feign ignorance as I climb out of the car and walk around to open her door before she can. She knows to wait for me but I wouldn't put it past her to try to prove herself now that she knows what I've got in store for us today. I offer her my hand. "Come on, you don't know you'll hate it unless you try," I urge.

"Sam, you know I'm afraid of heights," she whines. "Is it not enough to push me out of my comfort zone in every other way?"

I grab her hand and pull her to a stop so that she's looking at me. "Are you telling me this is red for you?"

She turns her head in confusion as if she didn't hear me, and then her eyes widen with understanding, and she shakes her head.

"Because safe words apply in all contexts of this lifestyle, Magnolia. I want you to know that I respect your boundaries. I want to push you, but I won't make you do anything you don't want to do."

"No, I'm sorry. I was just being dramatic." She shakes her head and smiles. "I'm just nervous, and I am afraid of heights, but I trust you, Sam. I want you to know that."

"Good." I push her hair behind her ear. "Now, let's get you geared up and climbing some walls." I wrap my arm around her shoulders and tuck her into me, shielding her from the cold wind as I grin like a thief who never gets caught.

SIXTEEN

Maggie

I stare at the twenty-foot rock wall before me, palms sweaty and heart racing as Sam tightens the climbing harness around my hips and thighs. He's positioned on his knees in front of me, taking extra care to ensure everything is just as it should be. It feels a little strange, almost intimate, but this isn't anything special. I'm not special here. This is a rock-climbing gym, and hundreds of people come here every week and put on the same gear, take the same precautions, climb the same walls.

"There you go. You're all set," he announces as he stands.

I clench my fists nervously in my fingerless climbing gloves that Sam insisted I wear. Unlike Sam, my hands are soft, and I don't have the protective callouses from years of climbing.

"Come on. We'll start you on the bubblegum wall. It's the easiest one, and we'll go from there." His eyes sparkle, and I can't tell if he's serious or teasing as he clamps me on the shoulder and moves me to a bubble gum pink wall with baby blue grips.

Maybe I should be embarrassed that I'm climbing in the kiddie section, but considering we're the only two people here, with the exception of the person running the front desk, I have a feeling Sam already thought of that. It's kind of sweet, actually. I can't imagine how much it must've cost to rent out the gym for the day, but Sam doesn't seem like he's hurting financially, so I try not to feel guilty that he did this for me.

"Here's your carabiner." He twists it open, then places the large metal clasp in my hand. "You open it like this and always clamp it here before you climb." He stares at me until I realize he's looking for my acknowledgment.

"Oh, yeah. Right," I stammer, but he doesn't move, only quirks an eyebrow. "I mean... yes, sir," I add.

A faint hint of a smile pulls on his lips as his pupils dilate, looking like he's ready to swallow me whole. I don't know if I'm more aroused or terrified when he looks at me that way. My body warms at the thought, and suddenly, the fear of climbing the rock wall takes a back seat. I'm in so over my head, but I can't make myself stop. Call it morbid curiosity or plain stupidity, but after the bathtub last night, I haven't been able to think of anything besides our next lesson. I don't know what will happen next, and I feel like I'm constantly on high alert when I'm near him. A part of me hates not knowing what to expect, but I think a bigger part of me loves the thrill of relinquishing control. Handing all my trust over to someone else and letting them decide what I need.

"What are you waiting for? Let's see what you've got." Sam's question startles me from my spiraling thoughts. I blink several times, then clamp my carabiner to the bottom clamp just as he showed me. I step up to the bubble gum wall and very carefully grab the highest blue rock I can reach while stepping on another.

The concept of rock climbing is easy enough. It seems

pretty intuitive to climb, and I move up the wall fairly easily. It certainly helps that I'm an adult tackling the kiddie wall, but I'm proud of myself nonetheless. A few moments later, I'm ringing the bell at the top of the wall, and I hear Sam clapping and cheering below.

"What do I do now?" I call out, terrified to look down.

"You're doing great, Maggie! Now, you just need to lean back and trust your rope. Push off the wall with your legs, and I'll be right here waiting for you!" Sam shouts from the bottom.

Though it goes against everything in my nature, I listen to Sam and immediately lean back, trusting the rope to do its job. My stomach flutters with the falling sensation for only a second, but then it's replaced by a shot of adrenaline. Before I know it, my feet are back on solid ground, and Sam scoops me into a bear hug.

"I'm so proud of you. That was incredible. You did amazing," he whispers into my neck before planting a kiss on my forehead.

I can't help my giant grin as I beam with pride, and suddenly, I feel like I can do anything. "Enough of the kiddie section. I want you to show me the course you take."

Sam's smile falls a little, and he studies me, "Are you sure you're ready for that? We could stay here a little longer and let you gain some confidence."

"No way, I'm tougher than I look. See?" I flex my bicep, and Sam squeezes it and laughs.

"That's a pretty impressive goose egg you've got there. Come on, Hulk Hogan, let's see what those bulging muscles can do." He grips my waist, playfully pinching my exposed stomach on each side as he leads me to the other side of the gym.

"Here we are. What do you think?"

I stare at the most terrifyingly tall and chaotic rock-climbing course my mind can even fathom as my confidence shrivels in terror. "This is a thing people do for fun?"

Sam strips off his shirt, then tightens his climbing harness around his thighs and waist. His lean muscles ripple with every movement. It's only the second time I've seen him shirtless, and I now realize just how he built those muscles. My forearms already ache from my kiddie course, and Sam's got muscles on top of his forearm muscles.

He tilts his head to each side in a stretch and winks as he notices me watching him. My mouth actually waters at the sight of him, and I don't even know what that means. It's like my body's acting on impulses that my brain knows nothing about.

I watch as he approaches the wall, clamps his carabiner on the safety latch, then climbs up the wall so fast you'd think a radioactive spider bit him. Sam's moves are fluid and calculated as he scales the wall. Somehow he makes it look easy as he uses his legs to push himself up while reaching the most challenging positions.

Within a few seconds, he reaches the top of the wall, then propels himself back down, landing just in front of me.

A thin sheen of sweat coats his body, and his muscles are somehow even more defined than they were a moment ago. His veins bulge in his hands and forearms, and I try my best to memorize everything about him. I can't imagine they make them any hotter than him.

He takes a step toward me and pulls me into him, grabbing my ass possessively before kissing me like he owns me. And I guess he does. I can practically feel the testosterone oozing off him as he deepens our kiss into something sinful and hungry.

Every nerve in my body is awake and reeling with desire as he kisses me like I'm his last meal, his last breath of air. I let myself go, chasing the sensations. I let myself feel everything he's doing to me, the way his rough, calloused hands grip my hips. The way his thumb traces over my stomach just below my belly button. The way he stops himself just as his fingertip brushes under the hem of my yoga pants.

I'm putty in Sam's hands, and I don't care that we're probably being recorded for surveillance footage. I'd let him take me right here in this rock-climbing gym if that's what he wanted to do. I feel so alive when I'm with him. Like I've lived in a black-and-white world and am seeing color for the first time.

When he finally pulls away from me, I swear he actually growls under his breath. He holds my face in his hands and wipes his thumb over my bottom lip. "I'm starting to think this whole thing is a conspiracy you've derived to kill me. There's no other logical explanation."

I look down and blush at the compliment. Oh, how I wish that were true.

"What do you think? Are you ready to tackle big boy here?" Sam nods to the massive rock wall beside us, then smacks me on the ass. "Let's see what you've got."

I look up at the wall that's easily three times as tall and far more difficult than the kiddie wall and then back to Sam. "Do I have to make it all the way to the top?"

He scans me up and down and moves closer, pulling my hair to one side, so I feel his breath tickling my neck. "I'll tell you what. Why don't you start climbing and just do as I say? If I don't think you can do it, I'll tell you to come down." He pauses and nods his head at the wall. "But you don't stop climbing until I tell you to, do you understand?"

And just like that, I know my dom is back, and my friend is long gone. This isn't just a fun day at the rock-climbing gym anymore, this is a lesson in submission, and for some reason that I don't quite understand, I really want to please him.

"Yes, sir." I reach for the first rock, surprised by how narrow it is. I can't grip my whole hand around this one like the last time, so I have to use my fingertips.

I do my best to leverage my weight up with my legs since it's easier to balance with my feet as I move up the wall. My arms shake as I push myself, using muscles I didn't even know I had. I start to slow when I get about halfway up, pausing to catch my breath.

"You're doing great, Maggie," Sam calls. "But you're not even close to being done. Take a break, catch your breath, and keep going."

I look up, seeing I've still got a way to go, and then down to measure how far I've climbed. Bad idea. That was a very bad idea.

I swallow the lump in my throat as my body begins to quiver with exhaustion and pure terror.

"Sam! I don't think I can do this!" I yell, my face smashed flat against the wall as I cling to the small rocks.

"You can do it. Keep going!" he calls back.

I shake my head as my breath begins to quicken. "No, I don't think you understand. I think I'm tapped out. Can I please come down?" I beg and hold my breath as I wait for his response.

"No. You cannot," he calls. "You're so close, Maggie. You're strong enough. You've got the strength and agility already to do this. You just need to believe in yourself. You're stronger than your fear. I can't do it for you. You have to dig down deep and pull it out of yourself."

I breathe deeply, listening to his encouragement and calming my racing heart. I want to make him proud; I want to show him that I can do it. I release my left hand and shake it out, then look ahead for my next rock. I choose one slightly out of reach and stretch my arm as I push myself up on my toes. When

I make contact, I transition my weight and push myself higher with my feet, finding my next step.

"Thatta girl!" Sam claps below me, and my heart swells with pride at his praise. It feels so good to make him proud. It's not a feeling I've experienced very often in my life, having someone cheer for me.

A new wave of determination ignites in me as I push myself higher and higher. My muscles scream in protest, but I'm so close to the top.

I pause again to catch my breath and decide my next move when I hear Sam call up to me. "You're so close, Maggie. You're so damn close. Don't you dare drop, or I swear I'll make you climb the whole thing again."

My throat tightens as tears burn behind my eyes and I grit my teeth in annoyance because I believe him. I want to cry and give up. Everything hurts, and it's getting hard to keep my grip as the muscles in my hand spasm. I'm hurting and frustrated. This is stupid, and I don't know why I care at all. It's not like I'm doing anything important. It's a made-up activity that people do for fun. It's supposed to be a fun workout, not some life-altering rite of passage. But that's exactly how it feels, like a rite of passage.

As I inch myself up a little farther, my foot slips from underneath me. My fingertips tighten their grip, catching all of my weight reflexively, and my heart races from my near fall. That was close. Too close. I move my feet around until I find better footing and let myself calm down.

It's at that moment, as I'm sweaty and shaking, pressed against that rock wall, that I realize why this feels so important to me. It's not because I don't want to disappoint Sam. The wall is just a metaphor for everything I've had stacked against me in my life, and I'll never know what waits for me at the top unless I conquer it. I imagine all the people who've caused me pain standing at the bottom, booing and mocking me, waiting for me to fall. The foster parents, the kids at school who teased me and pretended like I didn't exist, and all the men who hurt me and shamed me into thinking something was wrong with me.

All the pain that had torn me down and prevented me from healing turns into my fuel.

I close my eyes and calm my mind as everything goes still, and the world falls away. I don't think about Sam standing at the bottom waiting for me or anything he says to cheer me on. It's only me and this man-made mountain, and I'm going to give it everything I've got.

With renewed determination, I bite my lip as I reach for the next rock, slowly inching myself higher and higher. The only sounds I hear are my heavy breaths, and I focus all my energy on moving my body up that wall. After what feels like hours, I finally see the last rock within my reach. I take a deep breath and push myself harder than I thought possible. My fingers cling to the small stone, and I finish the climb, only satisfied when my hand grips the rope and I hear the sharp ding of the bell.

I don't want to let go. This moment is so much bigger than a rock wall. I found the courage to see my pain for what it was and to finally release it. The sound of the bell is a sweet reminder of letting go of the past and moving forward to all that life has to offer.

I look down and see Sam's arms lifted high, clapping and cheering me on as if it was his plan all along... and I wouldn't be surprised if it were.

I propel myself down the wall, the feeling of butterflies a reward rather than a caution sign, and Sam scoops me up into a hug before my feet can touch the ground. He squeezes me tight, holding my head against him protectively as he whispers, "I am so fucking proud of you, Magnolia. You're fucking incredible. I hope you're starting to realize that."

The tears are back, flowing hot and fast down my cheeks like a release valve from every pent-up emotion in my body. I soak in Sam's adorning hug.

"Come on, gorgeous. Let's get cleaned up. I've got another surprise for you tonight."

SEVENTEEN

Sam

After leaving the climbing gym, I drop Maggie off at home and tell her I need to get some supplies for our surprise date tonight. I spend the rest of the afternoon running around town to different sporting goods stores until I check everything off my list.

Who am I kidding? I take my time running those errands because I need space to calm down after everything today. I need to clear my head and remember why I'm doing this in the first place. Maggie may belong to me temporarily, but the reality is that I'm preparing her for another man.

Trent Cain is the complete opposite of me in almost every way. I'd be lying if I said I hadn't fully stalked him on all his social platforms. It's just too easy these days, and I couldn't help myself. I may have also run a background check on the guy, just to make sure he didn't have a history of domestic violence or any other red flags.

He's got that whole jock look to him, even though his

football captain days are long past. He's wholesome, still lives in a suburb outside his hometown, and wears pastels and khakis on Easter. He's as vanilla as they come and probably doesn't shy away from his trusted missionary position. After taking one look at him, I have no idea what Maggie's even worried about. The guy married his high school girlfriend at nineteen. Surely he doesn't have much to compare her to.

But to my disdain, it all came back perfectly clean. No outstanding warrants, flags on his license, or lapse in insurance coverage. Nothing. I saw that he filed for divorce early this year after nine years of marriage. No kids, which surprised me, but who am I to judge?

My guess is that they realized something was off because they were finally in a place to have kids, and that's what led to the divorce, which according to the court document, was filed as *irreconcilable differences*. But I'm no expert, just a career bachelor who's been around the block a time or two.

The more I think about it, the angrier I become. Not because he's not good enough for her but because he's exactly the type of person she needs. Sure, she'd have to suffer through boring sex for the rest of her life, but I'm sure he'd treat her well. He's stable and has a great career; he'd be able to commit to her, give her babies and provide a life where she could stay home with them if she wanted.

All the things that I can't and won't do.

Maggie deserves a low-stress life. I only know a portion of her story, but from what she's told me, it's safe to say she comes from chaos, and now she deserves the world. She deserves someone who doesn't have all the fucked-up baggage that I have. So, as irritating as it may be, handing her over to some square who'll probably never understand how lucky he is, I know it's what's best for her, and isn't that the whole point of this anyway?

I check my weather app for the millionth time, making sure everything is as perfect as it can be. Normally, I would never put in so much effort for a creative date. I'm usually content with a nice dinner and a show before the night really begins when we get home, but I want to dazzle Maggie. I want to show her what kind of effort she should expect from men she dates, so she doesn't ever compromise for the bare minimum.

That reminds me, I'll need a little backup if I want to pull this off. I pull out my phone and text the only two shitheads I can count on to cash in one of the many favors I'm owed.

Hey, guys. I know it's late notice, but I need your help tonight.

JACK

Sorry, bro, Gwen and I are binging the Harry Potter movies this weekend. We're only three movies in, so...

You know, that sounds really nice. I'm so glad the two of you are together and safe back home. I'd hate the thought of what could've happened without your two pals Maggie and Sam there to HELP FIND YOU IN THE MIDDLE OF THE FUCKING OCEAN!

JACK

Yeah, you know what they say about good friends. They look out for you just because they care, not because they expect anything in return. I'm glad you understand.

I swear to god, next time you're stuck on a deserted island and you need my help to make it back home, I'm just going to rewatch Harry Potter.

JACK

I'm not saying my leg being amputated was entirely your fault ... but I think we all know if Benjamin were there, I'd probably still have a foot.

Not this again. You can't blame me for approving a life-saving procedure! Besides, you like all the variety that comes with changing your prosthetic! You even told me you bought a wooden peg leg for your pirate costume this year!

JACK

That's beside the point. That's just me making chicken salad out of chicken shit!

BENJAMIN

Alright, children, that's enough. Jack, your metaphor is disgusting. Sam, what exactly do you need?

JACK

You always take his side!

I've got a truckload of camping gear. I need you to meet me and set up a romantic scene on the rooftop of my building...

JACK

Absolutely not.

BENJAMIN

Is this for Maggie???

Yes. Please don't pry...

JACK

Are you kidding me! What are you planning on doing to our sweet Magnolia with a romantic gesture like this!?

BENJAMIN

Count me in. Oh, and Elliot wants to help, too.

Perfect. Thanks, man.

JACK

Gwen here. Jack would be happy to help his best friends spend a magical night together. Why hasn't anyone told me this is a thing!?

It's not a thing. Please don't tell her. We're just friends, and she asked me for a little… help. Don't get your hopes up.

JACK

She asked you for help, huh? Well, you know that I'm obligated to tell you that I'm well-read on murder documentaries, and I know exactly how I'd do it…

Sorry, Gwen is just kidding about the murdering thing. You know, those pregnancy hormones really keep you on your toes sometimes.

I completely understand. I promise I'm not in the business of breaking hearts. I'd welcome Gwen's rage if I knew I ever hurt Mags.

BENJAMIN

Elliot wants to know if you bought some of those little twinkling lights?

I've got an industrial-size box. Tell her she can knock herself out. Can you meet me in front of my building in an hour?

BENJAMIN

Ten-four

JACK

I'll do it, but I want you to know that I'm going to be grumbling under my breath the entire time.

I'd expect nothing less. Thanks, guys.

After handing off the date setup to the crew, I return to the apartment to freshen up, sneaking in while Maggie is in her room. Normally, I would just set everything up myself, but having Elliot's help really puts my mind at ease. I know those two buffoons are capable of putting in real effort for their ladies, but leaving them alone to handle something like this would really test my control issues.

I'm a simple man who knows what I want. It's not that I'm a perfectionist, but... Well I suppose that's exactly what I am. Life taught me a long time ago that if I want something done right, I'm better off doing it myself.

It's not like I'm setting up a proposal or anything. I just want tonight to feel special. I feel like Maggie's already come so far in learning to love herself, and I want to celebrate the small victories along the way. Besides, I'm a sucker for making her happy and have been since the moment I met her.

I think sometimes like recognizes like. Though we've experienced different types of pain, and mine was mostly self-inflicted, our souls recognize it in each other. I know she's really into astronomy, and though I have no clue what any of it means, a picnic under the stars feels like the perfect way to connect before we move forward physically. It's not entirely unlike me to make an effort to connect with my submissives, but I want to know Maggie on a cellular level. It's like I can't get enough of her. I want to know everything about her.

I'm opening a glass of wine in the kitchen when Maggie comes around the corner. She's wearing fitted fleece yoga pants and a green long-sleeve henley that hangs down just long enough to cover her ass. It's slightly oversized, and the wide neck hangs off her shoulder, showing a thin black bra strap. Her long hair's pinned up in a clip with little strands that have fallen loose, framing her face.

She's a walking wet dream of the girl next door, the perfect blend of sexy and sweet. I suppress a growl as I hand her a glass of wine. "You look stunning, good enough to eat."

She takes the glass and rolls her eyes. "Now, you're just lying. I look painfully ordinary at best. I had no idea if comfy really meant comfy, so I overthought it for two hours before finally settling on this."

She playfully shoves me, but I catch her hand and hold it to me, keeping my gaze trained on her. "I don't lie, Magnolia. I wouldn't have said it if I didn't mean it, and I don't like when you speak about yourself that way."

She sucks in a breath, recognizing the shift in my demeanor. Her eyes widen, her gaze curious, and I'm happy she doesn't look quite as terrified as she used to, though I'll admit I enjoy keeping her on her toes.

I pull the red silk eye-mask from my pocket and hold it out in front of me, "You remember this, don't you?"

She buries her face behind her hands. "Sam! Are you ever going to let that go?"

"Not anytime soon." I twirl my finger in a circle motioning

for her to turn, and she immediately listens, turning her back to me without protest. My chest swells with excitement as I secure the silky fabric around her eyes, knowing she trusts me so much already. "You're such a quick learner."

"Or maybe I just have a really persistent teacher?"

"Persistent. Thorough. Hard..." I let my hands trail down her neck and then her arms before finally resting them firmly on her hips. "Willing to go above and beyond the call of duty," I whisper in her ear as I lead her upstairs to my private rooftop terrace.

Chills spread over Maggie's exposed forearms when I open the outside door, but as we move closer to the standing outdoor heaters, it feels more comfortable. I guide her to sit atop a pile of throw pillows next to a charcuterie board covered in specialty cheeses, meats, and fruits.

"Are you ready to see your surprise?"

Maggie nods excitedly, her smile spreading from ear to ear. I remove her blindfold, pocketing it in case I want to use it later, and watch her misty eyes take everything in. Elliot really outdid herself. I'd imagined a cozy campsite vibe, but this is more than anything I could've asked for. They moved all my outdoor furniture off to the side and put a fully made inflatable mattress in the center of the space, sitting atop a layered rug.

String lights hang in a circle, framing the space without blocking the sky's view, and throw pillows are placed around for comfortable seating. They even lined the railing with rows of lit white candles in all different sizes.

"Sam, how did you have time to do all this?" Maggie covers her mouth in shock as she twirls around, taking it all in.

"I may have enlisted a little help from our friends." I reach for her and pull her to me. "Do you like it?"

Her eyes sparkle as she beams. "I love it. It's perfect, almost like a dream..." Her voice trails off, and I wish I could bottle up her delight and save it for a gloomy day.

I pour us each a glass of wine as we take our seats by the fire. "Oh, I almost forgot the best part." I pull out a giant salted pretzel from a small heated bag and a bowl of nacho cheese for dipping.

"You didn't!" She dives in, pinching off a piece of the pretzel and dunking it in the cheese. "Did you go to the mall to get this for me?"

"I did. I even waited for them to make a fresh batch," I say with a grin.

"How is this real life? A romantic rooftop picnic under the stars and my favorite snacks?" She raises a brow and tilts her head. "Are you buttering me up for something terrifying? Because there's no way I'm ready for the butt plug..."

I shake my head and laugh. "No, Maggie, I'm not veering off the contract–though the more you bring it up, the more I'm tempted to work it in."

"This pretzel is amazing, maybe the best one I've ever eaten." She licks the cheese off her fingers, making my dick harden.

Who knew eating a mall pretzel could look so erotic?

I decide to pull the conversation back to safer territory. "I've been meaning to ask you, how do you feel about everything between us? Do you still feel comfortable?"

She pauses mid-bite, eyebrows pulling down in concern. "Of course I am. Why? Are you changing your mind? Because it's totally fine if you want to stop–"

I hold my hand out in a stop motion and laugh, "No, Maggie, I don't want to stop." I help myself to a piece of cheese, propping my arm on my bent knee. "I just wanted to check in with you, that's all. It's important you're comfortable. I know I pushed you pretty hard today."

She nods. "You did, but I'm so happy you encouraged me. No one's ever talked to me that way, you know, motivating me." She scoffs, "I guess I've never had anyone care so much. I've always had to cheer for myself..."

"You deserve so much more than someone just cheering for you. You deserve someone sitting in your corner and picking you up when you don't have the strength, someone reminding you of how strong you are daily, not just when you feel like giving up. I'm really proud of you, Maggie. I want you to know that I recognize how challenging that climb was, and you shocked the hell out of me." I laugh. "Those yoga muscles are no joke."

She flexes her bicep playfully, then winces, shaking her sore arm out. "Yeah, I think I shocked myself, too. I don't know what came over me. I was completely gassed three-quarters of the way up, but suddenly, I wanted it more than I've ever wanted anything." She places her wine glass down and crosses her arms over her chest. "I began trying to please you like I always do, but then something changed, and suddenly, I didn't care as much if you were proud of me or not. It was like I couldn't even hear you or even think of you. It was just me and that giant wall; everything else just disappeared."

She brings her fingertips to cover her mouth as if she's ashamed of what she just admitted. "Is that okay? I mean... I didn't mean to say I didn't care about you. I just–"

I lean forward and take her hand in mine. "That's the best thing I've ever heard you say. You did something for yourself. That's all I wanted. I wanted you to be proud of yourself, love."

"Thank you," she says in a whisper, voice cracking with emotion. "I'll never forget that feeling as long as I live." She smiles with glassy eyes. "You're so much more than a friend, Sam. I'm so glad to have you in my life."

My chest aches at the reminder of what this is, but I force a smile to cover my discomfort. "Anytime. Speaking of our arrangement," I change the subject, "what's the deal with you and whats-his-name? Things going well?"

Her smile fades, and she pulls her hand away and picks at the charcuterie board. "Things are good. I haven't heard from him since he sent me the venue information." She pops a strawberry in her mouth and nearly moans.

"What do you mean the venue? For the reunion?" My question comes out quickly.

She takes another bite, this time of chocolate, and licks it from her finger before responding. "Yeah, he said he was stressed out about planning everything, so I offered to help. It's no big deal."

"And he just agreed?"

"I mean... yeah." She pauses sucking the chocolate from her fingertips and looks at me. "Was I not supposed to offer to help?"

I sit back with a sigh, crossing my clasped hands over my knees. "No, I guess I'm just surprised he took you up on it. That's all." I scratch the back of my neck. "So, what are you helping him with exactly?"

"Oh, you know, just catering, checking everyone's RSVPs, and helping with the venue." She counts off on her fingers. "There was a huge misunderstanding with the place he originally booked. He had the right time and place and even enough seating, but he booked it for the wrong year. Can you believe that?" She pops a grape in her mouth and laughs. "If I didn't call to ask where to set up the catering, I don't know if he would've caught it."

My jaw flexes in annoyance, but I keep my comments to myself, even though it goes against everything I stand for. I don't know that the guy's taking advantage of Maggie, but if I were a betting man, I'd have my money on it. It seems far too ironic that they've only spoken briefly, and she's suddenly doing the brunt of the work for him. Typical guy.

"I want you to be mindful of your stress level," I remind her. "With everything going on with the studio renovation, I'm not so sure you need to be taking on so much of someone else's responsibility."

"Oh, it's nothing. I'm just–"

"Helping." I clasp my hands together and lean forward. "I know you're helping, but this was his responsibility. You do too much for everyone else. I'd like to see you focus on yourself for a little while, at least while you belong to me."

I watch her fumble with her napkin, dropping her cracker accidentally, then overreacting as she tries to wipe the crumbs away. I can't help but laugh. "Why don't we move over here, and you can teach me about the stars?

She perks up at my suggestion. "You really want me to talk about the stars?" She looks around, gesturing to the whole scene around us.

"Of course I do. I've nowhere else to be, and I'm curious about your hobbies. What do you say?" I wink.

"I guess I'm just surprised. No man has ever even pretended to care about my hobbies. I know it can be boring, and I don't want to bore you."

Her voice trails off, and I place my fingertip on her lips. "That's enough talking back, or I'll have to come up with another punishment for you."

She sucks in a breath, "If I remember correctly, it wasn't so bad." She bats her eyelashes and smiles, then tugs me by the arm.

I don't think she knows just how much I'd love another opportunity to punish her again, but for now, maybe I'll just settle with pleasuring her.

EIGHTEEN

Maggie

We lay on our backs, staring up at the night sky for what seems like hours. Sam never once interrupts me or tries to change the subject. He just lays next to me and listens. It's cold out, especially when the wind gusts around us, but between Sam's warm body snuggled next to me and the outdoor heaters around us, I'm perfectly cozy in only a long sleeve t-shirt and throw blanket.

We discuss our thoughts on the universe, religion, and the meaning of life. It's surprising to find someone so willing to talk openly about the deep stuff. I've never met someone who could match my enthusiasm, but Sam seems to enjoy our conversation as much as I am.

"Tell me something about yourself that you've never told anyone," he says after a moment of silence. He turns to face me, propping his head on his hand, and I mimic his position.

"Something I've never told anyone? Let's see..." I tap my

finger to my lip as I try to think. "I've never been on a roller coaster. Never even been to an amusement park, actually."

Sam sits up, his eyebrows pulled together in confusion. "You're kidding. How have you never been to an amusement park? That's like childhood 101 or something."

I force a smile and shrug. "I think you and I have very different ideas of what childhood looks like."

Sam winces. "Oh, shit, I'm sorry, Mags. I'm such a dick. I'm sorry." He adjusts his pillow underneath him and scoots toward me. "So, why haven't you gone as an adult? I feel like everyone needs to experience puking their chili dogs up from a rollercoaster ride. It's one of the most basic human experiences."

I throw my head back and laugh, picturing a perfectly put-together Sam puking in the bushes at a theme park. "Well, now that you put it that way, I don't know what I was thinking. I guess I should've come to you for help a long time ago."

Sam's smile falls a little. "What was it like growing up in foster care? I mean, if you feel like talking about it." He stares at me like I'm the only one in the world, giving me all his attention.

I twist the tassel on the throw pillow as I consider how deep I want to go. I don't want to derail the evening with tales from my sad childhood, but no one has ever asked me about it before either, and it feels nice.

"As you know, my mom surrendered me as soon as I was born. She wanted to put me up for adoption, but my grandmother wouldn't have it. So, she kept me, and by the time I was home from the hospital, my mom had moved out—not wanting anything to do with me. That's the story my foster family told me anyway." I shrug. "My grandmother raised me until she suffered a stroke when I was five. There was no one to care for either of us, so she went to live in a nursing home while I was sent to a foster home.

"The family was nice, from what I can remember, but they were only a temporary placement. I was lucky to stay there for nearly a year. Foster homes are hard to come by, especially in the small town I'm from. People usually take care of their own. When I was around eight, I was sent to live with another family, although they were waiting for a baby, so as soon as they got the call for newborn twins, I got the boot. They were only certified to have two foster kids, so there wasn't a place for me anymore. Anyway, by that time, I was already ten, going on eleven. I'd bounced around schools so many times I was terribly shy. I didn't exactly make a warm impression. My next placement was at a larger home with several foster kids, and I was the oldest. I got to know all the other kids and hear their stories. I had to watch them go through therapy and give testimonials for their abuse, and I quickly realized just how easy I had it. I started helping take care of the kids in the home, and that's how I was able to earn my spot. I realized that the more I helped, the longer I could stay in the same place." I shrug and hug the pillow to my chest."

Sam places his hand over mine, offering me comfort. "You must've felt so lonely, moving around all the time like that. Feeling like you were constantly being rejected by everyone."

"Yeah, I was lonely, but I realized early on that I was lucky since I didn't have to go through all the trauma the other kids did. I tried not to take it personally, all the moving. I knew the nature of it was that people wanted babies. Little babies who hadn't been damaged by the world yet."

"You're hardly damaged, Maggie. I wish you could see yourself the way I see you. It kills me to think of how you've always cared for everyone else, even when you were just a kid. You had to grow up too fast, and I'm so sorry about that."

I wipe a tear away. "It all worked out in the end. I found Elliot and Gwen in college and then met you through Benjamin. I have a deep appreciation for the people in my life that I may not have otherwise."

"You don't always have to be so fucking positive all the time, Maggie. I hope you know that you don't have to put on a show for me. I'm in this with you for as long as you need me..."

"I know, Sam, and it means more than you'll ever know." I prop my head on my hand and turn to face him. "What about you? What's something you've never told anyone?"

He quirks his lips, and his eyes shift away from mine as if looking around us for the answer, and then he finally speaks. "I feel like most everyone knows my secrets, or did anyway. I grew up in a small town with three younger brothers. There wasn't much I could keep secret from any of them."

I lean in a little closer, desperate to hear whatever he's about to confess because everyone else may know Sam's secrets, but I feel like I haven't even scratched the surface of really getting to know him.

"I guess that's why I'm such a private person these days." He rubs his hand across his stubbled chin and forces a laugh. "Something no one else knows about me is that I'm not as calm as I appear to be most of the time." He pauses, and I place my hand on his, offering encouragement. "I, uh... I used to be really shy and anxious when I was a kid. I was convinced that everyone was staring at me all the time. When I did something good, bad, it didn't matter. I perceived any attention as bad like I was being made fun of."

"Sam, that's horrible." I brush my hand up his arm, and my chest aches at his confession. I feel as if I can physically feel his pain in my heart and want to take it away from him.

"My mom was the only one who understood it. She protected me in a way, always stood in front of me when I needed her to, and made sure no one commented if I had to get new clothes for an event. I think she even emailed my teachers and prepared them before school started every year. I was lucky to be average in every way during school, so I easily blended into the background." He shrugs. "I made decent grades, and it wasn't until middle school when I froze during a presentation that I realized how big of a problem it was."

"How did you get over it?"

"I don't know, really. I guess I just sucked it up. After my mom died when I was twelve, my dad needed me to help out with my younger brothers. There wasn't any room for my brokenness any longer, so I just sort of just pushed it all down."

"That doesn't seem very healthy... You didn't have any friends or a girlfriend you could talk to..."

"Attachments only make complicated things worse. I learned that the hard way a long time ago."

"Oh, I'm sorry. I didn't mean to pry."

"It's fine." He tucks a piece of hair behind my ear. "I'm just one of those people who needs to learn lessons the hard way."

I glance down at his lips. "Is that why you became a dominant?"

"One of the reasons. I like to be in control in more ways than one." He pulls my pursuing hand away from his shoulder peppering it with kisses and inches his way up my arm at a slow, tortuous pace.

"What about your brothers and your dad? How did they fare after losing your mother?"

Sam stops his perusal, his dark eyes meeting mine. "My father and brothers are doing just fine. My dad lives in the same town, though now he's got a nice beachfront property. My two younger brothers live there as well, and my second brother lives in Louisiana with his wife. They're expecting their first child in the spring."

"That's nice. So the kids were alright," I say more to myself than to him.

"Yes, they were." He leans up on his elbow, studying me for

a moment before tracing along my nose. "Your freckles are so distracting, like specs of stardust sprinkled across your face."

I giggle, and his eyes flick to my lips. My breath hitches as I watch him, unsure of what happens next.

As he wets his lips, my body inches closer to his, instinctually closing the gap between us. "Speaking of my family. I've been meaning to ask you something."

My heavy eyes flutter open in surprise as I wait.

"My stepmom's throwing my dad this retirement party back home, and I was wondering if you'd come with me?" His fingers trail from my nose down to my lips, then my chin, as if trying to touch every inch of me.

"Of course, I'd love to!" I practically blurt. "I'd love to meet your family." I push myself up to a seated position and pull him into a hug. I don't think he realizes how much something like this means to me. Other than Elliot and the occasional visit from her parents, no one's ever offered to include me in something like this.

"It would be the same weekend as your reunion." His words are a cold glass of water, snapping me back to reality.

I shake my head, "It's fine. I'd love to meet your parents... and your brothers."

My smile fades as I remember the shit show of a renovation my studio's undergoing, and it's as if he can read my mind because, before I can protest, he holds up his hands and says, "Don't worry about the studio or the travel. We've got the best crew in the city working on it. So I don't want to hear any arguments. Besides, as a business owner, how many opportunities do you get to have a worry-free vacation?"

I consider him for a moment and finally relax. "You're right. I haven't seen the beach in at least a decade. It would feel so good to get away and feel the sand in between my toes and listen to the waves."

"Good. It's decided, then. My parent's beach house is only a two-hour drive from Bramville. I'll drive you there myself. I can book your flight home straight from there." He looks down at the space between us. "That is, if you decide to come back home."

My brows pull together in confusion at the comment. I guess I never considered what would happen if Trent and I hit it off. He lives in Georgia, and I've built my life and career here. My mind begins to race with how fast things are moving in my non-existent relationship, and Sam must recognize the panic bubbling beneath the surface.

His hand wraps around the nape of my neck, gentle at first, as he runs his fingers through my hair. His touch feels so amazing. Like he's able to hit a button and shut off everything in my mind. I close my eyes, and then his soft, wet lips are on mine, and he's pulling me into him, wrapping me up in his strong arms, ridding me of every ounce of worry.

I melt into him as relief and desire wash over me. "Let's not waste this night on that stuff." He pulls away a little and turns up the music before offering me his hand. "May I have this dance?"

I throw my head back and laugh as I place my hand in his. I swear this man loves to give me whiplash. Just when I think he's going to jump my bones for good, he switches it up on me, determined to keep me shaking in my boots.

He leads me underneath the twinkling lights as "Wildflowers and Wine" by Marcus King plays over the speakers. When he pulls me tight against him, planting a kiss in the crook of my neck before righting his stance, every hair on my body stands on end. He twirls me around on the rooftop underneath the full moon, and it feels like I'm dreaming, floating on air as we move and sway to the music.

"Would you mind if we started our next lesson out here?" he whispers.

I nod as I bite my lip, but Sam's feet still as he waits for a proper response.

I can't believe I still feel shy in front of him, but this feels different, like we're doing something bad, being outside in the open, and the thought alone burns like wildfire in my belly. "Yes, please."

"So fucking polite." He kisses me softly, then bites me before pulling away.

My eyes go wide. I knew it was coming, but somehow, I wasn't prepared for it to be tonight. I haven't even memorized the most common sexual positions in the kama sutra or practiced what to do with my hands...

"Stop freaking out and dance with me." Sam pulls me into him and playfully slaps me on the ass. "We'll go as slow as you want." He moves his hands to the small of my back, settling on my hips with a firm, steady grip.

It's possessive and commanding and immediately puts me at ease. I trust this man with everything. I just hope I'm able to walk away from this with our friendship intact because the lines are so blurred I don't know where our friendship ends and this arrangement begins anymore. And strangely, I'm having a really hard time worrying about that right now.

NINETEEN

Sam

I don't think I've been this nervous with a woman since my first time when I was sixteen. My heart's pounding so hard that it may as well be part of the song.

My mind and body are doing weird things, teaming up on me, trying to convince me that this is something else entirely. But I know it's not. I tighten my grip to mask the tremble in my hands and then twirl her in a spin, bringing her body flush against mine, where it belongs.

I didn't think it was possible to like her any more than I already did, but after our conversation this evening, I don't see how men aren't throwing themselves at her feet. She's incredibly strong, kind, and smart, not to mention drop-dead gorgeous. Her bright red hair stands out like a rose in a world full of daisies, and her warm skin is lit up with the cutest freckles that magnify her bright hazel eyes.

Any man would be lucky to be on the receiving end of her smile. And when she laughs, especially when I cause it, I feel like I've just climbed Mt. Everest. And yet, she came to me, asking for help. I still can't wrap my head around it, and I'm equally thankful to be so goddamn lucky and pissed that she felt so desperate that she needed to do it.

I let out a slow, controlled breath. I already knew she was too good for me, but I'm thankful for the reminder she gave me tonight because there's no way in hell I've done anything to deserve her. So, tonight, I will savor and relish every smile, every touch, and every whimper as I do my best to show her how she deserves to be treated. I may not be able to control how anything else goes in her life, but I can take control tonight. And I'll live off the memory for the rest of mine.

The song comes to an end and blends into another, and our feet pause as she looks up, eyes wide with wonder. "I'm really nervous, but I want you to know I trust you."

My chest swells, and I feel ten feet tall when she looks at me like she trusts me with her entire being. It's so innocently erotic because there's no way she knows what she's doing to me, and it's exactly what I need to hear. I release my grip on her waist, my fingers itching to trace her collarbone.

She leans her head to the side, granting me full access as my fingers trail across her soft skin. My cock swells at the sight of her so eager for my touch, and I pull her closer with my opposite hand, so she can feel what she's doing to me.

She lets out a little gasp and smiles, and her eyelids flutter closed. Her skin feels like velvet against my calloused fingers as I trace her collarbone, slowly sneaking my thumb lower on her chest. Her head falls back, granting me more access, and her breath quickens, her body hungry for more.

I suppress a growl as I watch her slowly unravel before me, letting down her guard and just being in her body. My thumb dips down a little lower, grazing the top of her perky breast, and she whimpers, pressing closer in response.

It's so fucking sexy to watch her let go and fully experience pleasure. I'm desperate for more, but I want to pace myself. Things could easily get out of hand if I let myself lose control, and I'm not ready for this night to end.

I dip my thumb down again, dangerously close to her nipple and she lets out moan of pleasure that goes straight to my already rock hard cock. As if I needed any more fuel for my already strained self-control, I lift her shirt at the hem and pull it from her body, rewarding myself with a view that will forever be burned in my memory. Maggie stands before me with hungry eyes in a thin strapped sports bra that dips a little in the middle.

It's nothing like the expensive lingerie I bought her, the kind I'm accustomed to taking off women, but somehow it's even sexier. She looks so much like herself tonight, which adds to everything I'm feeling. Pulling her arms up, she attempts to cover herself, and I shake my head. "Don't do that. Don't you dare try to hide the most goddamn beautiful view I've ever seen."

She drops her hands at her sides and blushes. "I can feel your eyes on my skin." She glances over her shoulder, no doubt checking to see if anyone else can see her. We're on top of one of the tallest buildings in the city, we may be outside, but we're definitely not in anyone's view. Though, that doesn't take away from the feeling of being exposed.

I study her, watching to see any indication that I've pushed her too far, but I can see by how she's breathing and how her nipples harden into tight little peaks that she's open to this and maybe even on her way to enjoying herself. I just may have a little exhibitionist on my hands. Only time will tell.

"So. Damn. Perfect," I say as my hand rests on her hip. "I need to see all of you. Stay still." I slide my hand over her shoulder and down her rib cage as she stands still before me, not daring to move while I trace her beautiful body with my fingertips. I take the opportunity to pull the waistband of her leggings away and drag them slowly down her long legs.

Helping her step out of her pants, I admire her body under the moonlight. It's by no means bright out here, but between the light of the moon and the twinkling lights around us, I'm pleased to have a clear view of her body. The heaters give a nice warm flow of air that mixes with cool breezes.

I plant a soft kiss on the top of her foot before tossing her leggings to the side. On my knees, I look up at her, and I'm struck with another wave of pure, unadulterated gratitude that this woman would trust a man like me to bear witness to any part of her, much less give me the joy of participation. This is how Maggie should be treated, standing before men as they kneel and worship the ground she walks on.

I continue kissing up the length of her leg as my hands explore her, stopping just before I reach the apex of her thighs. She parts her legs as my fingers glide dangerously close to her center and lets out a small whimper when I don't give her what she wants.

"Now, don't be greedy. I want to show my admiration to every part of you," I whisper as I move my mouth higher and higher until I've reached the top of her thighs.

Her only response is a frustrated pant. She moves her hands to my hair and tightens her grip, pulling it slightly as my kisses inch higher and higher. "You're so beautiful. I could taste every inch of you, and it wouldn't be enough."

She whimpers, and I know I've got her right where I want her. She's putty in my hands, but I'm having too much fun to stop now.

"I really want to taste you here." I slide the back of my knuckle over her wet center, and her body jumps in surprise. Her eyes fly open, and I look up at her for permission. I may be her dom, but she's the one in charge here, and I don't want to push her further than she wants to go, whether she asked me for it or not.

She nods slightly and closes her eyes, then her hands return to my hair, giving me all the encouragement I need. In a swift motion, I lift her, wrapping her legs around me, and move to the mattress. I lay her down gently, careful, so she doesn't hit her head as the air mattress shifts under our weight. As much as I loved my view, I want her to be as comfortable as possible because if I have it my way, she's never going to forget this.

I hover over her to pull off her bra and slide off her wet panties. Seeing Maggie lying bare before me isn't something I could've prepared myself for. Yeah, I saw hints of her in the bathtub, but holy shit, this woman is beautiful, and I could spend a lifetime exploring her every freckle and curve. "Fuck," I mutter under my breath as I shake my head in disbelief.

She tries to cover herself again, and I throw her hand to the side. "Do you need me to tie you up, or do you think you can keep your hands out of my way?" I quirk a brow, but my voice is stern. I don't think I've been this serious about anything in my life.

She shakes her head and smiles, then covers her eyes with her hands. "Why are you so good at all of this?"

Her question makes me smile because she doesn't have a clue about what I'm good at. "Maybe I'm just really enjoying myself? Have you ever thought of that?" I wink, then cover her mouth with my own as my hands roam freely over her taut body, so delicate and strong yet soft and feminine. My hand finds her soft, supple breast, and my eyes roll back in my head from the contact. She's so fucking perfect in every way. I don't think I could have designed her better myself.

I break my kiss from her lips and lick my way down her body, sucking her tight nipple into my mouth. She writhes beneath me, hands rubbing and scratching my back as she arches for more.

She tugs at my shirt, and I lean forward, pulling it off at the hem. Then I kick off my pants, so the heavy fabric of my jeans doesn't hurt her. Our hot skin touching feels like heaven when I come back down on top of her and she wraps her legs around me, pressing her bare pussy against me with only the fabric of my underwear separating us.

"Goddammit, Magnolia, you're driving me crazy." I adjust my growing erection as I lick and taste her body, inching my way down to the space between her legs.

Her pussy is so beautiful, and my mouth waters to taste her. I grip her ass in one hand while my other hand explores her every curve. She tightens her grip on my hair as she bucks up, arching her back, desperate for relief.

I kiss her gently at first, then slowly lick her up and down, keeping my tongue soft and flat. Her thighs wrap around my head, and she moans, her hands frantic in my hair, but I keep my slow pace.

"Oh, God, Sam. Don't stop!" she moans as she squirms beneath me.

A cocky smile pulls at my lips, and fuck, I've never been prouder than I am at this moment. Hearing her beg me, crying out my name as she squirms beneath me, I feel like I'm on top of the world. I don't answer her, though. Instead, I glide two fingers inside her, continuing my exploration with my mouth, finding that tender spot and pressing.

Her body jumps off the mattress, and her hands fly up to her face as her pussy tightens around my fingers. "Does that feel good, baby?"

"Mmm," she moans as she writhes beneath me, so desperate for relief.

"Your pussy's so wet for me and so goddamn tight. You taste

so fucking good." I pull my fingers out and press them to her lips. "Taste yourself."

Her lips part with a gasp, and she sucks my fingers into her hot mouth.

"Good girl, you're so fucking hot when you obey me. I can do anything I want to your perfect body because you belong to me." I pinch her nipple, and she lets out a cry. Then I caress her, rubbing my thumb softly over her tight peak.

Her pussy clenches, and she gets even wetter, if that's even possible, and I know she's close. I had a feeling my girl would like dirty talk, and I'm having the time of my life teasing and edging her.

"I could play with your body all day and never get tired. How does that sound to you, baby? You want me to keep going?" I croon before licking her harder, applying more pressure while keeping my tongue soft and my pace steady.

"Oh, God, please don't stop. Fuck, I'm so close. Please don't stop, Sam," she begs as she spreads her legs wider, and her body stiffens.

I slide my hand up to play with her tits, nearly exploding from the sound of her panting. "Are you ready to come for me? I want to hear you scream my name while you come on my face. Can you do that for me, baby?"

"Yes. Yes. Yes," she whines as she squirms, thighs tightening around my head, and I suck her clit into my mouth. I work my fingers into her sensitive spot in a steady rhythm, and her back arches as her body goes stiff. Then she's screaming my name as she completely falls apart.

I kiss my way back up her body and pull her into me in a hug. "You're so perfect, baby. So fucking perfect." As I tuck her into me, she buries her face in my chest and I rub her bare back, letting her calm down from the rush. Several moments pass before she pulls away with tears in her eyes.

"Thank you." She sniffles as she wipes a stray tear from her cheek. "Thank you for showing me that I'm not broken." She sniffles again as a sob catches in her throat.

I feel my heart cracking as I hold her, and I know that this is just a small step. I know we've still got a long way to go. I may not have much time left, but I'm determined to make the most of what I've been given.

"Shh," I whisper. "You aren't anywhere close to being broken. I promise you I'm going to prove that to you very soon." I kiss her temple and wrap a blanket around us as I hold her, rocking her like that until she finally falls asleep. It's only then that I close my eyes and let myself pretend this is real life.

TWENTY

Maggie

"Well, well, well, look who the cat dragged in. You've got some explaining to do, missy." Gwen calls from her cozy nest on the couch. Feeling light and refreshed, I step into her living room and hang my coat on the coat rack.

This morning, I woke up to a surprise breakfast on the rooftop after the most incredible night, even though it was interrupted when Jack called, practically begging Elliot and me to come to stay with Gwen for a few days. Apparently, he got a call to make a cameo for some new Discovery Channel show filming in Costa Rica.

As much as I enjoy hanging out with Sam—and our lessons—I was excited to get some time with my besties just to let loose and stop worrying about all the complications I've welcomed into my life.

I need this time to relax and have a little fun.

I help myself to a glass of wine. Elliot arrived before me and had already prepared a tray of snacks and drinks for our slumber party. She rounds the corner carrying a giant bowl of popcorn, and her eyes widen when she sees me.

"Mags! You look so good!" She sets the popcorn on the coffee table and rushes to me, pulling me into a tight hug. "Is this sweater new?" She leans back, still holding me at my elbows, "That green looks amazing on you. Ooh, and it's cashmere!" She runs her hand up my sweater sleeve and back down again.

"Thanks, Elliot. Yes, it's new." I feel the beginning of a blush burning on my cheeks. "Sam bought it for me."

"Oh, *Sam* bought it for you? How is *Sam*?" Gwen singsongs from behind us, and we spin to face her, not wanting her to feel left out of the conversation. She's been put on bed rest, and Elliot and I are under strict orders to give her whatever she wants and only to let her up to use the bathroom.

"Yes, he did." I wipe my sweaty palms on the legs of my jeans before grabbing the stem of my wine glass. "Sam's well. He's working late tonight." I tug at the neck of my turtleneck, loosening the tight fabric that suddenly feels a little claustrophobic, and take a seat on the opposite end of the sofa. Elliot carries the tray of snacks to the coffee table and sits in the armchair next to Gwen.

Gwen shoves her hand into a bowl of popcorn. "And how would you label your relationship with Sam these days?"

"Gwen! Let her at least finish her drink before you start the interrogation!" Elliot hisses, but Gwen doesn't relent. She just narrows her eyes as she waits for my answer.

I take a long gulp of my wine. I knew this was coming. After Sam told me he enlisted the help of our friends to set up the rooftop last night, I knew I'd be hearing about it. I just wasn't quite expecting it to happen so soon. "We're just friends. He's helping me become better acquainted with myself, but it's nothing more than that," I assure her.

"Uh huh," Gwen eyes me up and down. "I call bullshit."

"So, um, how's the renovation going on the studio?" Elliot pipes in nervously, and I'm thankful for the change in conversation.

I make myself a small plate of snacks, piling various crackers and dips on my plate. "Things are going great. I actually stopped by on my way here and spoke with my contractor. They plan on replacing all the damage and installing new top-of-the-line pipes and a hot water heater next week. After that, it'll mainly be cosmetic stuff, replacing drywall, laying new floor throughout, baseboards, painting, all that stuff." I relax a little as I pop a grape in my mouth.

"That's amazing! So, what are your plans until they finish? If you want to give Sam a break or need your own space, you know you're always welcome to stay with Benjamin and me. We've got a guest room, but fair warning, his family's staying with us, and my mother-in-law is kind of eccentric." She laughs. "I think she even makes me look normal sometimes."

I bite the side of my nail as I consider her offer. "I'll let you know, okay?" I don't know what will happen after my reunion, but it might be weird staying with Sam after I've gotten together with Trent. I know we're just friends, but I don't want to seem like I'm flaunting anything in front of him.

"Of course. Why don't we change into pajamas and get cozy for the movie?"

Elliot jumps up, and Gwen throws off her blanket, revealing a cute two-piece pajama set. "I've already beat you to it."

I look around nervously and bite my lip. "I'm good. Way too comfortable to change right now." I scoop a chip into the large bowl of dip and shove the whole thing in my mouth as a bead of sweat slides down my back. Suddenly, I regret the turtleneck and jean combo, but it's for the best.

Gwen narrows her eyes skeptically. "You know, Elliot, I'm

kind of chilly, actually. Do you think you could turn the fireplace up a little?"

Elliot whips around and rushes to Gwen's side. "Are you feeling okay? You're always so hot. Do you think you have a temp—"

Gwen rolls her eyes as she slaps Elliot's hand away. "Just turn the fireplace up, would you? I'm pregnant, and pregnancy hormones aren't always predictable."

"You got it." Elliot clicks on the fireplace, then skips off down the hall to change into her PJs.

"So, how are the sex lessons going, Mags?" I almost choke on my popcorn from Gwen's random question.

I'm chugging a bottle of water and coughing when Elliot comes back and plops down on the floor between the sofa and coffee table. "You okay?" she asks, and I give her a thumbs up between hacks.

They wait for me to catch my breath, and Gwen finally says, "You really thought you were going to get away with some half-response earlier? I have nothing going on in my life, Maggie. I've been on bed rest for two weeks, and I'm starting to run out of things to think about. I need this!" she practically begs. "Please, just tell me something. No, tell me everything. I need to know all of it. Start at the beginning. I'm so bored, and this is the most exciting thing that's happened since Jack knocked me up on a deserted island, and we both almost died."

Elliot looks between us. "Only share what you feel comfortable sharing, Mags..." She elbows Gwen, and they seem to have a silent conversation with their eyes. I wonder what they know... What has Sam told Benjamin and Jack?

I clear my throat, the blush creeping back to my cheeks. "It's nothing, really." A bead of sweat runs down my brow, and my upper lip is moist with perspiration. I wipe it away with the back of my hand and tug at my sweater again. "You know I haven't exactly had the best track record with guys..."

"What do you mean track record? You never date?" Gwen asks.

I shrug. "I mean, I do go on dates sometimes. I just don't tell you because I don't want to be asked about it if they don't go well..."

Elliot grabs my hand. "What? Why wouldn't you tell us this, Maggie? We could help you, give you advice, or whatever."

"It's embarrassing. I feel like I'm lightyears behind both of you. The truth is all the men I've been with have shared the same complaint." I look up and hold out my arms. "It's me."

"What do you mean it's you?" Elliot asks.

I count off on my fingers. "I suck at sex. I'm terrible in bed, comparable to spoiled milk, a catfish, I fuck like a plank of wood or an inflatable sex doll. Oh, and one time, I actually hissed because I saw someone do it in a porno, and the guy lost his erection completely and then asked me to leave."

"God, this is good," Gwen says as she shoves a handful of popcorn in her mouth. "Keep going."

"So, you approached Sam to help you get better at sex?" Elliot asks.

"Yeah, but it doesn't mean anything." I shake my head. "I reconnected with an old friend from high school, and... I just wanted a little help, so it didn't happen again."

"But you didn't have any friends in high school..." Elliot adds.

I wince because she isn't wrong. "I didn't, but I wanted to. Trent was the first person to ever make me feel chosen. He asked me to a dance before I moved foster homes, and when I moved back, he'd already moved on and was dating the head cheerleader," I explained. "I couldn't blame him. I mean, I was gone for over two years, but I guess I never really got over him.

Anyway, he reached out about our class reunion. He's divorced now, and he asked me to go with him. I really think this could lead somewhere, and I just want to feel confident enough should the opportunity present itself." I shrug.

Gwen narrows her eyes. "Sweetie, you know I'm all up for practicing sex, but... do you really think it's necessary? I mean, those other guys must've been high off their asses to think you weren't a good lay. I mean, look at you. You're a total bombshell."

"Yeah, I'd tap that," Elliot offers awkwardly.

Gwen adjusts herself, so she's sitting forward, a throw pillow shoved behind her back.

"So, tell us about the lessons? Have you learned anything new?"

"A few things." I take another sip of wine and clamp my mouth shut. My cheeks are flushed now but not only from embarrassment. I'm actually starting to accumulate some boob sweat. It must be eighty degrees in here. I push the sleeves of my sweater up to my elbows and stretch my turtleneck down when I hear Gwen gasp.

"Hickey! Mag's, you have a giant hickey on your neck! I fucking knew it!" Gwen points and shouts before tossing a handful of popcorn at my face.

I duck under my arm, so the popcorn doesn't hit me in the eye, and before I know it, Elliot's on top of me. We fall out of the chair as she pins me to the ground. The woman's got the strength of a chimpanzee, and I don't know where she keeps it.

"What the hell, Elliot!" I squeal as I squirm beneath her powerful thighs. She's got me pinned on the floor, laid out on my side, and her thighs gripped tightly around my face.

"Sorry, Mags, but Gwen asked me to help her get a better look. Just be honest, and I won't have to manhandle you..."

I blink my watery eyes open against the strain of Elliot's

thigh grip and see a swollen Gwen waddling toward me. "You made us do this." She tsks as she pulls the neck of my sweater away from my skin and gasps in surprise.

"Magnolia Anderson, you are covered in hickeys from your neck down to your..." She drops my sweater, stands, then waddles back to her seat on the couch.

Elliot follows suit, releasing me from her death grip, and I cough as I sit up carefully, dizzy from my near suffocation.

"Care to share with the class why you thought you could conceal a collection of hickeys from your best friends, who both know you hate turtleneck sweaters because they feel like they're made to be torture devices for your neck?" Gwen quirks a brow and crosses her arms over her chest.

I let out a frustrated sigh. "Ugh, fine! What do you want to know?"

Elliot scoots closer and looks to Gwen, who nods as if this is all somehow part of a larger plan I'm not privy to. "When did you get the hickeys?"

I hang my head as embarrassment rushes up my neck, but I force myself to answer. "Last night." I swallow a gulp. "Sam got a little carried away before he went down on me on the roof..."

Elliot jumps back and audibly gasps as she covers her mouth with her hand. "Magnolia!"

Gwen smiles ear to ear as she turns off the fireplace with the remote I take her silence as encouragement to keep going.

"So far, that's the furthest we've gone, but there's more." I pause, waiting until I have their full attention. "Did either of you know that Sam is a dominant?"

"He's a what!?" Gwen's voice comes out in a croak, and her eyes nearly bug out of her head as she grips her hands on the throw pillow in her lap.

I nod as I pick at the hangnail I've created since being put in the hot seat. "So, get this, his long-term submissive just ended things the night I bumped into him downtown..."

"Natalie?" Elliot asks, and I nod. "I think I remember hearing Benjamin talk about her. They were together for a while, weren't they? Benjamin said things weren't serious and that Sam didn't do relationships, so I never asked to meet her."

"Yeah, so when I asked him to help me the only way he'd agree was if I signed his contract to be his new submissive." I relax my shoulders and look up, meeting their stunned glares.

"What the fuck, Mags! You're Sam's submissive, and I'm only just learning about this!" Gwen tosses the throw pillow at my head, and I duck as it narrowly misses me. "What kind of kinky stuff is he doing to you? You little slut, you better spill!"

"What's it like? Does he like to hit you and stuff?" Unlike Gwen, Elliot gives me a worried look.

Suddenly, I feel a little less shy after getting that secret off my chest. "No, it's not like that at all. Actually, it's kind of the opposite."

"You have my attention..." Gwen practically drools.

I scoot forward on my seat and almost whisper even though we're the only one's here. "Basically, we have this contract that has all my hard limits and rules he wants me to follow–"

"What are the rules!?" Elliot interrupts.

I shrug. "Stuff like I need to eat two healthy meals a day. I can't ignore my phone without putting it in focus mode, so he knows I'm busy. I have to be in bed by ten on weeknights. Oh, and he gets really upset when I'm self-deprecating."

"What happens if you break a rule?" Gwen asks, now sitting on the edge of her seat.

I bite my lip and look down. "So far, I've only been punished once ..."

"Oh my God, Mags, I'm going to explode over here!" Gwen blurts. "What was your punishment?"

I squirm in my seat, unable to look her in the eye. "He bathed me," I mumble under my breath.

"He bathed you? Like in boiling water or something?" Elliot's eyebrows pull in confusion.

I sigh. "No, not like that at all. It was kind of nice, actually. He made me bathe in front of him, and he washed me... He told me how beautiful I was, and then he..." I bury my face in my hands, and I could die right now of embarrassment, but I'm kind of relieved to have someone to talk to about it, so I continue. "He showed me how to pleasure myself with the removable shower head. So I did, and he watched... while he jacked himself off..." My voice trails off, and I sigh, slacking back in my chair.

"Holy shit!" Gwen fans herself, then lifts her hair off the back of her neck. "Jeez Louise, Elly, can you get me a cup of ice? Jesus, Maggie, that's so hot! I have to say I'm jealous you're getting your world rocked. I have to get Jack drunk if I want him to really rail me because he's so scared of inducing labor." She laughs.

Elliot comes back with her cup of ice, and Gwen pops a piece in her mouth and rubs the glass on the back of her neck.

"And last night, he went down on you on the roof? So, does that mean sex is next on the list of lessons? Is he going in order?" Elliot asks.

"Hell if I know. If I know anything about Sam, it's that he likes to keep me on my toes and unexpecting." I laugh. "He even invited me to go home with him to his dad's retirement party next week."

I don't miss the way Gwen and Elliot's eyes dart to one another. "What? I mean as a friend. He just wants me to get a chance to relax at the beach before the reunion." I pour myself another glass of wine. "Why? Do you think that's a bad idea?"

Gwen looks to Elliot before speaking. "I guess I'm just surprised, that's all. You know, if he's trying to keep things casual, why would he bring you home to meet his family?" She shrugs. "But hey, what do I know? I'm just a knocked-up married woman. I may be out of touch with what the kids are doing these days." She waves me off.

Just then, my phone pings in my pocket, and my heart races. I pull it out and am a little disappointed to find a message from Trent.

TRENT

How's everything going? You have any fun plans tonight?

I study the message for a minute when Gwen finally asks. "What? Who is it? Is that Sam?"

I shake my head, still staring at my phone. "No. It's Trent, actually."

"What did he say?" Elliot asks.

"He wants to know if I have plans tonight." I shrug and start typing my response...

"Wait!" Gwen says, and I pause. "He's feeling you out. Why not give him something to work with?" Her eyes twinkle with mischief. "He's the end game here, right, Mags?" Her question hangs in the air between us.

I stare for a moment and shake to attention. "Uh, yeah. He is. What should I say?"

Gwen wiggles her fingers for me to give her the phone, and I hesitantly pass it over before sitting on the couch next to her. Elliot piles in beside me as we hover over the small screen.

I watch as Gwen types...

Thought I would meet my girlfriends for some drinks and then maybe go dancing...

His response comes almost immediately.

TRENT

Dancing? I'm sad I'll miss it.

Me, too. I could use someone to hold my purse and coat. What are you up to tonight?

TRENT

Aw, now, I think I'm more useful than that... I thought I'd head into town and meet up with some friends. Maybe grab some beers and play pool.

I'll have to decide that for myself. I'm a master pool player. Maybe I can kick your ass sometime?

TRENT

I'd love that. It's a date...

Well, I just pulled up to the bar. Have fun tonight... but not too much 😘

"Gwen!" I snatch the phone from her and slide it into my pocket without looking as it buzzes again. "I can't play pool, and you're making me sound like a... a..."

"A woman who's interested in his company?" Gwen answers for me as she quirks a brow. "Relax, Mags. You don't really have to be good at pool. No one actually cares about that game. It's just foreplay." She wraps her arm around my shoulder. "You should be learning all about that, right?"

"Yeah, I guess so." I wipe my hands on my jeans and then stand. "Since the cat's out of the bag, I'm going to change into my pajamas. Could we please crack a window, so I don't suffocate during the movie?"

Gwen laughs and fans herself with her shirt, "Yeah, I'm sweating my ass off over here."

"Oh, thank God!" Elliot says as she jumps up and cracks a window.

I grab my overnight bag and head to the bathroom, where I peel off my sweaty turtleneck and reveal dark hickeys all over my neck and chest. There are some on my lower stomach and inner thighs. I don't know the purpose of those, but it was almost like Sam was marking me...

I roll my eyes at my thought, dismissing the idea immediately. What would someone so experienced with women want with someone like me?

I pull on my sleep top and push my jeans down. The phone in my pocket buzzing hard on the tile. I pick it up and see the unread message. Only it's not from Trent.

SAM

I hope you're being a good girl tonight and remembering all the rules?

I smile as butterflies swarm in my belly and heat pricks across my fair skin as if every mark he left behind is its own heat source. I type out a quick response and then put my phone in my overnight bag.

Yes, sir.

TWENTY-ONE

Sam

I stare at the calendar on my phone screen as my heart skips a beat, panic brewing just below the surface. I've only got one more week before Maggie and I head to Florida, and then she'll no longer be mine.

It feels like a punch to the gut thinking about her wrapped in another man's arms, but she was never really mine to begin with. I don't know where I'm getting off believing she ever was. I pull open the drawer of my side table and pull out the contract. The paper's worn with little creases, having been studied so much. I stare at our rules and the end date highlighted in bright yellow before letting my eyes skim down to our signatures.

Time's passing too fast. I haven't even gotten a chance to have sex with her yet, and every new day feels like a giant clock ticking away, reminding me that our time is running out. I drop the contract on the bed beside me and shove my hands in my hair. What am I doing?

After our date on the roof, I lay awake all night, completely panicking. I fucking marked her like she was my own. I couldn't stop myself. Watching Maggie come apart like that, really owning her sexuality and letting me explore her in ways no one ever has... Fuck, it was like a drug to my ego. My infatuation with her lessons is starting to cross the line. Hell, I don't even know where the line is anymore. All I know is I can't stop thinking about her. Every minute of every day, I'm consumed with thoughts of her laugh, how she smiles so big when she really laughs at something, those goddamn freckles that drive me crazy, and her authenticity in everything she does. I could spend a lifetime trying to be good enough and wouldn't even come close to deserving her.

So, naturally, I had to call in a favor, so we could both have some space.

I reached out to a contact, a friend of a friend who scouts for reality TV for the Discovery Channel, and it just so happened they were filming a new survival show in Costa Rica. They jumped at the chance to have Jack, aka Wombat Willy as he's known on his YouTube channel, film a special guest appearance as a judge for one of the competitions. The offer was so perfect that he couldn't say no. He was calling looking for help before we were even finished with breakfast.

Of course, I was persuasive and offered to look after Gwen myself, which led him to remember Maggie was currently available to Gwen-sit. Everything fell into place after that. Maggie's been staying with Gwen and Elliot–having much-needed girl time, so I don't even feel guilty–and I've been wallowing, wrestling to gain back some control.

I glance at the clock. She'll be home any minute now, and I need to put on a good face. I don't want to lead her on, so I've got to figure out how to fulfill my duties without letting on that I'm struggling to keep our friendship at the forefront.

I press my hands to my mouth in prayer, not exactly sure who I'm praying to. I just know I need help. I know it may hurt like hell, but I have to protect her, even if it's from myself. I hear the front door open and close, followed by her sweet voice. "Sam! I'm home. Are you here?"

My heart tightens in my chest, and I take a long breath readying myself. I shove the contract in my side table drawer and pull on a t-shirt. "Yeah, I'll be right there!" I call as I make my way into the living room to greet her.

I bump into her in the hallway as she rolls her suitcase to her bedroom. She throws her arms around me, pulling me into a hug. Her hair smells like peaches and vanilla, and my fingers linger on her hips when she pulls away. "How have you been?" she says as she rubs her hands up and down my back. "I feel like I haven't seen you in forever. I know it's only been four days, but I missed you." Her eyes sparkle when she smiles, and I feel like I've been electrocuted. Sparks sizzle in my stomach, an annoying reminder of our chemistry.

I force a pained smile and pull away, taking her suitcase and storing it in her bedroom. "I've just been busy with work, getting ready for our trip. You haven't missed much. I've been home late every night this week." I push my hand through my hair and lead her into the living room, where I click on the TV, turning on *New Girl*. It's one of her favorite shows, and I have to admit that after she told me, I find myself watching it even when she's not around. It's quirky, funny, and light, perfect for playing in the background.

She curls into the sofa opposite me and pulls her long hair off her neck to one side, absentmindedly braiding it as she listens. I catch sight of a faded hickey on her neck, and my mouth waters as blood rushes to my cock. My mind flashes back to her back arching beneath me as I tasted every inch of her skin, marking her as my own as she writhed beneath me, begging for more.

I pinch the bridge of my nose and close my eyes, trying to regain control of my body's response. "Are you okay?" Maggie asks, leaning into me and placing her hand on my thigh.

Fuck. That's not helping.

"Do you have a headache? Want me to grab you some medicine?" Her innocent words tease me like a feather bringing me closer and closer to the edge.

"No, it's just allergies," I lie, blinking my eyes open. Maggie stares at me curiously as she squirms in her seat and bites her lip. There's clearly something she wants to tell me, but she's too afraid to say it. I love watching her fight against herself. It's so fucking cute watching her try to work up the courage to say something she finds uncomfortable. It's refreshing, actually. I'm so used to being fed bullshit at work all day that it's nice to see someone so genuinely authentic.

She runs her hand up my arm, which is draped over the top of the sofa, back and forth in a soothing motion. I watch her as she fidgets and then scoots closer to me. Only then do I realize the top two buttons on her oversized henley are undone, revealing the faintest glimpse of a black lace bra.

"I had so much fun with Gwen and Elliot," she purrs as she moves closer to me, her other hand moving to the back of my neck in a seductive touch.

I fight the urge to pull her into my lap and let her feel what she's doing to me. Instead, I steady my breathing as I try to gauge the situation.

"So, I was thinking." She moves closer, her shirt falling off her shoulder, revealing a hint of her supple breasts. I bite my cheek and suppress a groan, my fingers itching to touch her. How could I be so negligent not to jack myself off earlier today? I'm wound up so tightly after not seeing her for four days that I feel like one wrong move, and I'll blow a load right here in my pants just from looking at her.

"I want to show you how thankful I am for being so patient with me." She runs her hands up my thighs moving dangerously close to my zipper. "I can't stop thinking about having you in my mouth." She licks her lips, and all the breath is dragged from my lungs. I gasp as she slowly releases my zipper, my hard cock springing free.

"Mags? What are you–"

She fists my cock in her small hand, and I suck in a surprised breath. Oh, fuck. I'm not prepared for this. My willpower is dangerously low even when I'm in control, but having her take the initiative has my brain short-circuiting, and I can't even form the words to speak.

"I'm not sure you're ready–" My words trail off as she runs her hand along my hardened cock, rubbing me over my underwear before pulling them down. My rock-hard cock springs free, and her eyes widen as she bites her lip.

"Holy shit, that's big." She shakes her head, not tearing her eyes away as she moves to her knees on the floor and looks up at me.

Holy fuck. I grit my teeth as I stare down at her, so bravely helping herself to what she wants. Fuck, it's sexy seeing her on her knees in front of me, so hungry for my cock in her sweet mouth.

She rubs her thumb up the base of my cock with gentle pressure, and my head falls back to the couch. Christ, I'm so worked up that a well-placed breeze could finish me off at this point.

The sound of cracking bones brings me back to the moment, and I sneak one eye open, watching as she cracks her fingers, then stretches her head from side to side.

Then she opens her mouth wide like she's yawning, then closes it.

Is she... is she stretching her jaw?

What is she planning on doing to need so much mobility?

My eyebrows knit together, the rushing blood slowing its descent from my brain to my cock, giving me a brief moment of clear thinking.

When she takes the hair tie off her wrist and ties her soft curls away from her face, I panic.

"Red. Red. Red," I scream the only word I can think of as I pull my pants back up to cover myself. As curious as I am to see what she's going to do next—I mean, dangerously fucking curious–I can't go there with her. Our entire arrangement is about Maggie finding confidence in her own body. Sure, I could teach her to suck dick, but I'm far more concerned with her having her own orgasms during sex than worrying about getting her man off. As far as I'm concerned, blow job lessons are just the sprinkles on top, and selfishly, I'd rather not teach her how to pleasure a man—even if it means I have to miss out on this once-and-a-lifetime opportunity.

Maggie's face flushes bright red, and she buries her face in her hands. "Oh my God. I'm so sorry!" She pushes herself away from me and buries her face in her arms, shaking her head. "I don't know what I was thinking..."

I don't hesitate to pull her up into my lap, wrapping her in my arms and kissing her on the top of the head as I try to calm my rapid breathing. "It's fine. It's fine. I'm just not ready to go there yet." I kiss her again and again as I try to soothe her mortified whimpers. "You didn't do anything wrong. It's just me. I promise."

She wipes at her eyes and sniffles. "I'm so embarrassed. Gwen and Elliot said I should surprise you with a blow job because all men love blow jobs, and I guess I just thought..."

I pull her hand away so I can see her face. "I do love blow jobs. Don't be embarrassed. I just don't want to blur the lines any more than we already have, okay?"

She bites her lip as her chin quivers, and fuck, it kills me to see her so upset, especially at my doing. But this is for her own good, and I'd hate myself for doing anything more than she asked me to do and that we agreed upon in the contract.

I move her from my lap and tuck her into my side as I assure her she didn't do anything wrong. I want to explain myself further, but I can't do that without revealing my feelings. So, instead, I comfort her and promise that I'm fine.

After she's finally calmed down, I make her a cup of tea, pull her feet into my lap, and give her a massage. My balls ache in protest from the close call, and I know I'll have to finish myself off a few times if I want any chance of sleeping tonight.

We fall into a comfortable rhythm and watch a whole episode of *New Girl* in silence as I rub her feet and massage her legs. It's achingly perfect despite Maggie's original plan for the evening. Don't get me wrong, I love to fuck, but holding someone special and having a night in on the couch is probably the next best thing. My heart swells with something that feels a lot like love, but I'll be damned if I admit it to myself. I don't know how you can recover from something like that more than once.

There's a knock at the door, our food delivery, as the show ends. Another episode begins to play just as I get up to get the food. I catch sight of Maggie's phone lit up on the table as I pass by, showing a new text from Trent.

TRENT

I loved hearing from you the other night, and I can't stop thinking about you. Are you free tonight? Maybe we could video chat?

I clench the plastic containers as white-hot fury roars and rips through me, but I bite my tongue. I'm furious with jealousy and want to smash her phone into a million pieces and bury it, so she can never hear from the douchebag again. But as my balls ache and my stomach tightens, I'm reminded why I'm doing this to begin with.

He's the reason she wants help, and I wouldn't be fulfilling my end of the bargain if I forbid her from talking to him, as much as it goes against the very nature of who I am. The reason why I'm a dominant.

I grit my teeth and purse my lips. As much as it tastes like vinegar in my mouth, I offer, "Hey, Mags, I didn't mean to look, but I just saw you got a text from Trent." I bring the food to the coffee table and pour us each a glass of wine. "Do you want some help... you know, sexting with him or something?" I regret my words the moment they leave my lips, and it feels like I've just stabbed myself with a thousand needles. But her eyes go wide and she looks stunned. She chews on her nail—one of her obvious signs of nervousness. I really need to enlist a punishment for that behavior. She won't have any nails left by the time the event rolls around at this rate.

"Um... yeah, actually." Her bright hazel eyes search my face as if trying to read me. I do my best to keep my face still and neutral, so I don't sway her or contradict my words. "Gwen texted him for me a little the other night, and for the life of me, I can't think of anything to say."

I pass her the phone, and she types in her passcode and opens the text exchanges. I sit next to her on the sofa, guzzling half a glass of wine as I read through the messages. It looks like Gwen's set her up with some mild flirting and suggestive messages, but nothing crazy.

My muscles relax in my stomach as I take the offered phone

from her. My fingers hover over the screen as I contemplate what I want her to say.

Is it strange that I'm a dude, texting a dude, pretending to be the woman I'm falling in love with? Yeah.

But this is what I signed up for, and this woman has me wrapped so tightly around her little finger that I'd sell my soul to the devil for a do-over life where we could actually be together. But since I'm the only devil in this situation, I suppose that's out of the cards. It's a penance worthy of the crime, and I deserve every bit of anguish that comes my way.

"Okay, let's see... What do you want to learn about him from this exchange?" I ask as I try to formulate a response.

"I... I don't really know." Maggie shrugs. "I guess I want to know if he sees me as a woman rather than the awkward teenager I was in high school? Is he interested in a relationship with me, or is he just looking for a good time? Is he tied to his location for his job? Will his family be okay with him moving on after his divorce? Will they like me?" She blurts her questions off rapid fire.

I try to suppress my laugh with a cough. "Oh, is that all?"

Her bright eyes look at mine, and then she looks down at her wringing hands. "Is that too much? See, that's why I need help. I don't know what to say or how to even begin."

I wink. "How about we start with the most basic question? I begin typing.

"What's the most basic question?" she asks.

I answer her without looking away from the phone. "If he's even into you like that... and more importantly, if you're really into him."

I hit send on the message and pass her the phone.

> You may be able to talk me into a video chat, but you're going to have to warm me up for it first.

Maggie gasps as she reads the message, her neck bright red and splotchy. "Sam! Oh my God, he's going to think I'm asking him for nudes or something!" She squeals as she playfully punches me in the arm.

I laugh at her embarrassment. "Come on, Mags, what do you say? You wanted my help. Let me help you do this." I look into her eyes, trying to gauge her.

She shakes her head and smiles. "I can't believe I'm letting you help me sext someone."

This whole arrangement just went from weird to downright ludicrous.

I give her my best devilish grin and pour her a fresh glass of wine. I excuse myself and come back with a whiskey on the rocks because it's going to take something a little stiffer than white wine to give me the strength to go through with this.

"Cheers!" I clink my glass to hers just as Trent's response pops up on the screen.

TRENT

> You have my attention ... What are you wearing?

TWENTY-TWO

Maggie

"What are you wearing? Seriously?" Sam scoffs and rolls his eyes. He opens his hand for the phone, and I hesitate only for a moment before handing it over to him. I trust him, but who knows what this may put into motion. Am I ready to take the next step with Trent? It feels so scary, but I guess that's what I've been missing, why I haven't been successful in any of my relationships... why I'm such a terrible lay.

Anxiousness swirls around in my belly at the thought of Sam being so willing to help me flirt with Trent. It's unsettling, and I kind of feel like I've got whiplash from his typically possessive nature. I guess this really is just a friend helping a friend and nothing more. All the confusing feelings are just a reflection of my naïvety. Of course, I'd start to feel something for the first man to give me a positive sexual experience. I blow out a frustrated sigh. I'm so thankful Sam isn't a mind reader because he'd be running for the hills if he had any idea what I was thinking. *Feelings are not facts. They are visitors and nothing more,* I remind myself.

I've got to woman up and let loose for a change. This is how adults behave in relationships. Not everything is special and meaningful. Sometimes people just like to have fun, and what Sam and I are doing is just that.

My bruised ego feels a little better after my internal pep-talk. I hope I'll eventually figure out how to stop believing every little butterfly I feel in my belly when a man gives me attention. I guess the feelings just magnify when it comes from a close friend.

Go home, butterflies. You're drunk.

I finish my wine with a newfound boldness and reach for Sam's whiskey glass.Taking a long sip I watch him as the liquid burns my throat in the best way.

The faintest hint of smirk pulls at the corner of Sam's mouth as he watches me. "Can I get you another drink?" His eyebrows lift.

"That's up to you. I've already had four drinks this week at Gwen's. I don't want to break another rule." I offer him a shy smile as I twirl my hair.

His eyes grow dark, and his nostrils flare, and just when I think he's going to protest, he gets up and goes into the kitchen. The sound of cabinets opening and the clinking of ice dropping into glasses is answer enough.

Maybe he needs the liquid confidence as much as I do?

A moment later, he returns with two full glasses and places the bottle on the coffee table. "I think we can make an exception just this one time."

I take the glass, wrapping my hands around it and holding it close to my chest. "Thank you, sir."

"You're welcome," he grumbles, then picks up the phone and resumes texting.

Leaning over, I watch as he types. He's like a man on a mission and seems to know exactly what to do next. Did he learn these skills in school? Maybe I was absent that day...

When he's satisfied with his response, he hits send, then holds the phone out for me to read his response.

> I'm having a cozy night in, so it's not anything to write home about. I'm wearing long fuzzy socks that come up to my knees and an oversized plain white t-shirt...

Trent's response is immediate.

TRENT

> That sounds sexy as hell. Do you think I could see a picture for myself? I'm having trouble imagining it.

I grab Sam's arm in a panicked grip as my mouth goes dry. "I knew this was a bad idea! What are we going to do? He wants proof, and I don't even have long socks! I don't know how to take a sexy picture. He's going to know I'm lying and–"

Sam smiles, but it looks pained, and he lifts my chin commanding me to look at him. "Take off your pants, and I'll do the rest."

"But I–" I start to protest, but he cuts me off.

"Are you questioning me, Magnolia?" He quirks a brow, pinning me with a devious glare that knocks the breath from my lungs.

Without another word, I slide my pants down my legs, extremely thankful I shaved last night. I don't know what kind of weird control Sam has over me, but it's more than just a contract. I want to please him with every fiber of my being. He's awakening something inside me I never knew existed. It's terrifying and exhilarating, yet somehow, I can't get enough.

"Good girl," he coos. "Now, spread your thighs a little and pull your foot underneath your thigh." He moves behind me and lifts my shirt, so my boyshorts are exposed, as well as a little bit of my stomach.

"Just like that," he says as he presses my legs to open a little wider, his fingertips grazing across my pussy for just a second. But that's all it takes. Heat floods my body, pooling in my stomach as my sex swells in arousal.

I suck in a heavy breath as my head falls back to the couch beneath him. My whole body softens as desire flows through me. My skin is on fire, and I need him to touch me again.

He snaps a picture, stares at it, and actually groans. When he sits back down, he takes another long gulp of his whiskey, hissing from the burn. His hair is disheveled like it's been pulled in frustration. I have to force myself not to run my fingers through it as the memory of my hands gripping his hair in fistfuls as my body rocked beneath his talented mouth flashes in my mind.

Trent's message pops up, interrupting me from my daydream.

TRENT

Holy shit, girl. I think I found my new lock screen.

"I hope you know how painful this is for me." He clears his throat as he types another message beneath.

Now show me yours. Fair is fair.

He hits send, then tosses the phone down and rubs his eyes with the palms of his hand. "I can't believe my life has come to this." He laughs and shakes his head.

"You know, this was your idea," I remind him and nudge

him with my elbow. "You don't have to do this. I can go to my room and talk to him. I'll figure it out–"

"The fuck you will," he barks. His jaw clenches, his face hardening. "I'm allowing you to get to know him under my supervision. Don't forget you belong to me until October second and not a minute sooner."

"Yes, sir," I whisper as a fresh swarm of butterflies springs to life in my belly.

My phone lights up with another message, and Sam grabs the phone before I can see. He huffs a breath in amusement and relaxes a little. I glance at the phone and see a picture of a shirtless Trent wearing tube socks and baggy light blue boxers decorated with tacos standing in front of a full-length mirror. His blond hair is combed to the side, and he's drinking a beer. There's a small patch of chest hair in the center of his chest and another sprinkle just below his belly button. He's of medium build and has a nice body, but I can't help but notice how his skin seems so bare without any tattoos.

Sam texts another response.

Nice. You must be turning women away left and right when you go out.

I read the message and look at Sam in confusion, and he shrugs. "I'm just feeling him out. Trying to answer that list of questions."

TRENT

I've been known to turn a few heads. It's hard stepping back into the dating world after being out of it for so long. I feel like I'm miles behind the times even though I'm only 28. It's freeing, though.

Trent: What can a guy do to get a better view? 🤞

I'm sure it is...

What view did you have in mind? I'm a lady, after all, Trent...

Sam groans and tosses the phone down, steam practically spewing from his ears as he drags his hand down his face.

I smile because I don't know what other face to make. This is absolutely insanity, and a part of me enjoys seeing him so bothered by it while the other part feels guilty. The two emotions play tug of war in my chest, and I take another swig of whiskey to quiet both sides.

Trent responds quickly.

TRENT

I'm usually a boob man 🤷

My mouth drops open, and my breath hitches at his straightforward response. Sam's wearing a pained expression and is practically sitting on his hands to keep from throwing my phone across the room.

Biting my lip nervously, I wait for Sam's directions.

He avoids my gaze and unbuttons his collared shirt, revealing a white undershirt underneath, then collapses back on the couch with his arms spread wide. His fist is clenched around his glass of whiskey.

Maybe it's the booze making me feel braver than I am, but I climb into his lap, straddling him and wrapping my bare legs around him completely. "Hey, if you insist on us doing this, why don't we have a little fun?" I lift my chin and offer him a cheeky grin.

He grips my ass and pulls me flush to him before running his hands up my back and underneath my white t-shirt, stopping just below the sheer black lace bra he bought me on our shopping trip. His eyes grow hazy with lust as he slowly grazes over my curves as if trying to memorize my body with his hands.

"Are you trying to kill me, sweetheart?" He laughs, but his hands pause and his hungry eyes meet mine. "What did you have in mind?"

I explore his body in return, enjoying how his hard muscle flexes and ripples as he moves. My fingers drift up his abdomen until they find his broad chest, which is so perfect it could be sculpted from stone. Unlike Trent, Sam's body drips with masculinity. He's got the sexiest coating of chest hair sprinkled over his pecks and a line of hair leading down his stomach until it disappears under the waist of his pants.

He's chiseled and hard built with muscles he earned climbing and pushing his body to the limits. As a yoga instructor, I'm quite familiar with human anatomy, but Sam's physique is on a whole new level. His tanned skin and deep brown eyes contrast his light brown hair, which has a touch of curl when it grows out.

Lost in my thoughts, my hands drift lower toward the waist of his jeans as if they have a mind of their own. He clears his throat and grips my hand, halting my curious perusal. "I asked you a question."

"Oh... right..." I strain to remember what we were talking about. "I thought we could have a little fun, make a game out of it, you know, to keep ourselves entertained while we press Trent for the answers to my questions."

He narrows his eyes, still holding my wrist in his firm grip. "What kind of game?"

I shrug and bat my eyes, laying on the innocence. "We could bet on his answers. Loser has to strip?"

He releases my hand and rubs the stubble on his jaw as he considers me. Setting his glass down, he pours himself more whiskey, and I recognize the glimmer of mischief in his eye. "I must warn you, I'm pretty good at reading people. I'm not sure it'll be a fair competition. He tugs his shirt away from his chest.

As I consider him, I let my eyes drift over his broad chest and then back down. "I think I'm willing to take that risk." I move to the other side of the couch and sit crisscross as I face him. The alcohol warms me from the inside out, and my neck feels flushed as I pick up my phone. "Let's start with something easy."

I'd be willing to send you a peek if you agree to answer some basic get-to-know-you questions. I should at least feel like I'm caught up on your life before I send nudes.

TRENT

Sounds reasonable. What did you have in mind?

Sam watches over my shoulder as I type, his thigh pressed against my knee. I dart my eyes over and scan his face, looking for his approval, and when he gives me a slight nod, I type out my first question.

I feel like I already know some of the basics, so how about... When was the last time you jerked yourself off?

Sam chokes on his whiskey and snatches the phone out of my hand, but I'm too quick. I already hit send.

"Hurry, you have to guess!" I giggle, holding my hands up as he moves over me.

He backs away and shakes his head, the muscles in his jaw flexing with annoyance. "He jerked off to your picture. He did it less than ten minutes ago." He looks at me as he grips the phone face down.

I scrunch my nose in disbelief. "No..." I shake my hand and

answer confidently. "My guess is last night before he went to sleep." I grin wide and add, "He used a dirty sock and fell asleep five minutes later."

Sam's face contorts into a look of utter disgust at my answer. "I guess we'll just have to see," he says as he flips the phone over.

TRENT

You're just coming right out with it, aren't you?
Last night before I went to sleep.

Am I allowed to ask you the same question???

Waggling my eyebrows, I turn to Sam. "Looks like someone doesn't read people as well as he thinks he does," I tease.

"He's either a fucking liar, or I'm worried about his testosterone levels," he says as he strips off his button-up.

"What's that supposed to mean?"

"You just sent him a picture of your thighs spread wide open." He widens his eyes to add emphasis. "I took the fucking picture, and I..." He stops. "You know what? Never mind." He crosses his arms over his chest and gestures for me to proceed.

No. That's not how the game works. I'm a lady, remember?

Sam scoffs a laugh over my shoulder.

"What?" I turn to see what's so funny.

He covers his smile with his hand. "What's wrong? You didn't want to tell him the truth? You may be a lady in the streets, sweet Magnolia, but I'm afraid there's more to you than that, and I'm determined to prove it to you." His eyes bore into mine like he's looking straight through me, sneaking a glimpse into my soul.

I shiver, and my mouth goes dry. He can't possibly know how much I want that, too. I pour myself another drink, my head starting to feel floaty, and my body tingles all over. I pick up the phone and ask my next question.

Moving on... would you rather... give or receive.

Be honest!

Sam's hand grips my thigh, his large palm swallowing it up.

"I remember Trent being so kind. He's definitely a giver," I say with confidence.

Sam rolls his eyes. "There's no way he doesn't say receive." He tightens his grip on my thigh, sliding it a little higher.

Every muscle in my body tenses in anticipation of his next touch, the next stroke of his hand on my skin, but he doesn't move. He just stares at me with that annoyed look. I don't know what this energy is between us. All I know is it's thick and sticky. It makes me want to do questionable things that I've never even thought about before.

I flip the phone over and interrupt the thought before I do something I regret.

TRENT

I enjoy giving...

"See!" I squeal as I point at the screen and clap my hands.

Sam shakes his head. "He's fucking lying." He laughs as he pulls his t-shirt over his head and tosses it to the side. "It's a simple answer. There's no reason for the ellipsis after." He pushes his tousled hair back from his face in frustration, and I drink in the way his muscles flex in annoyance.

This game was a really good idea. I don't think I've ever had such a good idea.

I lick my lips as my gaze drifts to his abs. I narrow my eyes to focus as I lean in and start counting them. "One. Two. Three. Four. Five. Six..."

"What are you doing now?" Sam laughs, swatting my finger away from his stomach.

I sit up and laugh. "I was counting your abs. There are so many of them. I needed a closer look," I say like it's obvious.

"No more whiskey for you." He tries to take the cup out of my hand, but I'm too quick.

I hold up my finger, "Just let me finish this glass." I hold it to my chest protectively, and he finally relents. "Maybe you should stop worrying about what I'm doing and worry about yourself," I joke.

"I don't think that's possible even if I wanted to." Sam's voice lowers, but he pours another for himself. "Ask him to elaborate on the question," he demands when I pick the phone back up.

For a moment, I'm lost, having completely forgotten what we were talking about before his shirt came off, but I scan the messages and remember. "What do you want me to say?"

"Ask him if he has any caveats about giving since he added the ellipsis." He pulls me closer to him again, ensuring no space between us. "If he says no, I'll take off my jeans."

"Done," I say as I ask for clarification.

Why the... ? Do you love giving no matter what?"

I mean, mostly ... I don't want to be the only one giving. I'd like a little reciprocation every now and then.

Sam snatches the phone from me and types out...

Is that all? That's your only caveat?

Wow, I feel like I'm under interrogation.

I promise it'll be worth it. Answer the question.

I'm not the biggest fan of pubic hair, and my tongue hurts after a while sometimes, but other than that, I love it.

"Aha!" Sam drops the phone and punches the air in victory. "I fucking told you there was a caveat!"

"That's not exactly unreasonable!" I cross my arms over my chest and roll my eyes.

"I'd eat pussy for every meal if I could." He leans in and whispers, "I would eat it with some hair. I would eat it on a chair. I would eat it soft and bare. I would eat it on a dare..."

"You are so ridiculous–"

He moves closer, and I scoot back until I'm lying down on the couch, and he's hovering over me. "You wouldn't even have to prepare. I wouldn't need to come up for air. I would eat your pussy anywhere."

The tingles in my belly transform into full-on lightning bolts as I stare into his deep brown eyes that threaten to suck me right up. Before I can offer myself to him for the taking, whichever way he'd prefer, his lips pull into a devilish grin. "Take it off, baby."

He sits up, still straddling me, and watches as I pull off my shirt. I can feel the heat of his stare as his eyes scan my body. Then, as if remembering something, he moves back to his end of the couch and hands me the phone.

It takes me a minute to remember what I was doing before Sam recited his erotic Dr. Seuss poem, which was quite impressive off the top of his head, I may add. I twist my hair to the side and type out another question.

Do you have any kinks I should know about?

I don't know why I ask. It's not like I've ever thought of kinks before. I certainly don't identify as kinky in the bedroom, but call it morbid curiosity or something else entirely. I want to know what I'm getting myself into with him.

Sam's fingers draw a line down my spine, and I suck in a breath at his touch.

"I think you know the answer to that one already." He rubs the skin underneath my bra strap, and I close my eyes, the sensation relaxing yet exciting. My head rolls to the side as his hand moves up the nape of my neck, granting him full access as his hands explore my skin.

"What's your answer? What do you think he's going to say?"

It's hard to think about anything but how his hands feel on my body. I'm so relaxed and aroused in the strangest way. "The more I'm learning, the more I'm starting to think everybody has a kinky side to them. I say yes," I answer.

Sam stifles a groan. "That's where you're wrong, sweetheart. But let's see what he says."

He flips the phone over and reads the text aloud.

TRENT

I'm just happy to be invited at all.

"Thank God," Sam says as he flicks the clasps of my bra open, and it falls to the floor, leaving me topless and panting.

The next thing I know, he's on top of me, and both my arms are pinned above my head.

TWENTY-THREE

Sam

"Fuck, I can't take it anymore," I growl as I pin her hands above her head, drinking in her slight frame beneath me. The phone crashes to the ground with a thunk, but I don't care. I can't think about anything right now except my carnal desires. She's so fragile lying beneath me, and I'm careful not to squish her as my instinct takes control. "Don't move your hands. Keep them just like this." I cover her wrists with my hand and push down.

She gasps as I slide my free hand up her rib cage and cover her breast. My eyes nearly roll back in my head at the feeling of her. Her pink nipples harden into peaks, and I pinch one, making her yelp. Her eyes go wild, and she bucks against me, arching her back, needy for more. "You liked that, didn't you?" I pinch her other nipple eliciting the sexiest moan I've ever heard.

I don't know what's come over me. I wasn't planning on crossing this line with her tonight, but I'm only capable of so much restraint. Watching her text another man, even though it was my idea, has triggered my every possessive instinct and brought it to the surface. I want to have her, mark her as my own, even if it's the only chance I ever get. I want to brand this vision of her into my memory, so I can revisit it again and again because there's no one I've ever found so appealing.

"You knew exactly what you were doing to me. Asking those questions tonight. I should punish you right now for being such a fucking tease." She bites her lip and looks up at me, her eyes full of wonder, but she doesn't say anything. She just lays there like the good girl she is. So. Fucking. Perfect.

I slide my hand over her wet panties, covering her with my palm and applying the slightest pressure. Her panties are soaked, and she spreads her thighs apart, showing me just where she wants to be touched. "You're so wet for me. Your pussy is begging for a release, isn't it?"

"Yes, sir. Please," she pants as I tease her, her face flushed pink with desire, and my cock threatens to break through the zipper of my jeans, my erection so swollen it's painful.

"So polite." I reward her manners by sliding my finger underneath her panties, finding her slick, swollen nub, and rubbing it in slow circles. She bucks against me, then tries to lean up and wrap her arms around my neck, hungry for more. But I pull my hand away completely.

"Ah, ah, ah," I scold as I move her hands back above her head. "If you want me to touch you, you have to obey the rules. You're such a good girl all the time, aren't you?" I pause my movement as I wait for her response.

She nods, her arms straining to break free, but she doesn't move them again. A fresh hit of dopamine floods my system at the sight of her so needy yet obedient. Being in control gives me a high like nothing else, and Maggie is turning out to be a damn good submissive.

Fuck, I wish I could keep her.

"But you know what I think?" My belt clinks as I unbuckle

it and slide off my jeans, kicking them to the floor. "I think that there's more to you than that. You're not really a good girl, are you?" I groan as I grind my cock into her, and I'm surprised when she hooks her legs around my waist, pulling me in closer. I can't imagine what fucking her would feel like if it's already this good. It's taking everything in me not to take her right now.

"You've been holding back, not giving yourself what you really want, haven't you?" I pinch her nipple harder this time, and she yelps, her head falling back as she arches her tits up for more. A wicked smile pulls on my lips, and I repeat the motion, loving how her body reacts to my touch. I suck her nipple into my mouth and thrust two fingers inside her tight little pussy.

"You like being told what to do," I whisper as I curl my fingers inside her stroking her g-spot. Her pussy clenches in response. "You like being dominated. You'd even like it if I got a little rough with you, wouldn't you?" I slide my free hand up her body until I reach her neck. I'm careful as I begin to tighten my grip.

"Yellow?" I ask, my eyes searching her face for any sign of discomfort.

Her trusting eyes stare into mine, and it's as if she's letting me glimpse her soul. "Green," she pants.

Pure, erotic adrenaline shoots through my veins, and I suck in a deep breath as I feel myself expand to all I am, no longer confined to the nice guy I present to the world. It feels incredible to unleash myself for the first time, and I'm so turned on that the only way I'll stop is if I hear her safe word. I'm like a wild animal finally set free. My muscles ache to stretch and run wild, to give into every carnal urge.

I tighten my fist around her thin neck, suppressing her blood flow as I continue my strokes. "You look so perfect wearing my hand as a necklace. I could do anything I wanted to you right now, and you'd let me." I slide a third finger inside her only for a moment until it's wet before sliding it into her tight ass.

Her eyes widen at the sensation, the fullness bringing her closer to the edge as she loses the fight of keeping her hands pinned down. "Oh my God," she moans as she covers her eyes with her arms, hips bucking with need.

I bite her nipple as I increase my pressure around her throat and curl my fingers into her soft sweet spot, playing her body like an instrument until she's quivering beneath me, her orgasm just out of reach.

"So fucking perfect," I whisper as I rub her clit with my thumb, and she nearly bucks off the couch. "I knew you'd like it in the ass if you tried it. You're so fucking sexy when you lose control. I'll never get tired of watching you fall apart."

She raises her legs, laying them on my shoulders as her head thrashes to each side, her orgasm dangerously close. "That's it, baby. You're such a good girl letting me play with your pussy..."

I circle her clit with a little more pressure until she's screaming my name, and her entire body stiffens, her pussy tightening around my fingers in pulsing waves as she rides out her orgasm.

She collapses beneath me as her heavy breathing starts to slow. My lips come crashing down on hers as I lick and suck, starving for more. My hand moves to the back of her head as I grab a fistful of her hair and pull her head back. I nibble and kiss her throat, savoring her scent of vanilla and citrus and something unique to her.

"I should really stop. I don't know if you're ready for all of me. I don't want to hurt you," I say more to myself than to her.

She takes my face between her hands. "No. Please. Sam, I'm begging you. Please don't stop."

"Fuck." I groan and tighten my grip around her soft hair. In one swift motion, I flip her over onto her knees. Then I kick off my underwear, my cock achingly hard as I maneuver myself to her entrance. "I'm going to try to go easy on you, but I can't make any promises." I slap her ass, and she arches her back, pressing her pussy into me as I thrust into her.

My vision blurs as white-hot pleasure squeezes me from every side. I blink several times, urging my soul back into my body as I take her in deep, slow thrusts. "Holy shit, baby, you're so tight." I groan, gripping her hips as I drive into her.

I knew the sex would be good with her after we first kissed, but nothing could've prepared me for this. I feel like I'm toggling between earth and somewhere unknown, where the only thing that exists is pleasure. I slide my hand up her spine, damp with perspiration, as I fuck her hard burying myself inside her again and again.

A tingle builds at the base of my spine as pleasure spreads through every nerve in my body. It's almost too much, but I'm not ready for this to end just yet. On my next thrust, I push her back so she's face down on the sofa with her ass up, and she lets out a muffled scream. I reach around and squeeze her bouncing tits, and the sound of our bodies slapping together fills the air. "That's my girl. You take me so well. So obedient, letting me fuck you however I want." I slap her ass and make her whimper as she turns her head to the side.

I notice her biting her lip and follow her eyes to our reflection in the glare of the black TV screen. She's watching us fuck.

I gather her hair in a ponytail and wrap it around my arm as I pull her back up on all fours, then grip her face and turn her toward the TV screen. "You see something you like?"

She gasps as I stare at our reflection, positioning her so she can see herself as I drive into her harder and harder.

"You like watching yourself getting fucked, don't you, baby? You look so fucking beautiful on all fours. Your tits pressed together and your ass out as I fuck you. Your pussy is so wet for me, isn't it?"

"Yes. Fuck, Sam." she cries, and just like that, I come undone. The sound of my name on her lips as she moans her orgasm is my complete undoing. Warmth pools at the base of my spine as I grip her hips, and bright light flashes, my orgasm exploding in pure ecstasy. She moans, her pussy squeezing painfully tight as I empty myself into her.

"Holy shit."

She collapses beneath me and shivers as I gently pull out of her and move to the floor, so we're face to face. The realization of what I just did comes crashing down on me as I'm suddenly able to think clearly for the first time since we started this.

I push her damp hair away from her forehead. "Sweetheart. Are you okay? Did I hurt you?"

She laughs. "No. You didn't hurt me at all. You were perfect." She offers me a sleepy smile.

"We'll see if you still feel that way tomorrow. Come on." I stand and lift her from the couch, cradling her against my chest. "Let's get you cleaned up."

I walk us to the bathroom and shut the door with my foot, setting her down on the toilet. "You need to pee so you don't get a UTI."

"Sam!" she shrieks, covering her face in embarrassment.

"Stop being embarrassed. I had my finger in your ass earlier. I'm not grossed out by the sound of you peeing," I tease.

"Oh my God. I think I may spontaneously combust from humiliation."

"If you don't hurry up, you'll leave me no choice but to punish you..." I warn. Then I turn around to give her privacy, busying myself as I adjust the shower temperature. The damp air fogs the bathroom as I let the hot water wash over me, and a minute later, I feel Maggie's arms wrap around my chest as she presses her body into me.

I spin around and pull her flush to me, guiding her underneath the shower stream, so she isn't cold as I kiss her soft and slow. I pour shampoo into my hand and move to wash her hair when she pulls back in confusion.

"What are you doing? I can do that myself."

I ignore her protest and massage the shampoo into her hair. "I know you can do it yourself, but I *want* to. I want to take care of you." I hold the nape of her neck as I move her back under the warm stream, rinsing the shampoo completely. Then I repeat the process, combing the conditioner through the ends of her hair.

She grabs the soap and lathers it in her hands before rubbing it down my back. "Magnolia," I warn, but she just gives me an innocent smile.

"What? Maybe I want to take care of you, too?" Her hands work the silky suds over my chest, and I let out a frustrated grunt when her slick hands grip the base of my cock, which is already rearing for round two. "There seems to be something else on your mind besides bathing me..." she whispers as she strokes me.

"Are you trying to kill me? Is that it? Or did you get a taste of something you liked?" I groan as she works me, but I only let her have a few strokes before pushing her back up against the cold tile wall and wrapping her legs around my waist as I drive into her.

"Ok, my greedy little slut. You can have one more round, but then you're going to let me bathe you like a good girl, do you understand?"

"Yes, sir," she whispers. Her moans of pleasure echo through the hot, steamy bathroom as I lose myself to her for the second time tonight.

I always knew women were magical creatures, but I may have just discovered the most powerful one. Our bodies move together in rhythm, and when she's screaming my name in a pitch only dogs can hear her, I let myself fall apart. And I swear I see God. And just as I've always suspected.

God is a woman.

TWENTY-FOUR

Maggie

I wake as the bright morning sun peeks through the sheer curtains. I blink my eyes open, realizing I'm not in the guest bed I've grown familiar with but in Sam's instead, tangled up in his loose sheets. I look to my left to see his side of the bed is empty, and I don't know whether to be relieved or disappointed.

I glance around the tidy space, drinking in all the small details scattered throughout the room, and notice the pillows on his side propped up and fluffed perfectly as if he attempted to make his side of the bed while I slept.

It's such a Sam thing to do. I'm learning he isn't just controlling in the bedroom. He has an order about things, not in a neurotic way, but more like he prides himself on doing everything the right way. He doesn't cut corners, and there isn't a lazy bone in his body.

He's not like anyone I've ever met. I'm learning he's a breed all his own.

I sit up and stretch, and every muscle in my body aches as

memories of last night come flooding back. I'm mortified when I remember him saying the safe word because I was too stupid to ask him before attempting to go rogue with my lessons. I drag my hands down my face as I try to remember if I said anything stupid or embarrassed myself beyond repair. Did I come on too strong? Did he feel obligated to *service* me, or did he enjoy it?

A vivid image of Sam's chiseled tattooed body driving into me as he pressed me against the cold shower tiles flashes through my memory, and I pull the sheet up to cover my face. I can't believe I let myself be so free with him. I didn't even know I was capable of feeling so passionate. I was drunk with desire and hardly recognizable.

My mind flashes with images of our bodies colliding, how he dominated me in every way, and how I enjoyed it. The way he forced me to watch our reflection and how it awakened something I didn't know existed.

Last night after round two in the shower, Sam insisted on washing me again. Then he carried me to bed, brushed my wet hair, and dressed me in one of his worn, cotton t-shirts. He held me against his chest, hands playing with my hair until I drifted asleep.

I feel so safe when I'm with him. Like I could be or do anything I want. He pushes me to be a better version of myself, and I trust him to be there to catch me if I fall. Maybe it's just the dominant thing, but it feels nice to be cared for, cherished even.

I'm afraid Sam may have unlocked something deep inside me that can never be undone, which terrifies me.

My head drops back to the headboard with a thud, and I let out a frustrated sigh. I'm way over my head, but all I can do now is stay above water. I force myself to get up and make the bed so that my side matches Sam's, then I pull on a pair of his boxers and make my way into the kitchen.

I find him sitting at the kitchen island reading the morning paper. He's dressed impeccably in a suit and tie, with his hair styled neatly. He looks so clean-cut and professional. You'd never guess the dirty things he was capable of.

"Good morning, gorgeous. How are you feeling?" Sam croons as he pushes away from the island and kisses me on the cheek.

"It's not the worst hangover I've ever had but don't ask me to run a marathon or anything." I laugh as I grab a coffee cup from the cabinet.

He takes the coffee cup from my hand and gestures for me to take a seat. "I didn't know how long you'd need to sleep, and I didn't want to wake you. Otherwise, I'd have brought you your breakfast in bed." He pours me a cup of coffee, adding the perfect amount of milk and sugar, then places it in front of me next to a glass of water and two Advil.

He raps his knuckles in front of the glass of water. "Drink this first. Then you can have your coffee." He turns back toward the kitchen, pulling out ingredients from the fridge. "How about an omelet and toast?"

"That sounds perfect. Thank you." I down my glass of water and Advil and take a small sip of my coffee, savoring the first delicious drops. Knowing someone's coffee order without being told is such a small thing, but it's another reason I feel so safe with him. It's like he actually sees me; he's always paying attention.

Sam cracks a few eggs in a bowl, then chops up some fresh veggies and meat, whisking them together before adding the mix to the pan. I watch as he moves confidently around the space, each movement deliberate and practiced. Is there anything this man isn't good at?

"I hope you don't mind, but I took the liberty of handling what we didn't finish last night." He glances over his shoulder and nods toward my phone sitting near the bowl of fruit in the center of the kitchen island.

How could I forget? The whole reason we got so *caught up* was that I asked him to help me get closer to *Trent*.

I reach for the phone and swipe the messages open to see a sexy selfie of a nice pair of breasts, wearing a thin black lace bra with an oversized green sweater hanging off her shoulders. There's even long red hair draped over her shoulder in a thick braid.

My eyebrows pull together as I read:

Sorry about last night. My neighbor stopped by and needed help with something unexpected, and by the time we were finished, it was too late. Enjoy the pic. You earned it. 😉

TRENT

Holy shit. I'd say the pic was worth it. I had fun last night. Maybe we can do it again sometime soon?

I'd like that, but I'll be traveling next week and completely out of pocket. I'll see you at the reunion, though. Save me a dance?

TRENT

Looking forward to it. See you very soon, Maggie.

"What do you mean I'm traveling all week? And whose boobs did you send him?"

Sam sets my omelet down in front of me and refills my water. He props himself up on his elbows, hands collapsed as he leans in. "My bathroom guy called me this morning and said he needed to shut off all the water for a few days to finish the renovations, and the whole place would be a mess with construction crews coming in and out... so I took the liberty of extending our trip to the beach." He stands up and adjusts his tie. "I figured we could use a little vacation anyway."

"But, I can't just leave. I've got the studio renovations to worry about, and it's going to be bad enough–"

Sam holds up his hand. "I already talked to Joey this morning, and he said the studio is coming along nicely. They're expecting to wrap up the job in two weeks. You should be all set to come home to a renovated studio and apartment after the reunion."

"But I–" I start to argue, but I see the muscle in Sam's jaw begin to flex, and my words trail off.

He moves behind me, shifting my hair off my neck to one side, and trails his fingers along my exposed skin as he whispers, "Let me spoil you a little longer. I promise you'll enjoy yourself, and you need a break from worrying about everything here."

I suck in a breath at his tender touch. How am I ever supposed to argue with that kind of logic? Besides, he's using his hands, playing my body like an instrument only he knows how to play. It's not fair.

"Fine, I'll let you take me away, but only because I haven't seen the ocean in over a decade," I huff.

His eyes sparkle with mischief, and he traces my jaw with his thumb. "Good girl. Pack a bag. We're leaving at five o'clock sharp."

"Wait, we're leaving today?" My eyes fly open, and I start to protest, but Sam just nods and kisses me on the forehead.

"I'll send a car to get you. I'm meeting you at the airport after work. Oh, and I've arranged for my masseuse and her team to come by and give you a full day of pampering. Have a good day, Magnolia. I'll see you this evening." He grabs his keys and coat, and then he's gone.

I guess I better get a move on... It looks like I've got a full day ahead.

When Sam said he was meeting me at the airport, I assumed he meant a *real* airport, not a tiny hangar in the middle of the country.

The car pulls up to a small airplane, and I catch sight of Sam talking to the pilot outside. The driver comes around and opens my door, and Sam comes over, pulling me into a hug. "You smell delicious. How was your spa day, Ms. Anderson?"

I laugh and swat him on the chest. "You didn't have to book me the royal treatment! I've been scrubbed, rubbed, and waxed everywhere. I think every surface of my skin has been polished. I should be glowing or something."

"You're welcome." He winks. "I hope you know you didn't have to wax anything for me." He pushes a stray hair behind my ear, and I blush.

"I wanted to. Besides, I'm going to the beach. When in Rome, right?"

"That could be arranged." He links my arm with his and leads me up the stairs of the small airplane. There's enough seating for about eight passengers, but it looks like we'll be the only ones flying, except for the pilot and the flight attendant.

"Welcome aboard. May I take your coats?" the flight attendant asks as we sit in two comfortable leather seats facing each other with a small table between us. After Sam passes her our coats and thanks her, he reaches over to buckle my seatbelt, pulling the strap taut across my hips.

"Sam, this is too much. I hope you know you don't have to do all of this for me. I'd be fine flying on a commercial flight like a regular person."

"Well, Magnolia, I don't much consider you to be a regular person. As I said this morning, let me spoil you while I can." He leans in, and whispers, "or I can have fun thinking of more ways to torture you... It's your choice."

I make a show of snapping my lips shut, but when I look outside the window as the plane takes off, I can't help but smile. If Sam's plan is to ruin me for all normal men, then I'm afraid it may be working. A girl could get used to all this pampering.

His hand finds my knee underneath the table, and he rubs my leg in soft, slow strokes as we watch the ground beneath drift farther and farther away.

"Champagne?" the flight attendant asks once we reach altitude.

"We'll have two ginger ales, please," Sam says as he looks up from his phone.

"Hey, maybe I wanted a glass of champagne for my first and probably only private plane ride."

He slides his phone into his pocket and pins me with a stare. "I was negligent with you last night, and I won't do it again. You need to let your body recover today, and that means no alcohol." He pulls my hands into his and turns them over, examining my wrists.

I pull my hands away. "I'm fine, Sam. You can stop checking me for bruises." I idly rub my hand over my wrist to replace the heat from his touch.

"I'm sorry I was so rough with you last night. I'm angry with myself for losing control like that. I shouldn't have pushed you so much. I guess I just got lost in the moment."

"You have nothing to apologize for. Really. Last night was incredible. I'll remember it for the rest of my life. I know that for sure."

The flight attendant arrives with our drinks, setting them down in front of us. "Here you are. I'll be back to check on you in a little while. Press the call button if you need anything until then."

I take a sip of the cold bubbly soda. I don't know what it is, but it somehow tastes better when you're flying three thousand miles above the ground in a private jet.

"So, are you always this charitable with your submissives, or is this just because we're friends?" I arch my brow as I ask the question that's been on the tip of my tongue for the last week.

Sam laces his fingers together, setting his hands on the small table between us. "I do enjoy pampering my submissives. Though I suppose I've never done it quite to this extent. I like to think I rise to the necessary occasion."

"And I needed more pampering than usual?"

"You were in desperate need of being shown what you deserve. I'm afraid I've only skimmed the surface of the things I'd like to do for you. But I understand this is only a temporary arrangement, and we simply don't have the time. I'm doing my best to give you the cliff notes version anyways."

His words hang in the air between us, and a sickening feeling pricks at my stomach at the mention of the timeline. Sam and my arrangement will be over soon, and I don't know what kind of heartache I'll walk away with. I can't be a fool and assume I'll walk away completely unscathed, but hearing him bring up the contract is the reality check I need to bring me back down to earth.

Sam is a generous guy. His kink is to pleasure women who submit to him. Sure, he may make me feel like I'm the only woman in the world, but that's because of our contract. I can't forget that I asked him for help, and he's simply fulfilling his end of the bargain. It's nothing more than that, no matter how much my heart aches from confusion.

His terms were clearly stated in the contract. He doesn't want a relationship outside of his arrangements. He doesn't want to settle down. He doesn't want a family. Without thinking, I start to chew on my nail-bed as my mind wanders to all the reasons he could be the way he is.

Of course, I could never ask him. Sam is so private that I feel lucky to know him as well as I do. If he wanted me to know, he would have told me, so I need to respect his boundaries and stop trying to figure him out.

"You're ruining your manicure." Sam reaches for my hand, gently kissing each of my fingers, then laces his fingers with mine. "What are you worrying about over there that's got you chewing your fingers to little nubs?"

"I... uh... I was just thinking how nervous I was to meet your family," I lie.

Sam's face relaxes, and his warm smile meets his eyes. "They're going to love you. Don't worry about that."

"Remind me again. Who will I be meeting?" I ask, genuinely curious. I may not have thought that at that particular moment, but they've certainly been in the rotation of things I've been worried about ever since he sprung the trip on me.

"My dad, James, and stepmother, Charlotte. My younger brother, Simon, and his wife, Wren. And my two baby brothers, Drew and Jamie. Everyone will be nice and welcoming, but I can't promise Drew and Jamie won't try to embarrass me. I haven't been home since last Christmas, so they'll probably give me a hard time about it."

Nervous energy bubbles up in my stomach. I don't know whether to be afraid that I'll disappoint them by not being Sam's real girlfriend or excited to be included in someone's family celebration for the first time ever.

"Are you and your brothers close? What about your dad?"

"My brother Simon is only a year and a half younger than me. We were always inseparable growing up. Not quite Irish twins, but close enough. He's a lot like me. Ex-military. Quiet.

Serious. But his wife, Wren, is the complete opposite. She brings out the best in him, so he may even be able to hold a conversation now, but I can't make any promises. He's had some trauma in the past, so he can be pretty distant."

"Wow. Thanks for the heads up. What about the other two?"

"Drew and Jamie are younger. They both inherited our mother's bubbly personality. They can be annoying as hell, but that's just because they remind us of all the fun we're missing out on."

"Aw, that sounds like a lot of fun. It must've been so chaotic growing up with all that testosterone."

"You can say that again. My poor dad; I think he was solid gray by the time he was forty after raising the four of us. There was always something going down in the Jordan house..." He shakes his head and laughs.

"Well, I can't wait to meet them. I hope they like me."

Sam traces his thumb over my collarbone, sending heat to my core. I press my thighs together and sigh. "They're going to love you. Don't even worry about that."

"What did you tell them about us?" It's a genuine question. Surely Sam's family doesn't know about his kinky lifestyle... unless they do, which would make this even more uncomfortable.

"I told them you were my girlfriend." He smiles and licks his lips as his gaze scans my body, eyes lingering on my cream-colored silk camisole as my hard nipples brush the soft fabric. It was a bold move to go braless for our flight, but I'd say it's worth it for how Sam's staring at me right now.

I press my arms together, giving him a better view of my cleavage as an idea pops into my mind. "You know, I've always wondered how one becomes part of the mile-high club?"

He sits back in his seat as his eyes scan all the way up my

body. "Are you sure you're up for that? I figured you'd be too sore."

"Then I guess you underestimated me, sir." I twirl my hair as I stare back.

"Fuck. I don't know how I'm supposed to say no to that." He stands and offers me his hand, wearing a wicked grin. "It would be my honor to initiate you, but you'll have to keep the screaming to a minimum. We don't want to be rude."

"I'll try my best, sir, but I can't make any promises."

"Christ, how did I get so lucky?

I hold his hand and follow him closely as he leads me to a private room in the back of the plane.

It's not even a cramped bathroom.

"And they say chivalry is dead."

TWENTY-FIVE

Maggie

A warm breeze blows my hair in my face, my long strands getting stuck in my lipgloss, and I do my best to tame it in the wind. It's eight o'clock, and we're standing on the front porch of the cutest three-story beach house right on the beach.

Crashing waves lull in the distance, and my stomach is in knots now that we're here. Fortunately, I didn't have much time to worry about anything on the flight. I was far too busy being ravished in the back room. If there's one thing I can say about Sam, the man is in no hurry when it comes to pleasuring a woman.

My mind flashes to the memory, and the knot in my stomach tightens even more.

"They're going to love you." Sam kisses me on the forehead as he rolls our bags behind him. Of course, he won't let me touch mine. "There's nothing to be intimidated about. Just remember to hold your breath when you walk through the door," he says as he turns the doorknob and steps in front of me just in time for the largest dog I've ever seen to jump on him. Its head is even with Sam's when it stands on its hind legs.

"Hey, Denver. Who's a good boy?" Sam coos as he rubs his ears. And just like that, Denver notices Sam isn't alone and abandons him, leaping up to greet me with a wet tongue straight up my nose.

Now I know why he said to hold my breath.

I stumble back, the dog's weight knocking me off balance, and Sam comes to stand behind me. "Whoa, now, Den. You're coming off a little strong. Let the lady warm up before you attempt second base."

"Goodness, it's very nice to meet you, Denver," I say as I wipe dog slobber off my face with the arm of my sweater.

"Denver, what have I told you about accosting visitors!" a man scolds as he pulls him away by his collar. Once released, Denver sniffs around our luggage.

"Hi, I'm Simon." The man looks eerily similar to Sam, except his tattoos stretch down his arms, and his hair is clean-cut and straight, whereas Sam's is a little longer and wavy.

I give his hand a tight squeeze. "Nice to meet you. I'm Maggie."

"Whoa, now! Do my eyes deceive me, or is that a woman on Sam's arm?" An older man pushes toward us. His eyes are warm like honey, and his hair is solid white. It's almost like I'm staring at Sam in the future. "I'm James." He claps Sam on the shoulder, then pulls him into a hug. When he breaks away, his smile covers his face. I can practically feel the joy beaming off him. "You must be the infamous Magnolia."

I reach out my hand to shake his, but he just laughs and pulls me into a tight hug, his large body enveloping me in a blanket of joy. "In this family, we hug. Welcome to our home. We're so happy to finally meet you!" He breaks away and runs his hands up and down my arms before releasing me fully.

I don't understand how, but I actually feel happier, as if some of his happiness transferred to me by osmosis.

"Hey, Charlotte! The kids just got here!" he calls over his shoulder as he attempts to grab one of the suitcases. Sam swats him away.

"I've got the bags, Dad. Why don't you show Maggie to the living room while I put these up?" Sam grins and darts his eyes to the side, telling me to follow him.

"Okay," I mouth as I rub my fingers on the hem of my sweater. I follow James through the entryway into a cozy open-concept living space with a giant off-white sectional. A cute woman with white hair, though it looks more platinum blonde than anything because her complexion is so stunning, squeals as she closes the oven door and rushes over to us.

"Oh, gracious, you're even more beautiful than Sam described. I'm so happy to meet you. I'm Charlotte." She grabs the sides of my face and squeals. "Samuel, you could have told us she looked like a supermodel!"

Charlotte's eyes well with tears as she looks at me and then hugs Sam. "It's been too long, Sam. We are so happy you're home."

"It's good to be back." His smile is soft and genuine, and I can't help but notice how his shoulders seem to have relaxed. "Something smells good." He looks toward the kitchen.

"I hope you're hungry. I know it's late, and you've probably already eaten dinner, but I had to make a little something." Charlotte walks back to the kitchen and pulls a dish out of the oven. "Fresh crab dip with homemade sourdough bread, Sam's favorite."

The moment the oven opens, the most delicious fragrances waft into the room. "Wow, that smells amazing," I say.

On cue, Denver bursts back into the room, knocking into the

back of everyone's legs as he heads straight to the kitchen, his tail knocking down anything in its path.

"Denver, I'm sorry, but I'm under strict orders not to feed you table food anymore." Charlotte holds up her hands. "How about a carrot?" She opens the fridge, pulls out a bag of carrots, feeding him a few, and then calls, "I'm feeding Denver a carrot!"

Simon appears again. His arms are crossed over his chest as he shakes his head. "Ok, buddy, that's enough snacks for you. Let's get out of this kitchen." He drags him to the living room once more, and I laugh, enjoying how everyone walks around chatting with each other with such ease.

Charlotte takes my hand and leads me toward the living room. "Maggie, this is Wren, Simon's wife." I find a gorgeous petite woman with pink and purple hair and a beachball-sized pregnant belly propped up on the sofa.

"Hi, Maggie! Sorry, I can't get up to hug you. Mr. Cranky Pants over there has given me strict orders to keep my feet up." She rolls her eyes and shakes her head, with arms circled around her large belly. "Just because I'm three centimeters dilated doesn't mean I can't move freely around the cabin!" she calls to her husband.

"You still have three weeks until your due date! You're not missing anything on the damn sofa. Dad even let you have full control of the remote," Simon yells back. He's grouped into conversation with Sam and his dad as Denver weaves between his legs, sniffing for any morsel of food.

"Hey there, bro!"

"What's up, Samsonite!" Two other men call as they enter the room and pull Sam into a hug. Sam smiles so wide I can practically see his molars as he playfully gives each of them a noogie.

"Hey. Ouch. Fuck, you're strong," one of the brothers yells as he tries to escape Sam's grip. "Okay, shit, I give up."

Sam releases him, and his brother doesn't miss a beat. In one swift motion, he twists Sam's nipple and takes off in a sprint, jumping over an excited Denver and landing on the couch next to Wren, her body nearly catching air from the force.

"Jesus Christ, Jamie, you almost crushed my wife and unborn child! Knock it off, or I'll give you a purple nurple that never goes away!" Simon yells.

"What does that even mean? Like a tattoo?" Jamie lifts his shirt to examine his normal-colored nipple.

Wren doesn't seem at all bothered by the energy. She just rubs her belly and scoots away from him, nestling deeper in the corner. "I wish I could say they don't normally act like this, but that would be a lie. You get used to it after a while, though."

Jamie rubs the stubble on his chin as he looks me up and down and nods in approval once his eyes land on my face. "I'm Jamie. Clearly, I'm the good-looking brother. I hope you're not disappointed with Sam now that you've seen me. It happens all the time." He rubs his palms together maniacally. "I'd be willing to look the other way about our meeting if you are..."

Just then, Sam appears behind his brother and snatches him up by the neck of his shirt. "Enough with the creepy shit. I just got here, and you're already ready for an ass beating?" Sam pulls Jamie's shirt a little tighter, and Jamie coughs with an exaggerated choke. "Apologize, now," Sam demands.

Cough. Cough. "Sorry. Maggie," he croaks. Then Sam releases him, shoving him to the side.

"It's very nice to meet you, Jamie. Sam's told me all about you–"

Jamie lifts his hands above his head, then folds over, propping his hands on his knees, a pained expression on his face. "Excuse me. I just lost all my breath. I just need a moment, maybe some fresh air... "

"Son, if you don't stop with the theatrics, I'm going to give your bed to Denver, and you can sleep on the porch with all the fresh air you want," James retorts as he grabs a beer from the fridge. "Maggie, can I get you something to drink? Wine? Beer? Soda? Lemonade?"

I look to Sam, curious to see what he'll do, considering he's already bent his own rules for me once.

"Can you grab Maggie an IPA and me a milk stout?" Sam answers. His dad passes me a beer, and Sam grabs it from him and opens it before handing it back to me. I feel like a princess the way he takes care of me, and knowing he loves it as much as I do makes it even hotter.

"Who's up for a game of Mexican Train?" James says as he shakes a tin of dominoes in his hands.

I clench my beer bottle tightly, my nerves fluttering back at the suggestion of playing a family game. This is all I ever wanted growing up, and it's a lot to take in. I've been here less than ten minutes, and I've already been offered food and a drink, and now, we're going to sit around a table and play a game. I didn't know families like this still existed because I've certainly never seen one.

We all move to the expansive dining room table, and I pause as everyone seems to find their designated seats.

"Come on, Maggie. You can sit right here. It's the best seat in the house," James says as he pats the chair beside him.

"Thank you." As I sit, Sam moves to the chair across from me.

"Relax," he mouths, giving me a sexy wink.

"Eat up now. I know how everyone gets cranky when they're hungry, and we don't want to scare Maggie away on her first night." Charlotte places the hot, bubbling dip in the center of the table with a stack of appetizer plates and two platters of freshly cut bread.

The words have barely left her mouth before everyone

reaches for the food. Spooning heaping piles of dip on their plates like a pack of wild dogs fighting over their prey.

Sam snatches the plate from Jamie's grip, overpowering him in the short battle of strength, and hands me the plate with a wink. "Here, baby, Jamie made you a plate."

I take it apprehensively, watching as everyone tries to contain their snickers. "Thank you, Jamie. You're too kind."

James dumps out the tin tray of dominoes, and they clash onto the wooden table. "Maggie, have you ever played Mexican Train before?"

I cover my mouth, now full of the cheesy crab dip, and shake my head. My mouth waters for another bite as soon as I swallow.

"Drew, why don't you explain the rules," James says to his dark-haired brother sitting beside Sam. Out of everyone, Drew's dark brown hair and ocean-glass green eyes are almost too extreme of a contrast. His coloring is mesmerizing. It's so different from the others, but when he smiles, I can see the family resemblance. It seems he's managed to clone himself four times over, and I can't help but wonder what Sam's mom must have looked like. No doubt she was beautiful. I feel like I'm sitting at the table with the Hemsworth brothers, I didn't know every child could be so attractive, but I guess they've got good genes.

Sam winks at me as he takes a pull of his beer, and I listen as Drew reads the directions to the game, stopping to clarify certain rules and give examples with random dominoes.

I look around and take in the scene before me, with my heart feeling like it's going to explode in my chest. It's puzzling to think this family, all of them grown, still fall into place here and feel at home like a deck of cards that's been shuffled together. I've never experienced anything like it in all my twenty-nine years. I ache for the loss of something I never had, but at the same time, I feel so lucky to be included. I almost feel like I'm one of them... and that thought terrifies me to my bones.

When this is over, will I be left with *two* giant holes in my heart?

"Alright, then, who's got the double twelve?" James asks over the sound of everyone shuffling and organizing their lines of dominoes.

I look down and see the domino in question. "Oh, I've got it!" I hold it up above my head.

"Great, put it down there. You're off to a good start. Maybe you can give Sam here a run for his money." James says as he makes his move, everyone falling in line behind me.

"Oh? Is Sam really good or something?" I quirk my brow, my eyes meeting his, and he gives me a wicked grin.

"The reigning champion, I'm afraid," James says.

"That's because he cheats," Jamie adds, sliding a domino at the end of the line.

"Just because I can keep a running count in my head and you can't doesn't make it cheating." Sam laughs.

"It was cheating when Rain Man did it–"

"Enough, you two. I'd like one goddamn minute of peace while I soak in this moment with all the people I love underneath the same roof," James scolds, and Sam and Jamie grow quiet, trying their best to conceal their grins.

I have a feeling they enjoy riling up their dad. And though I can't imagine having a dad, much less giving him a hard time just for fun, it's a testament to how close they are.

I feel like a stranger peeking in through the window, watching them goof off and laugh, the easy comfort in the space between them even though they haven't seen each other in so long. What must that feel like? No wonder Sam is so put together and sure of himself. He came from a home surrounded by love. It oozes out in every direction and with every exchange, like an oil that coats your skin and seals everything bad out.

A few rounds pass, and we fall into a comfortable rhythm, the game giving us a nice focal point that's not too difficult to play as we chat. I mostly listen unless asked a direct question as I watch Sam come to life, laughing and teasing his brothers. I feel as if I'm really seeing him for the first time, and it's almost like I'm intruding on something private.

"What do you think, Maggie?" Jamie's question jars me back to the moment.

I shake the fog from my head. "I'm sorry. What was the question?"

"I asked who you think, out of the four of us," he gestures to himself and all his brothers, "who would look the best—like the coolest and most authentic in real life–with a mullet?"

All eyes fall on me as the room goes quiet, and I feel immense pressure to choose correctly. I may not know much, but I've gathered that these brothers are highly competitive with one another... about everything, apparently.

I tap my finger to my lip as I consider. "Jamie, turn your head to the side. I need to see your neck." He does as I instruct, eager to please. I quirk my lips. "I need to see more. Can you pull the neck of your shirt down a little so I can see your shoulder?" I model the motion, and he mimics my pose, turning his head so that his invisible mullet blows in the wind.

"That's good." I nod in approval, then look at Drew and narrow my eyes. "How about you? How would it look if you were on the back of a motorcycle–"

Before I can give him any direction, he spins in his seat and widens his legs, arms coming up to hold the handles of his invisible motorcycle. He tousles his hair in the wind like an eighties supermodel, flicking his invisible long curls—because I imagine his hair would be on the curlier side if it were long—behind him.

"It's a tough call." I try to keep a straight face as I look between them, glancing over at Sam, who looks so proud he's practically beaming, and Simon, who's biting his knuckle to hold in a laugh.

When Drew pinches his nipples and licks his lips, apparently lost in the daydream, I have to cough to cover my laughter. "Drew wins," I declare, slapping the table for emphasis.

"What? HOW?" Jamie protests.

"Fuck yes! I'm doing it now!" Drew flashes me a shit-eating grin.

"How can you say he wins when my neck is clearly longer?" Jamie argues as he pulls his shirt down to show me.

James makes a show of sliding his domino into place, and Simon follows suit.

I slide my domino to my train as I explain. "I just think mullets ultimately look better with wavy hair. It's more mysterious and interesting."

"I can't believe this. Samuel, are you happy? Your girlfriend just crushed my dreams. It's almost like you planned it before you came." His head turns to glare between us. "Is that what this is about?"

His question falls on deaf ears because the only word I heard was *girlfriend,* and now, my whole body is lit up.

Sam's eyes sparkle, and he winks. "You know what, we actually did. Don't blame Maggie, though, it was all my idea. I figured you could use a little humbling. I don't want your head getting too big to fit inside your parents' house... that you still live in–"

"I've been saving money! It's called being financially responsible!" Jamie yells, slamming his beer onto the table.

"Slam that bottle down again on my brand-new table, and I'm going to break it off in your ass." James' threat comes out quiet and controlled as he takes his turn without looking up.

"Sorry, Dad. Sorry, Charlotte," Jamie says as he attempts to buff the nonexistent mark away with the hem of his shirt.

I bite my lip as I watch everyone play, and when it's my turn, I go out, laying down four dominoes at once. "I'm out," I announce.

The chatter grows quiet, and everyone's eyes fall on me as they look at Sam, who's twirling his final domino between his fingers.

"You did say I could play two doubles at once, right?"

James hoots in laughter as he claps Sam on the back, and everyone cheers. "Holy shit, son, I guess you really have met your match with this one!"

I'm not sure if they're excited that I won or just that Sam finally lost, but either way, it feels pretty exciting.

"This calls for a celebration! Who wants shots?" Jamie calls out as he pushes himself up from the table.

"I hate to be the fun police, but Maggie's had quite the day. I need to get her to bed. We've got a big day tomorrow, and I don't want everyone scaring her off on night one."

"Aw, come on, Sam!"

"Don't be a sore loser."

"You just got here!"

Everyone tries to argue, but he doesn't relent as he pulls out my chair and ushers me out of the dining room, protecting me from his wild family as if they're paparazzi.

"Good night, you two. We'll see you in the morning," Charlotte calls as she tucks herself under James' arm and whispers something in his ear. He smiles at whatever she says, wearing a look of peace. I don't need to have heard her to know they're happy that Sam seems so happy because I feel exactly the same way.

I just wish it wasn't coming to a screeching halt so soon.

"Our room is just back here," Sam says as he pulls me into him, wrapping his heavy arm around me. "My brothers call it the sex cave. It's the darkest, most secluded room in the house." He tickles my side playfully, and I let out a squeal.

"Don't worry, though. I meant what I said. You need some rest tonight." He flicks on the light, revealing a quaint room with a queen-sized bed and dark wooden headboard. It has a masculine feel but doesn't appear to belong to any one person.

"I'm going to snuggle the fuck out of you tonight." He grins as he pulls my sweater over my head and replaces it with a soft, modest pajama top. "But tomorrow, it's a whole different story."

He pulls back the blankets and gestures for me to get in, then turns off the lights and climbs in beside me. I curl into him, my head on his chest as he holds me, and a pinch of discomfort pricks in my chest as I realize that maybe I was shown this as a reminder of what I want... My very own family.

That may not be something Sam can give me, but maybe Trent can...

TWENTY-SIX

Sam

"Good morning, gorgeous." I pull Maggie's soft, warm body into me as I kiss her on the neck and she begins to stir. She slept like a rock last night. Actually, we both did. I don't know what it is about being home but I always get the best sleep when I'm under this roof. The faint sounds of chatter echo in the distance and I can hear the click-clack of Denver's nails pacing down the hall on the tile floor.

"Come on, if we don't get up for breakfast there won't be any left." I pull the covers down and walk around and help Maggie up.

She rubs her eyes and groans. "Who needs breakfast? I was sleeping so well." She tries to climb back under the covers but I stop her.

"You say that, but you haven't had Charlotte's French toast. Besides, we have plans today and I'd like to get a head start."

We make our way into the kitchen and find Charlotte busily

whipping something in a bowl while my dad works on a crossword puzzle in his favorite chair by the window.

A beam of golden morning light shines through the window illuminating Maggie's gorgeous red locks and in this light, it almost looks pink. I smile as I watch her, completely unaware of how devastatingly beautiful she is. She smiles warmly and does a little stretch looking so fucking happy and at peace and at that moment I almost forget to breathe.

How is it possible to be this fucking happy? The feeling is quickly replaced by dread. Our happy ending will be the shortest forever that will never be.

"Good morning, you two lovebirds," Charlotte coos as she pours us each a cup of coffee. Passing it to us across the countertop. "There's cream and sugar right over there. Breakfast will be ready in about five minutes. I'm just waiting for it to cool off."

I add the cream and sugar to Maggie's cup and give it a good stir before handing it to her. She makes the cutest moan of appreciation as she wraps both hands around the steaming mug and smells. "Everything smells so amazing. I wish I could bottle it up and save it."

"Well, you're welcome anytime, dear." Charlotte wipes her hands on a hand towel and throws it over her shoulder. "You don't even need this one if you don't want," she says as she whips the towel in my direction.

"Hey, I bring her home for less than twenty-four hours and you're already trying to replace me?" I hold my hand against my heart as if I'm deeply offended. But I get it. Maggie is incredible, and it's not hard to notice. She doesn't take anyone for granted. She's got this air about her that makes you feel like you're the only one in the room. It's not any one specific trait but a culmination of everything she stands for and everything she doesn't.

"Well, maybe if you'd come home more often we wouldn't need to," Charlotte retorts. She says it jokingly but I know she means it. Guilt pricks in my chest and I sigh. I know I should come visit more. But no one understands how painful it can be. Every time I'm here I'm reminded of the darkest parts of myself. As nice as it may be in the moment, it's like salt in the wound when I leave. It seems these days it takes longer and longer to recover from.

But my parents are getting older, Dad's hair has gone completely white since the last time I saw him nearly a year ago. Maybe it's time to suck it up and be more present, I'm all too familiar with living with regrets. I don't need to add to my ever-growing list.

Charlotte sets two plates down in front of us. "Here you are. I hope you like fresh berries, Maggie. I had a heap of them in the freezer from when we went picking this summer."

"This is delicious. It's like heaven exploded in my mouth!" Maggie closes her eyes letting out a little moan.

"That's what she said!" Jamie laughs as he walks in the room, eyes crusty and hair sticking up in every direction. He's bare foot wearing gray sweatpants pulled down low on his hips and no shirt. Drew gives him a high five from his seat on the couch as Jamie passes.

The real-life Beavis and Butthead.

"Oh Char, you know the way to my heart." Jamie singsongs as he makes himself a heaping plate.

Simon walks in and pours two cups of coffee, presumably bringing Wren her cup in bed. My brother is wrapped around her little finger so tightly, I can't imagine how he's going to be with a baby. "Save some for the rest of us, jerkoff! If my pregnant wife misses out on Charlotte's French toast, there will be blood and I don't think even I'm tough enough to stop her."

Jamie drops the metal spoon, and it clanks against the glass dish. "Fair enough."

I watch as Maggie's eyes ping-pong between my brothers like she's absorbing every word and can't get enough. What I would give to know what she's thinking right now...

"Do you think we could have one family meal where we don't use crude language? Or threaten to physically harm one another?" Charlotte barks as she pulls another batch of French toast from the oven. "We have plenty, there's no need to growl and hiss like wild animals."

"But we are wild animals," Drew teases as he scoots into the kitchen to make himself a plate.

"Believe me. I know. I'm just doing my best to make you all semi-polite humans." She dusts powdered sugar off her apron. "But one woman in a house full of males is no easy feat." She looks at Maggie as she sighs and shakes her head. "I did my best, dear, he's yours to break now."

Maggie smiles but looks down at her plate, pushing her food around with her fork. We both know that's not true but why does she look so sad about it?

"Well, I hate to eat and run but I've got a surprise planned for Maggie today." I stand and take mine and Maggie's dishes and load them in the dishwasher. "Dad, is it okay if I borrow your truck for the day? We're you planning on going anywhere?"

"I plan on enjoying my first official day of retirement from the comfort of this chair." He kicks his feet up on the coffee table and leans back, bringing the crossword puzzle closer to his face. "The keys are on the hook by the door."

"Thanks, Dad."

I turn to Maggie and waggle my eyebrows. "Are you ready for your surprise?"

"Sam, is this really necessary?" Maggie adjusts the silk eye mask I made her wear five minutes before we got here. I didn't want to risk the chance of her seeing something and it ruining the surprise.

It's not that kind of surprise but seeing her wearing it is bringing back all kinds of naughty memories plus a whole slew of new fantasies that I'll never have time to fulfill.

I push the thought to the back of my mind, today is not about sex but maybe we can squeeze that in tonight...

"Yes, it's necessary if I want you to be surprised. Now stop arguing with me and just walk. We're almost there," I say as I usher her forward, my hands firmly on her arms.

She blows out a frustrated sigh. "I look ridiculous and people are laughing at me."

I tighten my grip on her shoulders as I guide her around a large pothole. "How could you possibly know people are laughing at you? You can't see them."

"Because I can *hear* them, Sam! There was a kid back there that asked her parents if there was a piñata nearby that she missed out on."

I stifle a laugh. I did hear that little girl and it was cute as fuck when she thought her parents were holding out on her.

"What's that smell? It's almost like waffles but not..." Maggie asks as we finally make it to the gate.

"You'll see. Are you ready to see your surprise?" I unclasp the eye mask and watch as Maggie's eyes go wide taking in the large carousel front and center of the small amusement park. Families and groups of teenagers rush around carrying giant bags of cotton candy and light-up toys as the sounds of laughter and chatter surround us.

Her nose scrunches and then she breaks out into the biggest

smile and it's not hard for me to picture her as a tiny freckled little girl full of whimsy and wonder before the world robbed it from her. Her hands cover her face as she squeals in excitement. "You brought me to an amusement park? I've never been to one before–"

"I know." I pull her into a hug and brush her hair out of her face, my eyes trying to memorize her in this moment. "You told me. Obviously, that was unacceptable and needed to be remedied immediately." I take her hand and lead her closer to the carousel. "Every little kid should ride the carousel. How about we start there and then we'll work our way up to the bigger rides?"

She bites her lip, wiping the tears from her eyes, "This is the sweetest thing anyone has ever done for me, Sam. Thank you."

I snap a picture of her with my phone and pocket it. "You can thank me later. Let's get moving, we've got a whole childhood to make up for." I take her hand in mine and lead her to the carousel.

Two hours later we're sitting on a curve stuffing our faces with cotton candy. Maggie's eaten over half the bag washing it down with fresh lemonade wearing a smile that seems to be permanently attached to her face.

We knocked out all the kiddie rides and I don't know if it's the sugar overload but she hasn't stopped talking to take a breath for over five minutes. "You can have a little more but then I'm taking the sugar away from you." I say as I swipe the lemonade and steal a sip.

She pouts out her lip and looks at me with pleading puppy dog eyes. "I thought you wanted me to have the full experience?"

"You're going to be puking if you don't slow down. I'm doing you a favor."

"Fine." She passes me the bag and I spin it around sealing it for later.

I hear the loud dinging bells as a group of kids go wild in celebration. "Step right up and see if you have what it takes to beat the record! Five dollars gives you one minute." The park member calls from his booth.

Maggie's eyes dart to the source of the noise and she looks back at me, "Do you have five dollars?" She asks as she bats her eyes.

I stand and offer her my hand. "My pockets are loaded down and ready. You just lead the way, baby."

"Yess!" She pumps her hand in victory and jumps up and down. It's equally cute and heartwarming seeing her have so much fun. Her reaction has me wanting to buy her this whole fucking amusement park. Hell, if I'd known how happy it would make her I would've started with this to begin with.

We make our way over to the games and she points out the one she wants to try first. It's a basketball shooting game, the kind with the warped rim, a whole line of giant stuffed animals stretch across the top of the booth which I now realize is what attracted her in the first place.

"Give me my panda bear, bitch!"

A group of about eight teenage boys gather around the booth all whooping and cheering as a kid in the middle pounds his chest like King Kong.

They can't be older than fourteen and seem to be giving the park member a hard time, as they pull at random stuffed animals making them fall before he can stop them.

"Hey, guys, chill out would you?" I say as I walk up to the booth and the man dabs a handkerchief to his forehead.

"This game is rigged! He hit the buzzer earlier right before my last ball went in!" The kid screams as he tries to jump over the booth.

"Whoa, whoa, whoa." I grab him by the t-shirt and pull him back. "I suggest you and your snotty-nosed friends go find something else to do before I call security on you myself."

"Get your hands off me, perv!" The kid screams and pushes me back. "Help, the strange man in the sunglasses over here just tried to touch my wiener!"

Heads begin to turn all around us and I quickly realize if I need to play nice if I don't want to get thrown out of here before Maggie even gets a chance to ride a real roller coaster.

"Sam, let's just go." Maggie tries to pull me away but I don't budge. I'm not about to walk away before she gets to play this game because of some snot-nosed teenage pricks.

I turn the park member and pull out my wallet. "How much do you want for the panda?"

"Eh, thirty bucks?" He says with a shrug.

I pass him two twenties and his mouth pulls into a grin. "One panda for the shit stain and we'll each have a turn."

"Here you go." The man says as he passes me the stuffed animal.

I turn around and shove it at the kid. "There, now get lost."

"Fuck, yeah!" He screams as he holds it over his head like a trophy and all his friends cheer alongside him as if he actually won the prize himself.

He passes me the ball and I offer it to Maggie but she waves me off. "I'll let you go first. I want to take notes."

"Alright, let's win you that teddy bear." I give her a wink and ready myself.

"Time starts... now!" The man says as I shoot my first shot and the ball bounces off the rim. I grab the extra ball and shoot again, this time making it, shooting shot after shot in rapid succession.

"Look at this chump and his weak jump shot!" One of the kids says behind me and I turn to see they still haven't left.

"I said get lost, kid," I say as I shoot and it bounces off the rim to the side.

"And miss you looking like a chump in front of your hot girlfriend? Ha! Yeah right."

"Who taught you how to shoot, your mom?" Another kid shouts.

I squeeze the small ball so hard I'm afraid it's going to explode as I breathe through my nose. I grit my teeth and shoot again. This time sinking it.

"Lucky. I bet you can't do it again, you old man."

Maggie's hand comes to my back as she leans in and whispers, "Is this normal amusement park behavior?"

If I didn't have actual steam coming from my ears, I may have laughed at her innocent question. Instead, I try my best to focus on making the next basket.

"Oh, that's embarrassing right there. You trying to build a house with all those bricks?"

"I feel sorry for your girlfriend after seeing you struggling so hard to find the right spot... Hey rich guy's girlfriend, come over here and let a real man show you–"

"Ok, that's it." I drop the ball just as the buzzer goes off indicating my times up. I may not be able to legally hit a child but I sure as fuck can scare them. I spin around and the boys scatter like flies.

"Sam! What are you doing?" Maggie yells as I manage to grab the biggest one of the bunch by the shirt

"Look here, you little skid mark. I will rip the braces off your teeth and cut you with them if you talk to a woman like that again. I'll pay the best private investigator in the country to track you down and find every username you have and personally destroy every virtual world you've built. I will sabotage you in every way possible... Do you understand me?"

"Yes... Yes... Sir." I let go of his shirt and shove him and he falls to the ground then gets up and runs off to join his friends.

"Wow," Maggie snickers, "Gee, Sam, you really showed him." She covers her face as she tries to hold back her laughter.

I quirk my brow and shove my hands in my pockets. "You thought that was funny, did you?"

She nods her head and lets her smile loose. "You losing your temper to a group of fourteen-year-olds? Yeah, it was pretty funny."

"Those little shits had it coming. They've been posted up here tormenting every customer I've had today." The man working to booth says, and we turn back to face him. He holds up the ball, "How about a turn for the lady?"

"Thanks." Maggie takes the ball reluctantly. She widens her feet and bends her knees as she waits for the word.

"Ready. Set. Go!" The man rings the bell and she fires off shot after shot.

My mouth falls open as I watch her sink ball after ball with practiced form as if she's done this a million times. "Holy shit, you've been holding out of me..."

She shrugs her shoulders but doesn't look at me as she keeps on shooting, only missing a couple of shots here and there. "One of my foster homes had a basketball hoop. I used to stay out there all night when I needed a break from the chaos. I may have also played a little rec ball in college." She bites her lip and sinks her final shot just as the buzzer goes off.

The man behind the counter scratches his head. "You know, I'm usually pretty good at predicting things but I didn't see this coming."

He looks at his clipboard and points to me. "You can pick anything you want from here." Then he turns to Maggie, "I've actually never seen a score this high before..." He gestures to the small assortment of gigantic stuffed animals behind him. "The lady can pick anything she likes from the champion pile."

Maggie's grin spans across her face as she narrows her eyes and taps her lip. "How about the one in the back right there?"

"One pink and purple teddy bear coming right up." He passes her the giant stuffed animal and I snap a picture as she hugs it to her chest.

I don't know if anything could have prepared me for this strange combination of emotions. Guilt rips through me leaving a giant hole in its wake while a wave of joy flutters around my heart. I'll just have to lick my wounds when it's all over.

She heaves the giant bear on my back, throwing an arm over each shoulder and I sink a little at its unexpected weight. "Jesus, is it made from actual bears?"

Maggie just giggles. "Can we eat chili dogs and hit the rest of the rides?"

I quirk a brow. "You know that's a recipe for disaster, don't you?"

She rolls her eyes. "I don't know, Sam... I think I may surprise you."

"You know what? You're not wrong."

TWENTY-SEVEN

Maggie

"Are you sure you want to do this?" Sam asks as we stare up at the Twisted Splitter rollercoaster, the largest one in the entire park.

He's got a giant teddy bear propped on his back in a piggyback carry, and he looks absolutely ridiculous with his polished cool guy appearance in light wash jeans, a fitted dark gray t-shirt, and aviators carrying the most obnoxious stuffed animal ever created. And yet the fact that he's doing it at all has me covered in goosebumps from head to toe.

Seeing Sam laugh and let loose today has only made my confusing feelings for him grow stronger. I feel like I'm getting a sneak peek at the most intimate side of him, actually seeing the real Sam. He's got this wall built up around his heart, and I didn't even realize how high it was until I saw him opening up around his family. I can't stop wondering why, though.

I know it's not my business, so I don't ask.

"Hell yeah, I want to do it. I have to redeem myself after

that twenty-story drop back there." I attempt to smooth my wild hair and twist it to the side.

Sam sticks his finger in his ear and squints his eye. "Yeah, I don't know if I'll ever regain hearing in my left ear after those blood-curdling screams."

I shove him playfully. "My harness felt wiggly! What was I supposed to do, just accept death by rollercoaster? Am I really supposed to trust some sixteen-year-old kid to properly restrain me? I wasn't even touching the seat during that fall."

Sam laughs and shakes his head. "You sounded like you were being tortured. I think the people behind us really thought you were dying."

"I could've died of a heart attack, and all you could do was laugh." I cross my arms over my chest.

"You were fine. I checked your restraints before I even sat down. You were completely safe. It's one thing to free fall and entirely different going upside down and spun through loops." He hoists the stuffed animal up and nods toward the scary roller coaster. "This one's a beast. I don't know if you're ready but if you think you are, let's do it." He winks.

"Oh, I'm ready. This time, you're going to be the one squealing." I suck in a breath and puff out my chest. "Let's do this."

Sam just laughs and follows my lead as we wind our way to the ride. We've been lucky to have a small crowd—Sam says anyway—and haven't had to wait longer than a couple of minutes for each ride.

When we reach the top of the loading station, Sam drops the teddy bear by the cubbies, where we store our shoes, sunglasses, and phones. "Come on. We're riding on the front row for this one. The best seat in the house," he tells me.

Nervous excitement swirls in my belly, but I follow him to the front. When it's our turn, he lets me get in first and double-checks my restraint before buckling himself in. I know he's not technically trained in rollercoaster safety, but he's meticulous to a fault, and it makes me feel at ease, anyway. I think I'd try just about anything if Sam were by my side.

"Hey, Maggie, try not to scream so loud this time," he says as the rollercoaster shoots us forward, sending me flying back against my seat.

Exhilaration and thrill flood my nervous system, and my heart feels like it skips a beat as the momentum of the ride suspends me in mid-air. I let out a piercing scream from the pit of my stomach, feeling so alive. Sam squeezes my hand, and even though I can't see his face, I know he's smiling.

We go through a series of loops and upside-down spins, and I feel the skin on my face slide back from the speed. My stomach drops when the ride dips down, and my head sinks into the harness as the momentum throws us from side to side.

I don't know whether to laugh or scream, so I do a little of both, and it's so much fun. Our cart makes one final drop before coming back up to a flat, slow speed.

"Oh my God, that was amazing! I felt like an astronaut or something." When the chest restraints lift, I unbuckle myself. Sam follows suit, but he's moving a little slower.

We climb off the ride, and I throw my arms around his neck, burying my face in his chest. "Thank you so much for bringing me here! I've had the best time." We stumble back a little, with Sam caught off-balance from the force of my hug.

When I release him, I see his usual golden skin turn as white as a sheet. "Sam? Are you feeling okay? You look a little pale–"

Just as the words leave my mouth, he stumbles back and almost falls over. I grab him around the waist and still him as I study his face.

"I'm fine. Sorry, I just got really dizzy," he assures me as he walks toward the cubby area to collect our things. He bends down to grab the teddy bear and throws it over his back, stumbling as the weight falls to one side.

"Are you sure you're okay?" I grab his arm and lead him to the exit ramp, keeping my pace nice and slow, afraid that he'll fall if I let go of his arm.

"Yeah. I'm good. I just need to walk it off."

We make our way off the ride, and I lead him to a bench. I catch sight of the little asshole kids from earlier and immediately panic when I accidentally make eye contact with the kid Sam threatened.

As if he knows Sam's weak right now, he rushes over with his teenage posse in tow. "What's wrong, old man? Do you have a bellyache?" he singsongs in a taunting baby voice.

"Okay, kid, that's enough." I try to turn Sam in the opposite direction and lead him away, but he stumbles again, side stepping his weight from foot to foot like a newborn baby giraffe.

"Holy shit. It's better than I thought. What a pansy. Dude can't even handle a roller coaster." The kid laughs and shoves Sam with two of his fingers, making him stumble back again.

"That's enough," I warn. "Why are you so mean?" I huff a sigh as I tuck myself under Sam's arm, holding up most of his weight to keep him upright. My muscles burn from the exertion. "Come on, Sam. Let's go."

Before I can make a move, Sam's head sags to the side, and he falls out of my grip, landing on the hard pavement in front of the kid with a thud. He wrenches, spilling chili dogs and blue cotton candy all over the kid's white high-top sneakers.

"What the fuck–" the kid yells and jumps back as Sam starts to dry heave. "That's fucked up, dude. You owe me two hundred dollars! I just got these for my birthday!" His voice cracks.

Sam wretches again in response. Then very slowly, he raises

his arm and holds up his middle finger. I can't help but laugh at the absurdity.

The kid grits his teeth and balls his fists but eventually turns to leave, taking his crew of bullies right along with him.

Well, I guess that's one way to get rid of them.

"Come on, Sam." I try to help him stand, but he falls again, both him and the teddy bear rolling into the vomit pile.

I kneel down and push his hair back from his clammy forehead. "It's okay. Let's just sit here for a minute and see if you feel better." I look around and realize we're in the very back of the amusement park. There's no way I can carry him all the way to the car by myself.

I know he'll be furious later, but I don't really have an option. I take his phone out of his pocket and hold it up to his face to unlock it, then call his dad. Thankfully, he picks up on the third ring.

Three hours later, I'm sitting on the sofa sandwiched between Drew and Jamie as Dr. Gregory, James, and Charlotte's family doctor, explains vertigo to the family.

"I performed a simple technique called the Epely maneuver, and he responded well. He may be dizzy for a little while longer, so you should just let him rest as long as he's comfortable. Here's a prescription for some anti-nausea medicine." He lays the prescription on the coffee table. "But I expect him to be feeling much better by tomorrow. These things can happen anytime the head is jostled and shaken, but rest assured, it's very common."

"Thank you, Dr. Gregory." James stands and shakes his hand.

I've never seen anything like that before. He went from

being completely normal to being unable even to stand up. After I called James, I waited for what felt like hours. Though, it was really only twenty minutes for Drew and Jamie to show up.

I was able to get him up and on a bench, so we didn't cause any more of a scene. I knew Sam would be even more upset if I called the park medic or an ambulance.

Jamie and Drew were able to pick him up with no problem and helped him out of the park, and now that we all know he's fine, I don't know if Sam's ever going to hear the end of their teasing.

We all thank the doctor again as James walks him out, and I sag back on the couch with relief.

Charlotte walks in the kitchen and throws on her apron. "Why don't I heat us up some of the soup I made for lunch? I've got fresh bread ready to go in the oven."

Charlotte opens the spice cabinet and stands on her tippy toes to grab something at the top, and Jamie leaps up from the couch to help her. For a moment, I'm surprised by his kind gesture, but when I really think about it, everyone in this family appears to care deeply about one another. Despite all their playful bickering and teasing, they'd do anything to help their family.

I think of how Jamie and Drew rushed to help Sam today and how they didn't even tease him as they helped him get cleaned up and tucked into bed. There's no way I could've managed all of that on my own. What must it feel like to have people in your life who simply love you just because you're family?

I have friends who love and care for me, Sam being one of them, but that's an exchange. A tit for a tat. We're there for each other, so in a sense, I suppose I earn their love and care. It isn't unconditional.

The familiar pang of loneliness hits me in the chest like a

brick as I'm once again reminded of what I don't have. It doesn't seem fair, but life isn't meant to be. I guess I just wish I didn't have to have the reminder rubbed in my face quite so much.

"Drew, dear, would you mind getting the big soup bowls down from the cabinet." Charlotte sets a timer as she puts the bread in the oven, and Drew gets up to help her.

I watch in fascination as the threat of tears burns behind my eyes.

"They weren't always so polite," James says as if he can read my mind.

I clear my throat, suddenly embarrassed that I was caught getting emotional over something so silly. I start to tell him that's not what I was thinking, but he continues.

"When I met Charlotte, the boys were fourteen, twelve, six, and five. Jamie and Drew were practically feral animals at that point. What little good behavior they had, they learned from Sam." He nods toward the bedroom door where Sam sleeps. "I wasn't the best father to any of them, but I'm afraid Sam got the worst of it. He had to pick up my slack after his mom died, be the man of the family I couldn't be."

"That sounds exactly like Sam." I sigh. "It looks like you've made up for it. You have a beautiful family. Truly." I swallow a lump in my throat.

"Yeah, well, I guess age'll do that to you. Makes you realize what's really important. Charlotte lost her first husband very young, and I suppose we were both what each other needed to finish healing. I don't know if I could've done it without her. She's my angel sent by God." He smiles and glances over his shoulder, and I follow his eyes to see Charlotte stirring a big pot of soup as she orders Jamie and Drew around the kitchen.

"I can only hope to find love like that someday," I say with a sigh.

"Oh, come on, now. I think you may be a little closer than you realize." James winks.

I suck in a breath and force a smile. "Excuse me. I think I need some fresh air." I get up and walk out to the balcony that overlooks the ocean. I lean against the wooden railing and set my eyes on the bright orange sun setting on the horizon.

My soul longs for more from this life, and I'm not sure I can give it what it desires. I don't even know what I want anymore. I'm so turned around and upside down. I feel like I'm being tossed and tumbled in a riptide.

My peaceful moment alone comes to an abrupt halt when Denver shoves his big, wet nose straight into my crotch.

"Jesus, Denver, you're coming off too strong," Simon says as he pulls him back by the collar. "Sorry about that. I hope Den didn't ruin your only moment of peace..." He laughs, "I guess like I'm doing right now."

I bend down and rub Denver's ears. "You didn't interrupt anything," I say through giggles as he licks me.

Simon scratches the back of his head. "Thanks for taking care of Sam today. He really gave us a scare. You handled it really well. I know we're all grateful for that."

"Of course. It was no big deal. He'd have done it for me, too." I wave him off as Denver lays down and offers me his belly to rub, which I happily oblige.

"I know my brother doesn't have the most traditional dating life..."

My hands go still as I wait to hear what he's going to say.

"He has his reasons, as fucked up as they may be. I think you're good for him, though. Don't let him fuck it up, okay? He's definitely going to try. It's kind of his M.O." His eyes meet mine, and it's like he can see right through me.

"I'm not sure what you mean, Simon."

"Yeah, well, I guess you'll find out soon enough." He taps his leg, and Denver jumps up, eager to follow as he leads him down the steps to the beach. He pulls a tennis ball out of his pocket, and I watch as the giant clumsy dog chases it along the shore.

I can't help but wonder what happened to Sam to make him so guarded. I doubt he'll tell me himself, so I guess there's only one other way to find out...

TWENTY-EIGHT

Maggie

"Look who the cat dragged in," James calls from where he's sitting in his favorite leather chair. I glance behind me and see a messy-haired Sam approaching with squinting eyes.

"How are you feeling?" I abandon my post of peeling potatoes and rush to him, careful not to knock him off balance with my hug.

His large hand rubs my back, sending a shiver down my spine. "I'm feeling much better today. Thank you for everything yesterday." He stiffens. "It wasn't my proudest moment."

"Sam, you can't help that you got vertigo from a roller coaster," I scold. "Now, have a seat, and let *me* make *you* some coffee." I pull out the bar stool, and he sits hesitantly.

"Your Maggie is quite the little chef, Samuel. She's teaching me how to make boxty," Charlotte says as she bumps her hips to mine.

"Is she?" Sam sounds surprised as he eyes me. "I had no idea you could cook." He takes a sip of his black coffee. "I learn something new about you every day."

I roll my eyes and continue peeling the potatoes. "Well, in my defense, you're always so bossy, ordering dinner before I can offer." I shrug and wink at him.

"I suppose you're right," he says with a laugh.

"Now, Maggie, where was it you said you learned how to make this? A family recipe, perhaps?" Charlotte asks innocently, and Sam nearly chokes on his coffee.

"Well... um..."

"Maggie grew up in foster care. She aged out of the system when she turned eighteen," Sam answers for me. "I thought I told you that?" he says in a clipped tone.

Charlotte sucks in a gasp, her cheeks heating with embarrassment. "I'm so sorry, dear! I had no idea." She turns to Sam. "I feel certain I would've remembered a piece of crucial information like that," she scolds Sam. "I'm so sorry for asking such a stupid question. Please forgive my ignorance."

"It's fine." I wave her off. "I suppose I'm probably Irish or Scottish somewhere down the line." I pull at my long braid. "I was always the oldest kid in the homes, and the families depended on me to help out." I shrug. "I cooked dinner most nights and always liked to try new things with common household ingredients. The little kids loved it when I cooked. So that's how it all started."

Charlotte places her hand on top of mine, and I pause my peeling. "You really are a little diamond in the rough, aren't you?" A tender smile covers her face, and she points her dish towel at Sam. "You better not run this one off. We all just love her."

I swallow a gulp as silence fills the air between us. I hold my breath, waiting for Sam to reassure her, but he doesn't say a word. I can feel his eyes on me, heating my skin as if they're laser beams, but I don't meet his gaze. I just busy myself with cooking.

A few minutes later, Wren waddles in with Denver by her side, and Charlotte rushes to help her get settled on the couch, her questions forgotten. I suppose I'm thankful for the interruption. It makes things far less awkward for both of us.

After breakfast, I take a long, hot shower, letting the events of the last few days melt away. I can't help the confusion stirring in my gut as my mind and body fight over who should be in charge of my thinking. Being here with Sam's family has been so wonderful and painful at the same time. It's like tearing open a scab that I thought was almost healed but finding out the wound is still very raw and fresh. It makes me question everything I'm working toward in life, and suddenly, I feel like I'm running out of time to figure out what I really want.

I'm sitting cross-legged and braiding my damp hair into a French braid down my back in the corner of the room in front of a full-length mirror. In the background, I can hear Sam's deep laughter echoing, and it sends chills up my arms. Who knew his laugh was so full of life? I can't help but wonder what else I don't know about him. I feel like he knows everything there is to know about me at this point.

It's not that I expect him to change his mind about us... or having a real relationship with me. His limits were extremely clear when he presented me with the contract. But I suppose there was a piece of me deep down that I kept tucked away in my heart that hoped he'd discover something he liked about me. That I would be special enough to change him.

I shake my head and scoff at the thought. It sounds ridiculous. Like I've set myself up to be hurt. I can't let myself think that way, not if I want to walk away from this with any of my heart left to give. For once in my life, I'd like to be someone's first choice, but maybe that isn't in the cards for me. Maybe I'll always have to prove myself and work a little harder than everyone else to convince someone that I'm special. Maybe that's just how things are supposed to be for me.

My phone buzzes with a text message, and after I finish my braid, I cautiously lift the phone to see a new message from Trent. My eyes dart to the closed door as if afraid Sam's watching me. Why should it matter if he is anyway? I click open my texts.

TRENT

I can't believe I'm going to get to see you in real life in less than two days. I know you said not to message, but I couldn't help myself. I've been staring at the picture you sent every single night, and I wanted to give you a little something to think about, too.

The next message pops up, and my eyes nearly pop out of my head as I stare at a picture of what I presume is Trent's hard penis, his hand gripped firmly around his shaft.

I let out a scream, and my phone flies out of my hand from the shock. Holy shit. I just got my very first dick pic.

My eyes widen, and I cover my mouth, hoping no one heard my scream. But it's too late. Not three seconds later, Sam, Drew, and Jamie burst through the door.

"What's wrong?" Sam rushes to me on the floor as he assesses my face, his cool thumbs brushing over my burning cheeks.

Jamie grabs a baseball bat off one of the shelves and holds it up like he's ready to swing. "What is it? A mouse? I fucking hate mice. Where'd it go?" He pushes Drew in front of him slightly as he walks further into the room.

"Yes!" I agree. A little more enthusiastic than necessary. I'm grateful for the provided excuse. I can't let Sam know that I just got a dick pic from Trent. Who knows what he'd do with that information?

"I think I saw it run under the dresser."

"Oh, fuck. Ok." Jamie says as he jumps like he's doing high knees and swinging the bat over his shoulder. "I'm not scared of a tiny mouse." He says under his breath like he's trying to convince himself.

"Let's just move the dresser and kill it," Drew suggests as he starts to push the dresser to the side.

"It's more like a rat!" I scream, and he stops. "Yeah, it had this really long tail, as long and thick as my finger." I hold up my hand to show them, and Jamie gets a full-body shiver and starts hyperventilating as he high-knees in place.

"I can't fucking do rats. You know I'm terrified of Chuck E. Cheese." He shakes his head and shoves the bat at Drew, then takes off out of the room.

Sam laughs and brushes his finger over my bottom lip, his eyes dark and curious. "Why don't we go for a walk on the beach, and we can let Drew and Simon deal with the rat? That sound good to you?"

I don't know if he knows I'm lying, but suddenly, all the worries that have plagued me all morning are gone as Sam looks at me like that. My heart flutters in my chest, and I can't help but smile. "Yeah, that sounds perfect."

He tugs my braid and stands, then offers me a hand up. "Maggie and I are going for a walk. Please deal with the rodent issue before we get back."

I glance back at my phone lying in the corner of the room and decide to deal with Trent later.

We shed our shoes and walk down the steps along the winding footpath to the beach. Sam's large hand encompasses mine as we walk in comfortable silence, the waves crashing and breaking on the shore the only sounds.

The cool water nips at my feet, and I feel a sense of calm and grounding that you just don't get in the city. It's like all the noise of life is stripped away, and it's just our souls walking on the beach together.

"You're so different here with your family. You seem so happy, like you can let your guard down." I kick at the water pooling my feet, splashing it away. "I feel like you're keeping something from me." The confession comes out like the ocean itself is a truth serum, pulling it straight out of me.

Sam purses his lips, and his jaw flexes. "I don't realize I'm doing it. I just don't want to burden you with any of my pain. You've experienced enough on your own, and the last thing I want is for you to feel sorry for me and carry the weight of my issues." He stops and turns toward me, pulling my hands to his.

"I want to know everything about you, Sam. I'm a big girl. I can handle it." I shake my head. "You don't have to protect me from everything all the time. I'm strong enough to handle it."

"I know you are. You're the strongest person I've ever known. That's why I didn't want to tell you. You're so empathetic, Mags. You carry people's pain around with you. I don't want to add to that."

"Well, I want you to," I say. "I want to know everything about you. I feel like I've been so vulnerable with you all this time. It's only fair you open up to me." I don't know where my surge of confidence comes from, probably the ocean, but my words are true.

A pained look crosses his face, and he nods. "Yeah, you're right. I'm sorry about that. What would you like to know?" He starts walking again, and I keep pace beside him.

"Everything." I sigh. "How did your mother die?"

He sucks in a breath but doesn't miss a beat. "Cancer. She

fought it for four years before it finally won." He rubs his hand over his heart like it hurts to talk about it. "She was my favorite person. The nicest woman in the whole world." He nudges me with his shoulder, "You're a pretty close second, though."

I suck in a small gasp at his admission, but he continues.

"She was so thoughtful about everything for us kids. She had these extravagant holiday activities she used to make us do and cooked special meals for every occasion. I tried to keep it going for Drew and Jamie after she died, but it got harder and harder to manage. It started to feel like I was torturing myself the more I tried, and when I realized they didn't really remember, I decided it was best that they not know. That way, they didn't have to deal with the pain every time the holidays came around." He shrugs, and my heart aches for him. How much pressure little Sam must've felt to keep his mother's traditions alive.

"That sounds like it was really hard for you. Is that why you don't like to come home?"

"Mostly. It feels lame to feel the pressure after all these years still, and having Charlotte helps, too. I guess I just don't like feeling sad, and if I'm working, I don't have as much time to feel sad about missing her."

"That makes sense. Is that what led you to pursue a BDSM lifestyle, too?"

Sam huffs. "Maybe a little." He stops and sits on the sand, patting the spot next to him for me to sit.

I sit down on the warm sand and snuggle into him, unsure of where this is going but finally feeling like I'm meeting him for the first time and can't get enough.

"I'm going to tell you something only my family, Benjamin, and Jack know about. It's not something I share with just anyone."

I nod, encouraging him to go on.

"When I was in high school, I had this girlfriend. We dated for all four years, and I was madly in love with her. After graduation, I sat my parents down and told them I was going to propose. My dad warned me against it, said I had all the time in the world, and didn't understand what the rush was. But I couldn't describe how I felt. I just knew I needed her like I needed my next breath. Anyway, I was going to propose. I saved up all my money over the summer working on my dad's construction crew and bought a nice little diamond ring." He paused for a moment before continuing, "I was on my way to her house to surprise her with a picnic on the beach and a proposal when I saw her making out in her bedroom window with my best friend. It fucking hurt. Everything in me fucking hurt, and I saw red as my heart burst into a million pieces. Blinded by rage, I picked up a rock and threw it at the window, and broke it. The glass shards cut both of them, but a piece hit her in the eye. She had to have surgery and almost lost her vision." He looks down at his shaking hands, gripped into fists.

"I just meant to get their attention. Let them know I saw them. I didn't realize how hard I threw the rock. I didn't mean to hurt anyone..."

"Oh, Sam." I take his shaking fist, covering it between my hands.

"Her parents were furious. They sued my family for medical expenses and dragged out the whole ordeal in court for years. My dad had to refinance the house and almost lost his business." He shakes his head. "After that, I found out she'd been sleeping with him behind my back for almost a year. Their family played up the injury and painted me as a criminal, dragging my family's name through the mud. I've never forgiven myself for being so stupid and weak. After that, I went to the farthest college I could get into and never looked back." He sighed. "For the longest time, I didn't date, didn't trust myself to fall in love ever again because I didn't trust myself to be so lost in someone else. Then I discovered BDSM and found comfort in the dominant/submissive lifestyle. I knew it was the only way I could let myself get involved with women. If I could control the relationship with rules and clear expectations from both parties, then that's the only way I could allow myself to be with a woman." His eyes, rimmed with tears, search mine as his confession hangs in the space between us.

Suddenly, it all makes sense. Sam isn't being cruel by keeping a barrier between us. He's protecting me from the ugliest parts of himself, or so he thinks. I place my hand on his pounding heart and unbutton his shirt revealing the tattoos painted across his skin. "Is that what this is for?" I trace the image of a dagger stabbed through a heart, a snake threatening to bite coiled around his shoulder disappearing behind his arm, an eye with tears streaming down. It's as if he's branded himself with reminders of every painful memory of his past.

He nods. "They remind me what I have to lose if I lose myself again. Plus, there are some fun ones, too." His lips pull into a half smile, but it doesn't meet his eyes.

"You made a mistake, Sam. You need to forgive yourself and stop punishing yourself for something you did when you were a kid. No matter how horrible the consequences were. You're not that hurt kid anymore. You're so much stronger and wiser. You are a good person–"

"I'm not a good person, Magnolia. I'm a selfish bastard, and I've made peace with it." He kisses the top of my hand, his lips lingering. "You, on the other hand, are the sweetest soul I've ever met. I don't know how I got so lucky that you'd ask me for my help, but if you take anything away from our time together, I hope you realize your worth. I hope you never settle for anything less than perfect, on paper and otherwise."

I don't know what to say. Sam's confession feels like the final line in the sand between us. Sadness washes over me as I look into his warm brown eyes that are so opposite to mine. "I'm not ready for this to be over," I confess with a whisper.

"Then let's just enjoy the time we have left and stop thinking about the timeline." He jumps up and pulls me with him. "Come on. I've got an idea."

"Where are we going?" I ask as I try to keep his hurried pace in the sinking sand.

"You'll see." He grins and winks.

I follow him like a love-sick puppy down the beach, even though all the warning lights and sirens in my brain flash for me to stop before it's too late. But I know it's already too late. I've fallen in love with my best friend, my dominant whom I signed a contract clearly stating that this will never work between us. I've already dove headfirst into the deep end. I just hope I can walk away in one piece.

I'll just have to worry about that later.

TWENTY-NINE

Maggie

"What do you think?" Sam shouts over the loud music as we sit in an old beach bar, a sticky wooden table between us. The sound crew is setting up a small stage just in front of us as the speaker overhead plays a mix of nineties alternative and early two thousand's pop punk.

When the server comes over and places our drinks in front of us, Sam orders a platter of oysters. "What is this place?" I ask after she leaves.

"This is only the best bar on this side of the panhandle." Sam stirs his mixed drink with his straw and then slides it to the side. "Thursdays are emo night," he says with a wink.

Dashboard Confessional plays over the speakers, and I feel a strange pang of nostalgia in my chest. It's odd. There aren't many things I feel nostalgic over, but the music almost makes me feel like I've stepped back in time, reliving a memory or perhaps making a new one that never had the chance of being.

"There's this cover band. They know everything, and

they're pretty good. They play back up for the karaoke singers, so even if they suck, it still feels like you're at a concert," he tells me over the music.

My palms immediately start sweating at the mention of karaoke, and I wipe them on my shirt. I take another sip of my mixed drink, letting myself get lost in the lyrics as Sam's confession plays on repeat in the back of my mind.

"You got room for two more?"

I look up to see Jamie and Drew dressed in the cheesiest short sleeve, beachy button-up shirts and shorts that look almost too short to be men's but are strangely flattering on their muscular builds.

They sit down in unison before Sam can answer, and I see the look of amused annoyance in his eyes. He may act like he can't stand his little brothers, but a piece of him is happy to spend time with them, even if it means they're crashing whatever kind of date we're on.

Our server comes back with oysters, and Drew and Jamie dig in. "Could you put in another order of these and maybe a basket of cheese fries?" Sam asks patiently.

"Maggie, I think you're going to need to get your eyes checked," Jamie says as he sucks juice from his fingers between bites. "We tore that whole room apart and didn't see a trace of a rat." His smile breaks into a wicked grin as he holds up my phone. "I did find this, though, and damn girl... I didn't mean to see, but you left the screen open." He giggles and elbows Drew, who appears to be trying to conceal his own laughter.

"What is it?" Sam asks before taking the phone.

"It's nothing. It's just–" I start to explain, but his eyes go wide as he sees the dick pic.

"I see." His lips form a hard line, but he quickly erases the annoyance on his face as the bar manager steps on stage to introduce the band and the first singer.

Jamie and Drew turn in their seats, clapping and cheering as the band starts playing "Dirty Little Secret" by The All-American Rejects.

Sam's hand lands on my thigh under the table, and he leans in, his warm breath on my neck. "I thought I asked you not to engage with Trent any further while we were still under contract?" His voice comes out cool and stern.

"I didn't. I didn't know he was going to send that," I try to explain.

"But you looked at it. Is that what made you scream?" His grip on my thigh tightens, and I realize my friend Sam isn't here anymore, just my dom, and from the look on his face, he isn't too pleased with me.

My mouth goes dry, and I nod, unsure of what to say.

"You also didn't tell me he contacted you, did you?" He sneaks his hand up my thigh a little higher, fingers tracing the hem of my shorts.

"No... sir. I didn't. I'm sorry, I just didn't think you'd care–"

"You didn't think I'd care that you broke a rule? You didn't think I'd care that you belong to me," he looks at his watch, "for the next nineteen hours. And you looked at another man's cock?"

I swallow a gulp as his hand moves higher, fingers tracing over the top of my panties. Heat pools in my belly, and I close my eyes, terrified to move.

He slides his finger in my panties and grazes along my slick wet center, and I suppress a whimper as the awareness of the crowd around me builds. "What shall I do for your punishment, my sweet, sweet Magnolia." He pulls his hand away and sucks my arousal from his finger.

I suck in a gasp as the song comes to an end, and Jamie and Drew turn to face us. "That was awesome! I fucking love emo night!"

My cheeks burn hot, and I nod in agreement, offering my most convincing smile. The server returns with another order of oysters and cheese fries, and Jamie and Drew dig into the fries. My eyes widen as Sam takes an oyster and sucks it down, not taking his eyes off me.

Then he holds one up for me. "Eat," he commands. He squeezes a lemon on top of the oyster, and I do as I'm told, never taking my eyes off him.

Electric heat sizzles between us, and I don't know what's going through his mind. I don't know if I should be afraid, but I can't help but love the excitement brewing under my skin at the way he looks at me. I want to please him, be his good girl, and follow his commands, but another piece of me wants to prove to him that he doesn't always need to be in control.

I slap the table and push away, "Excuse me. I just need to use the restroom." Sam's eyes narrow, but he pulls his hand away from the back of my chair and gives me space to get up. I walk to the bathroom, and when Sam is finally out of view, I head straight to the DJ booth.

"Hi, my name is Maggie. I'd like to sign up for a spot to sing tonight."

I fill out the song form and head back to the table, giddy that I have my own little surprise for Sam. He's not the only one who can shake things up, now, is he?

I take my seat and yank my chair closer to his, his hand continuing its exploration of my body underneath the table. "I almost came looking for you," he growls in my ear.

"Long line," I lie and finish my mixed drink. I shake it in front of him and give him the best doe eyes I can manage. "May I have another drink, sir?"

His eyes narrow as he considers. "If you finish your entire glass of water."

I press my lips to my straw and begin drinking my water

without breaking eye contact. "Yes, sir." I don't know what's gotten into me or what kind of game I'm playing, but it sure is fun driving Sam wild.

His hand slides up my shorts again, fingers tickling and teasing me underneath my panties. "You're being cheeky tonight, aren't you? Well, you better not squeal too loudly, or my brothers will hear you. We can't have that, can we?" he drawls, his warm breath on my neck.

I suck in a breath as my body heats with pleasure from his touch, and I part my legs to give him better access.

"Fuck, you're wet for me. Your pussy is practically begging for it. I should take you right here in this bar, throw you over this table, and fuck you in front of all these people. Show them just how goddamn lucky I am," he growls in my ear.

"Yes," I whimper as my climax builds in my core. My clit throbs under his touch, begging for release, but he teases me keeping his pressure light. I want to feel his mouth on me, licking and sucking me. I want his cock inside me, burying himself so deep that it hurts as he loses himself inside me.

I bite my lip as the fantasy plays in my mind, and I'm pulled back to reality when the DJ announces, "Next up, we have Magnolia Anderson singing "Still Into You" by Paramore. Come on up here, Magnolia."

Sam slowly pulls his hand out of my panties, and I blush as Drew and Jamie turn to look at me in shock, the people sitting around us following their gaze. I clear my throat. "I... I've got to go." I squeeze Sam's hand as I head to the stage, nerves mingling with my arousal, creating a strange burst of calm confidence.

I adjust the mic on its stand, angling it down to my lips. "Sam, this one's for you."

The drummer taps his drumsticks together three times, and I tap my foot to the beat as the band begins, and I burst into song, all the angsty teenage feelings bubbling back to the surface.

I belt out the bridge, my voice powerful and commanding as I hit every note, and the crowd soars into applause, screaming and shouting on the floor. I let myself go as I belt out the notes of the song on stage, bearing my soul to Sam and everyone in the crowd.

Chills cover my body as the lyrics feel so true, as if I could've written them myself. I feel like art is the only thing that can unite people with a common emotion and make them feel seen for even the most unique of circumstances.

A crowd forms at the front of the stage as people jump up from their seats and jump up and down to the music. My eyes search the dark bar until they land on Sam, whose eyes are trained on me as he watches me with a look of pride and amusement.

I do my best Hayley Williams impersonation as I C-Walk and dance on the stage, feeling like I'm someone else entirely, and the crowd goes crazy. I don't think there was a timeline for this version of me to exist without Sam pushing me to start loving myself first.

Tears sting my eyes as I finish the last verse, my throat constricting around the words. Then the lights go down, and I bow. When I look up again, Sam's standing at the corner of the stage, waiting for me. He motions for me to come closer, and I grin as I make my way off the stage. The crowd spots him, too, and starts chanting his name.

"Come with me," he whispers with a mischievous grin.

I follow him out of the lively bar pulsing with energy onto the beach in the pitch-black night. I honestly don't care where he's taking me right now. I'd follow him anywhere because I trust him that much.

When we're finally out of eyesight of the bar, and there are no lights except from the moon, he pulls me into him and kisses me like he's suffocating and I'm his only source of air. "Fuck, that was hot, Maggie," he says between frantic kisses. "I wanted to punish you tonight, but you completely made up for it." He bites my lip and hisses, his hands cupping my ass like I'm anchoring him to the earth.

He drops to his knees, and I follow, our mouths never separating as he pushes his hands up my shirt. My hands find the buttons of his shirt as I begin to undress him, pushing his shirt off and loving how his skin feels beneath my palm.

"We're in public, baby. I can't promise no one will see us," he warns as I unbuckle his belt and his shorts.

"Let them watch," I whisper in between kisses. Sam lets out a growl as he pulls my shirt off and unclasps my bra, his movements wild and hungry. I love this side of him and that I can bring out his inner monster, the part of himself that he fears the most because he can't control it. He pulls my shorts down along with my panties in one swift movement, and I stop him before he can pounce on me. "Wait."

He stills his hands on my hips, our heavy breathing and the ocean the only sounds between us.

I stand and pull him up with me and lead him toward the shore, the warm water lapping at our feet, sending a rush of adrenaline up my spine. "I've always wanted to go skinny dipping. I don't know if I'll ever get another chance like this," I admit, feeling embarrassed because it's such a silly thing.

Sam presses his hard cock against my back and wraps my braid around his hand, then licks the side of my neck. "What are you waiting for, then, Ariel?"

We slowly walk into the water, the rough waves lapping at our knees. It's a little chilly the deeper you get, but I feel so alive that I don't mind the cold. On the next wave, I force myself down so that it splashes over my head as Sam tightly holds me around my waist.

A giggly squeal escapes me, and I throw my head back and laugh, letting all the confidence and whimsy of the night cover my skin in a protective coating.

"What are you thinking?" Sam asks as he slides his hand up my belly, grazing underneath my breast.

"I'm thinking that this is fun, and I'm happy." I turn to face Sam, drinking in his features under the light of the moon. "You changed me, Sam. You showed me what it feels like to love myself, and you gave me space to discover everything I want." I brush my hands down his abdomen, feeling his hard pecks and abs before finally taking his long, thick cock in my hands. I pump him a couple of times, loving how he responds to my touch. It's like I wield the power of the universe.

"Fuck, baby," he mutters. "You changed yourself, don't give me credit for that. This is all you, Mags." He pushes my wet hair from my face and kisses me deeply, sucking my bottom lip into his mouth and giving it a tiny nibble. I deepen the kiss, wrapping my legs around his back and pulling his hard cock against me.

"You're playing with fire; you know that?" He growls as he grips my ass, and I wiggle so his cock perfectly lines up with my entrance.

"I'm not afraid of you, Sam," I whisper between kisses.

Sam's grip tightens, and he pushes into me right there in the ocean. I throw my head back and arch my back, relishing the burn of his cock stretching me, the way he fills me up, sliding in and out. "Yes," I cry as his hot lips suck my nipple into his mouth. Then he's carrying me out of the water, the cold air nipping my skin with each step to shore.

He's careful when he breaks us apart and lays down on the

rough, wet sand, stoking his cock with one hand and the other propped behind his head.

I stand for a moment in confusion. Why is he lying down?

He taps his thighs. "Come on, Maggie. This is your last lesson. You want to be a good lay? You need to know how to ride dick."

Anxiety starts to creep up, but I push it back down, reminding myself of just how badass I've become. I let my instincts take over and climb on top of him as I lower myself onto his hard length.

Sam grips my waist as I rock back and forth, loving how he feels so full inside of me as I explore different angles. "I wish I could have this view burned into my memory. You look so hot right now. Your full tits bouncing as you ride my cock." He slaps my ass, and I let out a little shriek in surprise grinding myself on him harder, until I find an angle that makes my eyes roll back in my head.

I rock my hips back and forth as the warm tingly sensation builds in my core. My clit throbs as the ocean breeze tickles and kisses my skin, and I feel like I'm a part of something so much bigger than sex. Life in every form circles around me as I move against Sam's body, feeling empowered and invigorated on a cellular level.

"You ride my dick so good, baby. Fuck, I'm so close." He pinches my nipples and grips my hips like a lifeline as I ride him. "Goddammit, Maggie, I lo–" He stops himself and falls silent, gripping me so tight I'm bound to have bruises in the morning, but I don't care.

I lean up a little, brushing my clit across him before grinding myself in a circle, and the orgasm builds just under the surface. I do it again and again, my movements growing harder each time until every muscle in my body tightens and warmth floods from my feet all the way up my body. An explosion erupts inside me so strong that I can't control myself as I fall apart riding out the waves of pleasure. Just when I think it's come to an end, another rush finds me again and again.

I don't know what words I say or if any of it makes sense as I scream my pleasure, bouncing and grinding on Sam's hard cock. I don't care if anyone hears or sees us because, at this perfect moment, we're the only two people in the universe to exist.

Sam's cock clenches inside of me. "Fuck, baby, I'm coming," he tells me as we both ride out our orgasms in unison. At this moment, there is no past, there is no future, there is only now.

And right now, I am royally fucked, because I've just realized I fucked up and broke rule number one.

I fell in love with Sam.

THIRTY

Sam

I hover the mouse over the submit button for what feels like an eternity before finally mustering the courage. I click the button and close my laptop, breathing a sigh. This is what's best, and now that it's done, hundreds, no, thousands of people will be depending on me, so I can't back out now.

Anxiety bubbles up like acid in my throat. I try to wash it down with my bitter black coffee that has long gone cold. It doesn't help, just reminds me that every minute that passes brings me closer and closer to the end.

I'm sitting alone in the sunroom in my parents' house, watching the event crew set up tables and tents for my dad's retirement party tonight. I should've known they'd invite the whole town. I rap my fingers on the wooden chair arm as irritation simmers under my skin. The last thing I want to do on my last night with Maggie is share her with everyone from my hometown. After everything that happened, the way they treated my family, I don't know if even I'm that good of a bullshitter to fake pleasantries.

But my dad and Charlotte are better people than me. They've long moved on from it, forgiven and forgotten. It's just another blaring reminder that I don't belong here and never have. I belong in a big city where I can hide the monster inside me in plain sight. Deflect personal questions and spin them into getting others to talk about themselves. People love talking about themselves, especially the rich businessmen I deal with daily. That's why I'm so good. Being a good listener and never revealing any personal information is my secret weapon to being a successful businessman.

I had the perfect formula figured out. I was happy enough. At least I thought I was. Sex was easy. Work was easy. Everything was simple, laid out in black and white. My life was boiled down to the most basic process, and I could control the outcome with ninety-nine percent certainty. It was easy, exactly the way I liked it.

Not anymore.

If I wasn't already falling for Maggie, she hammered the nail in the coffin last night and sealed my fate. Watching her come alive singing on stage, the pure, magical confidence radiating off her felt like an angelic light that healed everything it touched.

It almost hurt to look at her, to be near her, to touch her. Like submerging yourself in ice water and immediately getting into a boiling hot bath.

Last night as I laid on the beach and she rode me within an inch of my undoing, I got so caught up in the moment that I almost slipped up and told her I loved her.

I sit up and prop my elbows on my knees, rubbing my temples as the dull headache pounds behind my eyes.

Fuck, I'm in over my head. I knew I was catching feelings, but I tried to convince myself it was because I cared so much about her, because she was my friend. I've always known she was special, but being intimate with her, getting to know what makes her tick, and learning about her past, my feelings snowballed so fast. I didn't even see it coming. Or maybe I didn't want to.

Maybe a small part of me wanted to see how bad it could get, how much pain I could cause myself. That's what I deserve, and like the selfish bastard I am, I'm happy I got to experience so much joy, even if it was stolen.

I just hope I don't hurt her in the process because that's the kind of pain I don't know if I can bear.

Releasing a sigh, I twirl my coffee mug between my fingers as I watch the crew below build the platform for the stage. Charlotte directs another crew about where to set up the tables. It won't be long now before the sun sets, bringing our last day to an end and turning that all into a memory, a painful splinter in my heart that will never heal.

Guilt gets the best of me when the crew struggles to move a large piece of the stage, and I sigh as I get up. I may be a piece of shit regarding relationships, but I can't sit by and watch when there's work to be done and not enough muscle to do it. Besides, my muscles could use a little physical exertion to get some of this frustration out of my system.

I place my coffee cup in the dishwasher before running outside to help with the grunt work. Anything to take my mind off of my reality, just for a little while.

I tighten the fabric of my bow tie and run my fingers through my styled wavy hair. I'm getting ready in the guest bathroom upstairs since Wren kicked me out of the room Maggie and I are staying in. She insisted that she do Maggie's hair and makeup, and they've been locked away in there just about all day.

I make my way down the stairs and knock on the bedroom door. "Hey, Mags, you about ready?"

The door cracks open just wide enough for Wren's face. "She's almost ready. Why don't you just go down, and I'll send her when I'm finished?" Her tone is mostly friendly, but it doesn't match the look on her face. My brother's wife is a feisty thing, and if I had to guess, I'm not the first person to rush her process.

I hold up my hands. "Take your time. There's no rush on my end." The last thing this party needs is an angry pregnant woman who's bound to explode at any minute. "I'll be just outside. Call me if you need anything."

She doesn't respond, just slams the door in my face. "And on that note, I think I'll make myself a drink."

I walk over to the bar cart and begin making myself a Sazerac when I hear footsteps approach behind me.

"Make it two, will you?" Simon says as he comes to stand beside me.

I grab an extra glass and make our drinks without a word.

"You know, Sam, you don't have to fuck things up with Maggie if you don't want to. There's no rule that you have to be a miserable asshole all your life," Simon says as I hand him his drink.

"Wow, Si, tell me how you really feel." I sip my whiskey and begin making my way downstairs to the party.

Simon stays in step and continues. "All I'm saying is I haven't seen you this fucking happy since–" He pauses. "It's been a long time. I just don't want to see you fuck this up because you're scared."

I grit my teeth and tense my jaw. "You have no idea what you're talking about. So, just drop it, okay?"

Simon drains the last of his whiskey and shakes his head. "Okay, man, I'm just calling it like I see it. But whatever you say." He claps his hand on my shoulder, then turns, greeting a group of dad's friends who just walked in.

The band starts playing some of my dad's favorite rock ballads from the eighties as swarms of people file into the courtyard. I take in all the friends who've shown up to celebrate my dad's retirement. Everyone here loves him. It's impossible not to love him. My dad is the most hardworking, generous guy who has ever lived. He'd give anyone the shirt off his back in a heartbeat, which is why so many people have come out to celebrate him.

Besides my immediate family, I can count my friends on one hand. I can't imagine touching so many people's lives as he has. Even after all the shit I caused with Claire, the way everyone in the community turned on my family for years, my dad continued to be generous and kind. Eventually, he proved that his heart of gold was the real deal, and people couldn't help but recognize that and love him for it.

I'll never understand how my parents were able to create a monster like me.

I tighten my grip around my glass as I watch everyone laugh and fawn over each other when I feel a slight tap on my shoulder. When I spin around, I see Maggie looking like an old Hollywood movie star. Her long red locks are pulled to the side in pin-up curls that cascade down her back. She's wearing a fitted floor-length emerald-green dress adorned with glass beads. The neckline reveals a touch of cleavage, clinging to her shapely breasts. The back is low-cut, dipping all the way to the top of her ass.

My mouth waters, and I'm instantly hard as I take her in. She's always beautiful in whatever she's wearing, with makeup or without, but this... this is a whole new level of gorgeous. I don't know if there's a word for how incredible she looks tonight.

Her hazel eyes stand out against her black cat-eye eyeliner, and she's wearing the most fuckable red lipstick on her gorgeous full lips.

"Wow. You look incredible, Mags." I pull her into me and spin her around, unable to keep my hands off her.

A blush creeps up on her cheeks, and she looks down at her fidgeting hands. "You think so? It's not too much?" She pulls the dress away from her, bearing most of her thigh in the dress' high slit.

I bite my knuckle to suppress a groan as images of fucking Maggie until she falls apart like putty in my hands flash through my mind. The way I'd like to smear that lipstick and remove her dress piece by piece...

"I mean, I know this isn't about me, and I'd hate to be dressed too flashy–"

"You're perfect. Stop worrying about it. Anyone would consider themselves lucky to lay eyes on you tonight. Your mere presence in this dress is a blessing to all mankind." I kiss her hand, unable to tear my eyes away from her stunning face. "Dance with me?" I offer her my hand, and she takes it, rolling her eyes and laughing.

We move to the center of the dance floor and begin swaying. Maggie looks around nervously. "Sam, it's not even a slow song. We look like idiots because we're the only ones dancing," she hisses in my ear.

I just keep dancing. "Just wait," I whisper as I turn her in a spin just as the band stops mid-song and begins to play "I was born to love you" by Ray LaMontagne. "See," I croon, "Who could deny you anything when you're wearing that dress?"

She rolls her eyes again, but I see her chest swell with confidence as I lead her. Our bodies fit together like a glove and move in an easy rhythm. That's the thing about Maggie and me, everything comes so easily. It's never been like this before, and I don't expect it ever to be the same again. She is a once-in-a-lifetime kind of love, and I'm just a thief who's rapidly running out of borrowed time.

I twirl her again and end the dance with a dip, planting a kiss on her exposed neck as the audience applauds us. Then I pull her up, take in the crowd forming a circle around us, and force a smile.

Maggie grits her teeth in a fake smile, eyeing me in confusion. "What in the worl–"

"Oh, Maggie, dear, you have to meet my best friend Doris," Charlotte squeals, pulling Maggie along to show her off to her group of friends.

"Nice," Cliff, one of my dad's buddies from work, calls.

I shake his hand and exchange pleasantries, doing my best to schmooze as I watch Maggie move around the space, greeting new people with a genuine smile. It's like watching a princess work a room. She's like a magnet attracting everyone with her authentically sweet personality. It's the kind of charm that can't be faked—it only exists in the pure of heart.

"Sam Jordan, will you look at that? Came here to flaunt that perfect piece of ass..." The familiar voice makes my hair stand on end, and I turn to find Jeremy Snider, my childhood best friend. The very one who went behind my back and slept with my girlfriend for over a year.

I bite my cheek so hard I taste blood, but I force a friendly smile. "I'm glad to see some people never change. I can't say I was expecting to see you tonight, Jeremy, considering everything in our past." My words hang like venom between us.

He shoves his hands in his jacket pockets and rocks on his heels. "Oh, you know, I couldn't turn down a good party."

"Well, please enjoy the complimentary food and drinks. I

didn't realize your situation was so dire..." I pull out my wallet, shuffling hundred dollar bills, and offer him six. "This is all the cash I have, but it should help cover a couple of weeks of groceries."

His jaw tightens as he looks from the wad of cash back to my face. "I don't need your fucking money, you piece of shit. I hope you rot alone in your house surrounded by piles of it, with no one around to love you. Your girl's going to realize real quick what mistake she's made and crawl off with the first guy with half a personality." He scoffs and spits at my feet. "You think you're so much better than all of us because you're a fancy pants rich boy, but everyone knows the truth that deep down, you're just an abusive monster with no impulse control." He makes a show of looking over his shoulder and takes a sip of his drink. "They really let you come out with no supervision?" He raises his brows and blows out a sigh. "I guess if you've got the money to pay people off, then..."

"Can I have everyone's attention, please? I'd like to say a few words," my dad says over the microphone, and I jerk my head to see him standing on the stage. I clench my fists at my sides and grit my teeth.

Jeremy's just looking for another payout, and I'll be damned if I'll give him one.

"Excuse me," I say as I slam my shoulder into his and make my way toward the stage. It takes a few deep breaths before my heart falls back into a normal rhythm, but I focus on my dad until I'm calm.

"... and after all these years, I couldn't have accomplished any of those things if it weren't for the people here tonight. Not only have you kept me in business, but your friendship is something I'll cherish for as long as I live. Few men are able to live their dream lives and make a living while doing it, and I know that none of that would be possible without a little help from my friends." He holds up his glass of champagne. "Thank you for coming tonight. Now let's party!"

Everyone clinks their glasses and applauds as my dad walks off the stage and joins them on the floor, where he's pulled into hugs and people clapping him on the back in congratulations.

The bands about to break into their next song when I walk on stage, "Sorry, guys, could I just say something real quick?" I ask the lead singer, and he steps away from the mic, giving me the floor.

I take the mic off the stand and loosen my tie, which feels like a noose around my throat as the chatter in the crowd dies down.

"Good evening, everyone. I'd like to thank you again for coming tonight to shower my dad with love. He's one of the good ones, and people like that deserve to be celebrated. My whole life I've watched my father embrace each day like it was brand new. No matter what kind of pain or heartache the previous day held, he'd start each day with a fresh slate, taking it just as it was. It's an inspiring thing to behold, really. My father showed me what it meant to work hard, even when times were tough, when I didn't feel like it and when the cards were stacked against me and things felt like they could implode at any moment. He taught me how to keep my mind set on what's important in life and what really matters. I watched him build his business from the ground up, then rebuild it from the ashes and make it into something better than it was before. Any man can work hard and put in the hours, but doing it with a heart of pure gold, giving more than you take, and seeing the best in everyone you deal with... that's the special sauce they don't just pass out to everyone. And that's something worth celebrating." I raise my glass and find my dad looking up at me with tears in his eyes. "I'd like to give a toast to the best man I've ever known. May his generosity and kindness rub off on us all."

Everyone cheers and toasts, and Charlotte hugs me as I make my way off the stage. "Oh, Sam, that was lovely. Thank you for saying such kind words. I know that means a lot to your dad, especially coming from you." She kisses me on the cheek.

I glance up to see Maggie staring at me with hearts in her eyes, which is like a punch to the gut. She saunters over and wraps her hands around my neck as she sways to the music.

"I knew you were just a big old softie deep down there. You just needed something to bring it out," she teases as she pokes me in the chest.

She feels so good pressed against me, but despite my poised speech, I'm still reeling from my exchange with Jeremy. My blood boils under my skin, and I yank at my tie, desperate for air.

Maggie's eyes search my face. "What's wrong, Sam? Is everything okay?"

Memories of Jeremy and Claire wrapped in each other's arms flash through my mind like a flip-book, drawing the rage of betrayal and humiliation to the surface. My skin burns hot as I feel the last ropes of control slide out of my grip, and panic rises in my chest.

I push away from Maggie. "I just need some air..."

"But, Sam, I–"

"Don't follow me, Maggie. I just need a minute to myself," I yell over my shoulder and walk off toward the pool, away from the crowd. My inner monster unleashed and terrified...

THIRTY-ONE

Maggie

I watch Sam walk away as tears burn behind my eyes. Something happened during the time I stepped away and when he made his speech, but for the life of me, I don't know what could have upset him so badly.

My eyes search the party, but all the faces are new. It's not like I know anyone here. I want to chase after him and help him calm down, but he told me to give him space. Maybe this is my last chance to fulfill my role as his submissive?

I grab a glass of champagne from a passing tray and down it as I take in the beautiful courtyard. Tents cover food stations in a circle around a large dance floor. Groups of round tables are set off to each side in clusters, and people wander the grounds, the beautiful beach house providing quaint spaces to be alone.

I never imagined people could live like this, and it's lit a fire of something I don't recognize in my belly. Not jealousy, per se. More like recognition that I'd like this someday, too. I can't imagine anything better than having a home surrounded by friends and family who love me and come together to celebrate life's little milestones.

Birthdays, anniversaries, graduation parties. I want it all. I want a big silly dog with floppy ears to play fetch with. I want a home set apart on a little piece of land overlooking the water. I want to share my life with someone I love and grow a garden, teach yoga, and revel in life's little magical moments. I want to have the amazing, toe-curling sex that I thought only existed in romance novels. And I want to grow old with the love of my life as we enjoy everything we've built together.

I don't realize I'm crying until a hot tear falls on my hand. I rub the stray tears from my cheeks with the back of my fingers, careful not to ruin my makeup.

"You must be the infamous Maggie," a soft feminine voice says, and I spin around to see a blonde, blue-eyed woman in a bright red dress. She's beautiful in her form-fitted gown, her breasts pushed together, nearly spilling out, and her fingernails painted to match.

"Yes... I'm Maggie." I extend my hand. "And what's your name?"

"You haven't heard about me?" The woman presses her lips into a pucker. "Consider me shocked." She tosses her sandy curls over her shoulder. "I'm just the poor girl Sam tried to maul."

Her words hit me like a freight train, and I'm taken aback.

A sly smile spreads over her lips at my reaction. "So, he *does* still talk about me. It's good to know he still feels guilty." She holds her hand up underneath her eye directing me to the faint vertical scar than spans from her cheek to her eyebrow. It's so faded and covered in makeup that I don't think I would've noticed it if she hadn't pointed it out.

I open my mouth to speak, but she interrupts me

"Now, Maggie," she coos, "Don't make excuses for him.

Only someone truly horrible could do something like this to a woman. We can't make excuses for a man's behavior just because he's pretty."

"Listen, Claire, it was very nice to meet you, but I should really get going–" I gesture to the party behind me, and she grabs my wrist.

"Oh, come on, don't leave. I'm only trying to warn you about him. Whatever good you see in him, just know it's all a show. This is what he's really like. The moment he doesn't get his way–"

"You don't even know him," I spit. "Sam was just a hurt kid back then, still healing from the loss of his mother. Then you... you cheated on him, and he messed up. He's not dangerous. He's kind and tender and loyal to a fault. Even when he doesn't realize it." I jerk my hand away.

Claire's lip curls in disgust. "You're even more delusional than I thought. Well, I can't say I didn't try to warn you." She pulls away and turns to leave, then calls over her shoulder. "He didn't happen to mention that he beat up Jeremy so badly that night that he broke his jaw and had to have it wired shut, did he?"

My face falls and confusion pulls at my brows.

"I didn't think so. He always seems to conveniently leave that little detail out. But you know, we got a house out of it after the lawsuit. We got enough money to put us both through college, and he even paid for our wedding." She shrugs. "I guess it wasn't too bad of a trade-off. Well, enjoy your life laced with domestic violence and bliss. I guess the sex *is* kind of worth it..."

I cross my arms over my chest as rage boils under my skin "You have no idea what you're talking about. Sam is the kindest, most gentle person I've ever known, and you've spent your whole life playing the victim." I step in closer and narrow my eyes. "Well, you aren't fooling anyone. Sam's done everything he could to make things right, yet you're still here at his family's home... If I didn't know any better, I'd say you're desperate for attention, and it's killing you that everyone's moved on." I let out a laugh of disgust. "Sam may have made a mistake when he was eighteen, but you're still downright pathetic. But I'm sure you already know that, too."

Her mouth drops open in shock as I turn on my heel. I need to find Sam and make sure he's okay. I lift my dress and tiptoe over the cobblestone path that leads to the pool, where I find him sitting alone, staring off into the distance with his arms propped on his knees. A pile of empty beer bottles lay at his feet as he dangles one from his fingers.

"I know you said to give you space, but I need to talk to you." I sit on the chair beside him, and he huffs out a groan.

"Maggie..." he warns, but I cut him off.

"I'm in love with you, Sam. I have been for a while now. I don't know why it took me so long to admit it."

"You don't mean that–"

"Yes, Sam, I do!" I turn to face him, trying to get him to look at me but, he keeps his eyes trained on the ground.

"You think that's how you feel, but it's all an illusion." He sits up, his dark eyes laden with anger. "You think this is real? It's all bullshit. You've been sold bullshit by the best player ever to play the game." His heavy words hang in the air between us like glue, and I feel like the air's been punched from my chest.

"Where's this coming from? Why are you saying–"

"I'm saying it was just sex for me. You're confusing your feelings. You don't have anyone else to compare to, so you think this is something it's not."

I shake my head, "No, you don't mean that. I felt it. I know what I felt. Stop trying to push me away, and let me in..."

He takes a gulp of his beer, turns to face me, and speaks. "I don't know what you want from me, I'm finally being honest with you. I didn't want it to come to this, but Jesus, Mags, you just keep digging in, trying to bore yourself into me." He releases an exasperated sigh. "You asked me to help you, to give you sex lessons, and that's exactly what I did. I never promised you anything more than that. We were friends, so I took pity on you and did my best to make you feel special. Hell, you are special. I meant every word I said. But this isn't a thing. It can't be a thing, and we both know it."

"Sam, you're drunk. Let's not talk about this tonight–" I start to get up, but he reaches out and grabs my hand.

"No, I'm not drunk, not yet anyway, but this is exactly the time to talk about it." He pulls out his phone, and we watch as 11:59 turns to midnight. "See, times up. The contract's come to an end and so have our lessons. You're a free woman, Maggie. Free to fuck whomever you please now."

"Sam, stop saying that. You know you're the only one I want to be with. Why are you doing this?"

"I lied to you," he whispers. "I told you that I threw the rock impulsively, and I never meant to hurt anyone, and while that's mostly true... I didn't tell you that I broke the window with my fist and pulled Jeremy through it and beat him until my arms went numb and Claire's dad had to pull me off of him." He turns and looks at me, his eyes full of pain and torment.

I shake my head as hot tears spill down my cheeks. "Sam, I–"

"See, I am a monster. I've been trying to tell you all this time. Do you finally believe me now?" He opens a fresh beer from his pile and tosses the aluminum lid. The sound of it clinking on the concrete rings in my ears.

"You don't scare me, Sam. You may have convinced yourself of that, but I've seen too much. I know you, and I know you're the furthest thing from evil. Let's go inside and drink some water. We can talk more when you calm down." I grab for his hand, but he jerks it away.

"Would you please just stop fighting me? I don't want to hurt you," he growls. "I'm trying to tell you this is over. I fulfilled the contract, and I wish you and Trent all the best. Trust me, he's a far better match for you than me."

"Is that what this is about? Trent? Because I don't–"

"Hasn't that been the plan all along? Don't you want to see for yourself? Give him a shot? Trust me, Mags, there's a big world out there full of guys who can give you what you deserve. I'm just not one of them. I'm sorry you thought I could be."

"You're just scared, Sam. You think you're so mysterious, but I can see right through you, and I have never been more disappointed in someone in all my life." I shake my head and wrap my arms around myself. "I'm not going to stand here and beg for you. If you're so determined to be miserable, then who am I to stop you? Maybe I am too good for you after all..."

"Simon can take you to Bramville tonight. Your bags are already loaded in the car."

I let out a scoff. "So, you planned this in advance? Nice work. Well, consider me gone. You won't have to worry about me inconveniencing you anymore."

His jaw ticks, but he doesn't speak, just stares down at his feet.

"Goodbye, Sam. Thanks for the sex lessons. I can't wait to show Trent all the new skills you taught me." I stomp off toward the house to find Simon, my heart cracking more and more with each step. When I reach the bottom of the steps I double over and let out a sob.

The sound of glass beer bottles crashing against the concrete echoes through the night like a soundtrack for my broken heart.

THIRTY-TWO

Maggie

I stare out the car window as the bright city lights disappear in the darkness, another town between us. The distance feels heavy and suffocating like a thick wool sweater that's been shrunk in the dryer.

I'm furious with Sam, but more than anything, I'm disappointed in myself. How could I have gotten so caught up when not falling in love was literally his most important rule? If I didn't know any better, I'd think I did it on purpose to torture myself. Hell, maybe I did. Maybe I wanted to see just how bad it could get. I guess now I know.

"There's heated seats if you want them." Simon presses the button on the front of the dash twice, showing me how to adjust them to my comfort.

"Thanks." I set it on high, not because I'm cold, but because my muscles are still sore from having sex on the beach. A cruel reminder of the most intense pleasure I've ever experienced, only to have it ripped away. I hope Sam's ass is chafed from the sand, at least.

"I'm, uh, I'm sorry about my brother." Simon's voice pulls me back to the present. "He's an idiot. I promise you he's going to regret it."

"Thanks." I give him a slight nod. It's awkward having your ex-dominant/friend's brother, who you only met a few days ago, drive you two hours to a hotel in the middle of the night, but at least he's giving me space. I guess I'm glad it was Simon and not Drew or Jamie. Who knows how those two would try to resolve the situation? A smirk pulls at my lips as I try to imagine it.

As sad as I am about everything, I'm so happy I met Sam's family. It was fun to pretend that I belonged among them for a little while anyway. It gives me hope for the future—hope that I can find something similar with someone who actually shares my feelings. Who knows? Maybe I'm driving toward that person right now. Isn't that what all this was about anyway? What if Sam was just the frog I needed to kiss before I met my true prince charming?

I roll my eyes at the thought. There's no way in any universe Sam Jordan could be considered a frog. A devil, perhaps? That seems more likely. The one who makes you trade for everything you've ever wanted in exchange for your soul. Only for you to realize you wanted the wrong thing, but by then, it's too late.

All of this is my fault, and now, I've lost one of my best friends in the entire world because I was too naïve, too weak, and too inexperienced to know that some people are just good at sex and it doesn't have to mean anything else. Falling for the first man to give me an orgasm makes me no better than I was at seventeen when I slept with the first guy who gave me attention. This whole time, I thought I'd matured, I thought Sam unlocked something inside me, but maybe it was just him? Maybe I really am broken.

I think back to how I felt on stage last night, singing in public for the very first time and letting myself soak up the rush of it all. There's no way I would've even considered getting up there before Sam. I've never felt so confident in my skin. The way we skinny-dipped and fucked on the beach—in public. It's like my body's been possessed by aliens but in the best way.

I dig my nails into the palms of my hands. I will not let myself go down that spiral and question how I got here. Sam may have hurt me, but I will forever be grateful for what he gave me, and if that's the trade I've made for a bruised ego and broken heart, I'll just have to be okay with that.

I hold my head a little higher as I stare at the bright full moon in the night sky. *No matter what life throws at me, the moon will always be there to ground me back to the present.*

I open my text messages and stare down at the last message Trent sent me shortly after midnight.

TRENT

I can't wait to see you today. I have to get there early to make sure things are set up, so if you don't mind, I'll swing by to pick you up around four o'clock.

I heart his message and send him a thumbs-up emoji. I'm just about to send him the address to my hotel when I look up to see Simon pulling underneath the overhang to a fancy hotel.

"Um, Simon... I don't think this is right." I crank my neck, trying to read the name of the hotel, but the awning is blocking my view. "I'm supposed to be at the Holiday Inn on Central." I pull out my phone to double-check my confirmation email and show him the screen.

He puts the car in park and sighs. "About that... Sam may have upgraded your reservation to Bramville Gardens." He opens his door and starts unloading my bags from the trunk as I sit there, annoyance brewing underneath my skin.

Simon opens my door and offers his hand to help me out. "I told him it's kind of fucked up to change someone's hotel accommodations after you break up with them... or whatever it was between you two–"

"He told you about our arrangement?" I blurt before he can finish his sentence.

Simon gives me a knowing grin. "It wasn't hard to put together. I know my brother's fucked up view on relationships, and you seemed way too *innocent* for him." He takes my purse off my shoulder and places it on top of my suitcase. "You're too good for him. He knows it. I know it. I certainly hope by now you know it."

He clicks his key fob, locking his car, then turns to head inside. I scramble after him, hanging on to each word like Simon's about to reveal some deep dark secret to help me understand Sam's psyche. "I do think he was different with you. You pulled out a piece of him that I haven't seen in a really long time." He pauses as we wait for the motion sensor doors to open, and then we step into the luxurious lobby. "Don't beat yourself up over this. Sam's a complicated guy, and sometimes I don't even think he's in control of his actions."

I follow Simon to the front desk, where he hands over Sam's credit card and checks me into the room.

"Welcome, Ms. Anderson," the receptionist says. You'll be staying upstairs in the penthouse suite. It's located on the twentieth floor. You'll need your key card to use the elevator. We have room service available with an award-winning restaurant from eight o'clock to midnight every day. I see you'll be staying with us for a full week. Please let me know if you need anything." She passes me the key card, and I look to Simon for clarification.

He leans in and whispers, "He had a work trip come up and didn't want you to be out of a place to stay. Your studio and apartment will be ready in a week. I'll send you the confirmation for your flight next Sunday."

I roll my eyes as I take the key card and thank the front desk attendant. "A work trip just came up? How incredibly convenient."

Simon shrugs. "Hey, his credit card is on the room. I say you take out your annoyance and live it up this week. Rack up that room service bill and enjoy your free vacation on his dime."

"Oh, believe me, I plan on doing just that." As I push the button to the elevator, Simon hands me my suitcase.

"It was very nice to meet you, Maggie. On behalf of the entire Jordan family, please don't judge us because of our dimwitted brother."

I hug Simon. "Thank you for driving me. Sam's lucky to have a brother who'll tell him like it is. Don't be too hard on him, okay? And tell Wren and Charlotte goodbye for me. Your family is lovely."

I step onto the glass elevator and stare down as the lobby below disappears, and before I know it, I'm kicking off my shoes in the fanciest suite I've ever laid eyes on. Downtown Bramville may not be much, but it's got its charm.

A huge glass window spans from the ceiling to the floor, taking up an entire wall. There's a bottle of champagne on ice with two glass flutes and a note sitting on a small table in the quaint seating area.

I pick up the note and read:

I'm sorry, Magnolia. You deserve so much better.

-Sam

It may be three in the morning, but I open the champagne anyway and pour myself a glass as I take in the extravagant room I get to call home for the next week.

Maybe I'll bring Trent up here tomorrow night and sleep with him in the bed Sam's paying for? Order some chocolate-covered strawberries? The friend in me is appalled at the thought, but my broken heart wants to make him hurt like he hurt me.

I'm at war with my emotions, but as the bubbly liquid coats my tongue, I realize I'm tired of always putting others' feelings before mine. For the very first time in my life, I want to be selfish with my emotions and let my inner fire run ablaze rather than putting it out at the first sign of smoke.

I drain my glass and pour myself another as I make my way to the bathroom and fill the large bathtub for a bubble bath.

I know one thing for sure, Sam taught me how to recognize my desires, and now that I know what I like, it's easy to see the things that I don't. As hurt as I am, I'm also angry as hell that I didn't see it coming. I'm now comfortable enough with myself to know my worth, and maybe that was the biggest lesson I got out of it. I'll never let a man make me feel like I'm anything less ever again.

I strip off my clothes and step into the hot bubbly water. Sinking slowly as the hot suds cling to my skin and the ache in my muscles relax, I stare up at the intricate copper tiles on the ceiling as my glass of champagne glass dangles from my fingers over the side of the tub.

I may be heartbroken and hurting, but it's lit a spark inside me that wasn't there before. It feels a lot like selfishness. And it feels pretty damn amazing.

I drain the last of my champagne and sink down lower as I use my newfound skill set to bring myself to orgasm. I don't think about anyone but myself the whole time.

This new Maggie is going to have so much fun...

THIRTY-THREE

Sam

Some moments in life hit a little harder than others, the kind of moments that stick around and cling in your memory whether you want them to or not. They alter your sense of self and remind you that everything happens in contrast–the good, the bad, the ugly, and everything in between. If you're lucky, the memories will feel like a warm blanket and a hot drink on a cold day, but if you're like me, it's more like the sting of a paper cut you didn't realize you had.

That's how my heart feels right now. Like it's covered in paper cuts, some of them so tiny you don't even notice they are there until someone comes along and submerges it in lime juice, and it burns everywhere, and you don't know how to make it stop.

My head hits the back of the seat with a thud as my dad's truck turns onto the road leading to the small regional airport.

"I hate that your visit is ending on such a sour note, son. I really do." My dad's concerned eyes shift to me, and I do my best to look casual.

"I know, Dad, but this opportunity came up, and I've been on a waitlist for over a year. I want to do this, and they're counting on me." It's a lie, but he doesn't need to know any details.

I'm heading to Africa for three months to help dig wells for a nonprofit. There normally is a waitlist since the organization can only staff ten people at a time, but since I'm one of the investors, I can pretty much decide when I want to go. I've been meaning to sign up for a shift, but disappearing for three months with no cell service hasn't been feasible for me in the past. Now, it sounds like exactly what I need to do to give Maggie some space to fall in love with her new beau and for me to lick my wounds and attempt to get over her.

I know there's no reality where I'm ever really over her. Hell, I hope the memories we created haunt me for the rest of my life, but I would like to have a semblance of self-control if I have to be near her. It killed me to send her away last night. It felt like my bones were splitting in two, but I knew every second she was near me would make the end that much more painful.

She deserves so much more than I can give her, and I hope she realizes that. I hope one day I can be in a room with her and not feel as if my heart could explode, but I know that kind of healing will only happen if I give myself time and space.

So, I'm heading to Africa to put all my frustration toward a good cause. To put my muscles to use and dig wells until I'm so utterly exhausted that all I can do is sleep. Then I'll wake up and do it all over again. Hopefully, three months will put a dent in my healing process, but if by the end of this, I'm still unsure, I guess I'll just have to sign up for another group. I'll do it again and again as long as it takes for me to feel like I'm back in control.

My dad pulls the truck into the drop-off area and hugs me. "You promised Charlotte you'd be home for Christmas this year, and we're going to hold you to it. I want to see you more, and if that means we have to take the RV up to Chicago, you know we'll do it." My dad pats me on the back before pulling away, and I have to fight back the tears that burn behind my eyes. What's happening to me? I never get emotional telling my family goodbye.

"Thanks for everything, Dad. Tell Charlotte thanks for me. I love you, and I'll see you for Christmas. I promise."

I step out and watch my dad's truck disappear into the distance.

My phone buzzes in my pocket, and I answer the call, wedging it between my face and shoulder.

"Is this email serious?" Benjamin says.

"As a heart attack." I print my boarding pass at the kiosk, shove it in my pocket, then make my way to the security line.

"So, I take it things with Mags didn't end well? What the fuck happened, man? Last time I saw you, you had actual hearts in your eyes."

"Nothing happened." I throw my bag on the conveyer belt and slide my shoes off. "Hang on just a sec..." I lay my phone down in the bucket, walk through the metal detector, and pick it back up. "We had an agreement, and it ended. It's nothing more or less than that." I slide my shoes back on and grab my suitcase.

"You're so full of shit, and you know it. Sam, you're really trying to convince me—and yourself—that you weren't falling for her. What am I supposed to tell Elliot? What's going to happen when we celebrate something and want you both to be there?"

With a sigh, I collapse into a seat, my eyes trained on the flight schedule across from me. "Listen, I'm not saying it won't be weird at first, but that's why I'm leaving. I'm giving her space, and when I come back, it'll be like nothing ever happened. I promise I'm not going to fuck up the group–"

"You're just going to disappear for three months and come back and pretend like nothing happened? That's seriously your *adult* plan, Sam?" He emphasizes adult as he scolds me.

"It's the best I can do," I snap.

"Well, I hope you know what you're doing. And I hope this isn't the beginning of you disappearing on us for good." Benjamin lowers his voice to nearly a whisper. "You can't run from this, Sam. Not really. You know how well that worked out for you last time..."

"Yeah, well, I don't really have a ton of options, now, do I? Will you just keep an eye on things? Call and check in with Joey and triple check everyone will be out of there by Sunday? And make sure he sends the bill to my assistant?"

Benjamin sighs. "Yeah, man, I'll look out for her."

"Good. I'll try to email and check in when I can, but I don't expect to have much cell service the whole time. Tell Jack I'm sorry I'll miss the baby's birth, but I'll send a good enough gift to make up for it."

"We're now boarding flight 408 to Denver. Passengers flying first class may begin boarding the aircraft," the flight attendant announces over the speaker.

"I've got to go. My flight's boarding. I'll see you after Christmas." I stand and make my way to board the plane.

"Alright, man, I'll see you then." Benjamin sighs. "Oh, and Sam..."

The flight attendant scans my boarding pass with a beep. "Yeah?"

"You're a dumbass and a coward for running away, but I feel like you're going to realize that soon enough. Take care of yourself. We're going to miss you."

I laugh at Benjamin's frank words. "I'm going to miss you

guys, too. See you around." I slide my phone into my pocket as I board the plane and take my seat in my first-class suite. I scratch my fingers along the smooth leather armrest as the memories of initiating Maggie into the mile-high club come flooding back.

I squeeze my eyes shut to ward them off as the pain in my heart burns like acid.

"Sir, could I get you something to drink?" a flight attendant asks and my eyes spring open.

"Whiskey, please. And keep 'em coming."

THIRTY-FOUR

Maggie

I smooth down my dress and stare at my reflection. I'm wearing a one-strap hot pink fitted sheath dress and patent leather white booties. It's a far cry from my usual comfortable wardrobe, but I felt like celebrating myself tonight, and I wanted a dress that embodied the same energy.

So, this morning, after a good five hours of sleep, I pulled myself out of bed, treated myself to brunch, and went shopping.

I yank the price tag off the dress and try not to squirm as I look at it. The new Maggie splurges on herself from time to time, and this is a part of that. Besides, I wanted to wear a dress that was my own. I didn't want to put on anything that Sam helped me pick out or paid for.

The bright pink bow on the back of the dress sticks out on each side and makes the teenage version of me so happy. I decided that since I'm going to my high school reunion, I might as well dress up for my inner teenager who never got to experience having cute clothes, much less fancy dresses.

My whole life I've just taken everyone's leftovers, completely grateful for the scraps of what was left, never asking for more because I didn't want to seem ungrateful. I've realized that people only see you as worthy when you value yourself first. By being so agreeable all the time, I've made it easy for people to take advantage of me. Not only have I made it easy for them, I've taught them to treat me as less than. All because I didn't value myself.

Not anymore.

Tonight, I'm going to walk into that reunion as the new me, and this is only the beginning.

I spin around, loving the way my long orange hair contrasts against the magenta fabric. It's a color combination I've always been warned away from, but my inner teenager is squealing from the excitement that I'm finally dressing her in her favorite color.

My phone buzzes on the wooden side table with a text from Trent.

TRENT

Hey gorgeous. I'm downstairs waiting when you're ready. No rush though.

I apply my bright pink lipstick and make sure I don't get any on my teeth before throwing my purse over my shoulder. It's go time.

Be right down.

I hit send just as I step into the elevator. A swarm of butterflies erupts in my belly as the the elevator carries me twenty stories down. My stomach tickles, and it reminds me of the ride at the amusement park where I screamed the whole way down. Sam couldn't stop laughing at me when I ran out of breath and started up again and again.

Suddenly, the butterflies feel more like trapped gas.

As I step out into the lobby, I push the sick feeling down, and a genuine smile breaks across my face when I see Trent holding a bouquet of lilies.

"I can't believe this is finally happening." He rushes toward me and pulls me into a hug, smoothing my hair down as he pulls away and studies my face. "Maggie, you look... incredible."

His grin is huge, and his blue eyes soak me in.

Trent's only a couple of inches taller than me with heels. I notice the height difference immediately because his eyes seem so much closer. I can feel him staring at me, and it feels so... intense.

"Thank you." I take the flowers from him and follow him to his car, idling under the overhang.

Trent walks around the driver's side and climbs in, and I stand there like an idiot before he rolls down my window and calls, "You coming or what?"

I shake my head, open the door, and climb in, feeling like an idiot. Not every man is so pretentious about opening doors for women like Sam. I think I've spent a little too much time with him, and I must've forgotten.

"We've got to get moving. This hotel was way farther out of the way than I realized." Trent puts the car in gear and takes off in a rush. I flinch when he pulls out in front of a car and lays on the gas.

"You really look incredible. That dress looks like something a model would wear." He holds out his hand with his palm up, and I eye it before placing my hand in his. His palms are clammy and soft, unlike Sam's strong, calloused hands.

"I can't wait to walk in with you on my arm." Trent whistles. "Palmer and Malone are going to shit themselves when they see you." The mention of his best friends sparks a memory of the three of them throwing balls of paper around the classroom every time our teacher turned her back. They were always so mischievous, but somehow managed never to get caught...

"I've got the catering company scheduled to arrive in ten minutes, but we'll be lucky if we can beat them."

I glance at the GPS that says our ETA is in twenty minutes just as Trent turns on the freeway and hits the gas, weaving between lanes and passing cars on both sides.

I tense and try to calm my breathing as my heart races. I feel completely out of control and have a twinge of guilt that I made us late. Trent passes the last car in front of him, and though he doesn't slow down, I let myself relax for a moment.

I take the opportunity to study him, his blond hair cut short, a receding hairline. He's filled out a lot since high school. All of his sharp edges softened with age. He's still handsome but in a responsible adult kind of way. He looks like he keeps his finances in order and knows what a Roth IRA is. Not that Sam doesn't... I guess it just isn't the first descriptor that comes to mind when you look at him. His sexy forearms, chiseled jaw, and those deep brown eyes that look at you like he could swallow you whole... Those are the features that stand out when you see Sam.

I shake my head, pushing away his image.

It's not a bad thing that Trent is so different than Sam. If anything, it's good. Trent doesn't play games. Trent doesn't come with contracts, rules, and agreements. Trent is easy.

"This feels so natural, doesn't it?" Trent tightens his grip and kisses the back of my hand.

I glance at the speedometer and try not to panic when I see we're nearly going ninety. I force myself to smile through the anxiety. "Yeah, it feels good."

"You know, I have that picture of your boobs set as my phone's background." He waggles his eyebrows suggestively.

I don't know if that means he thinks he's going to get to meet my boobs in person tonight or if he's just being flirty. Either way, I don't know what to say, so I just laugh.

I cross my ankles and turn toward him in my seat, suddenly aware of my tense body language, and smile as a pop punk song plays on the radio.

Almost instantly, Trent changes the channel to a country station. "I hate that emo stuff. Those guys are all whiney, and all the songs sound the same."

I deflate a little because it's not that I don't like country, too, but just another reminder of how different Trent is from Sam. That was one of Sam's favorites, and he would've turned up the volume.

I have to stop comparing them because it isn't fair to anyone to be compared to Sam. He's not even real. Nothing we had was real, so it's a losing battle to hold anyone to a standard not even Sam could meet.

I urge myself to relax as I sing along to the song, harmonizing with the female vocalist during the chorus.

"You sound great, Maggie. I didn't know you could sing," Trent says, impressed.

I pick at my fingernails with my free hand. "I love singing. I just never let myself do it in front of anyone until recently."

"Well, I'm glad you decided to start." Trent smiles and kisses my hand again before weaving through another line of vehicles.

I hold my breath and squeeze my eyes shut, my whole body tight with fear. Hopefully, the ride home won't be quite so *intense*...

"Are you shitting me right now? You're telling me this bombshell on your arm is Gaggy Maggie!" Alison Davis wolf whistles with her fingers and claps her hands. She's drunk out of her mind. Everyone is, actually. Since I'm Trent's date, I've had the privilege of sitting with Bramville High's cool kids. It's something I would've killed to do in high school, but as I look around at everyone reminiscing about the good old days, I realize they don't really have anything new to brag about. It seems like all their accomplishments happened during their glory days.

Gaggy Maggie. I almost forgot all about that little nickname... I blocked out a lot of my childhood memories after moving away because it was easier to start fresh than dwell in the past. But leave it to Alison to reopen that wound.

I force a smile and curtsey before taking my seat in the plastic folding chair. It may not be the best delivery, but I realize she's giving me a compliment, so I choose to focus on that rather than letting myself get upset. Trent and I are the only sober ones sitting at the two round tables that the guys pulled together.

The drinks are flowing, and everyone seems to be having a great time catching up, but if I have to hear one more recount of the football team's game-winning hail mary or the senior pranks they pulled, I may actually injure my eyeballs from rolling them so hard.

It's not that I'm not having fun. I am. I'm just tired from not getting enough sleep last night and the physical exertion of setting up all the tables and chairs in the gym.

We planned to have the reunion in a hotel conference room —I even set it up. But after Sam instructed me to stop helping so much, things sort of fell apart at the seams. Trent paid a DJ and booked a mobile bar to provide free booze, not realizing he went over budget. One expense led to another, and he decided to move the reunion to the high school gym and do the setup himself.

Translation: I carried over three hundred chairs across the gymnasium by myself when we got here because Trent needed to make a phone call to check on the catering.

I may be a teeny bit bitter as I look around at all the ex-football players bragging about their bench press records while my arms and upper back ache from the manual labor, but it's not like they had any control over it. It's just one of those things that happen. I'm happy I was here to help because this whole gathering would've been a nightmare if I hadn't been there.

Trent moves behind me, massaging my shoulders with a pinching motion and yanking a strand of my hair. I wince as he digs a finger into my shoulder bone, which he then pushes harder because he thinks my reaction was one of pleasure or relief.

I feel a little disappointed as I look around the space. I don't know what I expected exactly, it's not like I has a ton of friends in high school anyway, but everything seems to be falling flat. I haven't genuinely laughed once, and even though I'm sitting at the most lively table in the whole place, I can't help but feel like the lonely teenager I was all those years ago.

I'm starting to wonder why I wanted to come to begin with...

Originally, I wanted to come back to this space and create new memories to replace the old ones because I've changed so much since high school. I thought if they could just see the adult Maggie, who owns her own business and makes enough money to buy herself nice clothes and a decent haircut, then they'd accept me as one of them. But I still feel like an outsider.

"So, how about you, Maggie? I know you're with this loser tonight, but do you have any kids yet? An ex-husband or two?" Malone, one of Trent's best friends, asks, and the conversation dies as everyone looks at me.

I swallow a gulp, suddenly nervous about being put on the spot. "Well, no. I don't have any kids or ex-husbands... I do own my own yoga studio back in Chicago, though. That takes up most of my time." I press my lips together, hoping I said enough but didn't ramble on too much about myself.

"That's so strange you haven't been married at least once by now," Alison giggles and whispers loudly behind her hand. "Maybe she is still Gaggy Maggie..." She pretends to stick her finger down her throat and laughs.

My shoulders stiffen, and I shift in my seat but don't respond.

"You two look great together," one of the other ex-cheerleaders chimes in. "How long have you been an item?"

I look over my shoulder and meet Trent's gaze, and he startles. "Oh, um, not long... I don't really know that we're officially an item. Just trying things on to see how it goes." He shoves his hands in his pockets and rocks on his heels.

If I didn't know any better, I'd think he was more nervous than me... which is weird since he's always been the confident, attention-seeking football star. Maybe he's embarrassed about his divorce? Samantha didn't show up tonight, which was surprising, but since they shared a friend group, I guess there was only room for one of them. Since Trent planned the reunion, I suppose it was an easy decision.

"Right. Well, here's to finding the perfect fit!" Alison holds up her wine and everyone clinks their glasses together.

I bite my lip and try to ignore the suggestive innuendo. Is that what Trent's thinking about tonight, too?

"Excuse me, I've got to make my speech. Then I can officially check off my presidential to-do list for the evening, and we can really get this party started." Trent slaps his hands on the table and runs up to the stage.

He taps the microphone a few times and clears his throat.

"Thank you all so much for coming tonight. It's great to see some new faces around here." He points at one of the cheerleaders, "I'm talking about you, Melanie!"

Everyone at her table erupts with laughter, and she flips him off as she chugs the rest of her wine.

"I'm kidding. You look great. Listen, it was a lot of work planning this event. I don't know what I was thinking when I ran for student council president, but it all managed to work out in the end. Like many of you, my last ten years were filled with lots of growing pains with plenty of happy memories mixed in. The older I get, the more I realize you've got to hold on to the good times and treasure all the little moments you can get because you never know when you'll hit your next speed bump and be thrown from the vehicle." Trent laughs and shrugs at the mention of the inside joke about him flying out of the back of a pickup truck during an outdoor pep rally. One of our classes' funnier memories that year.

"Anyway, none of this would've been possible if I didn't have the beautiful Magnolia Anderson helping me out. Gaggy Maggy as most of you know her."

My smile falls, and I purse my lips in annoyance as everyone laughs. I don't even remember how the nickname started, just that it plagued me... and apparently still does.

"Stand up and take a bow, Maggie. Seriously, guys, you should see her glow up." Trent claps his hands, and everyone joins in to shower me with applause. I grit my teeth and stand as I wave, then quickly sit back down. My skin burns bright red, and I wish I could crawl under the table and hide. I'm mortified, and I can't help but wonder how I was so okay with it the other night, but now I just feel like an insecure child all over again.

"Okay, I've kept you all long enough. Let's have fun tonight and make some great memories, so when we all come back here in another ten years, we have some new stories to tell!" Trent holds up his drink. "Cheers everybody!"

He runs off the stage, practically jumps in his seat, and wraps his arm around me. "Now that that's over, how about we let loose?"

One hour later, I tighten my hands on the fabric of Trent's shirt as he leads our group, plus a few other tables, in a conga line around the gym. I don't think he's drunk...yet... but he's certainly reverted to the charismatic version of himself that I remember.

Everyone seems to be having a blast, and I have to admit, Trent knows how to throw a good party. We just ran out of alcohol, so I'm grateful that the party should be dying down soonish...

I wince as Malone grips my waist behind me, sending a warm gust of drunken breath over my shoulder every now and again as we dance around the gym. This *should* be fun. I should be able to let loose and enjoy myself. But it feels like I keep noticing everything that irritates me... like Malone's sour beer breath or how Trent's managed to step on my toes at least five times with the heel of his shoe or the fact that we ran out of food within the first hour because Trent didn't order enough...

Why am I so determined to be in a bad mood? Why can't I just let myself relax and enjoy this party?

I think back to Kyle's words when after I slept with him. *"You're just bland, Maggie. You just laid there like a plank of wood. I just don't have any physical connection with you..."*

Maybe he was right. Am I just a bland person who doesn't know how to have fun? I'm in a conga line surrounded by drunken idiots who seem to be enjoying themselves. Why can't

I turn off my bitch switch and just enjoy myself? How was it that Sam was able to get me to relax?

My heart aches at the thought of Sam, and I have to fight to hold back tears. He hurt me so badly, but I still miss him. I miss how he took control and how I felt so safe when I was with him. I didn't realize what a relief his dominance provided—in more ways than sexually. Because I trusted him so fully, I was actually able to let myself loose and experience true pleasure.

I realize now that I'll never have that feeling again, so I'm just going to have to try to be that for myself. I bite my lip as I consider what Sam would tell me to do right now.

He'd probably be upset that I was surrounded by so many drunk people, and he'd be worried about my safety. Just then, Malone slides his thumbs over my hips, making my skin crawl. Sam would be furious I was letting someone touch me that made me feel uncomfortable...

And just like that, I step out of the conga line. Malone doesn't miss a beat as he grabs Trent by the waist and continues dancing. I grab a bottle of water from the ice chest and drink half of it then start cleaning up the food the best I can, more to keep myself busy than anything else, as the party begins to die down.

I was right. Once everyone ran out of booze, they began sobering up and taking their parties elsewhere. Trent's nearly sober now as he waves the last group of his friends goodbye. He wraps his arm around me and kisses me on the head. "We did it! We fucking did it!" He grabs the trash out of my hand and throws it back on the table. "Don't worry about cleaning up. I've got a community service group coming in the morning." Trent twirls his keys around his finger. "Come on. Let's get out of here."

"Yeah, okay. Let's go," I agree.

THIRTY-FIVE

Maggie

I convinced Trent to let me drive back to the hotel, and he was hesitant at first, but I think he knew it was the only hope of him having any chance with me tonight, so he finally relented. He was probably okay to drive, but after the drive over, I wasn't going to take any chances.

"Wow, this is incredible," Trent says as he steps into the suite. "I guess yoga studios are more profitable than I realized. You must really be doing well for yourself." He sits on the sofa and rubs the cushion next to him.

I kick off my shoes and remove my earrings, placing them in a glass bowl by the sink. I don't want to tell him about Sam, but I don't want to lie to him and say that I paid for this outlandish suite either. If this does turn into something, he'll eventually find out that hotel rooms like this are not in my price range. I decide to go with a half-truth. "This is actually a gift from a close friend of mine. He knew I needed somewhere to stay for the week because my apartment and yoga studio are under construction, so he offered me this. He's pretty rich, so it's not really a big deal."

I smile as I sit down beside him, unsure of what to do with my arms. I try to lean one on the couch's arm, but it's too low, and the back of the sofa is too high to feel natural. I finally just cross them in my lap. Great, now I look like a debutante sitting pretty at a ball, not sexy at all...

"That's cool. I wish I had rich friends to buy me stuff." Trent laughs as he props his feet on the coffee table, making himself at home.

The gesture irritates me. How does he feel so comfortable right now? Meanwhile, I can't even figure out what to do with my hands?

"I couldn't help but notice Samantha wasn't at the reunion." I blurt out the first thing that comes to mind. As soon as I hear the words, my stomach recoils in embarrassment, but Trent doesn't seem to be bothered.

"Yeah, she's been traveling a good bit since the divorce. I guess she's doing all the things she wanted to do before she settled down. She met someone, I think. I guess she was too good for me after all." He scoots closer and brushes his thumb over my cheek, and my shoulders tense for a moment before I force myself to relax.

"That must be hard to end such a long relationship. I'm sorry you've had to deal with that."

Trent shrugs. "It's fine. I mean, what are you going to do? It's annoying when two people agree to something, and someone decides they want something different, but all I can control is me, you know? She's the one who changed the rules on me. I held up my end of the bargain."

I feel a rush of defensiveness wash over me at his words, and even though I realize he's talking about his situation, I can't help but compare what he said to my own. "Yeah, but don't you think you should be flexible and reevaluate your goals together rather than sticking to rules you made when you were eighteen?" My tone is sharp, and Trent jumps in surprise.

His eyebrows knit together, and he rubs his hand over my knee. "Wedding vows aren't exactly rules. We both knew what we were signing up for when we said, 'I do.' Sometimes people realize they want different things, and they're better off alone–"

"Or they could have a conversation and be open to hearing alternatives and create a new plan that works for both of them. Things don't always have to be black and white all the time. You never know. Things could work out better than you ever imagined if you're open-minded..." My voice trails off, and I wipe a fallen tear with the back of my hand.

"I'm sorry, Maggie. I don't know what you're saying. Are you trying to convince me to get back together with Samantha? Because we're both happier now and–"

"No, I'm sorry, Trent." I shake my head. "I was out of line. Forget I said anything. I'm obviously not the relationship expert, now, am I?"

His eyes narrow as he studies me, glancing down at my lips. "Maggie, would it be okay if I kissed you?"

I suck in a breath and nod, ignoring how my stomach twists into a knot as Trent leans in. His wet lips brush against mine, and I have to fight the urge to wipe the excess spit from my mouth. He opens his mouth and drives in his tongue, then pulls it out, licking my lips before pressing his mouth back to mine.

My eyes fly open in shock as I try to settle into the kiss and kiss him back, soft and slow. If he notices our differing kissing strategies, he doesn't show it because he just shoves his tongue in my mouth again and makes the licking motion repeatedly, no matter how much I try to show him what I like.

Then he's on top of me, hands pulling at my dress as he pushes himself closer and closer. My head sinks into the side of the couch arm as I realize I've backed away from him as far as I can. Now, we're both laying down on the couch... or he's lying on top of me rather.

Trent slides his clammy palms up my leg as he grinds his hard length into me, reading my squirming as desire.

"Trent–" I try to speak, but he sucks my tongue and moans in pleasure at the sound of his name.

His hands feel wrong, and everything tonight feels wrong, but I still want to wash myself of Sam's touch and replace it. I want to make a new memory around sex, so I can get over him and move on with my life. If that means I need to be patient with Trent, then that's what I'll do.

I hook my leg around his waist and spin myself so that I'm on top of him, finally able to breathe. "Whoa, you really know what you're doing." He waggles his eyebrows, and I inwardly cringe, but I'm committed, so I kiss him slowly and finally give up after he licks me again. I'm just going to have to take what I want. I don't need all the foreplay and dirty talk. I just need to close my eyes and focus.

I push myself up and try to unzip my dress, but my hands can't reach the zipper, so I unbuckle his belt and start removing his pants. Trent lets out an excited giggle, and I feel my vagina dry up as repulsion rips through me. I stare at his average-sized penis, and time seems to come to a standstill. The reality of the moment hits me like a tidal wave, and I crawl off him, unable to tear my gaze away.

There's nothing wrong with him, but it just feels wrong. That's not my dick. I don't want to put it in my mouth. I don't even want to touch it. I want nothing more than to wrap it back up and send it on its way with a polite yet firm goodbye.

"You okay?" Trent asks, staring at me with confusion as I realize I'm still staring at his dick in terror like it's an intruder in my home.

I shake my head and smooth down my dress. "Yeah. I'm fine." My eyes meet his, and I hate that I can't follow through with it. "I'm so sorry, Trent. I can't do this." I climb off the sofa and cross my arms over my chest, looking down at my feet to give him some privacy to adjust his clothing. "I thought I could do it, but I'm not ready." I look up for a moment to see him zipping his pants. "It's not you. I'm in love with someone else, and I'm not ready..." I let out a sigh as I admit, "I don't know that I'll ever be ready."

When I look up again, Trent's fully clothed, and his cheeks are pink with embarrassment. I feel awful, but I won't sleep with him just because he wants to. That's the old Maggie.

"It's... uh... it's fine, Maggie. Really." Trent shoves his hands in his pocket and walks toward the door. "You know, I... never mind. It's your loss." He picks up his keys and gives me an awkward salute. "For the record, the guys and I had a bet that one of us could hook up with you at the reunion. I guess I'll have to tell Malone he won." He shakes his head, and my jaw drops at his confession.

"I guess the rumors were true. Gaggy Maggy is as bland as white toast. Nice tits, though." The door clinks closed, and I stand there in shocked silence.

I want to be mad. I want to chase after him and stab him with the heel of my shoe... but all I can do is laugh. I shake my head and laugh as tears fall down my cheeks because that was the last thing I ever expected after everything that's happened over the last month. I realize his words don't hurt me because I don't agree with him. Trent can take his mediocre penis and Supercuts haircut back to his high school buddies and tell them anything he wants about me because if anyone in this scenario is bland, it's him.

I fall back on my cozy bed and playback the memories of the worst date of my life and laugh at his audacity to say *I'm* bland.

It's strange to realize you've changed, that you respond to things differently than you used to. It's like I'm looking at myself from the outside, finally seeing the bigger picture. I will never let a man—or anyone for that matter—make me believe I'm anything less than amazing ever again.

With six more days in this suite, I fully intend to make the most of it.

I roll over and pick up the phone. "Hi, would you mind sending up an order of the street tacos, chips and queso, and a large Pepsi? Oh, and what do you have for dessert?"

THIRTY-SIX

Sam

Three months later ...

I collapse into my seat as I try to adjust to the rushed business of the airport during the holiday season. Having spent the last ninety days around the same group of about twenty men, working from sun up to sun down under the hot African sun, I'm exhausted even navigating this terminal.

My face feels oddly bare, and my clothes feel restrictive as I try to get comfortable in the stiff seat. Last night, I thought I'd died and gone to heaven when I stepped under a shower's hot stream for the first time in three months. I didn't realize what luxury hot showers were, and after this experience, I swear I'll never take them for granted ever again.

My olive skin's more of a golden bronze, and my hands are covered in a whole new set of calluses. I'm leaner, stronger, and more at peace than I've ever been in my life. I thought it would be hard to be cut off from the world, but it was exactly what I needed. Being able to immerse myself into a good cause while exerting myself to the point of exhaustion every day left me little time to overthink the laundry list of my past mistakes—not to mention the new ones. For the first time in my life, I could fall asleep without fighting off my inner demons.

Of course, the minute I stepped back into my hotel room last night, all the memories of what I was running from came flooding back to me like a tsunami. So, naturally, I let myself pretend for one more night that I didn't completely fuck myself over by running away. It didn't really work.

Despite the hot shower and real mattress, I slept like shit last night.

But now I'm sitting in the airport, waiting on my next connection and watching everyone buzz around me with excitement and determination as they try to get home for the holidays. I snicker as I watch large families bicker and argue while trying to run to catch their flights. There's so much stress and anxiety in the air that it's almost palpable. I feel like an alien observing another species entirely, as my thoughts couldn't be further from the upcoming holiday.

I glance at the dirt under my fingernails that I failed to scrub away, and I'm reminded of something so much bigger than a holiday. Maybe it has to take something major like isolating yourself and giving back through hard labor to realize what's really important. Or maybe that's just what it took to get through for me because I was so closed off.

I pull my phone out of my pocket and stare at it. It's fully charged, but I haven't been able to bring myself to power it on just yet. I know that once I do, all my clear thinking will be polluted with all the things I ran away from. But I can't run forever. I need to face reality, and I'll probably spend the next three months playing catch-up on just my emails, not to mention everything else.

I suck in a breath and power the phone on, letting myself get reacquainted with the tiny computer that seems to run my life whether I like it or not.

My eyes widen as my email icon lights up with a red five-digit number, and my missed texts and voicemails follow closely behind.

Fuck me. This will take forever. I push my fingers through my wavy hair and sigh making a mental note to have my assistant schedule a haircut as soon as I return to Chicago.

I'm flying straight to Panama City since I promised my family I'd be home for Christmas. I even bought my plane tickets ahead of time and told them about it just so I wouldn't back out. I haven't seen or talked to anyone since the day my dad drove me to the airport.

I meant to call and keep in touch, but there wasn't any service where we were staying, and I didn't venture out to the city on the weekends like some of the other guys. I used my rare moments of free time to sit in the silence of nature and soak up whatever healing the universe had to spare. A smirk pulls at my lips as an image of Maggie sitting cross-legged on the beach, the wind swirling her hair around her as she sat there for what felt like hours refilling her depleted well.

I didn't understand it at the time—I still don't, actually—but she was on to something. So while I tried not to think about her, it seemed like nature constantly brought her up anyway.

It was cruel at first, and I was angry that I couldn't shake the memories, that they seemed to haunt me more when all I wanted was to escape, but after a while, the loneliness took over, and I felt comforted by her memory. I found myself thinking of her when the sun came up, how the orange and pink hues mingled, reminding me of her bright ginger hair. I found myself staring at the stars many nights as they reminded me of the freckles spanning her nose. I tried not to think about the night we spent on the rooftop or any night we spent together, actually, but the memories always crept in anyway when I let my guard down.

So, while I was alone and there was no one there to see or know what I was thinking, I let myself dream of what it would've been like in an alternate universe. I let myself feel loved by her without judgment, and I kept it tucked away deep inside me while I worked until my hands bled and my muscles shook.

The hardest part was making myself stop after indulging in daydreaming for so long. I can't know the pain I caused her, but I don't deserve the pleasure of allowing myself to forget any of it. At least I could give her the space she needed to heal. It was the least I could do.

My finger's still hovering over the email icon when the flight attendant announces it's time to board. I sigh and shove my phone back in my pocket as I make my way on the plane.

Maybe I'll let myself enjoy a little bit more fantasy before I rip the Band-Aid off.

I stare out my window as passengers slowly start to fill in the space around me

---

"Will you look at that? He's actually here." My dad hugs me and then opens the trunk for my bag.

Drew punches me on the shoulder, then hugs me. "Good to see you, bro."

I groan as I climb into the passenger seat and fasten my seat belt.

"What? Are you tired or something?" Dad teases and smiles,

studying me for a minute. "Hard work looks good on you, son." He finally says as he drives off.

"What's with the shaggy hair? Are you trying to grow a mullet, too? Jamie's going to be pissed." Drew says as he rubs his hand over my hair.

"I didn't exactly have time to get a haircut while I was out there. But now that I know it'll annoy Jamie, maybe I'll keep it like this for a little while longer." I pull out my phone and stare at it, afraid to see what lies inside my inbox.

Would she have written me?

The thought's barely left my mind when Drew clears his throat. "Ahem, whatcha doing?"

"Nothing." I shake my head. "I just can't make myself check my emails. I'm probably going to be drowning in work for the next two years..."

"So, you haven't heard from her?" Drew asks.

My chest constricts at the mention of her, and I whip my gaze to Drew. "I don't know what you're talking about."

"Oh, so we're all supposed to just pretend like we didn't watch you fall in love right before our eyes and completely fuck it up and run away?" He lets out an annoyed laugh. "Cool, I wasn't sure which way we were going to play it, but now I know delusional is what you had in mind..."

"Drew," my dad warns as he tightens his grip on the steering wheel. "Can we at least get home before you start your shit? You promised not to antagonize him if I let you come."

"I'm sorry. I shouldn't point out when my brother's being an idiot even though we're all thinking it."

I grit my teeth and sink into my seat, my eyes trained on the road as I simmer with annoyance.

When my dad finally pulls up to the house, I can't get out of the car fast enough. I don't need this from him right now. He has no idea how much I've already tortured myself. I don't need the entire family to dog pile on top of me, too.

The smell of apples and cinnamon drifts around me as I step through the door. Charlotte's in the kitchen baking, her apron covered in flour or powdered sugar, and she squeals when she sees me. "Oh, Sam! I'm so happy you made it!"

I kiss her on the cheek as I hug her. Then I jump in surprise when I'm stabbed in the ass by Denver's long nose. "Jesus, Simon, control your dog!" I yelp, petting his floppy ears. His long tail stings as he wacks it against my legs with excitement.

"Ouch, now, you shoo. You know you're not supposed to be in the kitchen when I'm cooking," Charlotte scolds as she pops him with a hand towel.

I watch him run off, his nails slipping on the tile floor as he tries to hurry, and see Simon cradling a pink bundle to his chest. Wren's curled into the sofa beside him with a computer on her lap typing.

"Oh, wow. Congratulations." I rush to him as all my irritation melts away when I see my brother holding his baby.

"Sam, I'd like you to meet your niece." He pushes the blanket away from her face to give me a better view. "This is Annie. She was born on November first."

My eyes well with tears, and I trace her little hand covering one of her eyes. She's a wrinkly little thing and so freaking tiny. I can't really tell who she looks like, but my brother is beaming with pride as he looks down at her. I don't think I've ever seen him so happy, and it almost feels like staring too long into the sun.

Wren scoots over, and I take the seat next to him as he passes me the tiny bundle. She smells like lavender and baby powder and feels so small, like she could slip through my hands. I bounce her a little, and she coos, then sucks one of her fingers in her mouth.

It's incredible coming home to a new life and a new family member I already love so much even though I've only just met her. At that moment, I'm so jealous of Simon that I almost can't stand it. But I'm so happy for him, too. I wish I could feel a sliver of his obvious joy.

My chest aches as I realize why it hurts so badly. I had that and I sent her away. I shake my head as I stare at baby Annie as if she holds all the answers like she's some kind of baby Yoda.

What if it really is that simple? What if by trying to control the situation and protect us both from pain, I caused it to hurt so much worse? What if the resistance I have to falling in love is really just the feeling of getting hurt? And hurting her? Didn't I cause all of that anyway?

I look up at Simon, who's studying me.

"What's wrong? Did you poop again? I just changed her like five minutes ago–" He tries to take her back to check her diaper, but I shake my head.

"I think I fucked up. I think I monumentally fucked everything up."

Simon rolls his eyes and laughs. "No shit, dumbass. So, what are you going to do about it?"

I shake my head and hand Wren the baby as a wave of nausea rises in my gut. I curl over and prop my head on my hands as I stare down at my feet, my mind swirling a thousand miles a minute.

"Have you talked to her since–"

I sit up and pull my phone from my pocket, hands shaking as I struggle to open my email folder. I swipe down the screen as I search for her name in the sea of messages.

"Give me that, you idiot." Simon snatches the phone out of my hand and types her name in the search bar. I don't know why I didn't think to do that. I blame the adrenaline rush.

He hands me back the phone. "There. I think this is what you're looking for."

I stare down at the screen and see an email from Maggie that was sent one week after I left. I suck in a breath as I open it.

To: Samuel Jordan

From: Magnolia Anderson

Subject: Thank you.

Dear Sam,

I'm writing you this email from the first-class lounge on my flight back to Chicago. Thank you for the upgrade btw. I've enjoyed my week of splurging. (I may have gotten a bit carried away with the room service... you'll understand when you get the bill... but I'm not apologizing for that!)

Anyway, I've had some realizations over the last week, and I wanted to thank you for all you did to help me with our *lessons*.

I wanted you to teach me to be better at sex to impress men, but instead, you taught me that it's more important that I'm impressed with myself. You showed me what it looks like to put myself first for the first time in my life and not let people walk all over me. You helped me realize what I wanted and how I wanted to be treated and that I have complete control over how I allow people to treat me.

Sam, you gave me the best gift that anyone could give me, you gave me the gift of insight of what I've always wanted.

I'm sorry I pushed you to change. I realize now that we want different things, and that doesn't make either of us wrong. I will not compromise anymore, and I hope you don't either.

I know you'll probably torture yourself for a long time to come—over everything you did or didn't do—but I hope that every once in a while, you stop and let yourself enjoy a nice whiskey or the way the air smells just before it rains. Promise me you'll allow yourself to be happy again. The world needs a little more of the carefree Sam you keep tucked away from everyone but your close friends and family.

I don't know if we'll ever be able to go back to what we were before my crazy suggestion, but I hope you don't let my presence deter you from spending time with your friends. Maybe we can draw up a new arrangement?

I'm still pissed at you, but I realized the last thing I want is to be with someone who doesn't want me back. I deserve more than that. I deserve to be with someone who chooses me first, so that's exactly what I plan on doing.

Goodbye, Sam. I guess I'll see you around.

–Maggie.

P.S. Thanks for everything you did to help me with the studio. I can't wait to get back to my life with a clean slate.

I press my fingers against my temples and rub as I finish reading the email. I don't know whether to be happy she sounds so good or upset that she doesn't seem to miss me at all... If she sounded that good three months ago, what must she be like now? She probably doesn't even remember I exist.

My shoulders sag in defeat, and I let out a frustrated sigh.

Simon claps me on the shoulder, and I jump. "Welcome to rock bottom, brother. The good news is you can only go up from here."

"I don't know, Si. I think I may just have to build myself a little house down here because I don't think I'm climbing out of this hole anytime soon."

"So, you're just going to give up?" Dad's voice comes from behind me, and I turn to find him staring at me with Charlotte tucked under his arm. Jamie stands beside him, shirtless with a whole-ass permed mullet, a mustache, and his arms crossed judgmentally over his chest.

I have to shake my head to check if I'm hallucinating because he looks so ridiculous, but I guess people really can change a lot in three months.

"Were you all just standing there waiting for me to admit I fucked up?"

"Son, we've been planning this intervention since your punk-ass ran off to Africa. Do you know how hard it was for me to not slap the shit out of you when I saw you?" Dad snaps.

Charlotte elbows my dad. "We just don't like seeing you so miserable."

"Well, too late." I drop the phone and shake my head. "There's no telling what she's up to now. She's probably dating that douche-bag, Trent, or someone else by now."

"I guess you won't know until you see for yourself," Wren pipes up, and my eyes dart to her as she nurses Annie.

"So, what am I supposed to do? Get on a plane and go to her?" I scoff. "It's Christmas Eve. I don't think I can even call in any favors to get a flight out tonight."

"Well, then, I guess we'll just have to take this party on the road," Jamie says as he waggles his eyebrows.

I shake my head, but everyone jumps up at once.

"I'll pack you some snacks for the road," Charlotte calls as she pulls food from the refrigerator and shoves it into a bag.

"I'll go fill up the tank and make sure there's air in the tires," Dad says. "When was the last time you got the oil changed?"

"Two weeks ago. I told you, Dad, you don't need to treat me like a little kid," Jamie calls.

I hold my hand up in protest. "Whoa, whoa, whoa. What are you doing? I just got here. I don't need to be chauffeured in a death mobile by Beavis and Butthead, okay? I'll figure it out."

"We don't have time for that!" Charlotte yells as she shoves a loaf of bread into the bag. "Besides, it would do you boys some good to spend some time together. You can get there by tomorrow morning and surprise her on Christmas if you leave now."

I look down at my phone and open my photos, finding a candid picture I snapped of Maggie eating cotton candy for the first time as a rush of hope flutters in my chest.

All I can do is try... right? If she says no, then it won't be any more painful than it already is...

I just hope I'm not too late.

THIRTY-SEVEN

Sam

I can't believe I'm actually getting in this rundown van with my two moron brothers, but I don't have time to think of a plan B.

I'm sitting in the van, waiting for Drew to finish shitting since that's not something any of us want to deal with on this god-awful drive.

I look at my phone for the hundredth time to see if she's called me back or responded to any of my texts, but no luck. She must really be upset still. It's not like her not to answer her phone... I try to suppress my fear that something must be wrong. It's likely nothing, and she's just ignoring me for all I know. It's not completely out of the realm of possibility after how I left things.

I dial Benjamin and catch him up to speed.

"I can't get ahold of her. Do you have any idea where she is? If she's okay?"

Silence fills the other end of the line, and a beat passes before Benjamin sighs. "Elliot just dropped her off at the bus station. She... uh... she left her phone with Elliot because it's all a part of the healing experience, and she asked us to look after the studio while she's gone. You really fucked up this time, Sam..."

"What do you mean? Is she seeing someone? Has she already moved on?"

"She's not seeing any one person... consistently... but she's been on a lot of dates." He sighs again. "She's happy, dude. She's got this glow about her she didn't have before. I don't mean to be cynical or anything, but I don't know how this is going to play out for you. I don't want you to get your hopes up and shut down again."

I suck in a hiss and clench my fist, half relieved that she's doing so well—proud, even—and half gutted that she's not hurting like I am. "I'm already too far gone, Benjamin. It doesn't matter at this point. I'll regret it for the rest of my life if I don't at least try to get her back."

"Okay, then. Well, I know the bus is stopping overnight in Nebraska. If you hurry, you may be able to catch up to them before they get to Lotus Haven. Once they open the gates, there's no getting in or out for two weeks."

"What the fuck is she going to do, cut off from everyone she knows for two weeks?"

"Gee... I don't know. Maybe she needs some *space* to find herself? Apparently, that's what the kids are doing these days, running away from their problems and doing mushrooms in the wilderness—"

"I was doing charity work!" I cut him off. "Wait, are they really planning on doing drugs out there? How could you let her do this! What if she gets hurt—"

"I can see your time away did wonders for your control issues. She's a grown woman, Sam. I don't know what she's doing, and I frankly don't have time to worry about it. Maybe you should've thought about that before you left..."

His words burn me like a hot fire poker. "You're right. Call me if you hear from her, okay? And do you think you can find out information about where they're staying? Maybe a license plate number for the bus she's on?"

"I'll see what I can do."

I end the call with an exhausted sigh and let my head fall back against the seat just as Drew struts out of the bathroom like a new man. Good, at least that's another stop we can avoid. He climbs in the back and shivers as he buckles his seatbelt. "Now, I'm ready to go."

Jamie's backing out of the driveway when my Dad runs out of the house waving his arms. I roll down my window... manually... and stick out my head. "What's wrong? What'd I forget?"

Dad runs up to the window, panting from his sprint, and reaches into his pocket. He pulls out a small red velvet ring case shaped like a heart. I shake my head. "No. Dad, I can't take that. She would want you to keep that. It's the only thing you have to remember her by."

Dad winces as he leans forward holding his side and shakes his head. "No, son." He gasps and coughs. "She wanted you to have it. It was always going to be for you. I was just waiting for you to bring the right girl home to give it to you." He shoves the velvet box in my hand.

I tighten my hand around the small box. "You're sure? You think I should do this?"

My dad laughs and ruffles my hair. "I think you'd be the biggest idiot on the planet if you didn't—and that's saying a lot considering you're sitting in a Red Vine candy-wrapped camper van next to your twenty-five-year-old brother with a permed mullet and a porno-stash..." He nods to Jamie. "I love you, son, but you look like if Tom Seleck and Billy Ray Cyrus had a baby."

"Thanks, Dad! Love you, too!" Jamie yells a little louder than necessary. He put the van in reverse and begins backing out of the driveway. "Who's ready for an old-fashioned Jordan family cross-country road trip? We've got plenty of food and drinks and bottles to pee in. What more do three brothers need?"

Before I can respond, he turns on the stereo, and the song "Stacy's Mom" blares through the speakers. Drew and Jamie sing along, playing air drums and guitar like a modern-day Wayne and Garth.

I sink lower in my seat as my anxiety builds. What if I don't make it in time? What if I'm already too late?

I can't control what happens next, which scares the shit out of me. All I can do is try to beat her before she reaches her destination.

"Will you pass me some gravy for my mashed potatoes?" Jamie calls to Drew in the backseat, who's sitting cross-legged in the back, heating Christmas Eve dinner on an electric stovetop. Charlotte hated the idea of us missing her big dinner, so she whipped up a few to-go containers and sent us on the way with whatever else she could grab from the fridge.

"I'm going as fast as I can! I've still got to finish heating the mac and cheese, and the dressing is next in the queue. I asked you if you wanted gravy earlier, and you said 'no,' so you'll just have to wait like the rest of us," Drew calls before tossing two dinner rolls to us in the front.

In my wildest dreams, I don't think I could've imagined a more ridiculous road trip if I tried. We're driving nonstop, trying to turn a twenty-seven-hour drive into twenty-four in a Red Vine candy-wrapped van from the 1990s, eating Christmas dinner…

We've only been on the road for five hours, and I don't know how much more I can take.

"Could you give me a little more sparkling cider?" Jamie asks as he reaches behind him to pass Drew his glass.

Yes. His glass. These two idiots have real dishes in this shitty camper van because, and I quote, 'plastic bottles and paper plates are terrible for the environment.' If I weren't absolutely desperate for their help, I wouldn't be sitting here, but since time is not on my side, I have no choice but to endure it.

Drew passes the refilled glass of sparkling cider back to Jamie, who slurps a sip. "Ah! Refreshing. Don't lose that bottle, Drew. I'm going to need to whizz in it before too long."

We drive all night long in that van, and just like Jamie promised, we only stop for gas. The sun's coming up, and it's Christmas morning. I look over at my brothers, both of whom are snoring, sleeping like babies. It's pretty cool to see how much they've grown since they were little and I was still at home taking care of them. They're so different now, but also strangely the same. It's like I knew they'd turn out just as they have. I'm not surprised by any of this in the least bit… and I also know they've both got a long way to go before they're done growing into the men they'll eventually become. I can see that future potential for them, and it makes my big brother's heart swell with pride.

Last night, Benjamin sent me the license plate number and the location of where they stayed overnight, along with their itinerary for today. I glance at the clock. We're only two hours away. Now, we just have to stick to the route—which Benjamin was also able to give me—and catch them before they go through those gates.

I tighten my grip on the steering wheel, fueled with renewed determination and a sprinkle of delusional hope. It's all I've got right now, so I'm clinging to it. Everything about this is out of my comfort zone, yet somehow, it feels perfectly right.

Falling in love feels like pure terror, like when you're at the very top of the rollercoaster, staring down at the first big drop. Or when bungee jumping, and you look down from the bridge just before you dive off. The fall is scary and feels out of control, but the rush you get after it is like nothing else in the world.

All of this time, I was scared of feeling out of control. I didn't even realize that feeling is what makes life worth living. What's the point of any of it if you don't have love?

I rehearse what I want to say over and over in my mind as I close the distance between us.

"Shouldn't we have caught up to them by now? What if Benjamin was wrong and we're too late?" I swipe my credit card and pay for the gas, so Jamie can fill up. It's the least I can do to cover his gas. I fully intend to replace his tires, too, before he makes the trip home.

Jamie sets the pump and leans against the van, pulling his coat tighter to block the wind. "Dude, just chill. It's all going to work out. You'll see. Look around, how can today go any less than perfect? We're practically inside a snow globe."

Jamie's always been the optimistic one in the family. He's the only one of us who inherited that particular trait from our mother. I used to think he was naïve, always looking on the bright side of things, but now, I envy him. How much time have I wasted because I was too stubborn to see an alternate solution?

Things aren't always black and white, Sam. The magic happens in all the colors in between.

That was one of the last things she said to me, and it took too many years for that little piece of wisdom to sink into my hard head.

My ears perk up when I hear the woosh of an engine in the distance. I glance around for the source of the noise, thinking it's probably just an eighteen-wheeler, when I see a large bus fly by and merge onto the highway.

My eyes go wide as I look at Jamie. "Come on. Let's go. That could be it!"

"Okay, let me just finish filling up the tank–"

I snatch the gas pump out of the tank and shove it back in the holder. "We don't have time for that. Let's go before we miss them!"

I run around the back of the van and climb into the passenger side, slipping on the icy concrete beneath my feet. Jamie turns the keys in the engine, and it makes a sad puttering sound.

"What was that?" My voice comes out panicked.

Jamie mumbles under his breath, "She can be finicky when the gas gets too low." He looks at me like I'm an idiot, even though he's the one using pronouns for his Red Vine Van. "That's why I wanted to fill up."

I reach over and turn the key myself, swearing under my breath as Jamie slaps my hand in protest. I don't relent though, and after a few turns, Van-essa finally comes to life.

"Keep your paws off." Jamie gives me a final slap before peeling out of the gas station.

"Just go, hurry up before we lose them!" I hold the oh-shit handle as Jamie swerves onto the highway and lays on the gas.

It feels as if every tire is a different height as the van shakes in an unnatural rhythm as we gain speed. I can't believe we've survived this long, and I have half a mind to drive Van-essa into a ditch and buy my brother a new vehicle before he attempts to return home.

Several minutes pass before the large bus finally comes into view. I squint my eyes as we get closer and compare the license plate number to the one Benjamin sent me.

"That's it! **VN76-T5.** That's the bus!"

Jamie lays on the gas and pulls up next to the bus, matching its speed. "Ok, now, what?"

"I think we need to get their attention, get them to pull over?" I shrug. I didn't really plan out what to do if we actually caught up to them. I roll down my window and wave, trying to flag down the driver, but he's not paying attention. He's fully immersed in whatever song he's singing, tapping his fingers on the steering wheel like a drum set.

"Maybe you should moon him?"

I whip around at Jamie's suggestion. "How would that get his attention?"

"I don't know, I feel like people can sense nudity. It's in our nature."

"I'm not mooning a bus full of strangers."

"A bus full of strangers and the love of your life... All I'm saying is it's never not worked for me..."

"Because you've done this before!?" I snap as I wave my arms through the window, but the driver doesn't even flinch.

"Trust me, bro, I'm like a sensei when it comes to getting people's attention." Jamie circles his hand around his mulleted head.

I bite my lip and consider him for a moment, then Drew says. "Fuck it. I'll moon them."

Before I can argue, he's got his pants dropped around his ankles with his bare ass sticking out the window.

"Fuck, it's cold out there! I think my ding dong's getting frostbite!"

And just as Jamie said, I see the bus driver jerk the wheel in a startle as he looks at Drew's bare ass...

Jamie punches the air in excitement. "I told you! Humans can sense nudity. It's simple evolution..."

I shake my head in astonishment. It's not anything I would've considered, but a win is a win. I wave my arms in a windshield-wiper motion and scream for him to pull over the bus.

Phase one of the plan is complete.

Now, I just need to get to my girl.

THIRTY-EIGHT

Maggie

My back aches from sitting in this cramped seat, and I try to stretch it the best I can without disturbing the older gentleman sleeping next to me. I don't know much about him, just that his name is Carl and he's newly widowed. He smells like cigars and peppermint and falls asleep within minutes every time we stop.

In the brief moments when he was awake, he told me that my red hair reminded him of one of his great-granddaughters. He's the sweetest old man I've ever met, so I'm careful not to disturb him as I wiggle in my seat.

After returning to Chicago, I found my yoga studio in far better shape than ever. Apparently, Sam made a few upgrades without my knowledge. I tried to have Joey send me the bill, but he refused and said he'd already been paid in full. There was no arguing with him, so I just thanked him for doing such a good job and treated the crew to cupcakes.

I started classes back immediately, and the new facelift caught the eye of a group of mommy influencers. They all bought annual memberships and began posting daily vlogs of some of my classes, and before I knew it, my clientele doubled in only a month of reopening.

It's been a whirlwind of growth and the busiest season in my career. We've had a few growing pains along the way, and I eventually had to hire five new instructors and a couple of front desk workers to keep things running smoothly.

I would never have been able to capitalize on this growth six months ago. I would've been too afraid to take chances and try new things. I would've been afraid of disappointing my older members with the fresh spin on my classes, the very thing that most everyone now loves.

The version of myself that existed four months ago would've been too afraid of the risk of changing in fear of not pleasing *everyone*. Now, I realize what I thought was my greatest strength—my gentle agreeableness—was actually my greatest weakness.

You can't please everyone, believe me, I've tried for twenty-nine years to do just that. But once I realized the cost of putting everyone else's dreams, preferences, ideas, and comfort before my own on my mental and physical health, it was like a switch flipped in my mind.

Maybe things with Trent were the straw that broke the camel's back, or maybe I'd already started to change slowly and could finally see things for how they were. Whatever the case, that was the moment I realized what I was doing wrong. That night at the reunion, I realized I deserved so much more. It was the first time I actually believed it.

Sam may have broken my heart, but I know I wouldn't be here had I not asked him to help me four months ago. It may be unconventional, but I wouldn't trade my heartache for anything. The things I felt when I was with him, the way I felt about myself, no one can ever take that away from me.

I always wanted to feel chosen. I used to think I'd get that from a boyfriend or future husband, but now I realize I can choose myself. And from now on, I'm doing just that.

I signed up for the Lotus Haven retreat two months ago after the major boom in business. It's not something I ever would have done before, but I need this for myself. I need to continue my personal development and growth. I need to arm myself with tools to sustain the growth of my business and maybe even my personal life.

I want to be selfish for once While I figure out how to be the best version of myself possible. From now on, I'm not taking a backseat to my one life, only reacting to others. I want to be behind the wheel taking chances and trusting myself to make mistakes and then fix them by doing what feels right in my soul.

My whole life, I've let my childhood define me, always putting everyone's needs before mine, even to my detriment. But not anymore.

I don't need rescuing. I'm not a damsel in distress.

I am my own goddamn heroine.

I flip the page in my yoga magazine, only looking up as the sound of gasps and laughter buzzes around me.

I look around the bus to see where the commotion is coming from.

Some of the people seem angry while others laugh hysterically, and one older woman even pulls out a camera to take pictures.

What could they all possibly be looking at?

I follow their gaze and squint as a strange van comes into view. It looks oddly familiar, and I stare for just a moment before recognition dawns on me.

Is that? No...

I stand in my seat to get a better view, then carefully step over Carl and rush toward the middle of the bus.

The next thing I know, I'm staring at a man's white ass hanging out of the window of the old camper van, and then I see Sam waving his arms like a maniac.

My stomach drops, and my immediate thought is something is wrong. Why would Sam be flagging down a bus... in Wyoming on Christmas morning? Isn't he supposed to be in Africa or something?

I rush to the front of the bus to get the bus driver's attention and stand there awkwardly when he doesn't acknowledge me.

I clear my throat. "Excuse me."

He doesn't turn around, just keeps his eyes trained on the road as Vanessa Carlton's "A Thousand Miles" plays over the radio.

I tap him on the shoulder. "Excuse me. I was wondering if you could stop the bus. It's... a... it's an emergency."

The bus driver grunts. "No can do, lady. I'm on a tight schedule here, and we're already ten minutes behind. No more stops."

I look out his window as the guys wave and honk their horn. I realize the mooner is none other than Sam's brother Drew. He's abandoned his mooning in favor of flashing his nipples...

I bite my lip. "Right, I get that, but you see, it's an emergency–"

"Sit down, lady. I ain't stoppin' this bus."

I purse my lips in a flat line as I turn on my heel heading back to my seat in defeat. I fall into the seat and Carl perks up.

"What'd he say? Is he going to stop?"

My shoulders sag and I sigh. "No, we're already behind schedule. He said he's not stopping..."

"And you're just going to take no for an answer? This is true love we're talking about."

"What else can I do? I can't make him stop the bus. Besides, we're in a hurry–"

"You just need to think outside the box. Don't you worry. I've got this. Just play along." Carl winks, then drops his head back against the seat and clenches his chest. He lets out a moan and makes a wincing noise.

"My chest," he groans before releasing a louder moan as he flails in his seat.

"Is he having a heart attack?" the woman behind us cries.

"Someone's having a heart attack!"

"Stop the bus! We've got a medical emergency!"

People spring to life, waving their arms and screaming to get the bus driver's attention.

"Someone dial 911!"

"We don't have our phones. How are we supposed to call for help!"

Then the bus starts to slow as we pull off the highway onto the shoulder. Carl winks at me and continues his act. I spring up from my seat and push my way to the front, past the other passengers coming to check on Carl in the opposite direction.

"Hey, lady, what're you do–" the bus driver says as I hit the exit button and leap down the steps.

The van pulls in behind us, sliding to a stop as Sam jumps out of the front and runs to me.

I crash into his arms and bury my head in his chest. He's warm and sturdy and feels like home. I didn't realize how much I missed him until now.

"What are you doing here?" I gasp as the cold air whips around us. My teeth are chattering violently as I realize I didn't grab my coat before running off the bus.

Sam pulls me into him and wraps me in his warmth. "Fuck, I'm an idiot for walking away from you. I was scared, Maggie. I was terrified of losing myself to love. Terrified of feeling out of control. I didn't know what to do, so I pushed you away."

I cross my arms over my chest and meet his pleading eyes.

"You hurt me, Sam. You shattered my heart and ran off across the world and left me alone to pick up the pieces."

"I know, baby, and I realized my mistake the moment I got on that plane. I fucked up bad." He takes my hands and steps closer. "I love you, Magnolia. I couldn't let another day go by without you knowing that. I love you so much it fucking hurts, and I think I always have."

I swallow the sob that threatens to escape. "How do I know you're not going to run when things get serious, Sam? How am I supposed to believe you?"

He runs his thumbs over my hands and moves a little closer. "Let me show you, give me a chance to prove it." He holds out his arms. "I've got all the time in the world. I'll wait for you if that's what you want. I'll wait a thousand lifetimes if that's what it takes. I'll be your friend if that's all you can give me. Hell, I'll be happy with whatever I can get..."

I shake my head, and he lifts my chin to meet my gaze.

"I'll be whatever you want me to be. I'll have my vasectomy reversed if that's what you want. I'll give you a family and live a normal life. I'll move. Tell me what you want, and I'll give it to you."

Tears well in my eyes as I watch his Adam's Apple bobble, his nervous hands trembling as he holds mine. "I don't want you to change anything, Sam. I just want to be with you... all of you. I want the real Sam, the one without the walls around his heart."

He pulls me into a hug, wrapping me up in warmth as he kisses me gently on top of my head and lets out a sigh of relief. "I fucking love you so much, Magnolia Anderson. You have changed me to my core and made me feel safe to be myself. From the moment we met, I knew you were special, too good for the rest of us. I choose you. I see you. I love you so much it scares the shit out of me, and I was a coward for running away. I thought I was protecting you from me, but I realize now I was really just afraid of getting hurt, so I pushed you away, hurting both of us."

I shake my head and laugh as he wraps his hand at the base of my neck and stares into my eyes.

"You make me a better person, and you inspire me to see the good in everything around me. I need you like I need air in my lungs."

He drops to his knees, and I gasp as he holds up a tiny red velvet box shaped like a heart.

"I know this is sudden, but I've never been more sure of anything in my life. Take this as my commitment to you that I'm in this forever. I'm not going anywhere. I want to spend the rest of my life showing you just how much you deserve, showering you with love and affection, and giving you whatever your heart desires."

He opens the box to reveal a classic round diamond ring with a dainty gold band. It's simple and timeless and absolutely perfect in every way.

"Magnolia Anderson, would you do me the honor of becoming my wife?"

"Of course, I will." I half laugh, half sob as I pull him up and kiss him right there on the side of the highway somewhere in the middle of Wyoming as snowflakes start to fall around us.

I remove the ring from the box and slide it on my finger.

"It was my mother's. My dad said she always intended for me to have it. I hope you don't mind..."

I suck in a breath and hold my hand to my heart. "No, it's perfect. I love it."

Our kiss is needy and raw, and suddenly, I don't feel cold anymore as passion ignites like a flame between us. Sam's hands move to the back of my head as he presses me against him and deepens our kiss.

We kiss until I'm dizzy and weak in the knees, my blood rushing like wildfire in every direction as peace and relief flood my body.

When we pull away, Sam's wearing a grin I've never seen before. "We'll have to draw up a new contract. One without an ending date this time."

"I think I can handle that. Besides, I've got some ideas I'd like to add..." I blush and kiss his soft lips.

Sam's eyes darken as he searches my face, "Why don't we start right now?"

I take two steps back and smile just as the bus driver yells, "Hey, lady, are you comin' or stayin'?"

"Just one second. I'll be right there." I spin back to see Sam wearing a confused look. I shrug and point over my shoulder. "I know it may seem tacky to leave right after an engagement... but I really need to do this."

Sam's shoulders sag, and I can see the disappointment flash across his face, but then he sighs and smiles. "You know how I feel about you not having a phone." He leans in and kisses me on the forehead. "But I trust you. I'll be waiting for you as soon as you're done."

"I love you, Sam."

"I love you more, Magnolia. Now, hurry along before I lose the last of my restraint," he whispers, sending a flood of butterflies to my belly.

I wave goodbye, blowing him a kiss as I climb on the bus, where I find a proud-looking Carl smiling back at me as I take my seat.

"Well, how'd it go?"

I stare out the window smiling as we pull away. "I think I just got everything I ever wanted."

EPILOGUE

Sam

Six months later ...

I stand from my seat and raise my glass in a toast. "If you had told me I would be a married man one year ago, I never would've believed you. The very thought of committing to anyone for more than a year was unspeakable... Hell, I even had a contract to enforce it. But there are forces more powerful than any will of man, even my own steel-clad stubbornness." I look at my beautiful bride sitting beside me, meeting her gaze. Her bright eyes see the best in everyone around her, and I still can't believe how I got so lucky.

"Falling in love with your soulmate is a magic all its own, and it's not something I ever believed until it happened to me. There isn't a doubt in my mind that this brilliant woman wasn't hand-crafted by God himself as the perfect counterpart to my imperfect soul. I could live a thousand lifetimes and still not deserve her love, but I'm happy I get the chance to try. To a long, happy life filled with laughter and all the good stuff that we don't even know about yet. I can't wait to grow old with you and look back on all the fun we had together. Cheers."

We clink our glasses and sip our champagne as the band begins playing "Come to Me" by the Goo Goo Dolls, and everyone rushes to the dance floor. It's the same cover band from the night at the bar, the night I officially fell head over heels for my wife. And she's crazy if she thinks I'm going to let this night go by without an encore performance. I'll have to save it for the end, though, because I don't think I'll be able to control myself, and I don't want to miss out on this party.

I tried to get Maggie to marry me the moment I picked her up from her retreat, but she wanted to share the moment with our friends and family. I look around at everyone I love laughing and dancing under the string lights in the courtyard of my parent's beach house, and my heart swells in my chest. I didn't know I could get any happier until I slid that ring on my wife's finger and we exchanged our vows in front of everyone who loves us the most.

I asked Benjamin and Simon to stand beside me as my best men while Jack stood on my other side as the officiant. He took a class just for the occasion and is even considering making it a part-time gig during the summer months... Gwen's thrilled about that little endeavor.

After I told Maggie the ball was in her court about us starting a family, we had a long discussion about what we both wanted in life. She said she realized she's spent her whole life taking care of everyone else, and marrying into my family was good enough for her.

And as long as she's happy, that's all I care about.

We bought a house near my parents in Florida and plan to split our time between here and Chicago. My family has embraced her as one of our own, and she's even taught Jamie and Drew a few table manners. I think there may be hope for them yet. Though, we still can't convince Jamie to give up the permed mullet. At least he shaved off the porn stash for the wedding photos... It's all about baby steps.

After the retreat, Maggie came back with a fire in her belly and a dream in her heart. She started a nonprofit called The Bridge, which all blew up and took off overnight. She partnered with several local and major corporations to create jobs and internship opportunities for seventeen and eighteen-year-olds aging out of the foster care system. She was able to get a grant funding therapists, social workers, and counselors to provide mental health services to all the children in the program weekly, and she's just opened her first dormitory in downtown Chicago with several others coming down the pipeline.

Between the support network and mentorship, she's made a dent in leveling the playing field, giving many kids a better chance at success. It all happened so fast, and Maggie's passion and insight have fanned the flame of its rapid growth. I'm so proud of her. Her compassion and generosity never cease to amaze me. She's making an impact on this world by building something she once needed, and it's incredible to watch.

As for the dominant/submissive lifestyle... I'm pleased to report that we are very much still enjoying our dynamic. I love that Maggie has embraced me for who I am and hasn't tried to change that part of me. I actually think she loves it more than I do.

We find balance in everything we do, from inside the bedroom to our businesses, and we get to redefine our roles as often as we like.

It turns out Maggie didn't actually need sex lessons; she just needed to learn to trust her body. Once she stopped letting other people determine her worth, she was able to own her sexuality, and I've watched her confidence soar because of it.

Though, we still enjoy our lessons. They're just usually more on the advanced spectrum of things. I could spend a lifetime exploring Maggie's body, and I plan on doing just that. I don't know what the future holds for us, but I know one thing for certain—as long as I get to call her mine, everything else is just the sprinkles on top.

When the band plays "At Last" by Etta James, I take her hand. "Mrs. Jordan, would you like to dance?" She smiles and takes my hand as I lead her onto the dance floor, our bodies swaying in rhythm to the music. "Have I told you how beautiful you look tonight?" I whisper into her neck, making her shiver.

"Only about two or three hundred times." She laughs. "What are the chances we can create a diversion and sneak away..."

I tighten my grip around her waist as I look around the crowded dance floor. Drinks are flowing, and people are dancing and having a good time. They'll hardly notice we're missing. "I may be able to make that happen... but we'd have to be quiet." I give her a knowing look because my bride is anything but quiet, and we both know it.

"I promise I won't make a peep," she assures me with a mischievous smile. "Pretty please, sir? I don't think I can wait another two hours, and I want to enjoy the party." She bats her eyes as my favorite shade of pink tints her cheeks.

Desire rips through me at those sweet manners escaping her perfect red lips. I rub my finger along her chin as I stare into her bright hazel eyes that seem to swallow me whole every time I look into them. "Go upstairs to the library and wait for me. We're going to have to be very careful not to smudge your lipstick... I plan on saving that for later."

I watch her scamper up the steps and disappear into the empty house as I turn and search the crowd.

My eyes bounce between Jamie and Jack, and I smile. If there's anything I can count on from these two, it's creating one epic diversion. Hell, I may even be able to work in round two before anyone notices we're missing.

I make my way over and tell them my plan. It may be a bit extravagant of an idea... but what am I supposed to do? She did use her manners, after all...

BE A BOOK BABE

Do you want to be my friend?

Join my reader group: Jeré Anthony's Bantering Book Babes Where it feels like an grown-up slumber party every day.

We discuss books/reading, I tell my embarrassing moments– that happen all too often, and those hilarious inappropriate stories that only women will understand. Plus Giveaways!

It's a place for positive vibes + laughter + community and all the book talk!

So if you love my books and that sounds like you jam, come join us!

ACKNOWLEDGMENTS

I would be doing myself a disservice if I didn't acknowledge how far I've come in the few short years that I've been publishing. It's insane to think of just how different my mindset is today versus what it was after releasing Drive Me Crazy.

So on that note, I'd like to thank myself for doing the work and digging into all the uncomfortable growing pains that come with being a published author. There were many times where it would've been easy to give up, and yet I recognized the call of a bigger purpose in this work and kept going.

I wouldn't have been able to do that without the help of my therapist, Jason, who has spent every Tuesday over the last two years listening to me gripe, complain, attempt to self-sabotage, and even wallow in self-pity from time to time. And yet, somehow, this book still exists, and I'm not sure it would otherwise. So, if you were ever curious if therapy worked, there's your answer.

To my husband, Stephen, who also endured my wallowing and whining like a champ – I'm really a joy to be around most of the time, but I have my moments. It's what makes me so creative! Without you alpha-reading and being there to bounce ideas off of, I don't think this book would be anywhere near as good as it is.

And lastly, I'd like to thank my daughter, Emma, for being my biggest hype girl, but mostly for showing me in real-time what it looks like to work hard toward a goal and hit it. Watching you show up to all your soccer practices – even the ones that are optional – and being the hardest working player on the field has been such an inspiration to me. Seeing you voted captain by your teammates and then live up to the role like the leader I've always known you would be will be one of the highlights of my life.

When I doubted my own talent, you showed me that hard work, consistency, and focused effort are the building blocks to greatness. I only hope I'm returning the favor in some way. We may not be able to control the outcome, but we can control our effort, and that's exactly what I plan on doing.

This is only the beginning, and I can't wait to see where it leads.

AUTHOR'S NOTE

Thank you so much for reading Pretty Please Me! Doing research for this book was the absolute worst! Having to listen to hours of BDSM podcasts, learning as much as I could about the lifestyle, listening to interviews, and reading articles about kink... a total drag.

Obviously, I'm joking. I had so much fun doing the research for this book, trying to do my best to represent the kink community in an accurate, positive way by showing another side than the masochist/sadism that is more commonly portrayed in the media. (Not that there's anything wrong with that!)

When it comes to Dominant/Submissive relationships, there really are no rules as long as everyone involved is a consenting adult. I wanted to touch on the experience of feeling broken as a woman because the female sexual experience is so different from the male's. It's not entirely uncommon for women to just accept that orgasms aren't something they're capable of experiencing (especially if they were raised to believe there was something dirty about women enjoying sex, whether that was explicitly taught or just implied).

It's certainly something that I've had to work to rewire in my own life, and if I can help even one woman realize she's not alone, then I consider that a success. If you're interested in learning more about the kink community, there are tons of resources out there, and I encourage you to consume as many different sources as possible.

Please understand that this book is a piece of fiction, and while I did my best to describe the acts and lifestyle as accurately as possible, it's still a work of fiction. Romance/Erotica novels are not user manuals, so do your research. Thank you again for reading! These characters showed up in my head one day, and it's been one of the biggest joys of my life getting to spend time with them and writing their stories. Closing this chapter has been more challenging than I expected... but that just means I get to meet a whole new cast of characters now. Thank you for coming along for the ride and supporting me.

If you want to stay up to date and be the first to know about new releases, sales, giveaways, and hilarious embarrassing moments from my life, join my newsletter!

XOXO

Jeré

BOOK CLUB QUESTIONS

Book Club Questions

1. At the beginning of the story, Maggie felt incredibly lonely as she watched her friends' lives move forward without her. Have you been in a similar situation? If so, how did you deal with the dynamic changes?
2. In the story, Maggie struggles with feeling like she's not good at sex. Do you think good sex can be independent of feelings? How did your upbringing influence your ability to enjoy sex?
3. If you feel comfortable sharing, discuss an embarrassing sex story from your past and how you handled it.
4. If you could give Maggie one piece of advice, what would it be?
5. Maggie struggled with putting herself first and asking for what she wanted in every aspect of her life because of her survivor's guilt from her time in foster care. What are the ways you devalue your

own needs/wants/desires because it feels selfish to want more when someone you know may have suffered or had a harder hand dealt to them? Do you think it all evens out in the end? How so?

6. How would you describe Maggie's character at the beginning? What was the major change that took place over the course of the story? How would you describe her in the end?
7. How did you feel about Sam at the beginning of the story? How did your opinion of him change when you learned about his past?
8. How were you surprised by the unfolding of the story's theme of self-love through Maggie and Sam?
9. If you were given an opportunity to become someone's Submissive would you do it? What rules would you agree to and what would you negotiate out?
10. Strong friendships/family are a central theme of this book and are what helped Maggie and Sam in their journeys. How has friendship/family helped you overcome hardships?
11. If you've read all 3 books in the series, which character to do identify with the most? Why?

ABOUT THE AUTHOR

JERÉ ANTHONY (PRONOUNCED like hooray with a J) writes steamy, swoony, and hilarious romantic comedies with depth.

She is a mental health advocate, a lifelong anxiety warrior, and is ADHD AF. Her quirks bleed out into her stories making for an exciting group of characters. Because of her undiagnosed ADHD, growing up she always felt different from everyone around her. Now she strives to create stories that give readers an escape from reality while also helping them feel seen.

She loves a strong cup of coffee and thinks beer + buffalo wings are a delicacy that is unmatched.

Jeré currently lives in NW Arkansas with her husband, three children, dog, and two cats. When she's not writing, you can find her reading, driving her kids all over for travel soccer games, watching cat videos on her phone, or trying to convince her husband to go on another family adventure somewhere new.

Connect with Jeré:
Join my Facebook Reader Group: https://www.facebook.com/groups/616896780151111
NEWSLETTER: https://mailchi.mp/87e346b13331/jere-anthonynewsletter
INSTAGRAM: @author_jere_anthony
TIKTOK: @author_jere_anthony
WEBSITE: JereAnthony.com
Sign up for my newsletter to stay up to date with future releases, sales, and freebies

Printed in Great Britain
by Amazon